Copyright ©JudithArnopp 2021
First Edition

The author has asserted their moral right under the Copyright, Designs and Patents Act, 1988, to be identified as the author of this work.

All Rights reserved. No part of this publication may be reproduced, copied, stored in a retrieval system, or transmitted, in any form or by any means, without the prior written consent of the copyright holder, nor be otherwise circulated in any form of binding or cover other than that in which it is published and without a similar condition being imposed on the subsequent purchaser.

A CIP catalogue record for this title is available from the British Library.

Cover images: Catherine of Aragon pleads her case against divorce from Henry VIII. Painting by Henry Nelson O'Neil. Contributor: Niday Picture Library / Alamy Stock Photo
Portrait of the knight by Bolyuk Studio (shutterstock)
Cover design: Covergirl

Please note: This novel is historical fiction. The thoughts and opinions expressed within are NOT the author's but are those of the characters, based upon known historical events and the social and moral conventions of the period.

For Simon, my king

With special thanks to John, my editor Cas, and all my friends at The Coffee Pot Book Club.

A MATTER OF CONSCIENCE:
The Aragon Years

JUDITH ARNOPP

PART ONE
MOST ACCOMPLISHED PRINCE

> In the midst stood prince Henry, then nine years old, and having already something
> of royalty in his demeanour, in which there was a certain dignity combined with
> singular courtesy. On his right was Margaret, about eleven years of age, afterwards
> married to James, king of Scots, and on his left played Mary, a child of four …
> (Erasmus 1499)

Eltham 1502

My sister and I have slipped away from our nurse and stolen into the garden. I run ahead, my spaniel, Beau, at my heels, and scramble over a low wall. I am already running across the meadow when Mary's cries call me back. Reluctantly, I retrace my steps.

"It is those clothes," I say scornfully. "How can anyone climb a wall in things like that?"

She scowls at me, brushing moss from her skirts.

"I can't help being a girl. Anyway, you should be glad I am not a boy, for if I were, you'd never beat me at wrestling."

This is probably true, but I don't admit it. I turn away.

"Come on; hurry up before someone sees us."

Although it is only April, the sun is bright today; it chases away the winter and makes it difficult to sit still. All morning I have been fighting the fancy to escape. Near the river, I stop running and flop into the long grass; Beau runs on, his nose full of rabbit smells. A few moments later Mary catches up and flops down beside me. Tendrils of hair cling damply to her forehead and she smells of honey and sweat, green grass and lichen.

"Oh look," she says, ducking her head toward the ground. "I've found an Our Lady's bird."

We both lean closer to watch a tiny scarlet insect labour up a blade of grass. "It is like one of Mother's enamelled jewels," she says, keeping her voice low so as not to startle it. I roll onto my back and look at the expanse of sky. I can feel damp seeping through my fine clothes and know I will be scolded later, but just now I don't care.

"He's nearly at the top now."

Mary is still watching the ladybird. I roll onto my front again and see the creature has reached the pinnacle of its journey, tiny antennae feeling the air.

"I wonder if it can see us…" Mary says. "We must look like giants."

I flick the creature with my fingertip and it falls into the grass again.

"Henry!" Mary thumps my arm. "Don't be horrid. Now it will have to begin the trek all over again."

But Mary is wrong, it doesn't. Instead, it takes off in a blur of tiny black wings. When I see the dismay on my sister's face I wish I had let it be, but I don't apologise.

She lies down, stretches out and looks at the sky. I do the same. Side by side, hidden from the world by long waving grass, we are quiet, happy.

"Look at that cloud. It looks like a crown."

"No, it doesn't." But as I watch, I begin to see what she means. For a long moment, I am absorbed into the blue. Then I point to another, slightly larger cloud.

"That one looks like a ship."

"Does it? Oh yes, I see what you mean … it is changing now, into an owl … no, now it looks like the king."

We turn to look at each other, mention of our father reminding us of the trouble that awaits us on our return to the palace.

The sun retreats behind the cloud.

I imagine the sun must feel as if it has been drenched in water, the same way I feel when I try really hard yet still fail to win my father's praise. No matter what I do, I can never please him. Every time he curls his lip at something I've done, I wither a little inside.

"Father doesn't like me."

Mary rolls on to her stomach again, looking intently into my face.

"Oh, he does really, Henry. He is just anxious and busy. Being king is such an important job. Besides, Mother loves you best of all of us, that should make up for it."

She is right. I am Mother's favourite. She often whispers that I am made in the image of her father, the warrior king, Edward IV. Of course, she is careful never to say so in the presence of Father, or my grandmother. They wouldn't like it.

Mary sits up, poking her head above the waving grass.

"I think they are looking for us. I can see Tom running about the gardens."

Tom is one of the pages. He is supposed to be beneath our notice but I don't know many boys my own age, so I sometimes play with him when there are no grown-ups in earshot.

Mary and me were both disappointed this morning when a message came from Mother saying she would not be visiting us today. I had drawn a picture that I was going to give her to take back to Richmond, but it will have to wait now.

It was the arrival of that message that upset the servants. All the household staff were in a strange mood that morning. The only reason we had managed to get away was because Jenny was weeping, and the maids were distracted trying to comfort her.

We were bored. There was nothing to do. Margaret was reading behind a curtain, so when their backs were turned, I grabbed Mary's hand and dragged her outside. Now, I wish I had thought to bring something to eat.

As if in response to my thoughts, my belly growls loudly. Mary laughs.

"I wonder why stomachs make that noise. It sounds as if you have a little bear in there who grumbles when he gets hungry."

Her own stomach rumbles as if in conversation with mine.

"You must have a full-grown bear in yours."

She snatches up a handful of grass and throws it at me and an intense fight ensues. Seeing the fun, Beau runs barking back from his foray and leaps up at us, wanting to be part of it. The air is full of Mary's squeals and Beau's teeth. Everything smells green, and I have grass in my hair; some of it creeps down my neck, and soon I have it in my mouth and ears …

"HENRY! MARY!"

We leap to attention, stand rigidly side by side, our hearts filled with dread. The sun runs to take refuge behind the clouds again.

I open one eye and squint up at Grandmother, who is the last person we want to have discovering our truancy. Her stiff black brocade looks out of place here in the wildness of the meadow. I grab for Beau's collar, forcing him to sit.

"What do you think you are doing? Look at your clothes. Look at your hair. And Mary … you should be ashamed."

"I'm sorry, Grandmother. It – it was sunny and …"

"I did not ask for an explanation. I am in no mood to harken to lies and excuses. Come. You are needed at the house. Your nurse will be sorely punished for this."

Behind her back, we exchange glances as we follow her through the gardens that encircle the palace. We love Jenny and don't want her to suffer because of us.

"But it isn't Jenny's fault."

Grandmother halts so sharply I almost cannon into her. She turns and fixes me with a beady eye.

"I am aware of that, Henry, but since you are a prince and cannot be beaten like a common boy, I must find other ways to make you aware of the consequences of such behaviour."

"Yes, Grandmother."

I lower my head and try to look penitent. Her face softens and she holds out both hands. Mary takes her left hand, and I her right. We both know her bark is sharper than her bite, but many people don't.

"All the servants were being very odd this morning," Mary says, and Grandmother stops again and stares into the distance, her shoulders slumping.

"Yes," she says. "I know. We - we received some dreadful news during the night."

I stop scuffing my feet in the gravel and look up at her. The way her dark robes are outlined against the sky makes her look like a nun. Her eyes are clouded, her mouth drooping.

"What news?" I ask.

She swallows, as if her throat hurts, and her grip on my hand tightens. Bending down, she encircles us in her arms, drawing us both so close I can see the tiny lines surrounding her mouth.

"We had news from Ludlow that your brother Arthur, who as you know has been ailing.... Well, he did not survive. God saw fit to take him, and we have lost our son ... our bonny prince."

Her voice cracks, she takes a juddering breath, and I am terrified she is going to weep. As I watch her rapid blinking, her throat working as if she is trying to swallow something, my bones feel suddenly cold. My head spins as the import of the news strikes me.

Arthur has always lived in a different household to us, so I do not know him well, not the way I know Meg and Mary, but ...

"But Arthur is going to be king ..."

Grandmother looks at me. Her weary, hooded eyes are as sad as Beau's. Her hand trembles as she strokes my hair back from my brow.

"Not any longer, Henry. When the time comes, it is you who must now be king."

It is not until much later when we are lying in bed and Jenny has extinguished the candle that I remember Catalina. My brother's wife will be alone now, a widow at just sixteen years old.

It can never have been easy for her here, travelling all the way from Spain to a foreign country, trying to learn our ways, but at least she had Arthur. I wonder what will happen to her now. Had my brother lived she would have been queen one day, but now she has no future.

I turn onto my side, tuck one hand beneath my cheek and think how greatly surprised I had been when Father chose me to escort Catalina into the city shortly after she arrived.

It was a happy, proud day for me when, dressed in my fine new clothes, I rode out among the common people for the first time. I sat tall on my horse and waved at them and their answering cheer was deafening. It grew even louder when they laid eyes on Arthur's bride.

I had practised my welcoming speech until it was perfect but, when I saw her, I forgot the words … my tongue refused to obey my stuttering brain. The crowd also fell silent when they first saw her golden beauty. Everyone waited for me to speak but it was as though I had been turned to stone. Then she smiled and a dimple appeared on her right cheek. I found I couldn't stop looking at it.

Blinded by the splendour of her retinue, her fresh pretty face, for the first time I envied Arthur and wished I had been the elder son.

I had never hankered after the crown, never envied Arthur's status as heir. While my brother was forced to study kingship in the gloomy schoolroom, I was allowed the freedom of play. He seldom rode out on the hunt or played tennis in Father's court but, on that dull November day, I realized that perhaps there was more to life than idle sport. One day, I decided, when I reached manhood, I would marry just such a bride.

My mouth was dry. I ran my tongue across my teeth and cleared my throat before belatedly beginning my speech. I still don't know how much of it she understood but, as I manoeuvred my horse beside hers, I glimpsed the dimple on her cheek again.

By the time their wedding day arrived I had grown used to her, but whenever we met, I would go to great lengths to try to make her laugh.

Everyone, from the lowliest peasant to the king, loves Catalina. The last time I saw her was when she and Arthur set off for Ludlow. And now, just a few months later, Arthur is dead and Catalina is widowed.

If I were older, I would ride off to gallantly escort her home, but Father would never allow it. She will probably be sent back to Spain and I will never see her again.

I sigh so loudly it makes the night candle bob. Mary stirs in her bed.

"Are you awake too, Harry? I can't sleep either."

I roll onto my back. In the low light from the hearth, shadows pattern Mary's face.

"Yes. I was thinking."

"What about?"

I do not answer. I can hardly admit to thinking about Catalina. It would seem odd.

"Just … you know … about how sad Mother looked tonight."

"Poor Mother."

The king is unhappy too, of course, and so is Grandmother, but they are better at managing disappointment. Time and time again I have heard Grandmother say there is no point in worrying over things that cannot be altered, and nothing can change death.

"Do you want to be king, Harry?" Mary whispers.

"I don't know. I don't think so."

"It might be fun. You will have palaces and jewels, a big fleet of ships, and you can stay up late and order your favourite dinner every night. I think I'd like to be a queen."

"You'd have to marry a king."

A long silence before she shifts on her mattress.

"That will be all right, as long as he is handsome."

I chuckle and roll onto my side again.

"Night, Mary."

"Good night …"

Everything is changing. I am afraid; wary lest Mary be stricken down with something deadly, as Arthur was. We take to playing beneath tables or in closets as if the air itself is full of demons. Our big sister, Margaret, is too grand to play with us now. She is preoccupied with the arrangements for her wedding to the King of the Scots. She goes about the palace with a pinched white face, a slight frown between her brows.

Mary says Margaret is cross because she has to go and live in Scotland among strangers. If I were Margaret, I would not want to leave England either. The idea of living forever at the rough Scottish court is terrifying. Thank God I will never have to leave.

I stay close to Mary, hold tightly to her hand and hope she is with me forever. Just lately, I have lost so much.

I was still small when my little sister Elizabeth died. She was my playmate, closer to me in age than my other sisters. She just disappeared one night. When I woke in the morning, she was gone. I could not understand why she was no longer here. It was Grandmother who dried my tears and explained that only the good die young, and that she is in a better place now.

I cannot imagine a better place than Eltham.

Now Arthur has gone too, but if it is a better place, why is everyone so sad? The sorrow of the adults compounds my own. It is hard to laugh and be merry so I misbehave; even the harsh side of Grandmother's tongue is preferable to being ignored.

"You must learn to be good. You are the heir now, Henry," she says. "Shortly you will be made Prince of Wales. It is an honour you must live up to. You must not let your father down. You must prove your worthiness."

Am I worthy? Just a short time ago, the king was the proud father of three sons, the Tudor line was secure, and my mother always smiled. Now, I am the only one left of those three princes.

What if I am the next to die?

My father goes about the court with a long face, his white fingers constantly plucking at his velvet sleeve. He doesn't seem to notice me unless it is to reprimand. My hours of play are cut short and some days I only see Mary at suppertime, or when it is time for bed. On the nights when Mother manages to come to the nursery to bid us good night, I cling to her soft fragrant neck and beg her to sing songs of brave Arthur and Lancelot.

Her voice is not as merry as it used to be. It croaks when she speaks, as if she is trying not to weep. I feel safer when Mother is with me; she loves me even when I behave badly. Once, when I was younger, she overheard me say a very bad word. She didn't scold me or tell my father of it, she just frowned at me, and her disappointment stung as hard as a spanking.

I know that whatever I do she will always love me. Her faith in me makes me want to be good. I try so hard to be more like Arthur. I pretend interest in my studies and feign attention to my tutor's lessons even while my mind gallops like a hound in pursuit of a hind. So, when Mother begins to sicken a few short months after Arthur's death, my heart fills with dread.

It is Mary who remarks upon it first. We are in the garden, taking the air before it is time for noon time prayer. Mother holds my hand while I chatter on about the mouse that our nurse unaccountably discovered in her sewing basket. She knows I put it there, but she doesn't reproach me. Instead, she brushes my hair from my forehead and kisses me.

"Oh, my Henry," she says. "What am I going to do with you?"

I am just about to offer some ideas when Grandmother appears at the end of the path and calls

Mother away. Margaret and Mary stand beside me as we watch her go.

Mary rubs her nose.

"Mother doesn't seem well," she says, "and she is getting fat."

Margaret jerks Mary's arm. "Mary! She is with child again. Didn't you know? She has promised to give Father another son to replace Arthur."

My jaw drops; we turn in unison to our knowledgeable sister.

What about me?

"Is that true?"

"Of course it is. Don't you know that a queen's primary duty is to bear sons? A royal nursery must be full, and preferably full of boys."

"But I will still be king one day?"

She looks at me as if I am a fool.

"Yes, Henry, you will be King of England and I will be Queen of Scotland …"

"What about me?" Mary interrupts. "Where shall I be queen of?"

"Spain? France? Take your pick; it won't be your decision when the time comes anyway."

Margaret lifts her skirts from the wet path and begins to walk away, her head high. Mary runs a little way along the path after her, stopping in a puddle to shriek in Margaret's wake

"I won't marry a man I have no liking for! You wait and see!" She puts her hands on her hips, her bottom lip thrust forward.

Jenny appears from nowhere. "Mary! A lady, and most especially a royal lady, never raises her voice." Taking Mary's arm, she marches her back to the nursery.

1503

Since Arthur's death, I now have my own household. I have fewer female attendants because Grandmother says I must learn to be a man … learn to be a king. The lessons are daunting and I am not sure I will be able to master them all, even if I study for a lifetime.

Mother visits me less frequently now and, shortly after the day when I learn she is going to have another son, she journeys into Wales, leaving me and my sisters behind. I miss her so much, and the months seem long without her. To make it worse, my studies begin in earnest and the king works me so hard that I miss most of the summer. Winter is almost upon us before Mother comes home.

As soon as I learn of her return, I send a messenger to seek permission for me to see her straight away. She sends my page back with a scribbled note, saying she will be with us as soon as she can. The intervening hours seem endless.

I cannot settle to my lessons, I keep looking from the window, running to the door to see if she is on her way. I keep imagining her footstep, thinking I hear her voice. About the fourth time I do this, she is suddenly there, walking toward me, her smile wide. She is puffing, as if she carries a heavy weight upon her back. She sinks gratefully into a chair and opens her arms.

It is as if she has never been away.

"Henry," she murmurs, her hands caressing my hair, her lips brushing my cheek. I want to cast myself onto her lap. Before I was heir, when I was small, I would climb up and snuggle into her bosom. But I know I must display the good manners I have learned, and so I bow and give her a courtly greeting. She smiles wanly, blinking as though there is something in her eye.

"How you have grown," she says, and I lift my chin and inflate my chest, making myself as tall as I can.

"I will be as big as your father, King Edward, one day," I say, and she smiles, her eyes brimming.

"Indeed, you will."

She pats the seat beside her and I clamber up to join her. She slips her arm around me while I tell her about my tutors and all the newly appointed household gentlemen.

"I am glad Compton will still be with me. He is quite a few years older than I, but I am mature for my years, so they tell me."

Mother laughs gently and ruffles my hair.

"And your schooling; you are working hard as well as playing?"

"I enjoy some of my lessons, but the statesmanship is difficult to master – Mother, did you hear of Father's plan for my marriage?"

Her smile becomes fixed.

"I did. Does it please you?"

I frown. I am not sure I am ready for marriage but Father's choice of bride both pleases and confuses me. The woman I once greeted as sister is now to become my wife. Father has approached Spain with the proposal that Catalina, my brother's widow, should now be married to me.

I wonder how she feels about it, or whether they've even told her of the plan. I daresay she is glad she will still be queen one day. I half close my eyes and try to remember her face.

"I have not seen Catalina since she went to Ludlow. I imagine she still looks the same."

"I am sure she does, my son. She will make you a merry bride."

Catalina may be my senior by several years, but she is not old. The sudden memory of her high-pitched, youthful laughter makes me smile. I recall our easy companionship; our friendship sealed when she declared how pleased she was to call me 'brother.'

Will she be as pleased to call me 'husband'?

Mother's voice pulls me from my thoughts.

"Don't look so concerned, Henry. The marriage will not take place for years yet. Not until you are a man. Until then, Catalina will remain in England as our honoured guest."

I nod, comforted by the intervening years; years in which I can study hard and become the man I have always dreamed of being – a man like my grandfather, King Edward of York. Mother says he was a golden giant with a sword, a generous, benevolent king, beloved of the people, feared by his enemies, adored by his children. When I am grown, I swear I will be just such a king.

It saddens me when Mother enters confinement for what Margaret calls her 'lying-in.' It is to take place at the Tower of London. I wave her farewell, sad that it will be a month or so until I see her again. I long for the child to be born so Mother can be merry. It has been hard seeing her so sickly and sad.

I watch from the window as she is helped onto the waiting barge. Before she settles herself among the cushions, she turns and raises her hand to wave. She probably cannot see me, but she knows I am here. I dash a tear from my eyes and wave back, blowing her kisses as we did in my infancy. I watch until the barge is out of sight and, when I finally turn away, I realise Margaret has been watching me.

I sniff, wipe my face and smile blithely, as if nothing is amiss. She laughs, but not unkindly, and places a hand on my shoulder, guiding me from the room. We pass along the dimly lit corridor where the torches leap and dance, casting strange shadows on the walls. A mouse scurries across our path and my sister stops, grabs her skirts and waits while it disappears through a tiny crack in the wall. When we reach the door to my apartments, Margaret grasps my sleeve, preventing me from entering.

"You must strengthen your heart against such sentimentality, Harry," she says. "If you want to be a good king, you must learn not to let your emotions show. You must keep your heart's desires to yourself and never allow anyone to suspect that you bleed as lesser mortals do."

She smiles tightly and walks away. I watch her go, frowning as I fumble for the meaning of her words. Margaret is due to leave court for Scotland soon, probably never to return to England. She has spent the last few months with Grandmother, learning etiquette and the appropriate behaviour for a queen. I imagine there are similar rules for a future king. As Margaret turns the corner, I rub my nose. Deep in my heart, emotions tumble and turn like a chaotic game of catch-as-catch-can. How can I ever contain them?

Left to my own devices, I am a happy fellow. I enjoy good company, love the courtly dances, and the jesters that entertain us in the great hall make me bellow with laughter. It is only when life goes wrong that my spirit rebels. I am sore that Mother has left me again so soon and, now I come to think on it, I am resentful of all the honours and attention being lavished on Margaret just because she is to marry some old Scottish king.

As she disappears from view, I wonder if perhaps Margaret conceals her true feelings too. Perhaps she is not as content to leave England as she pretends. The king of Scotland is old, about sixteen years older than my sister and, so I have discovered, is the father of many *bastard* children. I wonder how Margaret will like that? I cannot imagine her taking it well, for beneath the veneer of obedience, she is always opinionated … and often rebellious.

The guard throws open the door to my apartment and I find my companions waiting for me. They look up at my entrance and, abandoning their game of chess, get to their feet to greet me.

"I am so glad I will never have to leave England," I announce as I enter the chamber. Compton sketches a slight bow.

"And we are glad of it too. I can think of none better to lead England into a new era."

My gentlemen are expected to praise me; it is their duty. I move toward the window, look out across the gardens. I can just glimpse the serpentine route of the river that bears my mother away. Concealing my sorrow, I turn a blithe face on my friends.

I am not given time to mope. Grandmother embarks on another round of schooling and appoints Sir Henry Marney to oversee my household. My whole life now centres on learning. A prince must know all there is to know of the far-flung places of the world; I must memorise their leaders, their customs, their politics. It seems a waste of time to me; should the need arise, all I need do is ask one of my tutors to advise me.

Father has a league of advisors and I am quite sure he doesn't spend too much time studying foreign policy. His mind is ever on the running of England, the hunting down of rebels, and keeping his beady eyes open for the merest hint of treason.

All I seem to do is work, sleep and pray. I look from my window at the bright blue winter sky and yearn to hunt, to walk with Beau in the gardens as I used to. I want to run in the meadow with Mary and the spaniel, feel the cold air reach the bottom of my lungs. I want to scream into the vastness of the January sky. Instead, for the best part of the day, I stay cooped indoors with my tutors.

But I do learn. My handwriting is no longer crabbed and crooked but uniform and neat. I no longer blot ink each time I prime my pen. I can name the heads of state, I can discuss theology as well as any man, yet … I am lonely, and sometimes feel so sad even the antics of my fool, John Goose, cannot raise a smile.

And then something happens that makes me realise I was not miserable after all. Before this, I have never known true grief, not even when Elizabeth and Arthur died. Dusk is approaching when the door opens. Mary looks up from her sewing and nudges me.

"Grandmother looks like a ghost," she whispers. And she is right. She glides unsmiling into the room.

"Put down your book, Henry," she says, and I take my thumb from it and place it on the table. It is as if I know what she is going to tell me before she says it and a deep dragging sickness consumes me. I fumble for Mary's hand and we wait, hand in hand, for Grandmother to speak.

"I have some news," she says at last, blinking rapidly, her throat working as if there is something she cannot swallow. She looks from me to Mary and back again. Her head lowers and she utters a prayer. "I am afraid your mother has been taken to God."

The flames crackle in the hearth. Our servants begin weeping but I feel nothing, not right away. I just stare at my grandmother and notice that her face seems to have turned to wax. It is an odd colour and there are deep lines scored into it.

Beside me, Mary begins to bawl. I put my arm about her but still I do not cry. I nod but say nothing even though my heart feels as if it has been cloven in two. Nothing, *nothing,* will ever be as it was before.

I am lost. I am quite, quite lost.

To cheer me, they tell me I have a baby sister, Katherine, but then, a few days later, I learn that she is dead too. I feel little grief for the child. It is just as well she did not live, for life without a mother is no life at all … and I should know.

Her loss makes me feel very small, inadequate against the trials God has seen fit to lay before me. I am like a beetle, squashed on the path, yet inside I rage against fate, rage against her leaving me.

I cannot speak of it for I am suffocating, as if someone is holding a pillow over my face. I cannot scream as I need to, for sorrow will not let me breathe.

Late one afternoon, I slip away from the constant vigilance of my attendants and creep into Mother's bedchamber. No fire has been lit and my breath is visible in the frigid air. I halt just inside the door and look about the room.

It is as it always is. Beneath a chair, I notice her embroidered slippers side by side, her robe thrown across the settle. On the nightstand sit a few books. I move deeper into the room, pick up one of the books and see that she has placed a marker between the pages to keep her place. When she placed it there, she believed she would come back and pick it up again to read from the page where she left off. Looking closer at the marker I realise it is one of the letters I wrote to her while she was in Wales.

I recall how hard I worked to make my characters as neat as possible, but now the ink blurs, merging beneath my tears. Something tightens in my throat, as if the hard ball that has been lodged there has suddenly come free. It is pain such as I have never felt. I blink to clear my tears and fall to my knees beside her bed. *Oh God, why did you take my mother? How will I go on without her?*

Grandmother is always harking on about God's ways being unfathomable and she is right. I can make no sense of this. I have always imagined Him as a kind, loving father looking down on me, guiding me, careful lest I fall, but now ... I wonder if he cares about me at all.

I grasp the embroidered coverlet and bury my face in it. Her fragrance fills my head; I feel her touch, hear her voice, her merry laughter.

Henry, I seem to hear her say, *you are greater and stronger than you know.*

But she is wrong. I am not great or strong at all. I am just a boy who has lost his mother and my future without her looms huge and black and terrifying.

Richmond 1504

When Arthur became Prince of Wales and married Catalina, they were sent away to learn all the things that royal heirs must learn. He had his own castle at Ludlow with a huge household and I had always imagined he had a say in how he spent his leisure time. It is different for me. Instead of the world opening up to welcome me, it closes. My freedom is so limited that sometimes I long to scream.

"It isn't fair," I complain to Guildford when we are alone. "I am shut away, treated like a maid. If I am to be king, I must learn about the world as it is now, but all I hear is how it was for my father. His view of things is as dour as ditch water."

"He is afraid." Guildford leans back on his chair and puts his feet on the table. I do the same; we never stand on ceremony when we are alone. That is why I enjoy the company of boys a little older than I; when we are alone, we forget ceremony and they treat me almost as an equal. For a short space, I can forget who I am and what is expected of me.

"Afraid of what?" I reply belatedly. Beau leaps up, his claws snagging at my hose, but instead of pushing him down, I caress his silken ears, looking into his brown trusting eyes. If only men were as loyal as dogs …

"Well, the sweating sickness is running amok again, and the King is terrified you will fall victim to it. He has lost his son, and now … well, now the queen has passed, he cannot afford to lose his heir."

"Who told you that?"

"Nobody. It is obvious. One only has to look at him to realise how anxious he is."

Our eyes meet briefly, long enough for me to recognise a kinship before I look away. I shift uncomfortably in my seat, reluctant to betray my own fear of contagion.

"I'm not going to die. Look at me; I am already almost as tall as Father. Arthur was never as hale as me."

"Old men are more aware of death. The king forgets the risks he took in his youth, or perhaps, being so much older, he realises how narrow is the divide between earth and heaven. Where we regard the tiltyard as a release for our pent-up energies, he sees only the dangers. Look at the accidents that have occurred. You could lose an eye, or an arm, or be killed outright – then where would the country be? Without an heir, contenders for the throne would swarm from the far reaches of the kingdom. No man wants a return to civil war."

He is right. Now I see how important I am, but it doesn't make my life easier. Father is constantly telling me the duties of a prince, Grandmother is ever prattling on about religion, etiquette and courtly rules. It is as if they think I am a peasant just crawled from the gutter.

My mother taught me the ways of a gentleman and I much prefer the things she taught me of her father. Now, he was a king to emulate. Edward IV never hid from his subjects and they loved him for it. They didn't deride him when he sported and drank and womanised. He didn't flee from court every time the threat of plague came too close.

But Father is sick. That is why he closets himself away. He is fearful of the people discovering his infirmity because he feels I am not yet ready to take his place. With just one son, he sees himself as having failed, and fears for the succession, the continuance of the House of Tudor that must at all costs perpetuate.

It is a lesson Father and Grandmother drum into me and, sometimes of a night, their voices creep into my dreaming. I can hear their constant refrain at every moment.

"A king must beget as many legitimate sons as he can, and a few daughters too for the forming of political alliances. I cannot stress enough how important it is to get a son, yearly if you can."

I picture Catalina, plump with my child, another on her knee, several more boys tumbling on the floor beside her. It is a pretty image. One day, I will make it so, but for now, I need to indulge the demands of youth.

I want to wrestle with my companions. I want to learn the steps of the dance, leap and twist in the air as I did at Arthur's wedding. I want the court to throw up their hands and marvel at my prowess. But how can I do so when they treat me like a girl?

When I am king, England will be renewed. I am determined to throw off the megrims of my father's reign and fill the court with light and laughter.

I don't know whether it is Guildford's doing but slowly Father relents, just a little, and allows me a little more freedom. Albeit reluctantly, he allows me to undertake military training, swordplay and fighting with axes. I excel in this and enjoy it far more than the dusty hours in the schoolroom. I grow stronger, happier, fleet of foot, and as agile as the best of them.

Of all my companions, there is only one I cannot guarantee to beat. My great friend, Charles Brandon, seven years my senior, equals me in strength, height and looks. Some say we are so much alike we could be brothers, and we encourage that by dressing alike, wearing identical armour so none can tell who they are facing in the tilting yard.

Whenever I beat him at any sport, I crow about it for hours, lording my prowess but, if he should have the victory over me, I scowl at him should he even dare mention it.

1505

As I grow older, I come to realise the power that will one day lie in my hands. Father ... and presumably Grandmother ... will no longer be here. They will no longer watch me. All decisions will be mine, although, of course, I will have to win the approval of my council. But people love me. My ministers will eat out of my hand, and the commoners will too.

My father is not loved, he never has been, but the more he shuts himself away, the more they speculate, the louder the whispers and plots against him become. When my time comes to be king, I swear I will wipe all that away. I will be the people's king, and I will make England merry again, as it was in my grandfather's day.

Although we are to be married, I have not been allowed to meet formally with Catalina. Occasionally, we see each other from a distance. Whenever we do so, I bow to her politely across the hall, but I cannot reach her for she is guarded by a flotilla of gentlewomen.

Mary tells me that she complains of not receiving an allowance. The king is still battling with the Spanish on the payment of her dowry and so she is living in what she calls 'poverty'.

She did not seem impoverished when I saw her last. She was plump and pretty, dressed in a shade that I describe as purple but Mary says is mauve. At supper, although we are seated far from one another, I feel her eyes on me and wonder what she sees. Is she pleased with the idea of our marriage? I return her scrutiny and she does not lower her eyes but looks right into mine, a smile spreading across her face.

It makes me feel quite odd.

Brandon says she is eager for me. Spanish women are passionate, he says, and he should know. He is fond of women and, despite his youth, has already had a string of mistresses. A regular visitor to the stews across the river, he does not restrict himself to lowborn women and is currently trying to coax Margaret Neville into dalliance. I am quite shocked at this. Margaret is very well born and an illicit affair with Brandon could be the ruin of her. No doubt she thinks she can tempt him into marriage, but the woman who snares Brandon will have to be more cunning than she.

Most of my companions, the older ones at least, have tasted the pleasures of women, but I have no desire to dally with whores. Instead, when the curtains are drawn about my bed at night, I think of Catalina and the delights we will one day enjoy. Since there are no tutors to instruct me on such matters, I listen to the tales my friends tell of their conquests. The prospect of bedding my future wife fills me with a mix of excitement and terror.

And then, on the eve of my fourteenth birthday, the king informs me that I must make a formal protest against the union with Spain.

"Why?" I exclaim. "I have no wish to protest against it!"

Father rubs his nose, dabs it with his kerchief which he rolls into a ball, and glares at me.

"Your wishes are of no moment. This is politics. You will do as you are told."

I am furious but I know better than to argue. It would do me no good. I can feel my ears growing red with resentment. I clench my teeth until I hear my jaw crack. Oblivious to my feelings, Father shuffles through the papers on his desk, picks one up and reads aloud the instruction he has written there.

"You must declare, before witnesses, that the agreement was made when you were a minor, and now that you have reached puberty you will not ratify the contract but denounce it as null and void. Your words will be set in writing and then signed and witnessed by six men."

Objections tumble in my mind but I cannot voice them. When he dismisses me with a flick of his fingers, I bow perfunctorily, turn on my heel and quit the room. I find Brandon in the tennis court, loudly protesting the score, while his opponent, Guildford, stands with his hands on his hips.

"You are wrong, Brandon, the point is mine. Isn't that so?"

He turns to the others, who are lounging nearby. Having only been half attending, they shrug and shake their heads noncommittally.

"My Lord Prince." Brandon, noticing my arrival, turns for my support. "You witnessed it, did you not? The point was mine. Back me up, Sir."

I pick up a racket, idly test it in my hand and, emitting a string of curses, hurl it across the court. Silence falls upon the company.

"What ails you, Sir?"

Brandon is the only one brave enough to come forward. He reaches out, his hand heavy on my shoulder. There are few men whom I permit to touch me. At the back of my mind I am aware that Brandon is merely proving to the others how high he stands in my regard.

I should shrug him off, but I don't.

"Walk with me," I mutter between my teeth, and then turn away, almost falling over Beau who dogs my every footstep.

"Out of my way!" I scream and he cowers from me, tail between his legs.

Tossing his racket to Thomas Knyvet, Brandon follows me.

"Henry, wait," he calls, and I slow my step until he has caught up.

"What has happened?"

"My accursed father."

I am so angry I can hardly speak; my lips feel tight against my teeth, my head pounds with repressed fury. "He demands that I denounce my union with Catalina."

I stop and rub my hands across my face, the blood thundering in my ears.

"I don't know if I am angry because I have lost her, or because I am so sick of being told what I must do. What will Catalina think? What will happen to her?"

He shrugs. "In all probability she will be sent home to Spain."

I think of her leaving, imagine her sad little figure boarding ship for the perilous journey to her homeland. For four years she has lived at the mercy of my father's generosity, which, as we all know, is greatly lacking, and now she is to be sent home like a misdirected package.

"Sometimes I feel this ... this limbo will never end, and I will spend my whole life under my father's jurisdiction."

He flings a brotherly arm about me and I am suddenly grateful to have a friend. He speaks quietly, with feeling, and I struggle not to weep like a woman.

"We are all told what to do by our fathers, Henry, and we are much alike, you and me. I am also the second son. Had my brother not died, I would like as not be languishing in the country, wed too young to some red-cheeked matron, yet here I am, your honoured servant. One day, you will be king, and I will still be at your side. The future will soon be ours, and the time for following orders will be over."

It is treason to even hint of the king's death, yet I do not reprimand him for, although it is a sin to say it, I also think of it ... often. When my father dies, my life will change a thousandfold.

I nod, half-convinced and more than a little cheered. I give a deep sigh. Brandon pats my arm.

"Come," he says. "I am sure I saw your sister, Mary, and Jane Popincourt heading for the gardens. Jane is a merry sort. Why don't we join them? There's nothing like female company to liven a dull afternoon."

I allow myself to be led outside into the bright winter day and, as the fresh air hits my lungs and the sound of female laughter wafts above the privet hedge, my heart lightens.

My sister and her tutor, Jane, are wandering between the barren flowerbeds. I smile when I notice Mary give a small hop as if she is struggling to contain her energy in the stately stroll. As they reach a corner, Mary hears our footsteps behind her and turns, her face lighting up when she sees me.

"Harry! It is an age since I saw you!"

Abandoning her attempt at serenity, she runs and leaps into my arms. I laugh and turn a circle, lifting her into the air, swinging her around.

"Oh, help! My cap!" She grabs for her veil, but it is too late; her finery lands in the gravel and my sister blushes to be caught wearing only her coif. Before I can retrieve it, Brandon scoops it up and brushes away imaginary dirt before returning it with a courtly bow.

"Your Royal Highness," he says formally, and my sister laughs.

"Thank you, sir." While we watch, the women fuss and fidget with pins to fasten the cap back in place.

"Has Father excused you from your lessons today?" Mary asks, taking her place at my side while Brandon falls into step with Jane Popincourt.

"I am meeting Master Skelton this afternoon but I don't wish to discuss my lessons. I want to forget all that. How are you, Mary? I rarely see you informally now."

Just shy of her ninth birthday, Mary is as bright and irrepressible as ever. Although she does her best to show herself as an obedient, decorous princess, I'd bet my favourite dagger she has bruises on her knees, and still steals dainties from the table and secretes them in her pocket. She is only a little taller than my elbow.

"I don't believe you have grown at all," I laugh, patting her head and almost dislodging her hood again. She scowls in the old familiar manner.

"Oh, indeed I have. Only a month ago my women had to order my seamstress to lengthen my gowns. Look, this contrasting border has been added to my skirt to provide the extra length. I shall be as tall as you one day."

"Then you will be a giantess indeed!"

I am little short of two yards high. I throw back my head, imagining my little sister with the height and build of an Amazon. She punches me lightly on the arm.

"And when I've grown as tall as you, you will have to watch out, king or no king, or I might knock you down."

"You'll have no need of large fists for you already slay people with your wit."

I take her hand and tuck it beneath my elbow. The trials of the morning melt away and my equilibrium is restored.

"You could mistake it for a spring day," I remark as we turn a corner and look up at the blue sky. Mary stops short. I look down at her.

"What is the matter? Why have we stopped?"

"Look," she says. "It is Catalina. I never know what to say to her ... despite her women, she always seems so alone and sad ..."

I take my eyes from her face and look across the garden to where Catalina too is taking the air. Mary puts her hand to her mouth and speaks behind it.

"Oh dear, I think she has been weeping ..."

Leaving go of Mary's arm, I hurry rudely away and, breaking with convention, make my bow before

Catalina. Straightening up, I am shocked to see, not the soft and pretty face I have dreamed of, but cold and angry eyes.

"Catalina, I …"

She leans toward me before I can finish. "How dare you speak to me?" she hisses. "How dare you even approach me? Do you think I have not been informed of your plan to reject our betrothal? I hope the devil takes you."

Before I can protest, she sweeps past me, her head high, and, as her ladies follow, each one regards me with such scorn that I feel as worthless as a worm.

Mary and Brandon catch up with me, noticing my shocked expression.

"She told me to go to the devil," I exclaim, and Brandon chuckles.

"Don't let it trouble you," he says. "Worrying will change nothing. You must make the best of the situation. Forget about Catalina and concentrate on the women you can have."

He does not understand. Reluctantly, I turn away, take Mary's arm and walk with her back to the hall. In my apartments, my gentlemen do their best to cheer me. Brandon calls for wine and we drink until late in the night. At first, I am morose and maudlin, but the Burgundy soon takes the edge off my disappointment. When Brandon and Percy kick off their shoes and do a madcap dance on the table, I am soon roaring with laughter.

"Come on, Henry…" Brandon grabs my hand, hauling me to my feet, and I begin to dance too. After a while, false joy consumes me. I throw off my jerkin and, in my shirtsleeves, I leap and frolic until my forehead is slick with sweat. I pay little heed to the music, give no thought of keeping time, and the musician cannot keep pace with me.

At last, when the players are dropping with fatigue, I collapse into my chair, my chest heaving, my heart thumping. I let my head loll against the back of the settle and turn to look at Brandon, whose face is gleaming red in the firelight. He laughs, his eyes crinkling at the corners, his handsome face somehow finer in disarray.

"By God, Henry, I have need of a woman now. There is nothing else to round off this fine evening so well."

I imagine feminine arms twining around my neck, soft kisses on my face, and find myself nodding agreement.

"Yes, a woman is just what I need," I reply and, when the face of Catalina rises before me, I thrust it away and think of another ... any other.

January 1506

Away from the eyes of my father and grandmother, my companions and I enjoy a rowdy festive season. Just as January dissolves into ennui, we learn of a ship, wrecked off the coast of Dorset. On board are the Archduke Philip and his wife, Juana, Catalina's elder sister. They had been en route to Spain to claim the throne of Castile when high winds forced them to seek shelter at Melcombe.

When the king summons me to his presence, I expect another reprimand, further orders to amend my attitude. So, when he tells me of the shipwreck and the plight of the royals on board, I am surprised, my interest piqued.

"You are to ride to welcome them to our country and escort them here. They will remain with us as our guests while the necessary repairs are made to their fleet. My master of horse will accompany you. See that you behave …"

"Of course, Father. I do know what is expected of me."

He looks up with a jaundiced eye.

"Indeed. Then it is a shame our expectations are so frequently disappointed."

I say nothing, clamping my jaw shut as he continues his instruction and provides a brief outline of Philip and his wife. As we ride toward Winchester, I quiz Sir Thomas further as to the archduke's nature.

"I have not met him, your Grace, but I am told he is young – less than thirty – and a lover of sports and fine clothes. While we accompany him at due speed back to Windsor, his wife is to travel more slowly. I expect the king will summon the dowager Princess of Wales to help entertain her."

Catalina. Of course, she should be there. It has been months since we met face to face. The last time I saw her, she was furious with me. I wonder if she has realised that in refuting our betrothal, I was obeying the order of the king. Perhaps ... if the opportunity presents itself, I will be able to convey my regret and help her to understand.

We clatter through the castle gate at Winchester and I spring from the saddle, tossing the reins at the groom. Without waiting for Sir Thomas, I ascend the stair and hurry into the hall. I blink to readjust my eyes after the brightness of the day, pull off my gauntlets and let my cloak slip to the floor.

As I hold out my hands to the blazing fire, my skin tingles and my nose begins to run. Someone claps their hands at a servant.

"Bring wine, bring wine!" he orders and, as they scurry to do his bidding, I speak to a trio of strangers who are warming their nethers at the flames. Richard Foxe hovers at my elbow.

"Ah, your Royal Highness, may I introduce you to the Archduke of Burgundy?"

A pair of laughing eyes meets my gaze. Instantly recognising a kindred spirit, my heart lightens. We clasp hands, his grip firm and strong; and his voice, when he addresses me, is warm. I know without question that I have met a friend.

Although Philip is some years my senior, we are well matched in height and strength.

"I am glad to see you have suffered no lasting ill from your ordeal," I say, and he laughs, the sound musical to my ears.

"It would take more than a little wind and rain to thwart me," he replies, "although my wife was shaken. In fact, she screamed and clung to me, wailing that we were going to die."

I laugh with him, wondering if I would have been so blasé were Catalina almost lost at sea.

A page appears with a tray of cups and I take one, handing it to Philip with a small inclination of my head. I hold my own cup aloft.

"To your very good health," I say, and he lifts his in reply.

"And may all our vessels be seaworthy!"

We drink deeply and in unison.

I had not expected to enjoy Philip's unplanned visit but, to my delight, we are almost immediate friends. We remain at Winchester for a few days, spending our time at tennis, hunting and jousting. Philip is strong, but he is impressed by my own prowess although, to my pique, I cannot quite best him. But, by the time we ride to Windsor to meet with the king, the archduke and I are firm friends.

It is a bright, cloudless day when we ride back to rejoin my father at Richmond. Sir Thomas stays behind with the rest of the entourage while my new friend and I gallop ahead. It is all I can do to keep abreast of Philip. I whip off my cap and use it to urge my mount faster and faster. The ground blurs beneath me, the wind whistling in my ears, my eyes streaming in the cold air. But, at last, our horses blown, we slow to a canter and then a walk.

Philip passes me a flask so I might refresh myself. When I offer it back, he draws close beside me, sitting easy in his saddle. He flicks at his hose to remove foam from his horse's bit.

"This is fine country," he says, sweeping his arm across the vista. "So green and fertile."

My chest swells with pride and I see the familiar landscape afresh. Since it is only January, the countryside seems bleak to me, the trees and meadows painted in sombre hues of browns, yellows and dark green. It will be a few months yet before it awakens from winter sleep.

"You should see it in the summer when it is much greener than this, and the meadows are spotted with flowers. This road we travel will be shaded in the summer from the thick canopy of the trees on either hand. Everything appears deeper and richer in summer

– this landscape is dormant. You should stay to see our country in its full glory …"

"Greener than this?" He looks around him, his forehead crinkled as he tries to imagine it. "I would stay if I could, just to see it."

"Why shouldn't you?" I lean toward him, my saddle creaking. "You are your own man …"

"I must leave as soon as my fleet is ready. My country awaits me, Henry, but, judging from what I've already seen, I like it here. I like you too, my friend, and will certainly return."

Although I am glad to hear him say so, I am deflated at the thought of him leaving. For a moment, I had imagined him staying to enjoy the summer sport with myself, Brandon and the others, but … it is not to be.

Philip puts a hand to his hip and rides with a long rein, his torso swaying in time with the motion of the horse. I adopt a similar stance, imagining how we must look together.

"You are not as I imagined, Henry. I have heard the King of England is a private, careful sort of fellow. Some say he is so reserved he is difficult to know. I imagined you would be the same."

He is too polite to say that he heard my father is a miser and a killjoy.

I stare toward the horizon.

"My father is troubled. He is on constant alert for treachery but once he has decided a man's worth, he is amenable enough. You may find him a little stiff at first but, given time, he will warm to you. How could he not?"

Philip throws back his head with a hearty laugh. I admire the long stretch of his neck, the firmness of his jaw. It is little wonder he has been named Philip the Fair. For a short while, we travel in silence as he drinks in the surroundings, and my own mind wanders.

I envy his glorious epithet; I have long determined that I will rule England differently to my father. I wonder what they will call me when I am king. I begin to toy with pleasing appellations. *Henry the Tall; Henry the Magnificent; Henry the Brave ... Henry the Valiant ... Henry the ...*

"PIG!"

Philip's voice tears me from my musing and instinctively I haul on the rein. In the road ahead, a large family of pigs are rooting and, as everyone is aware, horses and pigs make uncomfortable friends.

We halt, our mounts blowing and sidestepping, showing the whites of their eyes. Keeping my hand firmly on the reins, I twist in my saddle and urge the rest of the party to catch up with us.

"Have one of the grooms chase the beasts from the road. It will not do to worry our horses," I order.

We watch as a boy dismounts and warily approaches the swine. He flaps his arms, stamps his feet and makes tentative swooshing noises. Beside me, Philip begins to chuckle when the biggest pig stands his ground.

It blinks short-sightedly at its assailant, the sun shining through its twitching pink ears. It seems undecided whether to attack or flee. Nervously, the boy flaps his arms and, to his evident relief, the pig makes its decision, turns and lumbers after the rest of the herd, squealing as it goes.

We travel on, the whole party smiling and laughing.

"I wasn't afraid," I say, concerned that Philip might think me timid. "My father says horses hate pigs."

"Oh, they do, they do. When I was a boy, I was thrown from my horse when one appeared suddenly from beneath a hedge. I hit my head on a rock and was carried back to the castle. When my mother saw me, she thought me dead and squealed louder than any swine. It is the last real memory I have of her. Sometimes, when I think of my childhood, it is difficult to tell if I am remembering an actual event or merely recalling an account of something that happened."

My own mother's face floats in my mind; her eyes shining with love, her pretty mouth tilted upward in her smile. That is a *real* recollection. I know it. Her image is branded on my brain, her voice caught on a barb in my memory.

"I remember my mother very clearly. We spent much time together when I was a boy. She taught me my letters. I was very young when she died. I will never forget it; never forget her."

Our eyes meet; his are soft with understanding.

"Your mother was famous throughout Christendom for her beauty and piety ... and her strength of mind."

My throat closes and, for a moment, I think I will be unmanned but, thankfully, Philip remarks on a huge swathe of primroses clustered in the shelter of a ditch, and I have time to blink the tears away and compose myself.

The king puts himself out and offers Philip a royal welcome, ordering lavish entertainments and giving me free rein to keep him occupied with hunting, jousting and tennis. The better I come to know him, the more impressed I am by his bearing, his philosophies, and his purity of heart. I speak of very little else, and Brandon and the others grow weary of it. At first, I do not notice, and it is not until Brandon declines a tennis match, pleading a headache, that I sense anything amiss.

"A headache?" I cry. "I've never known you suffer a headache in your life. You sound like my grandmother; some activity will do you good. The sun is shining. Come along; the archduke will be waiting."

Brandon stands stiffly.

"If it is an order, then I must do as you ask."

I punch him playfully, but he doesn't laugh, doesn't pretend to fall down as he usually would. I peer closer. His expression is dark, his eyes dull, the spark of friendship absent. I draw back, wary of contagion.

"You must be ailing." I turn away. "Go seek my physician. It will not do for the rest of the court to catch it."

With Blount and Percy in my wake, I repair to the tennis court and find Philip already waiting.

"I managed to find some fellows to join us," I call. "Of course, Brandon is the toughest opponent, but he is ailing."

The words are strange on my tongue. In all the years I've known him, Brandon has never once even been slightly off-colour. I frown at Percy. "Has he been ill long?"

Percy rubs his nose, fixes his eye a little way to the left of my face.

"Not long, no; he began to sicken shortly after your return from Winchester."

It isn't often I am beaten at a tennis match, and when I am it usually spoils my afternoon. Losing makes me question my manhood, my ability to be the best, as a prince should always be. I would lay good coin that my grandfather, Edward IV, never lost a game in his life but somehow, when Philip bests me, I do not mind so much.

Although he is bigger and stronger and quicker than me, I am confident that it is due to his superiority of age. In a few years, I will beat him easily ... every time. We are returning to my apartments, Philip's arm around my neck, when we encounter my sister, Mary. I break convention by planting a smacking kiss on her cheek.

"My little sister, Mary." I turn her to face Philip. "The fairest lady of our court."

"I am honoured, your Highness."

Philip makes a gallant bow and bends over her hand. I see his lips actually touch her skin. Her eyes open wide in surprise.

"The honour is mine," she says, but I sense she is uneasy about something. Taking her elbow, I entreat her to accompany us.

"I will order up the musicians and we can play at cards until supper time."

She skims along at my side, her head barely reaching my shoulder, and I give her little opportunity to decline. Her ladies follow, muttering and giggling and making eyes at Philip and his attendants.

By the time I have washed my face and changed my linen, a fine company has gathered in my apartments. Brandon is notable by his absence and the other men of my household have joined Philip in flirtation with my sister's women. I lounge at Mary's side.

"Is anything the matter, Mary? You are quiet today."

She looks at me, and I am surprised at the disapproval in her eye.

"I am concerned, Harry, that you are neglecting those who love you for the sake of your new friend who will be gone from here the instant Father allows him to leave, never to be seen again."

"Who?" I sit up in surprise. "Philip? Whom do I offend?"

"Charles Brandon, of course." She waves her arm about the chamber. "Where is he? Do you really think him sick? Has it not occurred to you that he might be jealous of your new-found champion?"

I laugh shortly, my smile quickly fading. I grow serious.

"That is a girlish notion. He is not the sort of man who …"

"Charles adores you, Harry. He is always talking of how he is your devoted servant, your best friend and confidant. Now he feels usurped, no longer needed, no longer cherished. Who can blame him?"

"That is absurd."

"Well," she tosses her head, "I had it from his own lips."

Placing my cup on the table, I rub my knuckles, easing the rings that are cutting into my fingers.

"Don't you like him either?"

She shrugs. "He seems likeable enough, but you know what they say about friends. He is untested. Just now, he has nothing better to do with his time than be entertained by you. When he has returned to Spain, he may forget all about you. Brandon will never do that. He is your man and always will be … through thick and thin."

"But that doesn't mean I should have only one friend. He has no problem with Percy or Guildford – or Knyvet."

Her high laughter draws the attention of the other people in the room. She lowers her head toward mine.

"That, my dear Harry, is because he knows you love him the best of all of them. You've had years to prove it. Philip is a newcomer, a stranger to all of us, yet you have welcomed him into your company unreservedly, and with no regard for anyone else."

Mary is growing up. Her newfound confidence has not gone unnoticed, and it is not just in her burgeoning beauty but in her wit too.

"You are suddenly very wise, little sister," I say. When she smiles, twin dimples appear on her cheeks, belying her wisdom and making a child of her again. She taps the side of her nose with her forefinger.

"I take a keen interest in what goes on around me, Harry. You would be wise to concentrate on what the king is up to rather than investing all your interests on the outcome of a game of chance. Intelligence serves a man well."

Mary is not yet twelve, yet she speaks with the astuteness of a prophet.

"You sound like Grandmother." I nudge her with my elbow, meaning her to laugh, but instead she raises her eyebrows.

"I take that as a compliment. I can think of no better person to emulate." Tilting her head to one side, she frowns.

"You have no idea of the king's intentions regarding Philip, do you? You truly think he welcomes him; that he adores him as you do."

"He does! Look at the expense he has gone to for his entertainment."

"Ha ha, Harry! Our father sees Philip as an opportunity for political gain. Mark my words, his invitation to the court will be prolonged until Philip has been persuaded to agree to his terms."

"Regarding what?"

She shrugs. "I am not sure but, mark me, the king will gain from Philip's stay. Your friendship with him is encouraged only as an aid to softening the deal. By the way, did you know Catalina has been invited to join us all at Richmond? We are to 'help with the entertainments.' It will be interesting to meet with her sister – I wonder if she is as pretty - they say Juana is quite mad, you know."

I nod distractedly. Philip has already told me his wife can be unstable, but I wonder how Mary managed to discover all this information. She seems to know everything that goes on at court.

Later, I seek out Brandon and find him hunched over a book.

"That won't cure your headache," I say, hoping to raise a smile.

Keeping his thumb between the pages, he turns, gives me a fleeting smile and begins to rise. "I am slightly recovered but not enough for carousing."

"Don't get up."

I perch on the edge of the table, look down at my legs and flex my calf muscle, admiring the way it moves.

"I missed you at tennis. You are the best partner I have ever had."

"Because I let you win." The ghost of his old smile returns. I kick him playfully.

"You do not."

Silence falls between us, an awkward break in the conversation that we have never experienced before.

"You know, Brandon, the king ordered me to make a friend of Philip. He has some scheme up his sleeve. I would like you to know that you are, and always will be, my favourite."

With flushed cheeks, he looks toward the hearth. I see his throat move as if there is some obstruction. He shrugs his shoulders and cocks his head in the old arrogant way.

"I never imagined I wasn't."

Standing up, I hold out my hand.

"If you are recovered, why don't you join us in my chambers? My sister complains of lacking a dance partner."

I soon discover that Mary was right. Father's approval of Philip is all a pretence. Shortly after, with far less pomp than her husband, Juana is welcomed to the palace, and the entertainments are underway. As the hall fills with people, I search out Catalina, spotting her at once amid the sea of her attendants.

She is dressed in blue and silver. I am entranced by the style of the strange Spanish dance; the way her body moves, the graceful fluidity of her arms. She seems mysterious, exotic. I cannot stop watching.

As she dances, a gentle smile plays on her mouth, but she averts her eyes. Although she does not look at me, I sense that she 'sees' me. Something in the arrogant toss of her head, her haughty elegance, tells me her disdain is directed at me and me alone. When the dance ends and she returns to her seat, I watch as one of her ladies leans forward and whispers something in her ear. Catalina's face blossoms into smiles.

My heart fills. I long for that smile to shine upon me. I want to be the one to make her laugh so I can watch that dimple dance upon her cheek again. But I am so far from her I might as well be in another kingdom.

Standing stiffly at my father's side, given no opportunity to speak to her, I keep my eye on her throughout, willing her to glance my way … just once. But she doesn't. She is too stubborn. I will have to work hard to regain her approval.

While the musicians tune their instruments in readiness for the more informal dancing, my gaze follows Catalina as she approaches Philip. She curtseys, lower than etiquette demands, and says something I cannot hear. Neither can I hear his reply, but I am struck by the sudden change in his demeanour. His eyes are cold, his words brief, his handsomeness marred with dislike. Catalina's expression freezes and, red-cheeked, she turns on her heel and hurries back to Mary. When my sister leans forward, presumably to ask if all is well, Catalina replies with tight, unhappy lips.

Philip's words, whatever they were, have cut her and I am piqued that my friend should treat her with such rudeness. Mary reaches out and pats Catalina's hand and I am glad to see her squeeze it in return.

"Philip hates Catalina because she sided with her father over who should inherit the throne of Castile," Mary tells me when I question her later. "Catalina pretends she doesn't care but she is worried it will encourage him to treat her sister worse than he did before."

"Juana must be hard to live with; you can't place all the blame on Philip."

Mary sighs. "I don't believe Juana is mad at all. I believe she is unhappy and objects to things with a passion that Philip, being such a cold fish, cannot comprehend. To him, tears and tantrums equate to insanity when, really, she just loves him too well. She lives in terror of losing him. If he were just a little kinder, Juana would be calmer, and more manageable. That is what Catalina believes, anyway. I think they have both been raised to expect respect and when they don't get it ... well, they stand up for themselves."

"That doesn't make them mad."

"Exactly." Mary fixes me with a sagacious eye. "I am glad you realise that, Harry, and see that you remember it. If you should come to marry her, don't expect to be able to tell her what to do."

But, the next day, the court is buzzing with rumours of an explosive argument between Philip and Juana. I am desperate to learn the truth, but Philip doesn't appear all morning and I am left with my old companions, whose speculations run wild.

"Juana has quit the court," Brandon says gleefully, "and Philip is reputedly furious with her."

Catalina will be disappointed. I imagine she had been looking forward to an extended visit with her sister. I wish I could call on her to offer comfort. I wonder if Mary will help me arrange a chance encounter in the garden. But the king and Grandmother keep me occupied, issuing me with a list of instructions as to how my relationship with Philip must progress. As they ply me with a list of dos and don't dos, I am puzzled as to their concern.

"Why?" I ask at last. "Why does it matter? Philip is my friend; I have no need to be careful how I act and speak."

Father sighs, turns his eyes to Heaven in despair at my lack of intellect.

"I am working toward an alliance," he explains slowly, as if to an idiot. "An agreement with the archduke wherein I promise not to assist his enemies or allow any exile from Castile to enter our kingdom. Any of his enemies that fall into our hands will be turned over to Philip ..."

I open my mouth to speak but the king holds a finger aloft, silencing me.

"We have promised him an army should he need it and, in return, he will hand over Edmund de la Pole, who has for too long been given shelter in his realm."

At last, Father's motives are clear. For years he wanted to lay hands on the exiled Duke of Suffolk – the 'White Rose' as he is known. As the last surviving Yorkist and rival claimant to the throne, he has long been a bitter thorn in Father's side.

"And when you have him, do you mean to execute him?" I cannot help asking, but Father shakes his head.

"Oh no, I promised not to as part of the treaty but, of course ... you, Henry, have made no such promise. Once you are king, should you feel the need, there is nothing to stop you. It would probably be wise."

From the window of my father's privy chamber, I spy Catalina and her duenna walking in the gardens. Making some excuse, I escape the stifling jurisdiction and make my way outside. My heartbeat increases as I emerge into the brightness of the day, but it has nothing to do with the speed I have travelled.

Before I can persuade myself of the foolishness of my impulsive mission, I make straight for the part of the garden where I had seen her from the window. I almost run along the concentric paths, pausing at corners, judging which route will take me to her the quickest. Then, ducking through an arch cut in the yew hedge, I almost collide with Catalina. She cries out in alarm before she recognises me, and her duenna's face collapses into a mesh of wrinkled disapproval.

"Catalina," I gasp as eloquence deserts me. "I wanted to speak to you … alone."

Her chin is high, her eyes flashing resentment.

"That is not possible. I am not some … some …"

"I know what you are, Catalina." I snatch up her hand and cradle it in mine, placing my left over the top, trapping it there. Her fingers flutter in my palm like an ensnared lark. "Please, I beg just five minutes indulgence."

I have never begged for anything before. Her face remains impassive, but she makes no attempt to withdraw her hand.

"Very well, no more than five."

There is so much to say in the short time allowed and I fumble as to where to begin.

"F–first of all, it was no wish of mine to protest against our union. It was the king's order, and I have to do as I am told. He and your father are engaged in some wrangle over the dowry. I acted out of obedience. The matter is torture for me just now. One moment I am to marry you, the next it is some other European princess."

She snatches her hand away.

"How tiresome for you," she sneers, "and meanwhile I am kept in penury while your father argues over my marriage portion as if he has been sold some … some knock-kneed, broken down mare!"

In other circumstances I would have laughed at the analogy, but time is precious. I must persuade her. I reach for her hand again.

"My dear Catalina. I have no influence with my father. Everything I do is governed by him, but I swear to you, I was forced to make the protest. There is no woman on earth I would rather wed than you. I feel we are fated to be joined; you were sent here for me, not Arthur."

Her duenna loudly clears her throat in outrage. Catalina's cheeks are burning red now, her eyes moist. Realising I am still clutching her hand, I make so bold as to raise it to my lips. Her skin is so warm and fragrant I am reluctant to take them away.

"Pray, do not be cross with me, Catalina. If it were in my power, I'd wed you tomorrow, and I swear by the very moon and stars that you will one day be my queen."

"Moon and stars," she sneers. "What about the holy cross, will you swear on that?"

"Yes, I swear it, I …"

Withdrawing her hand again, she takes a deep breath and lowers her head.

"I am very lonely. Most of my countrywomen have been sent home and I have barely a gown that is not darned and mended. The king should be shamed for keeping a princess of Spain in such lowly estate. I have written to my father, and I have begged de Puebla to intervene with the king on my behalf. Do you know, I can barely feed my women now? Last week I was forced to sell some plate that was part of my dowry. I am in despair."

Her voice is full of tears. Her Spanish pride cast aside. My heart breaks for her.

"I will speak with the king, try to persuade him. Perhaps I can convince Grandmother to act in our defence; I know she thinks much of you. Since Mother died, the king has become more and more difficult. He listens to nobody and trusts no one. He lives as if there is an assassin behind every curtain."

Another cough from her duenna reminds us that our time together should not be prolonged. Her reputation is at stake. Made bold by the need for haste, I kiss her hand again, quickly and passionately this time, and look deep into her eyes as I give her my promise.

"Trust me, Catalina. Do not despair. I will do all I can …"

We leap apart at the sound of voices and approaching footsteps and, with one last smile, I sprint away. Spinning on my heel for one last look, I disappear behind the yew hedge and almost run into a group of courtiers. They laugh at the collision, beg pardon and give me good greeting.

"Well met, your Royal Highness, will you join us on our wanderings?" Unwillingly, I fall into step beside them, their conversation as lacking in substance as vapour in my ear. In my mind, I repeatedly relive my meeting with Catalina. I wonder if they notice my rapid breathing, the moistness of my brow on this chilly spring afternoon.

I can still smell the fragrance that clung to her clothes, I can feel the softness of her skin, suffer the moist sorrow of her eyes. What is she thinking now as she hurries back to the seclusion of her lowly rooms? I hope she will look a little kindlier on me now I have tried to express my feelings for her. I hope I have lessened her anxiety about her future ... our future.

***

Boyhood is behind me now. Something in my burgeoning romance with Catalina forces me to put immaturity aside. I find it difficult to concentrate. I see her face around every corner, hear her voice in the very breeze.

Brandon mocks me. "You have it bad, Henry. Who is the maid that has put such an arrow in your heart?"

For once, I do not confide in him. I would hate Brandon to sully her with innuendo and pry into how far our union has progressed. Were he to learn it has been nothing beyond a few words and a chaste, or not so chaste, kiss on the back of her hand, his mockery would be untenable.

He leans closer. "I will see what I can do to find a way to take your mind off this light of love. I will cheer you, Harry, you see if I don't."

That night, I follow Brandon to the dormitory he sometimes shares with the other young men of my household. Before we enter, he pauses.

"This should amuse you, Harry," he says with a quirky smile before throwing open the door. I halt just beyond the threshold, shocked to find a trio of women. They are young, still fresh looking, and unsure how to behave in our company. They cluster together near the hearth as if they have been waiting for me and, somehow, the way they are clothed suggests they are not ladies of the court but low women of the town. I have no idea what to say. I am not even sure I want to say anything. I would prefer to continue my dreams of Catalina.

Brandon watches my reaction. Unwilling to betray my lack of ease, I keep my face bland. In truth, every fibre of my body is suddenly alert to what might possibly lie ahead. I wet my lips, swallow something foreign and cough.

Knyvet, older than the rest of us, sees my lack of ease and pulls one of the girls onto his knee. He begins to kiss her neck. I am transfixed as she squirms and giggles and puts on a show of pulling away. When his hands creep up to her breasts, she stops struggling, relaxes against him, and closes her eyes. It is rather like when I'm trying to remove a tick from Beau's fur; he fights me for a while but then, realising I mean no harm, he rolls over and lets me have my way.

My loins stir. *But I love Catalina*. Brandon smirks as he takes a girl by the hand and brings her to stand before me.

"This is ... erm ... Harry." He winks at me, silently entreating me to keep my real identity quiet. She smiles shyly, and I realise she is just a year or two my senior and hardly a woman at all.

Brandon pulls off her cap and her hair tumbles about her shoulders, her eyes kindle. He pushes her closer, and she entwines her arms about my neck, her breasts soft against my torso. I should push her away, but my bones are melting, my resolve vanishing, my actions governed by the look in her eye.

"Come, my Lord," she says, her voice hoarse, her accent uncultured. "There's a quiet nook over 'ere." Her words are like some sort of charm and Brandon's chuckle follows as I trail after her across the chamber.

Such delight, such feelings I have never imagined. This is the thing that drives men mad. This is the thing that has broken treaties, initiated wars. It isn't love. It is lust, crude and glorious. It is the act that really governs the world.

She teaches me that it is women who possess the real power; they have the one single thing that all men crave. The girl takes me in hand, unbuttons my doublet, tears off my hose. As she strips away my innocence and rides me with unbridled energy into the dawn, I have neither the wit nor the will to stop her.

I forget Catalina, I forget Prince Henry, I forget England and unlearn every lesson I have ever been taught. All I know are the quick brown fingers and the moist red tongue of the girl whose name I never even asked.

***

Nothing alters in the months and years that follow. I continue my lessons; I aggravate my father and drive my grandmother to despair.

"I love you very much, Henry," she says, "but you must learn to listen. You must learn to consider the impact of your actions on others. You must heed your conscience, listen to that inner voice that tells you what is right and what is wrong. You have the rule book, stick to it at all times or … or …"

She throws up her hands and lets them fall to her lap again. Her sharp eye pierces mine. "I cannot be here forever to guide you, and neither can your father.

You must find it in yourself, Henry. Life isn't all about the sword play and dancing."

"No, Grandmother," I murmur, wondering if Brandon and the others have begun practising at the tilts yet. "I will do my best. Perhaps, if I had a wife to steady me ... Catalina ..."

She holds up a hand. "You know my thoughts on this, Henry. I have consulted many times with the king on the suitability of the match but, as yet, he does not agree. He is ailing ..."

Oh, I *know* he is ailing. Dying, some would say, although Grandmother will never admit to that. He is often abed, frail and sickly with a cough that wracks his skeletal frame. Sometimes, during an attack of coughing, it seems he will not breathe again. I wait in fear for him to fall back dead on his pillows, but each time he somehow manages to overcome it. When the fit is over, he glares sheepishly, wipes the drool from his chin and plucks the coverlet higher up his chest, before continuing to berate me.

I have the finest tutors in Christendom. I can discuss theology and politics with the greatest scholars in the Christian world yet, when I am with my father, I am as ineloquent as John Goose. His conviction that I will fail increases my inadequacy. I hate the disdain upon the king's face, his belief that I will never rule wisely. His sense of having produced an unviable heir is like a thorny crown and his lack of confidence infects me too, like a contagion. How can I, the *second* son, take on the heavy mantle of kingship?

As he clings to life like dying ivy to an oak, my confidence withers, but I let no one see it. I adopt a loud and merry countenance and try to drown my fear of the future with wine and women. And that just serves to make everything worse.

April 1509

There have been many instances over the last few years when I have believed my father to be on the brink of death but, when the time finally comes, there is no doubting it. I am summoned to his presence early one April morning, and as soon as I enter the foetid chamber, I can smell his imminent demise.

At my approach, his physicians melt away, and Grandmother stirs in the corner. She creeps toward me, crippled not by age but by grief. She senses his end is near although she doesn't voice it. Her hand clutches my robe, creeps up to find my hand. I squeeze her fingers; feel the crack of arthritic bone. I wet my lips but my voice is hoarse when I speak.

"What do the physicians say?"

She shakes her head, too overwhelmed to reply. My eyes wander back to the wreck of my father's body. The father who, since my infancy, has never shown me the least regard or affection.

While my mother was alive, I never noticed the lack, but when I needed comfort after her death, he turned away. He has shown in me only disappointment, regret, shame; my every effort to please him doomed to failure. Well, I only hope I do not fail him now.

While a priest reads the last rights and my father's soul passes from the earth, my grandmother sobs and I – well, I think of my future. A new and merry tomorrow for England, for myself … and for Catalina.

I always imagined that once I became king my life would be my own, but I see now I was quite wrong. Almost before her eyes are dry, Grandmother launches the arrangements for the king's funeral. Letters go out all over Christendom to announce the death of the old king and the advent of the new. She sends for my tailor and orders mourning clothes, and finery for my impending coronation. She does not seek my opinion or consult me on who should be present. Were it not for the fact of my late father's body, lying waxy in death, I would think I was still a mere prince.

And if Grandmother is offhand regarding my new status, my sister Mary is ten times worse. When I encounter her in the corridor, she does not sink into a curtsey or stand aside with her head bowed to let me pass. No, she stands in front of me, blocking my path, hands on hips, and mocks me as if we were children still.

"So," she says, "King Henry the Eighth; how does that feel, Hal?" Her laughter tinkles like a thousand irritating bells. I scowl at her, grab her upper arm and drag her along with me.

"Be quiet. You can at least show some respect before the court."

"And if I refuse, are you going to send for the guard and order them to take my head?"

Brandon sniggers behind me, drawing my sister's attention. When I turn and glare, he sobers, straightens his lips and bows low.

"Majesty," he says with great and feigned reverence. I look for mockery but find none. Taking Mary's arm again, I escort her to the great hall. As we approach, the doors open wide and we hear our names announced.

"Don't be a baggage, Madam," I mutter as we pass beneath the portal, "or I will have your head."

She smiles blithely, secure in my love for her. Before we take our seats at table, she leans close.

"I hear you ordered the arrest of Empson and Dudley. That should win you the approval of the people."

I shrug. "As I was advised. They are parasites. Nobody shall miss them. Half of Father's ministers are corrupt; they won't be the only ones who find their services are no longer required."

She pops a grape between her lips.

"Indeed? And by whom were you advised, Brother? Their enemies? Grandmother says it is a stringent move, and I agree. You must show the people your method of rule will be vastly different to Father's."

I nod. Of all my father's henchmen, Empson and Dudley are the most hated; their ruthless extortion of taxes won them no friends and many, many enemies. When they were discovered in a plot to hold and govern me, there was little I could do but heed my ministers' advice to order their arrest. I was unaware the news had yet reached the court, yet Mary knows of it. I wonder at the manner in which my little sister has grown so wise without me really noticing. She takes another grape, holding it before my mouth until I reluctantly part my lips. Sweetness bursts upon my tongue. She smiles and puts her face close to mine.

"Of course, Hal, you have realised there is nobody to prevent you from visiting Catalina now, or from marrying her either, if that still be your wish."

Turning her attention back to her platter, she samples a dainty morsel here, rejects another there. I had thought of it, of course. I have thought of little else since my father died. In the eyes of the world, if not my grandmother, I am king and, as such, the master of my own destiny.

Earlier this morning, only a few weeks after Father's death, a letter came from the Spanish court with Ferdinand's condolence and congratulations on my new status. In it, he urges me to wed his daughter as quickly as possible, to secure his protection against France. He calls himself my *ever-loving father* and hints that the ambassador will seek an audience soon. I imagine he has sent a similar letter to Catalina.

As I start to tear strips of meat from the bird before me, I wonder what her thoughts are on the matter. Does she still think of our tryst in the garden, when I declared myself?

Catalina is not present this evening. I wonder if she is ailing, or angry that I have not yet contacted her.

"Have you seen her today?" I ask.

Mary licks grease from her fingers.

"Who, Catalina? No. Do you want me to call upon her and discover her feelings on the question of marriage?"

That is exactly what I would like but I wish she had voiced it with more delicacy. I nod, shamefaced at her look of triumph.

"Then I shall do so immediately after supper. Never fear, Hal, if she baulks at the idea of being picked up after such a shameful rejection, I will talk her round. After all, who could resist you? I heard they are hailing you as the handsomest king in Christendom. All the unwed ladies of Europe will be hankering to marry you now. I will make sure she is aware that she has competition."

Mary is too pert and pretty by far and will lead her future husband a merry dance. She likes to be in control and her headstrong ways have long been the despair of our grandmother.

"And if you persuade her, I shall arrange a fine marriage for you, Mary; one that will knock our sister, the Scottish queen, into the shade."

She looks up from her meal, a trickle of gravy on her chin.

"Don't you dare, Henry. I am quite happy and intend to remain unwed for a good while yet."

Grandmother has covered the desk with slips of paper, lists of dignitaries, orders of velvet and fur. When I sigh for the third time, she puts down her pen, laces her fingers together and scowls at me.

"Are you not in the least interested, Henry?"

"Of course. Well, I am interested in the coronation, but I am happy to leave the arrangements to you. I would like to discuss one matter though …"

She presses her lips together, the wrinkles around them making her mouth look like a cat's arse.

"Catalina, yes. I was coming to that."

I lean forward in my seat.

"I am eager that the wedding should go ahead. We have the dispensation, and her father has agreed that the rest of the marriage settlement will be paid in full without delay. It is just … I do not know how Catalina herself feels about it. I never get to see her … not properly."

She begins to tidy the papers, piling them up around her like battlements.

"In my day, a girl had little say in whom or where she wed."

"Well, with all respect, you were not a princess of Spain."

"No, I wasn't, but I was heiress to the Beaufort estates, with a family line that stretches back to…"

"I know all that, but Catalina has the might of Spain behind her. I would prefer to seek her willing agreement."

Her lips twitch.

"You wish to woo her. How romantic of you."

"I believe a successful union should at least spring from mutual consent. The last time I spoke to Catalina she blamed me for rejecting her. I need to spend some time proving that my heart is true."

"And is it?" She arches her brows. "You have formed feelings for her?"

"Yes, I think so." My ears are hot, my face burning.

"How sweet. Sometimes I misremember how very young you are. You may seek an audience with her, but … keep your relationship within bounds until the deed is done."

I stand up and bow over her hand as I have always done and take my leave of her. It is not until I am outside the door and halfway along the corridor that I remember I have no need of her permission or her blessing.

I am king now.

As I make my way to Catalina's humble apartments, I practise what I shall say and how I shall say it. With only a page at my heel, I am more alone than is my custom. I could do with Brandon's company so I might ask his guidance, or Compton perhaps, who has such a way with women. But … the women they consort with are not princesses; they are trollops of the night or experienced women of the court. They will have no idea how one is supposed to woo a woman like Catalina – perhaps I should have written her a poem.

Assuming a confidence I do not feel, I stride through the palace, trying to calm my nerves, reminding myself that although she is a princess of Spain and several years my senior, I am now a king. She will pay me due respect.

I tug my tunic down, shrug the collar of my coat higher about my shoulders and puff out my chest. At my approach, the guards at her door throw open the portal and stand tall. I march into the room and, with my heart galloping, I cast about for my first glimpse of Catalina for a month.

The chamber is empty.

My carefully contrived confidence deflates. Only an aged woman sits sewing, her chair pulled close to the hearth on this chilly April afternoon. She hasn't heard my entrance.

"Where is your mistress?" I enquire, and she starts at the loudness of my voice, struggles to stand and, stifling a groan, makes a stumbling curtsey.

"My Lord King," she gasps, apparently overwhelmed by my company. "The princess is praying … that the king be granted swift ascension into Heaven."

Praying. Of course she is. I should have guessed. I turn on my heel, collide with my page and hurry toward the chapel. As I approach, my poise ebbs away. How should I greet her? What shall I say? Will she welcome me?

My footsteps slow. I hesitate, turn and begin to walk back the other way, my page trotting at my heel. I am on my fourth passage along the corridor when the chapel door opens, and Catalina emerges with a cluster of women. She halts when she sees me. Her women quietly nudge each other and giggle, while Kate's lips part, and her cheeks redden.

"Hen ... Your Majesty."

She sinks into a deep curtsey. I hasten forward, take her hand and help her rise. We are standing so close I can see wisps of hair that have escaped the confines of her hood, the fine sprinkling of freckles on her nose, and a tracery of veins on her temple. I swallow.

"Would you walk with me in the privy garden?" I ask, and she smiles, inclines her head and accepts my proffered arm.

With her women following at a short distance, we enter the garden, abundant with spring blooms, the birds busy in the trees. I point to a mass of flowers blooming beneath the hedge, and she halts.

"What are they called, Henry? I am ignorant of so many things here."

"Cowslips," I say, surprising myself at knowing the name. Perhaps my mother told me, and I have retained the information in some deep recess of my mind.

She laughs and I relax, suddenly happy in her company, no longer afraid that I will fail to win her.

"Cows lips," she repeats. "Such a funny name. They look nothing like the lips of a cow – or perhaps it is cow slips, so named because they make the cattle lose their footing. I have noticed that many English things have amusing names."

I have a sudden image of a herd of alarmed cattle tumbling, topsy-turvy, down a hill and suppress a bark of laughter.

"I've never noticed that, but now I come to think on it, you are right."

We move on, her head not even reaching my shoulder, which makes me feel manly, protective.

"I am sorry for your father, Henry," she says, and, to my astonishment, I see she has tears on her lashes. My father treated her in the worst possible way, how can she mourn his passing?

"It was expected," I murmur. "He is at peace now."

The last few days have taught me to utter the words by rote; I have felt little sorrow at the loss of my father but that is a sentiment I will never share with anyone. It would never do to appear heartless and nobody on earth would believe how harshly I was treated.

"My grandmother is distraught," I say to guide her from the question of my own feelings. "But she buries herself in the arrangements for the funeral and my coronation."

"I shall look forward to that day," she says, turning her round pink face up toward me. "It will be a happy time and we are all in need of some respite from our great grief."

I clutch at her hand, and the colour of her cheek deepens.

"The day could be made happier still."

She holds her breath. Slowly, she raises her eyes to mine. I do not smile as I try to let her see my emotion. I hope she can sense how desperate I am to persuade her, how eager I am to make her mine. A brief regretful image of my obscene dealings with the women of the night passes before me. I thrust it away and cling to the virginal perfection of Catalina. I cling to the here and now.

She shakes her head, confusion corrugating her brow.

"How could it be happier? I cannot think of anything more perfect."

"It could be *our* coronation day. I would be the happiest man ever born if you were at my side as they anoint me, if you could make your own vows as Queen of England as I make mine as King."

She stays silent, her head bowed as if there is some great event taking place on the hem of her skirt.

"Catalina." I press her hand. "Will you consent to be my wife? It is what everybody wants."

She looks up suddenly, slaying me with the longing in her eyes.

"Is it what you really want, Henry? What you truly desire, even were I not the Princess of Spain?"

"With all my heart."

I lift her hand, press my lips passionately against her fingers and, when I straighten up, she reaches out to touch my cheek. Her fingers are feather light. I cannot help myself and, heedless of the outraged protests of her women, I pull her to me and plant my lips on hers.

***

"You wish the wedding to take place before the coronation? Is that wise?"

"I see no impediment. We wish for a joint coronation. I intend Catalina to have an active role in the governance of our country."

Grandmother quirks her brow.

"Indeed. Then I suppose I will have to alter the arrangements that are already in place. There is scant time to have new clothes made for a public royal wedding and a double coronation."

"A private wedding will suffice. Here at Greenwich, in the Queen's closet, a couple of witnesses will be enough. It isn't as if we have to wait for anyone's permission; the papal dispensation has been in place for longer than I can remember."

"Don't exaggerate, Henry. Very well, I shall call on the princess and advise her on the selection of clothing. No doubt she will not mind a private wedding if there is the promise of the grand coronation to follow. She is a good biddable girl and still of an age to fill the royal nursery; you must both work hard to ensure plenty of heirs. The Tudor dynasty must continue."

I have heard those words my entire life. "Look how many sons your father had, yet in the end he was left with only one. A king can never have too many sons."

I spend a few moments contemplating Catalina's diminutive upright body, trying to envisage it without the layers of clothing. I fail.

Instead of Catalina, I can imagine only the whores I have sported with in the past; those over-used, voluptuous trulls. I blink to clear my sight and vow that those lewd days are past. With Catalina in my bed, I will have no need of light women. I can be the pious king I have always planned to be.

May 1509

I roll over, throw aside a pillow and look in wonder at the woman beside me. My wife; my brother's widow; my queen. Her bed cap has come adrift and her golden hair flows like water across the mattress.

I pick up a strand and bring it carefully to my lips. It slips through my fingers, writhing like a living thing between us – a sign of her vitality, her youth and fertility. Her breathing alters, her eyelids flicker, and she wets her lips with a small pink tongue. When she sighs, I hold my breath, wanting her to wake but reluctant to lose my private scrutiny.

While she sleeps, I can examine her; inspect her skin, her lashes, and the softness of her mouth. Her throat moves as she swallows and I want to kiss it, let my tongue play upon her Adam's apple, gently bite her white flawless neck. At the thought, I feel myself stiffen, hear my own heartbeat in my ears.

Stealthily, I slide the coverlet from her body, allowing my gaze to travel downward. Her breasts, high and firm, rise and fall gently as she breathes. Catalina is mine now; my wife, my property. In the eyes of God, I can do with her as I will.

There is no sin. When morning comes, there is no need to seek the absolution of my confessor. Last night, our wedding night, was like nothing I have known before. I realise now that coupling with whores is just a bodily function, like farting or – or – but loving Catalina involves every part of me, my heart and my soul as well as my body. Love is like religion.

She sighs again. I tear my eyes from her breasts and realise she has been watching me watching her. Her cheeks are pink, her eyes suffused with shy delight, and then her mouth stretches into a smile.

"Hal, how long have you been awake?" She gropes for the covers but I stay her hand, lean closer and lower my mouth to hers. As her arms slide around me and her fingers dig into my back, my lips find their way to her throat.

"Henry ..." As I lose myself in the fragrance of her arms, she mutters my name in my ear. My name, not Arthur's.

It is nigh on noon by the time we rise. I escape the chamber and leave her to the ministrations of her pink-faced women. At the door, I turn to blow her a kiss before strutting to my own apartments. My servants greet me with sly, knowing looks, but I do not care. Let them think what they will. I am ten feet taller than I was yesterday. After consummating my marriage, I am brimming with confidence.

"This morning," I announce, "I shall hunt. What say you, Brandon? Will you join me?"

"With joy," he replies. "Although I fear we are a little late for a morning ride, your Majesty, but we can make the best of the afternoon."

He grins and winks at his companions and I laugh along with them.

"I had state matters to attend to, Brandon. Very important matters. There is nothing more important than the begetting of a prince."

After much backslapping and congratulation, I break my fast before we set off from the palace. It is a high, blue day, energisingly cold; what my mother would have called a 'cheerful day.' If only Mother could see me now. As I gather my reins and lead my men on the chase, I am aware of the bright splash of colour we make against the awakening landscape. I feel like the king of the world.

In the weeks that follow, although I get little sleep and Catalina fills both my night and my day, I overflow with energy. Leaving the matters of state to my ministers, I fill the days with jousts, hawking and hunting, and our nights with dancing and romance. My queen and I are in love, and it is contagious; it spreads around the court and turns the palace into a garden of love.

My friend, William Blount, becomes enamoured of one of Catalina's favourite ladies, Inez de Venegas, and begs leave for them to marry.

"Love," I exclaim when I learn of it, "spreads as quickly as the plague, but the infection is far sweeter."

"It can leave as many scars, Your Majesty, if one does not love wisely."

"Nonsense, reckless love is not love at all, it is lust in disguise."

As if I am an expert on matters of the heart, I offer him advice on marriage, on how to treat his bride, how to make her smile as prettily as mine does.

While the courtiers look on, I slide my arm about Catalina's waist and draw her close.

"Mmm," I whisper. "How fares my pussy cat?"

She scowls and taps my nose with her fan.

"Do not call me that, Henry. I am not a cat. You make me sound like some flea-bitten tabby from the stable."

"Oh no," I croon. "Not a fat mouser but a sleek, elegant queen of cats. They are worshipped in some cultures, you know."

She pulls away. "Even so, I prefer Catalina."

"It is such a mouthful."

I pull her close again; tug back her veil so I can sniff her cheek. "And it is so foreign. Perhaps I shall call you Kate, instead. You are Queen of England now; you should have an English name."

She looks at me sideways while she considers.

"It is preferable to Cat, I suppose. If you cannot master your lax English tongue to form my proper name, Kate will have to suffice."

She squeals as I pull her down and kiss her soundly while her ladies murmur at the sweetness of our union. Her mouth moves against mine, her fragrance filling my head, her lashes fluttering against my cheek. I need her.

I need her now.

I pull suddenly away and she sits up, perplexed as I snap my fingers to dismiss the company from our presence. As the last of them backs out the door, and as their giggles fade along the corridor, I begin to loosen my sash. Playfully, Kate shakes her head.

"No, no. Everyone will know what we are doing…." She giggles as I fumble among her skirts. I find an ankle, my hand runs up her leg, and I revel in the softness of her thigh before discovering the hidden sweetness. Her protests cease and she grows compliant beneath my loving.

And so it continues. I cannot do enough to please her. I shower gifts upon her, and she does the same for me. She gives me a fine Sicilian horse; a jewelled collar; shirts she has worked herself in delicate blackwork and, eager to match her generosity, I order fine cushions and hangings for her chamber, jewels to adorn her perfect neck and her long pretty fingers. There is nothing I will not do to please her. When she requests it, I even agree that she can act as Spanish ambassador. I am confident she will now place the good of our country before that of her birth. She is English now and Spain is our ally and ever will be.

I am so content. A few short months ago, beneath the jurisdiction of my father and grandmother, I was miserable, but now, I am not only my own man but also a married man, and the king.

Grandmother approves of Kate; she loves her so much she invites us to call upon her. When we enter, she greets us warmly, and asks Kate to sit beside her at the fireside.

My eyes fasten upon her wizened hands and I wonder at the loose skin and rusty age spots. When she takes Kate's hand and asks if there is any sign yet of a child, I try and fail to imagine that Kate or I will ever grow so old.

Margaret Beaufort has lived a long and eventful life. She can relate stories of the kings of old – Henry VI who was her cousin; my grandfather, Edward IV; and the tyrant, Richard of Gloucester. It was she who helped my father to the throne, it was she who helped him rule, who encouraged him to wed my mother, the daughter of Edward, and mix the blood of York and Lancaster. It was Grandmother who masterminded the end of civil unrest in England.

All my life she has instilled in me the importance of lasting peace, of a royal nursery teeming with sons. Even in her dotage, she has not forgotten that a king without sons is an unstable monarch. Her rheumy eyes stare deep into Kate's.

"I will not be around to see it," she says, "yet I know you are fertile. England will soon welcome an infant prince and the Tudor line will thrive once more."

Kate flushes, her eyes flutter to mine and I smile, my loins stirring at the thought of making a prince with her. I tear my eyes away.

"You must not speak of death, Grandmother. You are haler than you look. It will take more than a chill to see you off."

"Even I cannot live forever, Henry," she sniffs, but I can see she is pleased. We sit for a while longer. I lean back in my seat and listen as she regales Kate with tales of her youth at the court of Henry VI, of her marriages to Edmund Tudor, Harry Stafford and Thomas Stanley. Her life deserves a chronicle of its own.

"They killed him, you know," she says. "Henry VI was a weak man, too saintly to be a leader, but he did not deserve to die."

Her mouth works as she chews her gums and peers into the hearth, as if she sees faces from days long past in the flickering flames; faces to which my wife and I are blind. "Everyone from my girlhood is gone now," she says, "I think I am the only one left alive."

A tear works its way down her furrowed cheek. With a courage I would have lacked a few weeks ago when I was a boy, I take her hand, feeling the fragile bones shift as I squeeze.

"God has spared you because you are blessed, and He knows I need and value you."

She lays her head on the back of her chair. "Ah, Henry, dear boy, I fear He cannot spare me for very much longer."

Kate clears her throat and I look up to see she is fighting against tears. She is sentimental, but we English are made of sterner stuff. I feel no great sorrow at Grandmother's approaching death. She has enjoyed a good life and we no longer need her. I am man enough to rule the country and her ideas are outdated; she echoes a dead era, the philosophies of a far-off place, a land of war and unrest.

My England will be a merry realm. My England will be hailed as the greatest in Christendom, and my sons and daughters will marry into the best royal families in Europe and take the name of Tudor with them across the world.

<u>23rd - 24th June 1509</u>

All England is merry. On midsummer's eve, my queen and I process through the streets of celebration. I have never seen London look so grand; the walls are covered with cloth of gold, the streets adorned with flowers. Women scatter petals from balconies, their cries of joy raining upon us. I turn in my saddle to where Catalina follows, resplendent on cushions in a litter of gold, drawn by white horses trapped in crimson velvet and glittering gems.

On every corner a bonfire burns; the inns and taverns are alive with music and dancing. Wine is flowing, the people are joyful. With the old king dead and another about to be crowned, a new dawn is breaking, a new regime is about to be born.

When our procession is over, Kate and I stand at the window, watching and listening to the celebration. She has discarded her heavy robes and wears a loose gown, her hair flowing free for my delectation. I move behind her, wrap my arms about her body and rest my chin on the top of her head. She reaches up to cradle my cheek and sighs with deep satisfaction.

"What a splendid day, my Henry. I shall never forget it."

I kiss her hair. "It will be even more splendid tomorrow. We should take early to our bed or you may be too tired to enjoy it."

I feel her torso shake with suppressed laughter. My wife has quickly come to understand me. She knows I am never tired. I often spend all day in the saddle, ride three horses until they drop with fatigue, and then dance all evening, but it never stops me from loving her until the sweet hours of dawn.

I pull away; she turns in my arms and kisses the cleft of my chin. "I am a little tired," she says, but the lusty gleam in her eye informs me otherwise.

***

Confronted by the huge crowd gathered at the gate, Kate hesitates, but I tuck her hand beneath my elbow and lead her forward along the red carpet. The people clamour around us, their voices making my ears ring, scattered petals falling like rain.

The people draw back to let us pass, and I beam at Kate and she smiles back, raising her free hand to the crowd as she warms to the festivity of the occasion.

The great doors of Westminster Abbey open wide to receive us. We step across the threshold into the coolness of the vestibule and the din outside fades. A few steps further in and the commotion is replaced by a vast echoing silence.

As a boy, I never yearned to be king, but since the death of my brother, almost every word spoken by my father and grandmother has been to ensure I become a good one. Now, now that it is about to happen, I desire the crown more than anything I have wanted in my life.

Grandmother does not turn at our approach. She sits tall, swathed in her habitual black, a kirtle of red beneath, a kerchief clasped tightly in her fist. Her unsmiling face is proud, her eyes moist with emotion. Few gathered here understand the iron will required to conceal the ailments of age that besiege her. I am the only one allowed close enough to hear the grate of bone on bone when she moves. She makes no complaint that the creaking gate at life's end is opening for her. I will do her proud this day. I lift my head, my mouth tilting into an imperceptible smile, and she nods. I have her unqualified approval ... at last.

As we progress deeper into the great abbey, the nave echoes with shuffling feet, every ill-concealed cough and murmured remark is amplified by the vast ancient space. My wife and I reach the altar and halt beneath the holy rood.

I am impatient for the moment of crowning, but the archbishop drones on for so long that I cease to listen, his voice fading as my mind conjures my predecessors gathered to witness the moment I become God's anointed.

If my father were here, I imagine he would remain unconvinced that I am fit to follow him. I picture my brother Arthur, standing a little behind Father, resentful that I now possess not just his life and his bride, but his crown too.

Mother is there, smiling and weeping in equal measure; and my grandfather, Edward IV, proud of his grandson, made in his image, rising to the throne. An invisible line of kings stretching far back to the time of

Arthur Pendragon crowds into the nave to do me honour, and witness the moment of my crowning.

Never-ending prayers are murmured, the oaths are taken, and then, finally, the holy oil anoints our breasts and Archbishop Wareham places the crown of England on my brow.

Beside me, I hear Kate's rapid breath, and know that if I were to take her into my arms, I would feel her heart pattering wildly, just as mine is. It is not fear that makes our hearts skip like a rabbit's. She likes to boast she is afraid of nothing, that as a daughter of Spain she is as fearless as I. No, it is not fear; it is excitement that our hour has finally come.

Kate has waited for this even longer than I. While I was still but Duke of York, with no expectation of this day, she was already just one step from the throne of England.

Of course, she expected to rule with Arthur, but she had no care for him, he was but a means to an end. As his queen, the rule of England would have been nothing but duty, while with me it will be a matter of the heart. Together, we shall lead our people into a new era – a time of peace, prosperity and security.

I swear, as King of England, that it shall be so.

A gentle cough calls me back to the matter in hand. Wareham's hollow, patient eyes are staring into mine. I realise I have not been listening.

"Will you grant and keep to the people of England the laws and customs to them, as old rightful and devout kings granted, and the same rarity and confirm by your oath, and especially the laws, customs and liberties granted to the clergy and people by your noble predecessor and glorious king, Saint Edward?"

"I grant and promise."

To my chagrin, having been silent for so long, my voice emerges in high-pitched discord. I sound like an unbedded boy. I clear my throat, and swallow phlegm.

"You shall keep, after your strength and power, to the church of God, to the clergy and people, holy peace and goodly concord."

"I shall keep." This time my voice is strong. I inflate my chest and stand taller.

"You shall make to be done, after your strength and power, equal and rightful justice in all your dooms and judgements, and discretion with mercy and truth."

"I shall do."

"Do you grant the rightful laws and customs to beholden and promise you, after your strength and power, such laws as to the worship of God shall be chosen by your people by you to be strengthened and defended?"

"I grant and promise…"

And so it goes on … and on. I look across the nave. Every face is turned toward me and, at Wareham's signal, the company rises to their feet and a great cheer breaks out.

Vivat, vivat Rex! Vivat, vivat, Rex! they cry and, shortly after, *Vivat, vivat, Regina!*

The voices shatter our ears, yet we stand tall, afraid to move for fear of dislodging our weighty crowns.

I glance at my queen; her cheeks are pink, but whether from pleasure or merely the cloying heat of our royal robes I cannot be certain. I beam upon the crowd, catch the eye of Brandon who is applauding loudly, as pleased as if it is he himself who is so honoured.

Finally, the applause dies down, people begin to chatter, and I realise the ceremony is finally drawing to a close. Soon, I can take my ease, loosen my clothing and break my fast. By the look of Kate, she will need to sleep for an hour or so before the evening festivities begin.

As we process from the abbey, I catch sight of my sister, Mary, surreptitiously wiping away a tear. When she sees me looking her way, she smirks affectionately and tosses her head as if she is not moved by this day, as if my being king changes nothing. But I know as well as she that nothing will be the same again.

29th June – Westminster Palace

Weeks of festivities ensue and, for a while, my court revels in the jousts and tournaments. We dance long into the night and everyone is merry; there is not a soul in the palace who rues the future with me as their king.

Early one morning, still jaded from the night before, I am relaxing with Brandon and Blount when a messenger arrives. I immediately know by his livery that he brings news from my grandmother. The boy hands me the note and, carelessly, I break the seal. I scan the words, expecting to see some admonishment or instruction for tomorrow's feast, but … I look up at Brandon, my former peace destroyed, my ears ringing with shock.

"My grandmother is sick …"

Brandon frowns, looking up from arranging chess pieces on the board.

"She was hale enough yesterday. Has she caught some chill? We were all up late …"

"*Mortal* sick, the message says. I must go to her."

I speak as if I am reluctant to go but, in truth, the news has unseated me. The thought of life without Grandmother overseeing my every move is … unimaginable.

I hurry to my chamber, push aside my attendants and pluck a clean doublet from the back of a settle. Turning sharply, I find Brandon has followed.

"Shall I attend you, your Majesty?"

"No, no." I place my hand on his arm by way of gratitude. "Go to Kate and tell her the news, explain that I might be late."

He bows low, all sign of his usual levity absent and, as I hurry from the room, Beau leaps up to follow, thinking I am off on the chase. Spinning on my heel, I call back into the chamber.

"Brandon! Call the dog back," and, at his whistle, Beau bounds away barking, tail wagging in expectation of a treat.

Since the coronation, Grandmother has been in residence at the deanery, here at Westminster, but I have not called upon her. She has, of course, attended every feast and tournament in honour of my crowning. I did not even make time to speak to her yesterday, on the day that marked my eighteenth year in this world. I had not even noticed she was ailing.

Now she is leaving me, the idea that she will not forever be on hand to scold and nurture me is inconceivable. I am not even certain that the palace, or the realm, can function without her; she is the captain of this great golden ship of state and has had a hand in every event since my father's accession in 1485.

"I must hurry …"

Halfway across the courtyard, I hesitate, momentarily doubting whether I will be permitted entry. But when the guard straightens his back and throws open the door, I remember that of course I will be permitted. I am the king; no one can prevent it.

My step slows; I fumble at the fastening of my cloak and let it fall to the floor. Soft footed, I ascend the stairs to the upper chambers, hurrying silently along the corridor to the great wooden doors of her apartment. When I enter, my newfound kingly confidence remains on the other side of the threshold.

I creep forward and peer at the great curtained bed in the centre of the room. Her attendants are huddled near the hearth and there is just one solitary figure at her bedside.

Bishop Fisher is praying, hands clasped, head bowed, and the figure of Grandmother is so tiny in the vastness of the bed that it could be a child. I step closer. He glances up and makes to rise when he recognises me, but I signal him to continue. I edge closer and look upon her face and know without doubt that she will not live out the night.

Somehow, I am on my knees; memories of other deathbeds, other losses, other pain come rushing in. I grope for her hand and clasp it in mine; the bones are as frail and as insubstantial as a bird's. I lower my head and place my lips upon the brown spotted skin.

Four hours I sit at her side, afraid to leave in case she passes in my absence. I do not want to be alone. I beg her to stay just a little longer, but she does not stir. She does not answer. She does not even rouse herself to make a last blessing upon me when I have never been more in need of her good counsel.

A thousand questions crowd my tongue; questions she will never now answer. I am at the helm of a great ship that is sailing into the dark. I have no idea how to navigate.

My throat closes. John Fisher's voice drones on, and Grandmother's breath rasps shallowly in her throat. I cling to her. This woman is a bridge to the past. The last link with the old England my mother knew.

Grandmother has known civil war, personal peril, torment, betrayal and so much grief. Since the age of thirteen, when she gave birth to my father, she has fought for the name of Tudor. I am sure that she dies with the name emblazoned on her heart. I clear my throat and whisper a vow, although she probably cannot hear.

"Grandmother. I know now why you bullied and badgered me to study. I realise that you sought only to reshape a foolish, pleasure-seeking boy into a king. I swear to you, Grandmother, on the name of Tudor, that I shall make you proud." My voice breaks.

She will be forever in my prayers.

I lean over and press my lips against her cold, clammy forehead. She reeks of death. Suppressing a shudder, I move back from the bed and stand with my head lowered while Bishop Fisher gives the last rites. In the presence of myself and her favourite, John Fisher, Margaret Beaufort breathes her last.

Her corpse lies unmoving. When they creep forward to reverently draw the sheet across her face, I want to scream at them to leave it. How can such energy be so suddenly extinguished? One minute she was here, her grating breath audible in the silent half-lit chamber, and now she is silenced.

She has gone.

"Kate! Kate!" I hurry back to the palace and head straight for the queen's chamber. Her women rise hastily to their feet, their blushes and giggles out of place on this day of death. But, of course, they have not yet been told. They do not know. Nobody does.

A girl steps forward and curtseys deeply. "The queen is at prayer in the chapel, your Majesty."

"Ah, yes ... of course she is."

I pace the floor, wrestling with my conscience, knowing it is unmannerly to disturb someone at prayer, but I urgently *need* to speak to my wife.

I pause at the window, look out across the park, biting the fleshy back of my thumb until my patience runs out.

"Go fetch your mistress," I snap, and the youngest of the ladies-in-waiting flees the room. The tension in the chamber increases. Kate's women watch me from their corner as I resume my pacing until I hear Kate's footstep. When she enters, as cool and composed as she ever is, I feel immediate relief and spring to her side.

"What is it, Henry? Are you ill? You look pale …"

"No."

I take her arm and lead her to the privacy of the window seat. "I am …unsettled, that is all."

She lowers herself beside me.

"About Lady Margaret …?"

"You heard, I suppose … that she is dead."

"Well, there have been whispers that she is ailing."

"She has gone," I whisper. "I was with her but I doubt she knew I was there."

The sympathy on her face almost unmans me. She pats my knee.

"We will all miss her. Of course you are unsettled."

Snatching off my cap, I throw it to the floor and shuffle closer beside her, taking up her hand.

"I don't know if I can do this alone."

She leans in closer to catch my quiet words and rests her hand atop mine.

"Do what alone?"

"This!" I wave about the chamber. "Be king. Rule England."

"Of course you can. Lady Margaret has spent years ensuring you are adequate to the task, and you have me to assist you. I was raised to be queen of England and am fully schooled in the matter. Together, we will prove to be just what this country needs. Whenever you are unsure, I will be there at your side to reassure you. There is no need for concern."

Wearily, I lay my head on her shoulder and listen to the birds outside the window. Of course, Kate is right. I have quickly learned that she usually is. We might be young, but what we lack in experience we make up for in determination. I sigh audibly, my breath making the gauze of her veil rise and fall.

We remain there with the warm sun on our faces, the murmured conversation of Kate's household women buzzing like a far-off swarm of bees. And as the afternoon slips into evening, the future rears ahead like an unscalable mountain.

Autumn –Winter 1509

The people adore me and Kate. Whenever the queen rides with me through the city streets, they cry out our names. Everyone is talking of the new mood that pervades the country, a feeling of hope for the future, of posterity and happiness for all.

When I ride at her side, I am pleased to see how much the commoners love my wife. They welcomed her when she first arrived in England all those years ago and they love her still. Although circumstances have altered, they are delighted to see her restored to her rightful place.

While I respond heartily to their cheers, she is more reserved, raising her hand majestically, accepting the applause as her due. She is proud and regal. They love her for her stately bearing just as they love me for my youthful exuberance. More than one courtier remarks that it is as though we have stepped from the tales of King Arthur. She is Kate the Magnificent, and I am Good King Hal.

On our return, the palace fires provide a welcome respite from the chill wind. Kate's cheeks are pink, her eyes bright. She draws off her gauntlets and passes them to one of her women before sinking into a chair at the hearth.

"You are glowing," I say. "The cold weather suits you."

She quirks her brow.

"Suits me? Brrrr, I don't think so, my Henry. I shall never grow used to it. I love England with my whole heart, but it would be dishonest to say that I do not wish the climate were more like Spain's. I remember when I first arrived; I thought I would be frozen to death."

I laugh and shuffle my chair closer to hers, sit down and cover her hand with mine.

"You are made of stronger stuff than that." I cast my eyes at her hovering women. "Why don't you send your women away. I know a sure method of warming you."

Her face reddens but she laughs and flaps her hand.

"Forgive me, my Lord, but I am weary from the ride and ..." she looks away, "... and my women tell me I should perhaps refrain from such things for a while ... considering my condition."

The stab of indignation at her rejection is quickly replaced by an explosion of hope. I grab her fingers.

"Kate, do you mean ...?"

She turns, laughing and smiling, but with tears in her eyes.

"I mean just that, my Henry. I wasn't going to tell you yet but ... I couldn't help myself."

"When? When will our prince be born?"

She shrugs.

"It is hard to be precise, but since we have been married for such a short while, I would think ... March perhaps, or April?"

"Ah, Catalina!" I leap from my chair and begin to pace about the chamber.

"We must consult my grandmother's book on the birth of princes. I will have it sent to our apartments. The best midwives must be summoned, and we must seek the most trusted of wet nurses. Oh, there will be such celebration – while you nurture our son in your womb, I will organise the greatest pageants to celebrate his birth; tournaments the like of which this country has never seen, Kate …"

I hurry back to her side and cast myself at her knee.

"Kate. Our boy will be like no other. He will be blessed. *We* are blessed! We have been wed for no time at all yet already we have a son, an heir! My grandmother would have been so proud, it is a wonder she hasn't risen to come and congratulate us in person."

Kate's pretty laughter fills the air. When I look at her, I am consumed with such love I really have no idea how to contain it. A surge of wanting washes over me. A few days ago, before she gave me this news, I would have borne her off to our chamber, but now … now I must think of our son, our prince!

For a while, I am overcome with exhilaration. I can think of nothing but the birth, of holding my son in my arms and showing the world that the Tudor line is flourishing. Kate, however, is less delighted. She loses her bloom and is sickly, unable to eat much at one sitting without calling for her women to bring her a vomiting bowl. I begin to eat in my own chambers, and she is so restless at night and unable to ease my needs that I rarely stay for long.

I hate to be kept waiting and the months of pregnancy are prolonged and tedious. Often, although I crave the first sight of my son, I think of the days before Kate's womb was blessed. I hate my vast empty bed and return to the sinful days of my youth when I would lie in the dark and think of her.

Sometimes, to my shame, I find myself thinking of others.

As Christmas approaches, I concentrate on providing the most lavish festivity the court has ever seen. I order up roast swan and peacock, dolphin and goose, as well as the biggest boar's head that could be found. Musicians arrive from Europe, tumblers from the four corners of the realm, and my master of revels sends for a troupe of players whose reputation has reached us from France.

My companions gather, each trying to outdo the other with suggestions for the celebrations. Brandon and Compton, their wine cups brimming, fill my private quarters with gaiety.

The musicians are so loud that I am straining to hear what Brandon is saying when my eye is caught by a woman. Her head is back, her throat is long and white in the light of the candles as she laughs at some joke Compton has made. Then she sobers, but her eye is still kindling when it catches mine and something jolts in my belly. I feel a stirring and she knows it.

Instead of looking quickly away as most women do, her eye lingers, a soft smile on her lips as she raises her cup and drinks from it. I know her. She is one of my many cousins; her mother is an aunt to mine. I narrow my eyes, trying to untangle the web of relations. Her name is Anne Stafford, sister to the Duke of Buckingham and wed to George Hastings. I raise my glass across the room and drink with her.

As the revel stretches toward midnight and my companions descend into varying states of befuddlement, I find myself in Anne's company. When I step back and bump into her, she pretends surprise.

"Oh, Your Majesty! Do forgive me, I am so clumsy ... may I?" When I nod consent, she pretends to stroke invisible droplets of wine from my doublet. "I fear I may have imbibed a little too much."

She sinks belatedly into a curtsey and, when she rises, leans against my arm, allowing me a waft of her fragrance and a tantalising glimpse down the neck of her gown. My interest rises.

I stammer for conversation. What does one say to a woman you have known all your life who has turned so suddenly into a temptress? If I were to ask that question of Brandon, he would laugh aloud.

Perhaps you should try asking her to bend over, Harry!

I smother a smile at the imagined response and tap my cup with restless fingers. The music staggers to a halt and starts up again; a simple pavane, which is a blessing given the easy steps and our current state of drunkenness.

"Do you dance, Mistress?"

She smiles blithely.

"I do, indeed, your Majesty."

Nobody pays us any heed as we take the floor. Her fingers are hot in my palm, her bold glances concealed beneath a falsely demure expression. Once or twice, as we move clumsily to the music, my hand brushes her cheek, her breast, and my eye is transfixed by the bounce of her goodly bosom. I wonder I have not noticed her before.

From time to time, she abandons good manners and smiles full in my face, letting me see the strength of her attraction. She is one of Kate's waiting women, and of excellent character. I have never heard a bad word said against her yet here she is, playing the part of a wanton. I can only suppose she has been taken by surprise and is as overwhelmed by our encounter as I.

It is widely acknowledged throughout Christendom that I am physically a cut above most men. I am six feet tall and can best any opponent in the lists. I am an athlete, a wit, and admired across the globe. Perhaps it is also rumoured I am skilled in the bedchamber. Perhaps her husband, Hastings, lacks in that department and she longs for a real man in her bed. No one can blame her for that. It does not make her a bawd. She is a lady, of good blood, a far cry from the harlots I dandled with in my single days.

Since Kate has been with child, I have ached for a woman in a way that no man should. If I were to lie with Anne tonight, the queen would be none the wiser. Indeed, it is the accepted thing that a man should take a mistress to ease his wife's pregnancy.

It would be no sin.

"Are you well, Your Majesty? You seem to be feverish. Do you feel the need to retire?"

I look down into her wide, pretty eyes, her moist parted lips, and I forget about Kate. I take out a kerchief, mop my forehead and smile.

"I do feel a little out of sorts. I wonder ... would you assist me?"

I dismiss my guard and we slip like naughty children from the hall, seeking the privacy of my inner chamber. Anne trips into the room, giggles and hiccups as she looks around. She is very drunk but perhaps that is just as well. I would hate her to think too clearly about what is to happen next. I would hate her to change her mind now.

I stand in the middle of the floor, watching as she wanders around the room. She tests the quality of the drapes and cushions, picks up a few of the favourite treasures I keep on my shelf. Then she turns to me.

"This is your private room, Your Majesty?"

I reach out and take her wrist, propelling her toward me.

"Henry. Call me Henry."

I drag her against my chest. Our mouths meet, her arms entwine about my neck as our tongues writhe, and space in my codpiece becomes a premium.

My hands begin a journey of their own, delving beneath her stiff skirts and layers of petticoats until I discover hose. I travel further, finding a garter and, by God, I almost explode when my fingers encounter the soft smooth flesh above.

"Henry!" she cries as I lift her and stagger toward the bed with her legs clamped like a vice about my waist. I throw her unceremoniously onto the mattress. While I fumble with my lacings, she wrenches up her petticoats to reveal her nethers, pink and welcoming in the flickering candlelight.

If this night makes me a sinner, then sinner I am, and the resulting punishment is welcome.

I expect to feel guilty but, when I wake, I am as full of lust as if I had never had her. I take her again, burying her face in a pillow so I do not have to look at her. Then I send her away with promises of another meeting soon. With the marks of my loving on her thigh, her hair matted at the back, and her bodice inexpertly laced, she sidles from the chamber, blowing kisses as she goes. As the door closes, I fall back on the pillow and sleep long into the afternoon.

All through Christmas, I am under some spell, consumed with thoughts of Anne. To conceal our amour, we construct a story that she is not in our company to be with me, but with Compton instead.

Compton is a good fellow and I reward him well for his discreet service.

On New Year's Day, I send her a princely gift, and it is that afternoon when I first become aware of Kate's displeasure.

From time to time throughout the festive tournament, I note her scowl and, when the entertainment is over, she quits my presence without speaking. I follow, wondering and worrying as to what I have done to offend her.

"Are you unwell, Kate?" I ask. "How does our prince?"

She passes me with her head high and I swear had the doors not been ten feet high and fashioned from oak, she would have slammed them in my face.

I trail after her, like Beau when he has been caught shitting in the chamber.

"What have I done?" I ask, splaying my hands, palms up, in supplication. She lowers herself into a chair, her belly perching like a rock on her knees. Sniffing with contempt, she says,

"Perhaps we should send for Elizabeth Stafford and you can ask her why I might be offended."

Elizabeth Stafford? My fear decreases. I am innocent of any dealings with her.

"What do you mean, Kate? You mustn't upset yourself over trivial matters. People love to gossip."

"Perhaps you should have thought of that before dallying with my household women."

"I – I..." I want to say *I haven't,* but Grandmother always said that lying is the worst sin of all. I wonder if it is worse than fornication. "I don't know what you mean ..." I end lamely.

She sits up straight, pulls her shawl tighter across her shoulders and looks at me. I feel like something disgusting stuck to the bottom of her shoe.

"My Lord of Buckingham is on his way to see you. I understand there are matters that need to be discussed."

I shrug, pretending ignorance of the situation and turn away, pour two cups of wine, one of which she refuses, the other I gulp as if it is aqua vitae. Then I take another cup.

It is ridiculous, of course it is. I am king of England not a schoolboy caught out in a misdemeanour. *What can they do?* Anne is a woman grown, old enough to make her own decisions, and I am the King of England!

Buckingham, when he comes, is seething with outrage. Try as he might to disguise it, he cannot speak but through gritted teeth. The words *Your Majesty* seem to be locked at the back of his throat, and I recall my father warning me that his whole family have lusted for the throne for generations.

Buckingham's own father was attainted for treason against Richard III. If he were able, this man would slice off my head and snatch the crown from it as it fell.

My inner fury increases.

"Well?"

Buckingham stands ramrod straight.

"Your Majesty, I have come to escort my sister, Anne, home. She is suffering from a malaise that we should hate to spread about the court."

I narrow my eyes. She was well enough this morning. This fellow knows my fear of contagion and is seeking to gull me. He fumbles for words and then continues. "I have arranged for a short stay in a nunnery, for the sake of her health, you understand, and then she will be returned to the care of her husband. I doubt she will recover enough to serve the queen again. I have spoken with Her Majesty and she endorses my decision. She wishes us well."

What can I say? I can hardly refuse, not without raising the suspicion of the entire court. Ugly rumours like this cannot be contained. But to have my mistress removed from my court! I will be the laughingstock of all Christendom.

They have all worked against me: Elizabeth Stafford running with tales to Kate, Buckingham and Hastings conspiring to part me from Anne. They should all be thrown into the Tower ... apart from Kate, of course.

I would not be without her.

Wolsey, when I tell him of it, shakes his head and clasps his hands.

"Unfortunately, Your Majesty, we cannot invent a reason to imprison either Buckingham or Stafford. We shall have to content ourselves with making them unwelcome at court and hindering any hopes they have of ... preferment."

To Wolsey, the lack of preferment is the worst punishment a man can have. I grunt a reluctant concurrence and swiftly sign a sheaf of papers he has placed before me. In the back of my mind, I hear my father's admonishment that I have neither read nor pondered on their subject matter. I can think of nothing but being denied the chance to resume my relations with Anne. God damn Buckingham and his pretensions to chastity. He is as ready to mix with whores as the rest of the court.

I bite the side of my thumb, tear a small strip of flesh and spit it out. Wolsey gathers up his papers, his mind already on other business.

"None of them are welcome at our court," I snap suddenly. "See to it that Elizabeth Stafford is sent away permanently. She must be used as an example to teach the queen's other women that it does not do to carry tales of their betters. God's teeth, Kate is not my mother. I am not her servant. As my wife, she is to do my bidding and learn to turn a blind eye."

He pauses, raising an eyebrow before bowing to my wish.

"I will see to it right away, Your Majesty."

It is almost dark when the doors are thrown open and the queen marches into my presence. Half asleep beside the fire, I look up startled at the sudden intrusion.

"Kate…" I mop spilled wine from my tunic.

"How dare you!" she growls through clenched teeth. Looking up from my task, I toss aside the soiled kerchief and meet her furious gaze.

In our short time together, we have seldom disagreed, but now I sense our first real argument is upon us. I decide to pretend ignorance of her errand and look nonchalantly away.

"How dare I what?"

I lean back in my chair. In her fury she seems somehow taller, somehow more beautiful. Presumably, the news of Elizabeth Stafford's dismissal reached her while she was making ready for the night. Her hair is uncovered, falling in waves about her shoulders, and she wears a loose informal gown.

"You know what I refer to, Henry. You have no right to banish my women from court. The queen's household is mine to control. You should see to your own affairs, but I must be left to oversee my own."

Abandoning my pretence, I lean forward, narrowing my eyes.

"But you didn't mind your own affairs, did you, Madam? And neither did your little spy."

Her lips part. "Spy? Lady Stafford acted as my loyal friend. Had you behaved as a loyal husband, she would have had no reason to bear tales to me."

She has me there. I relax back into my seat and stare into the flames, waving my hand dismissively.

"The matter is over with. I shall say no more of it and you will do the same."

"No. This must be dealt with. We must set rules now as to how we are to move on."

"Don't be ridiculous."

"My household is not some … some *brothel* to keep you amused when I am indisposed."

I ponder the idea. Most of her women are far too pious for my taste, elderly, moustachioed and overripe, but one or two of the younger ones are sweet enough. I refrain from making a reply.

She steps forward, clasping her hands placatingly.

"I thought you loved me, my Henry. I never thought you'd stoop …"

Her use of 'my Henry' informs me that fear is superseding her anger. I shrug.

"I am a man and a king. I have my needs and, unfortunately for you, there are many who seek to ease them."

"Promise me you will not stray from my bed again. Soon, our son will be born, and I can be a wife to you once more. Everything will be as it was before."

Our son. I picture Kate, rosy and fat after childbed, a sweet bonny prince tucked in her bosom. When that day arrives, I shall have everything I desire … apart from further sons and some daughters too for good measure.

I will miss Anne Stafford, but not for long. As Kate so rightly points out, she will soon be able to welcome me back to her bed. I never craved other women before and will probably not in the future. Recklessly, I give Kate my promise.

January 1510

It is a while before Kate smiles upon me again. As her belly expands, her temper grows shorter, and she complains of swollen ankles, digestive problems. At Yule I shower her with New Year gifts, pay for the best musicians in the realm. She thanks me but there is little joy in her and she retires to her chambers early, missing the best of the entertainments. At one such revel, I dress as Robin of the Wood, and my gentlemen become my merry men.

Garbed in green, we burst in upon the queen as she makes ready for the night, but my jest is taken amiss. When we rush in upon them, the chamber descends into chaos, screaming women, barking lap dogs, and Kate looks about to swoon from fright. I snatch off my mask and throw open my arms.

"Kate, it is me! I meant to amuse you, make you laugh, force you from this ennui."

"Henry!"

She sinks into a chair, a hand to her chest, and a small shard of guilt stabs me. What a fool I am to have alarmed her when she is at such an advanced state of pregnancy.

"Have I made you ill? I should have thought … I meant to … well, I thought, if the queen cannot attend the feast, the feast must attend the queen."

She laughs half-heartedly and, forcing a smile, waves a signal for the musicians to play. We turn her bedchamber into a place of revel; she watches from her bed while her women mingle with my gentlemen, and her apartment becomes a place of merriment.

"Come, Kate, dance with me." I pretend not to see her stifled sigh as she throws back the cover and takes my hand. I slow my pace to match hers, but she only manages a few stately steps before she halts and frowns, placing a hand to her back.

"I am sorry, Your Majesty, I am in some pain."

Concerned and contrite, I lead her to a chair, help her into it and call for a footstool. Instead of enjoying the revel as I had hoped, I am forced to sit at her feet and watch as my courtiers enjoy the feast that should have been ours.

But, for all that, it has been a good Christmas season and I prolong it for as long as I can. It would suit me well for our court to remain in a state of perpetual merriment.

The royal coffers are full, the winter is not too cruel and, in January when I finally sign the death warrant for my father's hated henchmen, Empson and Dudley, my popularity rises further still.

There are some on my council who advise mercy, claiming that now they have experienced a spell in the tower, Empson and Dudley will prove better servants than before. Some go as far as to suggest I pardon them.

"No!" I hit the desk so hard that pain shoots up my arm. "Their underhand dealings have no place in my England. I intend to rule with Godliness and justice."

I glare at the council, twelve startled faces gaping back at me as I continue. "The deaths of Empson and Dudley will benefit everyone, and I will brook no further delay."

My tirade is cut short when the door is thrown open. A servant runs into the room and falls to his knees.

"What is it? Why do you interrupt us?"

"It is the queen, Your Majesty. She has taken to her chamber."

For a moment, the import of his words does not penetrate. "Taken to her chamber? It is not yet noon …"

"The physician has been summoned."

The boy is terrified, his colourless face floats like a wraith in the belching smoke from the fire. I feel suddenly sick.

My prince! It is too early, far too early! I leap to my feet and my chair falls, its heavy oaken legs turned upward like a felled beast. In the speed of my departure, I cannon into the servant, the bearer of ill tidings, and he scrambles backward across the floor. As I run full tilt through the palace, the courtiers bend like wheat in the wind. Thomas More, his face lighting up at my approach, makes a knee, than swivels to watch me pass.

"Your Majesty, what has happened …?" His voice fades behind me as I hurry by without greeting.

Kate! Kate! Kate!

I must get to her. I must see her and tell her to stop this. She must not let loose our child before the proper time. She must not miscarry our son. My heir!

Hastening along the corridor, the door to her chambers looms large before me. The guards stare unseeing past my shoulder.

"Open the door."

Hearing the broken fear in my own voice, I burst into the chamber, flicking sweat from my brow. My heart plummets.

I see the usual bevy of women, but most of them are weeping; some pray aloud while the older women maintain a tight-faced vigil – their eyes fixed on the door of the inner bedchamber. Kate's sanctum. They do not seem to notice me.

A servant emerges from within; her head bowed over a covered bowl. Her step is weary and there is blood on her apron. I cannot move. Beyond that door, my son is in dire need. I blow out my cheeks, gathering strength, seeking resolve. My head is suddenly light. I need to stop this. I must *not* lose my son.

I take a tentative step and then another; my hand reaches for the latch and I throw the portal wide.

In all the chaos, they do not notice me enter. Nobody falls to their knees, nobody bows, Kate does not give her gentle smile or reach out her hand.

I am invisible.

I stand on her finest carpet and watch with terror in my heart as my queen thrashes in her bed. Her hair is damp, her face twisted, and her usually pristine white linen shift is scarlet with blood. The royal physician bends over the bed, shouting instruction to which Kate seems oblivious. She writhes and screams, a flood of

Spanish curses issuing from her usually sweet mouth. The physician frowns.

"Hold her still."

A midwife takes hold of her wrists and forces them fast to the mattress. I am in some nightmare. I will wake soon. *This is not my queen. That mangled bloodied form they are pulling from her is not my son!*

But it is.

As the horrific dream becomes real, I throw back my head and give vent to all my sorrow and rage and fear. I roar at God, at Kate, and at the twisted fickle hand of Fate that has dared to take my son from me.

We put away the royal crib, the swaddling bands so recently laid out in readiness for our firstborn. Wrapped in furs, Kate sits in a chair by the window and stares despondently at the frost-rimed garden. She is Kate, yet she is not Kate.

I can offer her nothing by way of comfort, so instead I call for my horse to be made ready. I escape the cloying air of the castle and ride like a demon across the frozen ground. Brandon, who follows unbidden, begs me to slow down, to take care, to give a thought to England.

England. As if I had forgotten her. Reluctantly, I ease my horse to a canter, a trot and finally to a walk. We come to a halt among a stand of trees. My mount lowers his head, his sides heaving as Brandon comes alongside. I knot and unknot the rein. Never in all my life have I felt less than a king, less than a man. Today, I am not simply a king without an heir. I am a bereaved father with a wife to comfort.

I should not be here at all.

I try to speak but my throat closes, my voice issuing in a croak. I cough to clear phlegm, look up at my friend and wince at the naked compassion on his face.

"There will be other sons, Harry."

I nod silently. Clear my throat again.

"It was a girl anyway. Not a boy at all, and we are young enough, Kate and I."

They are just words. I have no faith in them. It is as if I seek to console Brandon when it is I who needs comfort. But it is not just about an heir. Now that the fury at the loss of a son is fading, I am left with an overpowering grief for a child I will never meet.

Each time I close my eyes I see again the skinned rabbit that was my daughter's corpse. *I cannot unsee it.*

"I should be with Kate. We've hardly spoken since."

"It isn't her fault, you know."

"I know that." I nod fervently. "I know that, but I can't seem to … speak to her … about it. There is a wall between us. She blames me, I think … you know, all that trouble with Anne Stafford."

Brandon sighs gustily.

"It won't have been that. Men are unfaithful all the time. The queen understands such things. This loss can only have been God's will."

"But why? Why would He not want my child to live? There is no one on this earth Godlier than Kate."

He shrugs. I look at him and, although he meets my eye, I can see it is uncomfortable for him to do so.

"What would you do, if you were me, Brandon?"

He smiles, the ghost of his old self, and pushes back his cap and nods toward the palace.

"I'd go home and give comfort to my wife. In turn, it will comfort you too."

"I don't know what to say to her anymore."

"You'll think of something. Come, forget the past and look to the future. It can only get better. Do not waste your time in grief but go to work and beget another child on her!"

It is not as simple to tempt Kate from her megrim as Brandon might imagine. She is stubborn, clinging to her misery as if she is the only one to have lost a child. I bribe her with delicacies, with costly fabrics, with promises of a pilgrimage to the shrine at Walsingham when the weather improves. Slowly and reluctantly, she begins to respond. It might well be just to please me that she begins to smile again, laughing at my jests, listening to my plans for the forthcoming spring jousts. It is not until I see some semblance of her old self that I feel comfortable bedding her again.

Her body has changed. Although her arms and legs are still stick thin, her belly is softer, her breasts larger with a tracing of stretch marks that were not there before. It is strange at first, she feels like a different woman, but I grow used to it; in some ways, I prefer it.

By degrees, I inch her back to full enjoyment of our marriage bed and, when I am confident I will not be rebuffed, I use some of the skills I learned with Anne. God forbid she ever guesses where I perfected such things.

As every morning, I am roused by the sounds of the palace waking. Dogs barking in the yard, a voice calling for quiet, the soft tread of my servants making ready for the day. I open my eyes and look up at the canopy and realise I am still in Kate's bed. We must have both fallen asleep after our coupling last night.

I roll over, remove a skein of golden hair from my shoulder and look upon my slumbering wife. One arm is cast upon the pillow, the pale skin beneath as silken as the petal of a rose. She has lost her cap and her mouth is slightly open, her lips pink and plump ... inviting. Fumbling beneath the covers, my hand traverses the soft skin of her breast. She stirs and I feel her body quicken, but she does not wake. My fingers glide across her belly, creeping down to the warm recesses of her secret place. She jumps awake and slaps a hand over mine. My fingers quiet. Her eyes open and meet mine and she relaxes.

"Henry," she breathes, blinking away sleep. "I was dreaming. I wondered ..."

"Hush." I stop her words with my mouth and obediently she stops speaking, sliding her arms about my neck. For a short while, I am lost in the wonders of my wife, tangled in her hair, captured in her limbs and the soft sweetness of our union.

Summer 1510

It is early July when Kate confides that her courses are late for the second time. She clutches my sleeve, her cheeks pink with optimism, yet I see fear lurking behind her smile. My heart leaps but I quell it, unwilling to reveal the hope unfolding within me.

"Kate!" I place my lips on her forehead and draw her close, resting my chin on the gable of her hood. She is pliant in my embrace as I stare over her head across the garden, silently pleading with God to bring this child safely into the world.

As soon as she is certain, Kate once more embarks on the preparations for our prince. This time, I am more wary. I do not shout loudly of a miracle about to happen. I do not boast of my unborn son's future prowess in the tiltyard, his brilliance in the schoolroom. This time, I am uncertain. I pray more. I try and fail to remain chaste while Kate's belly expands and her temper grows short.

Having signed a treaty to extend the peace with France, I now sign a similar agreement with Spain. Then, fed up with affairs of state, I leave Kate at Eltham and embark on a summer progress.

After the feast of Pentecost, the court departs from Greenwich and takes up residence at Windsor, which holds the promise of hunting and shooting on fine days. In less clement weather, I occupy myself with wrestling and dancing, strumming my lute and composing new lays to delight the queen.

In August, Dudley and Empson finally go to the scaffold. Despite their pleas for mercy, I cannot forget the slights they aimed at me during my father's last few years. I allow them no leniency. They die penitent; no doubt wishing they had remembered that the prince they denigrated would one day become their king.

When I hear that the deed is done, I instruct my master secretary to look into their nefarious deeds of the last few decades and make reparation where appropriate.

During the last few months of progress, I have been busy, but I am still brimming with energy. I am glad when we reach the New Forest for a few days, for the woods there are full of quarry. My gentlemen and I hunt from dawn to dusk and then, when it is too dark to see, we repair to Beaulieu Abbey and feast until daybreak. But, whenever my hectic schedule allows, my thoughts stray to Kate and my child lying heavy in her belly at Eltham.

As we progress through Kent and the love of the people washes over me, I stand high in my stirrups and wave lustily, invigorating their joy even more. They shower me with rose petals, small gifts and tokens. Women run alongside my horse, begging me to touch their hands, to bless them. Being so close to the people always grounds me. They are my reason for being. The palaces and riches I possess are assets but cannot match the pleasure I receive from the love of my people.

When we reach our lodging, I sit before the warm fire, a cup of wine in my fist, while Brandon reflects on the past few weeks.

"And now we begin the last leg of the journey," he says, putting his feet up on a stool and crossing his ankles. "It has been a wearing few months."

"If it is too much for you, you can stay behind next time. I could do with a trustworthy eye kept on my womenfolk."

He lets loose a shout of laughter.

"I didn't say it was too much for me. I wager I am not too old to keep up with Your Grace just yet."

A boy tops up our cups and we both drink in silence, the crackle of the fire welcome now the nights are drawing in.

"Eltham is only a day's ride from here. It will be good to return and discover how the queen is faring. She will be glad to see me. We will leave directly after Mass."

As I predicted, Kate is indeed glad. As we canter through the parkland, a herd of deer dashes across our path and I wonder why I ever left. Eltham is my childhood home, and my mother's favourite palace that now houses my beloved wife, who in turn contains the nub of all my dreams.

Kate is waiting on the bridge over the moat. As I ride toward her, I see her wide, familiar smile and note that she is as fat and round as a partridge. Letting go the reins, I leap from the saddle before my mount has halted. I drag her into my arms. Her body vibrates with laughter; her breath is warm on my cheek. Before I kiss her, I run a forefinger along the line of her upturned nose. I close my eyes, for one short moment, perfectly and exquisitely content.

She is the first to pull away.

"Come, my husband. The whole court is watching. Come inside."

She slips her hand beneath my elbow and we turn toward the hall.

"How does the child?" I ask belatedly, and instinctively she places her hand on the prow of her belly.

"He kicks, my Lord, as lustily as a donkey."

"Oh pray, not a donkey! England won't tolerate another ass on the throne." I bellow happily with laughter, wondering if anyone noticed the subtle quip against my father.

We spend the afternoon with our closest friends in the privacy of our apartments. Kate rests on cushions while I lie beside her and place my head on her knees. I hold my palm against her belly to feel the prods and nudges of my son. Once satisfied that he is as strong as she claims, I lie down again and she brushes the hair from my forehead, her fingers cool on my skin. I close my eyes and allow her soft accents to wash over me as she relates the news of the months we have been apart.

She tells me of a letter from her father; a delivery of fine fabrics from the east; a plague of rats in the kitchens; the prayer cushions she has been embroidering. She also speaks of our son, of the festivities that will follow the birth, the joy we will share when we first behold him. I smile up at her, her gentle caressing fingers stirring urges that are best not stirred.

The company comprises our closest friends. They sit at a distance, murmuring among themselves. I hear a girlish giggle, turn my head and see Brandon teasing my sister again. In the presence of the court, his manner toward Mary is circumspect, but in private he is often too familiar. I rarely reprimand him for fear he will scorn me for a prude, but I do not like it.

As if dusting dirt from my hands, I leap up, brush my palms together and challenge Brampton, Knyvet and Compton to a game of tennis.

"Come, Kate, you must come and watch. You will be comfortable in the gallery."

I know she would rather remain here in idleness but I insist, and Mary and Brandon add their argument to mine. Reluctantly, she allows herself to be persuaded and we set off for the tennis court. As we go, Brandon falls into step with me, while Mary and Kate bring up the rear.

"I hope you are feeling agile, Brandon, for I mean to best you again. You are not going to spoil my unbroken record against you."

"I've been practising," he laughs. "You will not find me an easy opponent this time, Sire."

"Ha, would you care to wager?"

Knowing that Kate is watching, I strip off my jerkin and play in my shirtsleeves. Each time I show mastery over my opponent, I turn to my queen, and soak in the ripple of applause. My sister's praise is less effusive than the other women for she is out of sorts with me. Somehow, she has learned of the discussions taking place about a possible match between her and the French King. She says she will have none of it, but I beg to differ since, as her king, I am hers to obey.

Halfway through the game, when I have almost trounced the opposition, I turn for Kate's appreciation. She has a kerchief to her lips and has turned quite green. The next set begins but I am distracted, my eye constantly roaming to the queen.

Inadvertently, I concede a point to Brandon, and Mary leans over the balcony and applauds, slow and loud. Brandon beams, glorying in her attention, and gives an ironic bow. I glare at her, opening my mouth to chide her, but Kate forestalls me by drawing Mary back to her seat to whisper something in her ear. Slapping the racket against my palm, I turn my attention back to the game. I will have the best of Brandon and deal with my little sister when the eyes of the court are not upon us.

"Why should I show deference to you when we are among friends?" Mary says later when I complain of it. "It isn't as if there were ambassadors present to carry tales back to their masters."

Mary sniffs and examines her fingernails, buffing them on her velvet sleeve. She truly has no fear of me. While the rest of the court do their utmost to please their king, she behaves as if we are still in the nursery. Despite the honours and riches I have bestowed on her, she sees me as nothing more than a slightly ridiculous elder brother.

I doubt it will ever change and, in truth, there is some comfort in it for I sometimes grow weary of constant reverence. Even though I have dispensed with most of my father's household and engaged my old friends from the days at Eltham, I am treated differently. Only Brandon and Compton regard me as a man, a friend, and then only in the privacy of my inner sanctum.

Sometimes, when I tire of constant deference, my closest companions and I dress in plain clothes and go incognito among the populace. I revel in the rude company at the Southwark taverns; enjoy the bawdy lust of the women there and the dangers of the underworld. Of course, I do not go alone. Although I am big enough and strong enough to defeat any who should come against me, those I choose to accompany me are protection enough should the need arise.

While the queen is indisposed, it is hard for me to remain true to her. When we venture to the other side of the river, there are women who are not of the highest degree. In the lonely shadowy hours of the night they seem alluring, but the breaking day makes their former delight seem sordid. Such dalliances bring me little pleasure. I should find myself a proper mistress; someone decent, who is always on hand to soothe me when Kate is disinclined. Someone who can be on hand at court. I resolve to mention it to Compton. He acted as go between when I dallied with Anne Stafford; it is time he did so again.

As the pregnancy progresses without a hitch, I start to relax. All will be well. There are few monarchs in Christendom more pious than we, and God rewards those that treasure him. He is on our side.

I picture myself presenting my newborn son to the greatest in the land; holding him high before the court so all might look on him. I imagine them swearing fealty, praising his fine Tudor looks, the strength of his grip. This time, Kate will give me a strong son, and there will be more to come. The royal nursery will be full of boys ... and a few girls will be nice too, for securing diplomatic ties across the Christian world.

As winter approaches, Kate's belly swells into a globe. When she has settled in bed for the night, I visit her, not to bed her but just for the joy of feeling my son's robust kick.

The queen becomes more radiant by the day. Her hair is thick and red, her breasts are full and tempting; she smells of fruit and honey and I am sore tempted to love her. Only the thought of the child prevents me; no harm must come to my son.

Childbearing is as hard on the father as the mother. I love Kate, I want to bed her, but we can only go so far. Whenever I sample the weight of her dugs in my palm, I groan inwardly, intoxicated by the sweet aroma of her womanhood that fills my nose, fueling my lust. I do not want to seek easement from another, but I am a man, I have my needs. There is nothing else I can do if I am not to run mad.

Christmas 1510

The festivities are muted this year. For the first time since we wed, Kate is not at my side. She is great with child now and keeps to her chamber awaiting the birth.

There are entertainments, of course. I watch from the dais, applauding and bored in turns. My fool, John Goose, does his best but fails to raise my smile. I am jaded with the company, with his ancient jokes, and deeply in need of diversion.

As the music starts and the dancing begins, my eyes roam about the room. I should show willing. The court ladies are lined up waiting for the honour of being invited onto the floor by me. I drain my cup, wipe my lips and descend the steps to do my duty.

I care not with whom I dance. The sooner it is over, the sooner I can retire. I hold out my hand and cool fingers slip into my palm. My chosen partner sinks to her knees and it is not until she rises that I recognise Elizabeth Howard, the wife of Thomas Boleyn, an honest, valued member of my court.

She smiles, lowering her eyes, and our bodies move in graceful union. She speaks only when I rouse myself enough to address her, and I find her company easy, her silence soothing. There is nothing like a quiet pliant woman to relax the mind. Some women keep up an incessant babble I can do without.

Throughout the dance, and the two that follow, I keep her at my side. When I tire of dancing and retake my seat, I order a chair brought for her and she stays with me for the rest of the evening. I engage her company, not just because she is soothing, but because her presence will fend off others. There will be gossip, of course, but it will not last long. There is always speculation when I show a particular lady any undue attention. As soon as time allows, I take my leave of her and summon Brandon to retire to my private apartments.

"I've dragged you early from the festivities," I say, by way of apology. Brandon slumps into a chair.

"No, no. I was bored anyway."

He is not so drunk as to ignore the courtesy of hiding his pique. It is only a month or so since Brandon's wife, the mother of his two daughters, died of a fever. He does not seem to feel the loss, but I could wish he was more circumspect before the court.

I had noted his deep conversation – one might call it flirtation – with a newcomer to the queen's household. Had Kate not been in confinement, she would have had the girl sent early to her bed and urged Brandon to show more caution. It does not do to have the chief friend of the king become the butt of malicious gossip.

"You were so engrossed in that woman you didn't hear me summon you at first," I say, with the shadow of a frown.

"I like her," he replies, stretching his arm along the back of the settle. "She is a no-nonsense sort of a girl. I find her lack of pretence rather refreshing."

What he really means is that her lack of coyness promises a quick roll in the hay. My frown deepens.

"Well, the queen wouldn't like it. Find someone older, some kitchen wench or something, someone whose father won't kick up a rumpus if you deflower her."

He stands up, gives an ironic bow.

"And would Your Majesty like me to seek out a kitchen wench with a willing friend?"

His big laugh bounces around the chamber and I find it infectious; a slow smile twitches my lip. I pick up a cushion and throw it at him. He catches it deftly and hugs it to his torso.

"Henry, it is Christmas. Come, let us make merry. It will make you forget your temporary lack of a wife."

Reluctantly, I allow myself to be lured back to the fun of the feast.

January 1511 – Richmond Palace

A new day, a new year, and the world is crisp and the sky bright blue. We are preparing to ride out on the hunt. I am just pulling on my gauntlets and quaffing a cup of ale when the queen's messenger arrives. I break the seal impatiently and scan the page, my eye slowing as the import of the message becomes clear.

My heartbeat increases. I turn to Brandon, who waits with feigned patience at the door.

"The queen's pains have begun, her waters breached."

He straightens up, his eyes wide and hopeful. Fear clutches at my gut and sweat breaks out on my neck. I do not dare to hope. I have been this close before.

I cock my eye at the inviting day outside my window. I should cancel the hunt, seek the quiet of the chapel and await the announcement of the birth, but my body is restless. I need the exercise.

I clatter down the stair, the dogs at my heels, to the courtyard where our horses await us. The baying of the hounds increases when they see us; they strain at their leashes with hoarse, deafening barks. Spinning on my heel to say something to Compton, I come face to face with one of Kate's maids of honour.

She sinks to her knees, her head bowed. I reach out a hand.

"Get up, get up. You have news of the queen?"

She turns her face toward me, her eyes huge, her cheeks pink and dimpled.

"I do, Your Majesty. I am sent to tell you the prince's birth is imminent. He – he could be born at any moment … or now, as we speak."

My grip tightens; she squeaks beneath the pressure and I snatch my hand away.

"Forgive me," I say. She dips another curtsey, but I do not tarry. I run back into the hall, along corridors crowded with courtiers who fall like flayed hay. The hunt is cancelled. The lure of the whitest hind in all the forest pales to insignificance beside the promise of my son.

The passage outside Kate's apartments throngs with courtiers and servants eager for news. I stop, brush damp hair from my forehead and stride toward the doors. At the threshold, I am accosted by her women.

"Oh, Your Grace, the queen is …"

"Out of my way!"

I thrust them rudely aside and burst into the lying-in chamber. She is tiny in the vast bed, her face as pale as her linen sheet, but her mouth is wide, her eyes shining, and I know the news is good.

I take a step closer to the bed, peering at the bundle she cradles to her breast. With a coy smile, she eases the covering from his head and I look at my son. My living son.

He is no beauty. His face is as red as his hair, his nose is squashed, and a large bruise darkens his brow. But he is my son, and he is breathing and fat and healthy. He is the most beautiful thing I have ever seen.

Reaching out, I take him from her and carry him to the window where the light is brightest. He flinches, opening his mouth in a mew of protest.

"Henry ..." I unfurl his fingers, count them, marvelling at the perfectly formed nails. "Hello, Henry, my son ..."

The new year's feast is the merriest ever staged in England. We not only have a new month and a new year to celebrate, but a new prince too – an heir to our realm.

Our first son.

Kate must keep to her rooms until her churching but there are no such restrictions placed upon me. The celebrations continue until dawn, drinking health to my son, named in my honour. People shower gifts on him; ambassadors send messages across the Christian word, describing his perfection, his health and our utter joy.

At last, I have a boy to prolong the Tudor dynasty. I have done my duty. If Grandmother could see me, she would burst with pride, and even my father, could he witness this day, would be pleased.

A few days later, I ride to Walsingham to give thanks at the shrine, and so deep is my gratitude that I commission a great stained-glass window for the chapel there. For weeks, the whole of England celebrates; the church bells are ringing, prayers are said throughout the realm and bonfires are lit on every corner. To mark the gladness of England, I order the tower cannon to be fired and the city conduits to run with wine.

On the fifth day of his life, he is christened at the Church of the Observant Friars, where the Archbishop of Canterbury, William Wareham, stands as godfather and members of the court stand as surety for the absent King Louis of France, and Margaret of Savoy.

In the streets, the people are so full of elation that barriers have been put in place to keep a path clear along the route we follow. Afterwards, there is a banquet and a great pageant with glistening gold mountains, a golden tree hung with gold roses and pomegranates. Little children, dressed as Moors, dance barefoot to a cacophony of instruments and, to my shame, my eyes grow moist when I see them.

I am so very happy. God has blessed me and I hold nothing back in showing my gratitude.

In the weeks that follow, Kate and I gloat over the miracle that is our son. He is small yet lusty, his lungs are strong, and, at times, his voice is alarmingly loud.

"Henry," I murmur as I run a finger over the soft red down of hair and put my face close to his. *I wonder if he can see me.* He blinks slowly, squinting up at me as if trying to remember where we met.

"I am *Father*," I tell him. "Your sire, your king, but you will learn to call me 'Father'."

It is a word I long to hear on a boy's lips. Once the tedium of his infant days is over, there is so much I will teach him. He must excel at everything, as I do. He must learn to be better than his peers at learning, at sport and on the dance floor. He must be a great diplomat, a poet, and musician.

I lift him into my arms and whisper stories of King Arthur. The tales my mother told are still ripe in my mind. Kate watches with a smile from her seat at the window as my son and I stroll back and forth across the chamber floor.

Young Henry, lulled by my gentle tones, falls asleep, a trickle of drool collecting in the crook of my arm, but I do not halt the telling of the legends. I have no wish to return him to his nurse. I want never to put him down.

In his sleep, he snuffles and makes sucking noises that bring Kate to peer over my shoulder.

"He is very much like you, Henry," she says. "So sweet, so precious."

I smother a laugh.

"Nobody has called me 'sweet' or 'precious' in a long time."

She taps me playfully.

"Do not tease me, Henry, or I shall sulk."

A burst of laughter escapes me, startling the baby. He opens his mouth, exposes his milk-coated tongue and mews in annoyance before slumbering again.

"You should lay him down," Kate says, and reluctantly I hand him to his nurse. As we watch her tuck him firmly in his cot, I take my wife's hand. We repair to the window seat where the weak winter sunshine warms us through the thick glass.

"I wanted to talk to you, Kate. Now you are churched, I would have you join me when the court moves to Westminster."

Her face falls, her chin dropping.

"I am not yet ready to leave him ..." She glances regretfully toward the cradle.

"I know. I know ... but you may never be. It is your duty to be at my side. The court has missed you. We shall not be far away and can ride back at any instant. You know of the plans I have made for the joust. It is to honour our son, our heir. His mother must be present."

She bites her lip, nods again. "You have worked hard on it. Is everything arranged?"

"Yes." I let go of her hand and lean back, cross my ankles on a stool as I regale her with the details of the tournament.

"And you, as my queen," I say when I reach the end of a lengthy list, "are to distribute the prizes. They will love you more than ever now you've provided England with an heir."

She sighs, but she knows her duty. "Of course, you are right, Henry. I shall instruct my household to make preparation to leave."

Now that the months of waiting for the heir to be born are over, it seems no time at all. Both Kate and I would like to spend longer with him, but we can make regular visits. He is not far away.

We travel to Westminster a few days later, Kate turning wistfully in her seat every few moments until Richmond Palace disappears around a bend in the river. Her head lowers and she mangles a kerchief in her hands. It is clear she is fighting tears. One of her women picks up a lute and begins to play a merry tune. I turn away, tap my foot and concentrate my attention on the forthcoming joust.

February 1511 – Westminster Palace

The entire palace is in a fever of excitement when the day of the tournament arrives. My apartments swarm with gentlemen, already clad in their finest clothes as they help me into mine. The conversation is loud and boisterous; small pages dart about, fetching and carrying. Beau, hearing a sound outside, leaps onto my favourite seat, his front legs on the arm, his stumpy tail wagging, his barks adding to the chaos. I call him to me and he comes reluctantly, head low. He has been with me only a few months, brought as a replacement to his predecessor. I was heartbroken to lose my childhood friend and to fool myself he was still here, I named him in my old friend's honour. I swear I will always have a spaniel by me, named Beau. He has just calmed down on my lap when a noise outside sets him barking again. "Beau! Will you shut up!"

It was never like this in my father's day. Even the most carefully planned of entertainments were carried out with high ceremony. But I revel in the high spirits, the burgeoning excitement that promises so much.

We are lucky to have such a bright day in February; the air might be cold but the sun is dazzling, and I am confident it will be a tournament like no other. I sent out the challenge a few days ago, couched in the terms of a merrier time.

A queen of noble renown from the kingdom of Noble Heart is celebrating the birth of a new prince. Four knights are sent to joust all comers. The names of the knights are Cuere Loyall, Vailliaunt Desyre, Bon Voloyr and Joyous Panser.

These are, of course, knights taken from my favourite poem *The Romance of the Rose*, and I am to play my favourite character, Cuere Loyall - Sir Loyal Heart. Knyvet, Courtenay, and Neville are to play the other three knights. I can scarcely wait for the proceedings to begin.

"I shall see you later, my love," I say, kissing Kate farewell. "Do you think I look handsome?"

I hold out my arms, puffing out my chest and, gratifyingly, she puts her hands to her cheeks.

"Oh, yes, my husband. I don't know when you've looked finer."

I kiss her again and playfully smack her bottom before chivvying my attendants from the room. In the courtyard, the horses are tossing their heads impatiently. They are richly caparisoned, surrounded by an entourage of courtiers, dignitaries, footmen, officers of arms and a mace bearer to lead the way. I swing into the saddle, the bells on the harness tinkling, and look about me at the display.

The portcullis is raised; outside, the commoners are waiting to cheer us through the streets. The noise of the crowd is always deafening but today they outdo themselves. With one hand on the reins, I remove my cap and raise it above my head, making them cry my name all the louder.

It is a good day in England. Never has my father's reign seemed farther away. His dour rule is truly over and done. I am king, and England is how I planned it would be. The people love me, and I have a son and heir to follow me. Soon, Kate will give me more.

It is cramped on the cart that bears the garden of pleasure. I am shoulder to shoulder with my fellow challengers as the wagon is trundled in, drawn by golden beasts – a lion and an antelope with gilded horns. When it slows, I leap from the turret of a great golden castle. The crowd roars. I hold out my arms, resplendent in Kate's colours, while the court almost explodes with delight.

I outshine every other man with my purple and gold, the jewels on my doublet twinkling and shining in the light of the sun. I spy the queen, sitting with her ladies, her plump pink face glowing with pride when she recognises I am no longer Henry but Sir Loyal Heart – her devoted swain come to display his great devotion to her.

The music begins; a lively tune of my own devising. I leap in the air, twisting and twirling, the energy I have contained for so long now impossible to withhold.

As I turn and dart amid the throng, they begin to tear the spangles of gold from my sleeves, ripping at my clothes, stripping me of finery. I fall to one knee, laughing, but, thinking me in danger, the guards move swiftly in, halberds raised. I struggle to my feet and wave them away.

"Let them be," I cry. "It is all in good sport!"

And so it is. I could order their arrest but I am happy, merrier and more content than I have ever been. As they dart off with their spoils, I fall at Kate's feet, my tunic torn away and my shirt clinging to my damp torso. She blesses Sir Loyal Heart with her favour.

Over the next few weeks of tournament, I win almost every contest. There is no one, save Brandon, bigger or stronger than I, yet I vanquish him too. He wears a long false beard as part of his masque and, knowing himself beaten, throws down his weapon and grins at me, his face slick with sweat, his teeth gleaming white from the depths of his disguise.

Afterwards, the competitions over, my friends join me and the queen in our privy apartments and there is no suggestion of an early night. By the time we retire, poor Kate is worn to the bone and even I am glad of a little respite.

"Ah, Kate," I murmur into her hair as we lie beneath the covers. "What a time we've had. What a life lies ahead of us. I never knew such happiness was possible. It is more than I ever dreamed."

She rolls toward me and kisses me, pressing close and prompting me to make love to her again.

"I thought you were tired," I tease, with feigned reluctance, and she laughs. She knows very well that I am never too tired for her.

By the time we descend to the hall in the morning, most of the debris of the celebration has been cleared away. The servants creep around, grey beneath the eye, walking gingerly as if their heads are sore. Brandon appears with Compton, and both beg to be excused from our planned afternoon of tennis.

"My head, Sire, I feel as if I've been poleaxed," Brandon complains.

"You probably were!" I laugh. "You, sir, are womanish in your suffering. A gallop around the park will clear your head."

I put my hands on my hips, tipping backward on my heels as I mock him. He looks at me greenly before nodding agreement.

"Very well, Sire. I am well enough to play."

"Well," I say, in my final taunt, "enjoy your game. I will not be joining you for Wolsey has some urgent business and has requested an hour of my time." I sigh and reflect on how much I detest state affairs that keep me from my leisure. "I shall endeavour to be free of him quickly enough to join you."

Although I complain and mumble of Wolsey when he is absent, I would not be without him. He frees me of much of the tedium of governance; he deals with the minutiae and only consults me on matters of great import. He is waiting when I enter; he looks up from his papers and puts down his pen, rising to greet me with respect, as is his wont, despite our lengthy friendship.

"Your Majesty," he says. "I trust you enjoyed the entertainments?"

"Were you there? Did you see how soundly I beat every comer?"

"I was there for some of the time, Your Majesty. As ever, you were the brightest star."

"I ran twenty-eight courses, broke twelve lances and scored nine hits to the body and one on the helmet."

"Remarkable, Your Majesty."

He does not mention that Knyvet did, in fact, beat me on one such run, and neither do I.

I sit down, shuffle the papers he places before me, and make my mark on a few of them. I frown at another.

"What's this?"

He peers over my shoulder.

"This one concerns the household of our new prince, Your Majesty, and this …" he places a paper before me, "… is in regard to the charter for St John's College. Your grandmother …"

The door bursts open and a messenger hurtles into the room, falling to his knees, his head to the floor. I notice his clothes are mired, as if from a breakneck ride. My heartbeat increases. I stand up.

"What is it, man? Speak up!"

He raises his head, his face contorted with grief or fear …

"Your Majesty," he rasps. "I bring grave news. Dire news …"

His face twists; he knuckles his eye and looks anywhere but at me, as if wishing he were elsewhere.

"Your Majesty, it is the prince. Prince Henry was … this morning, he didn't … He is dead, Your Majesty."

My world tilts.

I hear Wolsey gasp, his hand coming to rest on the small of my back, daring to touch me.

I do not move. I do not fall to my knees or call upon God to change His decree. It is as if the earth and I have lost contact, as if my mind is reeling in the heavens, detached from my body.

Wolsey's voice comes from far away. The acrid smell of burning feathers assaults my nose.

"Drink this, Your Majesty." Wolsey holds a cup. I look down at it. The wine swills like blood. "Come, sit down. Drink this."

I come back to myself, fall into a chair. The world levels. I am going to be sick. The messenger is still snivelling on the floor.

"Get out!" I roar, and the boy flees, but Wolsey remains, hovering like a nursemaid. I regard him blankly, unable to feel anything. I should be weeping.

"I should inform the queen."

I try to stand, but Wolsey pushes me down.

"Forgive me, Your Majesty, but … I think … I think you should wait awhile. I will send for Charles Brandon."

I nod, close my eyes, and pinch the bridge of my nose. The vision of my son floats in my head; his fluff of hair, his hungry rosebud mouth. He was the culmination of all my dreams – my ambition. He cannot be dead!

My life's purpose – stolen from me before he can speak his own name. If I think too hard upon it, I will run mad. Launching myself from my seat, I push Wolsey aside. I must go to Kate.

Only she will understand.

For three days, we shut ourselves away from the intrusive eyes of the court. The whole country, the entire Christian world will be talking of our loss and I cannot endure their sympathy.

I slump on the bed while Kate vents her grief in my lap. She tears at her hair, writhing in unrelenting agony, but I cannot do the same.

Is her hurt greater than mine because it is more vocal?

Inside, my heart is cloven in two; it pumps salt tears instead of blood, yet I make no outward show. I am king. I must show only a brave face to the world, give voice to my certainty that God took our son because he was too perfect for this world.

Next time, I hear myself declare, *next time, our son shall survive.*

I lay my head back against the bed frame. *What must I do to win God's favour? What must I do to be blessed with a living child?* I ponder on the lengthy preparation for his birth; the prayers, the tiny garments Kate sewed. The royal crib, the same that gave me shelter, the same that my mother filled with child after child, is empty once more. What must I do?

Kate drifts into a restless slumber. I look at her knotted hair, her swollen nose, her ravaged eyes. I have seen her upset before. I have seen her weep, and, each month when she woke to a bloodied sheet, I shared her sorrow, but I have never seen her despair before. Not like this.

I must think of a way to calm her. This behaviour, this outward show of grief, is unseemly for a queen. She must stand tall and not allow our enemies to know how low this loss has brought us. I should wake her and tell her that the time for weeping has passed, but ... instead, I let her enjoy the only respite we have, and even then there are dreams.

I do not sleep. I watch the light fade, the fire slump. I witness the moment the first bats come out to flutter outside the window. I also watch the dawn creep over the horizon. I see the birds wake, hear the first crow of the cockerel, the early clatter as the palace begins to wake.

There is no respite for me.

On the fourth day, I emerge into the court again. My gentlemen are helping me dress when Wolsey asks to be admitted. He comes in, a sheaf of papers beneath his arm, his expression officious and concerned. He bows low.

"Your Majesty," he says, "may I express my ..."

"No!"

He halts mid-sentence, shaking his head in confusion. "Your Majesty, I merely sought to ..."

"Well, don't. I have no wish to hear it, and neither does the queen. You can instruct the court at large that we do not seek condolence of any kind. It was God's will, and we must accept it. Now, what business have we today?"

I wait while my man fastens the last few buttons of my doublet. I spend no time admiring my reflection, as is my usual habit. I turn from the looking glass, as ready as I will ever be to face the day.

"There is the matter we were discussing ..."

With a hand on his shoulder, I accompany Wolsey to the council chamber where all eyes turn sorrowfully upon me. Before they can speak, Wolsey raises his hand.

"His Majesty has expressed his wish that no word be said on the late grievous event. He wishes to look to state matters."

I take my seat in silence and wave at the company to do the same. A great shuffling and clattering of stools follows before Wolsey clears his throat.

"Your Majesty, the question of us joining Spain's campaign against the Moors. My colleagues agree that you should not travel to Cadiz yourself. You have reliable seasoned soldiers who can ride out in your stead ..."

I do not care. I nod reluctant agreement and Wolsey makes a scribbled note of my response. A chair scrapes and Thomas Howard, Duke of Norfolk, clears his throat.

"And, Your Majesty, I really feel – we all feel – that it is wiser to appease France than to prod them with an outward show of support for Spain."

Norfolk, as treasurer, thinks more about the royal purse than our honour. Our coffers are full, and although it would be preferable to keep them so, we cannot let France have everything her own way. Under my father's governance, our armies have grown flabby, fonder of ale and whoring than war. It is time they were beaten into shape.

Since I was a boy, I have longed to emulate my forebear: that other Henry. Henry V, who won long-lasting fame at Azincourt. Domination of France would earn me a similar accolade. I allow the council to persuade me to send Lord Darcy to fight the infidel while we turn our attention to undermining Louis XII in France.

I lean forward in my chair, link my fingers and press the tips of my thumbs together. Most of the council argue against rashness, fearing a move against France could spell disaster but, to my surprise, Wolsey offers his full support. A relative newcomer to the council, I sit back and regard him, absorbing his persuasive speech on the merits of giving the French a taste of our strength. I smile and stroke my beard. The more I come to know Wolsey, the more I like him. He shall go far in our service.

With thoughts of war dominating my mind, I have less time to dwell on the loss of my son. Yet each time I see Kate, my grief returns full force. She has ceased to mourn openly but she is listless now, where before she was energetic and bright. She prefers to sit quietly in her chambers, or pray in the darkness of her chapel than frolic with our courtiers in the hall.

Often, after remaining at the feast for as short a time as etiquette allows, she escapes to her chambers. When I follow her there, it is clear she has been weeping.

"Henry!" She dashes a hand across her cheek and turns a smiling face upon me, but I am not fooled. Her women retire to an adjoining room and I pull her from her seat, sit down in it and urge her onto my knee. But even our old closeness is tainted.

Whereas once she would have entwined her arms around me, whispered silliness in my ear, now she sits primly upright. The comforting warmth I need so much has been replaced by ice.

My hand slides downward and I squeeze her thigh, but although she does not pull away, she makes no response. For the first time, I wonder if she ever welcomed my attention, or if it was only ever duty.

I cast my mind back to the many times she has lain, pink and pretty, in my bed. No, I smile wryly. That was not pretence. That was delight. The memory stirs me and I pull her closer, nuzzling her neck. She tucks her chin against her shoulder and gasps. I am not sure if it is with pleasure or distaste, but I must get a son on her and there is only one way I can do so.

We have an hour before supper. I stand so suddenly that she almost falls from my knee. I catch her wrist.

"Got you!" I say, and she laughs nervously. She seems brittle, as if she will break if I am too rough with her, but I appreciate her attempt to regain her old self.

"I am not a fish, my husband," she says and, maintaining my grip on her hand, I pull her close again.

"If you were, and I was a fisherman, would you want to escape?"

"Oh no," she says, turning huge sad eyes upon me. "I'd never want to escape you, my husband."

Her lips quiver beneath mine and, as our hearts merge, my desire for her returns full measure. I pick her up and drop her on the counterpane, tearing off my tunic and bouncing down beside her.

"So many damn' petticoats!" I say, as I fumble beneath the layers. My fingers linger, tickling the warm softness of her inner thigh. It takes all my reserve to move slowly, stroking and gently pinching, teasing her desire from the darkness until it matches mine. When I take her, the rhythm of our loving echoes the same words repeated, again and again. *Give me a son. Give me a son. Give me a son.*

November 1511 - June 1512

"This schism is cruel, impious, criminal!" I thump the table and glare at the company. A ring of startled faces turns toward me, heads nodding agreement. "What will they think of us for joining the fray so late?"

"Your Majesty, the Archbishop of York begs your forgiveness for the unthinkable delays his messenger encountered on the road."

I growl disbelievingly. Louis has deliberately rent the church in two, but at least I have my excuse for a holy war. I have waited long enough.

I have waited all my life to don my armour and lead my men into battle, and now the moment is here. By the following April, all is in hand, and we have formally declared war on France. But, at the last minute, my hopes are dashed. My advisors are unanimous. I should not be the one to lead the troops. With no heir to follow me, I am too precious, too valuable to risk in battle.

I wish I could overturn their decision, thwart their argument but, deep down, I know they are right. I am invaluable and to ignore the threat to my person would endanger all England. I cannot subject my realm to a return to civil war. *I must get a son!*

That night, I leave the revellers in the hall and seek out Kate who, as is now her habit, has retired early with the beginnings of a headache.

I am not expected. Her women are in disarray. They scatter from my sight, blushing to be caught making their preparations for the night. I throw open Kate's chamber door and she raises her head from her pillow.

She is pale and her eyes are shadowed. I pause; I should leave her in peace but, from the dark recesses of my mind, my father's disappointment scuttles forward like a spider. *You have to get an heir.*

The begetting of a son supersedes her discomfort. With a click of my fingers, I send her chamberers away and begin to unbutton my shirt. She could complain at my intrusion but, instead, seeing the trouble I am having, she slides from bed to undo the fastenings herself. She smells of recent dreaming.

I look down on her linen cap and my former irritation seeps away. It is not her fault. She does all she can to give me an heir. Half her day and, I suspect, most of her night, is spent in prayer. She makes regular donations to the church, takes pilgrimage to Walsingham, and never denies me her bed. I have never once heard her disparage God for taking our children. Neither does she complain of fatigue when I keep her awake until the small hours, humping desperately to implant a child in her womb.

When I am dressed only in my small clothes, I lift her and carry her to the bed. She does not demur. I pull her shift over her head and she scrambles beneath the covers, declaring it is cold. I pull them aside.

The candlelight gleams on her milk white thighs, her plump breasts, and her belly that is still marked from when she carried our son. She is soft and willing and warm, as comfortable as a feather pillow after a long day in the saddle.

I pull off her cap and smile to see her hair fall in a red cascade. She waits, the picture of fertility, an icon of desire. *How can we fail?* A dart of longing spreads in my belly as I slide alongside her, my fingers stroking and searching. I close my eyes, lose myself in my wife, my queen, and pray God as I take her that this time, *this time*, He will bless us.

In the morning, I ride off to Southampton to inspect the troops before they embark. I doubt a finer army has ever been seen and, as I mingle with the men, my heart fills with envy. I should be with them.

It should be me, not the Marquis of Dorset who heads the twelve-thousand-strong troop. What I would not give to ride with them, to feel the thrill of the field, taste the blood of victory.

I spent my childhood training for war. Those infant campaigns with my wooden sword were to prepare me for battle: each turn on the lists, every challenge I've accepted, every sword I've wielded were to ready me for war; a war I am now denied.

Just as I am denied a son.

With a loose rein, I guide my horse among the ranks. The soldiers stand tall, their eyes gleaming with anticipation of a good fight. God and all His saints are on our side and the pope has promised each soldier a shorter spell in Purgatory should they die gloriously on the field.

My eyes mist, blurring the glint of steel, the gleam of silk pennants into a shining field of valour. My troops stretch as far as the eye can see and, beyond them, the masts on my warships; my proud royal navy flags flutter bravely in bright English skies.

I have not a single doubt that this gallant army will confound the malice and tyranny of those who oppress the church of God with this hateful schism. And when they take the victory, they shall do so without me.

As I watch my men march away, I bite my lip and fight the urge to ignore my councillors' advice and ride after them. Woodenly, I raise my salute, a tear in my eye and a lump in my throat, until it is time, with my stomach rolling with resentment, to turn my horse north.

As we gallop home, I rage against my lack of power. I crave war, yet am denied it. I crave an heir, yet am denied. What must I do to get my wife with child?

***

Sometimes, I suspect Wolsey has more to gain from this war than I do. None of the expected glory materialises. While I sit aimlessly at home, my carefully selected troops run amok overseas. My hopes of reconquering Guyenne are dashed when Ferdinand reneges on our agreement and he and Grey fall into dispute.

Reports come in from overseas, reports that sicken me and fill me with rage. The men, that brave army I was so proud of, are overcome by heat and too much strong wine. Discipline disintegrates as they fall sick and mutiny, abandoning their posts to crawl ignominiously home.

Ferdinand – that sneak, that rogue – deflects all the blame to Grey, who is now as grievously ill as those beneath his command. He is scarcely recovered when he is brought home, and into my presence.

He kneels like a bag of bones before me, still green about the gills, complaining of bad knees and begging to be allowed the comfort of rising. I consider his request while he sweats and shakes.

I have always liked Grey; he is some sort of uncle or cousin, on my mother's side. Despite my father's distrust of him, he has been loyal to me and dependable … until now.

I nod briefly, and his page assists him to his feet. He tilts his head back, swaying violently.

"I thank you for your compassion, Your Majesty," he gasps, glancing around the hall, determining who is present and who is absent, before looking at me.

"I am waiting for you to explain." I maintain a cold expression.

He wets his lips.

"King Ferdinand, having changed tactic, did bid me follow suit, Your Majesty, but I stood firm. I take orders only from you, Your Majesty, but when I fell sick … I was so very sick … I lost control. The men, lightheaded with wine and too much sun … everything descended into chaos. I couldn't stop them … I beg pardon for it, Your Majesty."

I rub my chin, pondering his words and, at length, decide to listen to my heart. I sense he is telling the truth. It does not excuse his incompetence, his loss of control, yet … Grey has always been my good servant while, despite being my father-in-law, Ferdinand has ever been wily and unreliable. Kate, of course, will think otherwise and place all blame on my kin rather than her own.

"It is the job of a commander to keep his troops in line. This is your second failing …"

"Your Grace, forgive me! I was sick unto *death*. Many of us were."

He holds out his hands, palms up, his fingers splayed. I decide to maintain a semblance of anger.

"Yet, you didn't die. It was born of too much carousing when you should have been fighting. Too much whoring when you should have been at council."

"Not I, Your Majesty. I remained at my post until I could no longer stand. This fever …"

His words fade, his face growing paler still, his eyes dark with terror. He moistens his lips again, speechlessly shakes his head, denying my accusation of neglect of duty. The power I hold over him is gratifying; his future completely at my whim.

I believe him. I know the problem. I should have been there. It was my duty. It is I who have failed. With me at their head, no man would slack in his obligation. No man would dare to slope off whoring when the King of England was looking on.

I inflate my chest and yawn loudly, a hand to my mouth.

"We are displeased with the result of this campaign, Dorset. I will have to ponder the matter. Take yourself to your estates and do not present yourself again until you are properly recovered."

He bows, almost falls and, with the support of his servant, shuffles from my presence. As the door closes, Wolsey steps forward, his paper and pen at the ready.

"Ah, Thomas," I say. "We will send our ambassador to the King of France. Warn him – gently, of course – that unless he forms an immediate peace with the pope, he will have to take the consequences."

Wolsey's eyebrows disappear into his cap, but he bows acquiescence as I continue. "It is all the fault of King Ferdinand, of course. He has ever been unreliable. You have only to consider his failure to send the queen's dowry … during my father's reign. If a man reneges on a deal that concerns his daughter's welfare, he'll renege on anything."

Wolsey bows in agreement and indicates the place on a document he wishes me to sign. I make my signature without reading it. He has my trust, and I am promised to a game of tennis with Brandon at noon.

As soon as he has rolled his papers away, I take hasty leave of Wolsey. Reaching the door, I encounter Kate and a gaggle of her women. She is wearing a fetching green gown, a pearl as big as a hen's egg, and a face like thunder.

"Kate!" I say. "What a lovely surprise."

There is no doubting she has overheard my comments regarding her father, but I decide to ignore the matter.

"Kate!" I say again, taking up her hands and kissing them. Her fingers stiffen, her shoulders are braced, and her frown is cut deep. I cast about for a way to deflect the brewing argument. "Would you care to walk with me in the garden?"

Her scowl does not falter.

"No, my Lord. I feel a headache coming."

Another one? I do not say this aloud but, instead, assume a sympathetic expression.

"Perhaps a turn about the garden would do you good but, if you do not care for it now, I am due to confound Brandon at tennis. You could come and watch."

She sniffs and regains possession of her hand.

"I wonder, my Lord, that you crave the company of a queen who failed to bring as much as a penny into the marriage. I am surprised you see fit to consort with the daughter of such an untrustworthy knave as King Ferdinand of Spain."

Her accent is always more pronounced when she is angry. It reminds me of the days of our first meeting, when she was a woman grown and I just a child of ten. It also brings to mind the passion she displays when I am in her favour. At the peak of pleasure, she always cries out in Spanish.

I would prefer to regain her favour with soft words, retract my condemnation of her father, but … it would be a *lie*. The man betrayed me, and the failure of the campaign lies directly at his feet. Even she cannot deny that. I bite my lip and, priming my mind for the prospect of a disagreement, I summon all the diplomacy I have been taught.

"You must agree, Madam, that our recent ignominy in France was directly due to Spain. He should, in decency, have kept to the agreement."

She raises her chin and glowers at me.

"I agree to no such thing. If my father changed his plan, then he must have had good reason to do so." My efforts for a peaceful negotiation shatter. She makes to turn away, but I grab her arm, pull her close, dislodge the ridiculous hood she wears and growl privately into her ear.

"You would do well, Madam, to remember where your allegiance lies … or should lie. You are Queen of England now. Any favouritism you show to Spain could be construed as treason."

Furiously, she struggles to snatch her arm away and curls her lip, speaking so rapidly in her native tongue that I cannot follow. It is clearly uncomplimentary.

I release her so suddenly that she stumbles, clutching at her attendant as I push past and cannon into one of her women. A girl so small and frail that she falls like a skittle.

"God save us!" I cry. "What are you doing?"

The young girl sprawls at my feet, her skirts about her knees. Hastily, she covers her modesty and, when I hold out my hand, shyly takes it. I haul her up, noting her scarlet cheeks.

"A thousand pardons, lady."

There is no need for me to make apology but she is pretty and very young, and clearly terrified. I do not recall seeing her before, so she must have recently come to court. "Are you hurt, Madam?"

She shakes her head, bobs her knees and averts her eyes. I notice the soft youthful glow of her skin, the dimple on her chin, the sweep of lashes on her cheek. I open my mouth to ask her name, but the queen intervenes.

"Straighten your skirts, Bessie," she snaps. "Come, we will return to our apartments. It is clear the king is too busy to heed my advice."

The girl bobs another curtsey and scurries in Kate's wake. Wolsey coughs behind me.

"Oh dear, Your Majesty. I hope the queen is not out of sorts for too long."

"She'll get over it," I say, moving closer to speak confidentially into his ear. "That girl, Bessie … who is she, do you know?"

"Erm … the daughter of Sir John Blount of Kinlet, you will remember him, Sire?"

"Yes, yes, of course, one of The Spears." I watch Bessie hurry after the queen and am rewarded when she turns at the last moment and smiles.

I raise my hand.

Usually, when I move about the palace, I am accompanied by an armed guard, a handful of courtiers, my fool and several servants and dogs, but today I crave solitude and bellow at them to fall back. I need some space to breathe. I am sick of ceremony. I must be allowed to think, to be myself, to consider what I must do. There is always so much to do.

The constant attention that is my due as king is often more of a hindrance than a benefit. Stifled by matters of state, as I draw near the tennis court, I fumble with the buttons of my doublet, eager for the game to begin.

Activity soothes me. It always does and I am determined to show everyone how the game of tennis should be played.

Brandon is waiting, lounging with a bevy of young women. His laughter drifts away when he sees me, but his broad smile remains.

"I thought you'd forgotten about me, Your Majesty. I was growing anxious."

He did not look anxious when flirting with the young ladies of the court. I pull off my doublet, and let it fall.

"Thought I lacked the courage for it, did you?"

His big laugh is accompanied now by the gentler laughter of the women. I spy my sister, Mary, whom I had thought to be in attendance to the queen. She leans forward over the gallery.

"Good morning, Sire. I will lay my coin against you, if you don't mind. Our father always warned me to have a care for my fortune."

I toss my sword belt to a waiting servant.

"Then I shall benefit from your loss, dear sister, for I mean to prove the better man."

She claps delightedly, her merry laughter just as it was in her girlhood. I could take umbrage that she bets against me, but I know she only does so to provoke me. I have had a lifetime of Mary's rag pulling. She will be sorry once her purse is lighter by a few shillings.

Of all the men at court, Brandon is my only real opponent, and I will have to work hard for victory. He will not allow me to win merely because I am his king. His competitiveness matches my own. I like that. If he beats me fairly, I will not hold it against him.

The gallery is crowded. One glance reveals that the gathering of courtiers has been swelled by the arrival of a company of foreign ambassadors. I smile, knowing they will carry tales of my prowess across Europe. I shall be known the world over as a strong, athletic king.

Taking up the racket, I bend low, twirl it in my fingers and slap it against my palm as I wait for the ball to come my way.

The crowd falls silent. Brandon takes his shot and the ball speeds toward me as if loosed from a cannon. I take half a step back, my eye on the target and, with all my strength, send it back across the net. It hits the gallery roof, bounces once before dropping into the court. Brandon returns it. I strike it again ... and so the game continues.

As we battle for supremacy, the stresses of the day dwindle. I forget Ferdinand and our humiliation in France. I forget Kate and her tantrums. I forget my need for a son and heir; all I crave now is to beat Brandon and hear the court hail me as champion.

I grow hot. My hair sticks to my scalp, my fine linen shirt clings, sweat trickles, drawing all eyes to my well-sculpted torso. There is not a woman in the gallery who does not admire me. I could have them all if I so desired. That would show Kate a thing or two.

For all Brandon's good looks, he lacks my power, my good fellowship. He is not king and never will be. I run my tongue around my arid mouth, searching for moisture. One more point and the sixth set, and thus the game, will be mine.

It has been hard won.

He is a worthy opponent, a worthy friend. Afterward, we will refresh ourselves; the wine will flow as freely as the conversation. I always enjoy the banter, the laughter with my good friends.

With a grunt, Brandon launches himself one more time, but he misses his footing and misguides the ball. It smashes into the net, drops, bounces twice in its trap, and the game and victory are mine.

I throw up my arms.

The assembly erupts in cheers, my name on every tongue as they swarm into the court to offer their congratulations. Laughing and exclaiming at the ease with which I won, I take the towel I am handed. I bury my face in it to wipe away the sweat and, when I look up, Brandon is before me, his face aglow.

"A good match, Your Majesty. I let you have that last point …"

I pull up short, look up from the towel again, about to call him out as a liar but, on seeing his expression, I throw my arm about his neck with a roar of laughter.

We are wending our way back to the palace when I spy the rich red hue of Mary's skirts. I spin on my heel and wait for her to catch up with us.

"Ah, sister!" I taunt as she draws near. The company pauses, giving us their full attention. She curtseys sullenly, pouting a little. "Let me relieve you of that purse, Mary," I say, holding out my hand. "Now, remind me: what was it you were saying about Brandon being the better sportsman?"

As the purse drops into my palm, reluctant laughter plays about her mouth. Fortunately, she is a better loser than a judge of men, and will not hold my victory against me.

She smiles wickedly.

"Your Majesty, my dear brother. I grant, you may be the better player but, in my opinion, it is the heart and not tennis that maketh the man."

Turning rudely on her heel, she leads her women away across the gardens while we all watch her go, open-mouthed at her impudence.

Her head is high, her bearing jaunty. She has grown into a handsome woman, a flower of my court, although I would never tell her so. One day, I will make her a fine match. A great English Duke perhaps, or maybe a king, if I can bear to part with her.

"Thomas!" I turn my head and, as if from nowhere, Wolsey appears breathlessly at my elbow.

"You called for me, Sire?"

"A word, if we may, about my sister." I beckon him to walk with me so we might speak quietly. "She is of an age to marry. We must cast around for a likely husband. Someone worthy of her."

***

Despite my best attempts to mollify her, Kate maintains her sulk for more than a week. Of course, she does her duty when I go to her chamber, but she takes no joy in it. In the end, fed up with her cold welcome and half-hearted coupling, I cease my visits and take my sport with others.

The women of the court admire me, think themselves lucky if I deign to take to the floor with them, or praise their ready wit. One or two allow me greater favours, but it leaves me jaded. After I have lain with them, I am driven by shame to seek the solace of my confessor the next morning.

It is hard for me to enjoy the bed of a reluctant woman and that is what Kate has become. How am I to ever get a child on her if she refuses to give me a proper welcome? It seems to me she should realise her good fortune at being queen of the realm, bedded by the handsomest king in Christendom. I long for a return to the way we were in the early days of our marriage. She saw no fault in me then. In the early days, our bedchamber rang with laughter ... before we lost our son.

Spring - Summer 1513

To the general disgruntlement of my council, I appoint Wolsey as chief minister. It irks them that one of lowly birth should be allowed to lord it over them. I dismiss their concern, laughing at their discomfort as they offer him false congratulations on his swift and steady rise.

He climbed the ladder from King's Almoner, shortly after my accession, to accepting a seat on the council. Now, he has become my most trusted advisor and I do not care how the rest of them mutter against him. I have no care for the secrets he keeps; I know he conceals his common-law wife and an infant child, but as long as he offers wise counsel, he will have my favour. I trust him as I trust no other.

When Kate looked like prolonging her sulks into the festive season, it was Wolsey who talked her round. Since old Louis of France responded sneeringly to my warning to make amends with the pope, the path is now clear for war. I understand that I am God's chosen instrument. Although he would prefer a peaceful route and is ostensibly against violent measures, Wolsey supports my desire to wage war on France.

He is a man who does my bidding.

To distract myself from the queen's continuing failure to conceive, I plan and plot our invasion of France and, this time … this time, I shall lead my men into battle myself.

In the great hall, a feast is underway. Kate is beside me, all smiles and graciousness, and a troop of fools has just finished their act. Laughter is still rumbling in my chest as they tumble from view and the poet John Skelton steps onto the floor. My laughter fades; I sit back in my seat, twirl my cup between my fingers and prepare to listen.

Skelton is my old tutor. I have long forgiven him for keeping me at my books until the light was too dim to see. I understand now the import of education but, at the time, I thought it merely a punishment inflicted by my father.

Now I no longer need a tutor, I retain Skelton's services at court. I send him on the odd diplomatic mission, consult him on all sorts of matters. Perhaps, one day, he will school my son; my heir will require the best tutors and, together, Skelton and I will scour Europe to find them.

John Skelton is something of a poet; he penned my father's epitaph but lauded him so much that I almost began to question his judgement. I prefer his chronicles, especially the one he wrote about Richard the Lionhearted on his third crusade. Most appropriately, it makes a pleasing mockery of the French.

As he clears his throat and stares soulfully at the great hall ceiling, I reach for Kate's hand and she allows her fingers to remain in my palm. While Skelton's words echo about the hall, my gaze runs around the company; they are mellow, well fed and content. The torchlight dances on their faces, highlighting their beards, making their jewels gleam, enhancing beauty and flaws alike. The visages of the women are softened, yet some of the men become grotesques. Compton's hooked nose is made monstrous, and Knyvet's deep set eyes become ghoulish. I turn my attention to the maids, whose fresh complexions and bright pretty colours are more soothing. A contented sigh escapes me.

The queen slides her hand from mine and indicates to her woman that she requires her cup filled. A girl rises. I hear the glug of poured wine, and her shadow passes across me as she returns the vessel to the queen. She curtseys before resuming her position at the queen's feet. My eye is taken by the movement and I realise it is Bessie Blount.

I watch her, noting how much she has ... matured since I noticed her last. Although she is still young, fourteen or so by my guess, the stark terror of being at court has vanished and she now bears herself with confidence. She notices me looking. I stroke my chin, incline my head and smile, delighted that she has not lost her delightful blush.

As my mind is drawn from thoughts of war, Skelton's voice drifts away, and I begin to ponder the mysteries of love. Later, while I strive to get a child on my unresponsive queen, Bessie's face floats in my mind's eye. The girl is so pretty, so full of admiration, so overwhelmed with gratitude at my notice. If it were Bessie, or someone like her, in Kate's place, my welcome would be so much warmer.

By April, I have persuaded all the men of the council to agree that we should finally declare war on France.

"This time," I tell them, "as your king, I will assume my proper place as Commander in Chief."

They nod grudging agreement and I launch into the preparations with a merry heart. At long last, I can realise my dream of riding in defence of England's honour. I will show the world I am not the penny-pinching king my father was.

If it empties the royal coffers, then so be it. The world shall see me as a king in my grandfather's image; Edward IV, the warrior king, or perhaps Henry V. This campaign will prove so successful it will put Azincourt in the shade.

I have put aside my distrust and am once more on good terms with Ferdinand. It is an uneasy truce, yet at least Kate's displeasure with me has passed. Things are almost like they were in the early days and, when I visit, she gives me a proper welcome. Her kisses are warmer now than they ever were.

"Ah, Kate," I whisper in her ear. "I hate it when we are not friends. I swear I shall never displease you again."

She laughs and snuggles against me, but I roll her over, tug the sheet down and reach for her duckies. They are larger since she carried our prince, brown-tipped now instead of pink, but I do not mind. I long to see them replete and blue veined with milk again. If she would only get with child, I would not even resent being denied the benefit of her bed. I bury my face between her breasts and blow a great raspberry to make her squeal.

It is near dawn when I take the private route back to my own bed. I am so weary I might have spent the night chasing a hind across the heath. Kate's scent clings to me, I am both spent and content and, as my chamberer tucks the cover beneath my chin, I reflect that if she is not with child after that amount of effort, she never will be.

I sleep until noon. Then, after I have broken my fast and said a rather late and hasty morning prayer, I attend the Privy Council.

I have kept them waiting for hours. The barrage of voices reaches me before I am halfway along the corridor. When I enter, it stops abruptly. They bow their heads, wish me good day and wait for me to take my seat.

I am impatient to rally my army and ride forth against King Louis, show him exactly the kind of warrior king he is up against, but my councillors drone on and on, obsessed with the minutiae. So much talk when we should be exchanging fire. War requires far more preparation than I had imagined.

The topic of the day is when the imminent invasion should take place. When we should embark? Where we should land? How many troops will be required? My mind drifts off.

I wonder if Kate's parts are as sore as mine after the lengthy night of loving. Brandon has suggested she is not as hale as I, and I should allow her some respite but ... it is not easy to stay away. I know it is too soon to visit her tonight, although I long to do so.

She has been looking tired of late. She eats too little and prays too much. She should be building her strength, not weakening it with fasting. I take up my pen and make a note to Wolsey to request some sweetmeats to tempt the queen's palate. I will order a private dinner, just the two of us, and write a short poem to accompany the gift. I will read it aloud to her and perhaps she will be tempted to invite me to stay.

***

I am a happy man. I am about to embark on my first campaign of war and my queen has informed me she is at last with child.

During the past months, the south of England has become a vast armoury as huge guns and ammunition are manufactured. Wolsey, who is in charge of it all, warily shows me the lists. I scan the page, which is as long as my arm; weapons, armour, wooden trebuchets to batter the French fortifications. I also note the white tunics with the cross of St George for the fighting men, the huge amount of harness, the many tons of victuals: oats, wheat and barley to feed and keep my army strong.

I flinch at the mounting costs, but I do not order that he scrimp on anything. I am not my father and I believe glory is more becoming to a king than a fat purse.

Our vanguard crosses the sea in May and waits in readiness for me to join them. Brandon and his army are already ensconced in Calais, awaiting my orders and, this day, my wife and I are to take horse to Dover, where she will see me off on my campaign.

It is a fine June morning. There is no sign of rain but neither does it promise to be excessively hot. It is prefect weather for a ride.

The perfect day for war.

Kate, as ever, keeps us waiting. The horses are restive in the yard and the retinue grows impatient. I stride back and forth in the chamber, waiting for her page to alert me when she is finally ready. My irritation vanishes when she appears, a vision in lilac and green.

"I am sorry, my husband, our son was ... he continues to make me nauseous of a morning..."

My son. My displeasure melts away at the thought of my heir curled in her womb. I kiss her fingers.

"No matter, my love. I would wait the whole day for you were it required."

She beams as she takes my arm, and we process to the waiting horses. The palace household has gathered to see us off. Once we are mounted, I raise my arm in farewell, whipping up their cheers that accompany us as we pass beneath the gate.

Behind me ride eleven thousand men at arms. We make a splendid cavalcade, and all along the route the commoners add their lusty good wishes for victory against the excommunicate – Louis of France.

God is on our side. The pope is on my side. This time, we shall not fail.

We make many stops along the way, to rest or change the horses, or to allow Kate the regular comforts that are more pressing when one is with child. My heart is still so softened with joy at the prospect of a son that I do not chafe outwardly against the delay. But the road is long, and progress is slow, and I ache to get there, to make this war real.

At Dover, I will make the formal announcement that Kate is to act as Regent in my absence. I may be God's anointed but even I cannot rule the kingdom and fight for God's honour at the same time. There are those who have murmured that it is foolhardy to leave a woman in charge of the realm, and a Spaniard at that, but … I shout them down. Kate is my queen. She is ripe with England's heir and will do all in her power to advance the good of the country for the sake of her husband and her unborn son. She has my absolute faith, my absolute devotion and my absolute love.

On the night before I take ship for Calais, she sheds tears at our imminent separation. I lift her chin and kiss the tip of her nose.

"Come, come," I say. "You are regent of England; this is no way to behave. You must think of our son."

She pulls away, sniffs and looks down at her shredded kerchief, nodding her head.

"It will be easier once you are gone," she croaks. "Just at this moment, I can hardly bear to let you go. Promise you will return to us, my husband."

I pull her back into my embrace.

"Of course I will. God is on our side, and I will keep myself safe. I want to see our son grow up … and his brothers, too."

She offers up a watery smile and I notice how pale she is. "Come and sit down," I say, leading her to a chair. "Perhaps you should sleep for an hour before the festivities begin. I will summon your women."

Amid the pious company who hurry to her bidding, I spy little Bessie Blount. She is wearing a gown of salmon pink and, beneath the gabled hood, her face is glowing. She glances at me, tears her eyes away before looking again. I wink and am delightfully rewarded by the flush that paints her cheeks.

We have been holding this silent flirtation for many weeks now. I am filled with delight by the fearful attraction I see in her eye. A maid should be fearful, especially when she is desired by a king. We have not yet spoken beyond a few words but, one day, I mean to find a way.

I watch as she and the other ladies fuss and flap about the queen. One woman fetches a stool for her feet, another carries a tray of cups. It is as if I am not present. They ignore their king in their fervour to serve the queen, but ... I cannot fault them for that. Kate is the vessel bearing the future of the realm.

I wait, somewhat disconcerted, by the window until I become aware of a figure at my elbow. "I thought you might crave some refreshment too, Your Majesty."

Bessie curtseys, almost spilling the brimming cup of wine she holds. Her voice is musical, with a hint of northern England in the accent. I reach out and take the cup and, as I do so, our fingers brush. She pulls back sharply, her cheeks turning scarlet, but she does not move away. I reach out with my other hand and dare to stroke her cheek. She gasps, her eyes grow wide, and I notice a pulse beating at the base of her throat. I wonder, were I to kiss it, how her skin would taste.

That night, a great storm lashes the south coast and, although her condition means I cannot show her the depth of my regard, I spend a final night with the queen. We both know it may be many months before we share a bed again. By the time I return, she may even have borne my heir.

The royal bed seems small in the centre of the great chamber. The castle walls are thick, the windows tiny, yet still the tempest seems strong enough to breach the defences. The wind howls about the towers, the tapestries shiver in the draught, and the fire leaps and burns like the flames of hell. Kate, putting aside her usual bravado, cowers beneath the covers, snuggled against my chest. I keep my arm tight around her.

I have no doubts as to our safety, but I am anxious for the royal fleet, anchored a little offshore and vulnerable to the storm. I stare sleepless into the darkness, imagining my beautiful vessels wrecked and torn, smashed helplessly against the rocks; my whole fleet turned to kindling.

God forbid I am vanquished before I have even put to sea.

Every few hours, I call for my man and send him to check that all is in order. I do not know how I expect him to see, for the night is as black as a crow's wing, but each time he returns, he assures me all is well.

When dawn breaks, I ease my arm from beneath Kate's slumbering head and go to assess the damage for myself. Followed by a handful of attendants, I step though storm debris; overturned chairs, torn pennants, scattered straw that yesterday was someone's thatch. When we reach the wharf, I stand, hands on hips, and peer out to sea.

The sea is pewter grey, sulky waves slapping against the sea wall. A dead gull floats, grey and bedraggled among the flotsam of the storm. I peer across the bay to where the fleet is anchored and sigh with relief when all appears to be intact. Just to be sure, I send a messenger to seek report of any damage. There can be no further delay. We must put to sea today.

We have waited long enough.

An hour later, I am assured all is well, and the fleet makes ready to sail. I send up a prayer of thanks and hasten to make ready for the journey. For appearances sake, I don upper body armour; a lightweight garment of German construction. Then they help me into a white tunic and a cloak of cloth of gold, before strapping on my favourite fighting sword.

"But, Henry," Kate protests when she sees me, "if the ship should founder ..."

I put my finger on her lips, stalling her warning. "God is with us, sweetheart. We shall not founder," I say, and she smiles sheepishly and folds away her fear.

I know how hard Kate fights to maintain composure. Every so often, she knuckles away a tear and swallows a fresh outburst of tears, but by the time we are all assembled on the dock, nobody but I would ever guess at her churning anxiety. We said our private goodbye earlier but now, before the crowd, I take her hand and kiss her fingers while the people shout approval.

"Take care of my son, and my realm, and remember, should there be any trouble from the Scots, heed the advice of the Earl of Surrey."

She nods resolutely, her eyes clear and bright, but does not give voice to the grief of parting. As I had known she would be, Kate is strong when necessity dictates. The country is in good hands. I trust this woman above all others.

The small vessel bobs and sways beneath my weight as I clamber on board. They urge me to sit but, instead, I stand tall so that all might watch as I am borne toward the waiting carrack.

My moment is here. The great warship rears above me; two men grab the ladder and hold it firm while I climb to the deck. I throw my head back, looking up at the sky where white gulls circle the mast, their mournful voices at odds with the jubilant crowd. Across the water, the royal party makes a bright splash of colour against the sombre quay, their calls for victory high and distant. The wind rises, the sails slap and crack and the sea swells as the ship slowly pulls into open water.

My stomach rolls.

Disguising the weakness of my belly, I cling to the ship's rail, my heart beating fast. I am exhilarated and fearful all at once. This is it. The moment I have waited for. I am no longer merely a king, but a warrior king; the leader of a vast army on his first step toward winning back our rightful territories in France.

On the last day of June, at nigh on seven of the clock, we make landing. A crowd has gathered to watch us disembark so I order the ships' captains to issue a gun salute. The cannons boom so loud I fear my ears must be bleeding but, despite being temporarily deafened, I grin defiantly at my companions. Our enemies will hear the great noise of our arrival and fear it hails the end of the world.

I wave both arms, calling ahoy to the neighbouring ships, and their captains and crew ahoy back. What a sight we must make – a fleet, four hundred strong, and a forest of masts, of brightly coloured pennons. A flotilla straight from legend with me, King Henry the Eighth, at the helm.

We landed a little west of Calais and, before we do anything else, I order everyone to attend Mass at St Nicholas' church before we process to the Princes' Inn, where supper is served.

As I eat my fill, I am regaled with news of the siege at Thérouanne. At first, I listen with good heart but, as the report sinks in and I learn of the death of Sir Edmund Carew, the loss of one hundred wagons of supplies and the two hundred strong escort who were with it, my mood lowers. So many men have been lost already, and the battle not even begun.

I retire early with a heavy heart, for the first time acknowledging that victory is not assured. God does not always reward the righteous.

My servants unbutton my doublet and, as they slide it from my shoulders, I wonder what England's fate would be should we be crushed. Defeat is unthinkable.

They draw off my hose, sit me on a chair and wash and dry my feet. What would my grandfather do, I ask myself? What would King Arthur do?

They ease my night rail over my head and place my feet in warm velvet slippers before bowing from my presence. I turn to the *prie dieu* and kneel before God to seek his guidance.

Sleep evades me. I lie awake while the French cavalry marches through my imagination. I see myself, divested of my crown, thrown into a French gaol, a French king on my throne, my queen besmirched, my unborn son....

I sit up sweating, and grope for the cup on my nightstand.

It was just a dream. *Dreams are not premonitions,* I tell myself, before thumping my pillow and lying down.

It takes a while for my mind to settle and I am just drifting off to sleep when a great clanging of bells has me leaping up again.

"What is happening?" I cry at my attendant, who stands blinking in surprise at finding himself so suddenly awake. "Go, man, and discover the cause."

He scurries out, still in his night clothes, and returns a while later, white-faced, his eyes bulging, his hair like a cock's comb.

"The French have infiltrated our lines."

I scramble from bed. "Quick! Help me dress."

A half hour later, hastily garbed in yesterday's clothes, I take to the town walls, a vantage point from which to watch events unfold.

Anxiously, I peer into the blackness of night. It is difficult to see. Dark clouds ride low across the moon but I can make out the faint light of bobbing torches, hastily extinguished fires and the cries of the enemy as our eagle-eyed archers pick them off one by one.

"They are from the port of Whitesands, a few miles away. We have them now, Your Majesty."

I nod, turning away from the dwindling action.

"I did not doubt it for a moment," I say. "We will have our revenge, be sure of that."

While two thirds of the army ride way, eager to make the most of the campaigning season, I linger in Calais to consult with the Imperial Ambassadors. The weather has settled and we are recovered from the recent storms, our bellies stable now after the sea crossing. I spend an afternoon practising archery with my guard and, of course, I am the victor.

The Spanish praise my victory, declaring there is not a man on English soil who can compare to me. I look at them sideways, searching for irony and take note that they do not mention men from other lands – their own king, for example.

I sometimes wonder at how easily I defeat all who dare stand against me in sport. It is true, I am bigger and stronger than most men I meet, but surely, men who have given their lives to archery should prove more of a challenge. Even Brandon has not bested me of late. I wonder how the French dauphin would fare against me in a contest. One day, I will send a challenge – a sword fight perhaps, or a wrestling match, or a turn at the butts.

As the end of July approaches, I depart from Calais, surrounded by a huge guard of three and a half thousand men. Such a precaution is unnecessary, of course, I can look after myself, but my advisors refuse to endorse a lighter force. The deeper we penetrate into enemy territory the more unstable the weather becomes, and cold slanting rain blows in from the west. Damnable rain that seeks out every breach in our clothing, drenches our hair, trickles down our necks and dampens our morale.

At four in the morning, unable to sleep, I hunch over a candle beneath flapping wet canvas, and write a letter to my queen.

To my most beloved queen,

I trust this finds you well and our child is thriving. This day, I rode into enemy territory in grievous weather. It goes hard with a man's spirits in such conditions but after we made camp I did not rest or take respite from the day until I had seen to the comfort of my troops.

I remember my mother's tales of Azincourt and how Henry V joined the men of his watch and warmed them with his words. I did the same. At first, they did not know me but although I wore a dark cloak and had left off all my rings, there was something about me that gave the game away. When they realised their king was in their midst, they left off their bawdy jokes and cynical criticism of their betters and fell to their knees in homage.

Sometimes, I wonder how it feels to be an ordinary man, but I suppose I shall never discover it.

We march on, deeper into enemy country. A band of renegade German mercenaries despoils a town, burning houses and doing hate upon the churches. I ride forth with my guard.

A woman is screaming; a lost child weeps near the town cross while all around is chaos. Horses, men, barking dogs, clashing swords, blood swirling in the gutters. I sit astride my horse and watch as my men ride forth in salvation. A ragged man, a mercenary by his looks, emerges from the church, his arms full of plate. He swivels his head, seeking escape, seeking sanctuary, although he has despoiled the only place that could ever offer him safety.

I unsheathe my sword and kick my horse forward.

"Your Majesty!"

I ignore the cry from my guard and ride full tilt, my weapon aimed at the villain's throat. He sees me coming, drops his contraband and opens his arms. I haul on the reins and halt before him. His wide eyes stare into mine. His chin judders. He cries out, but I do not understand the words he speaks. They could be foreign, or he could be speaking the language of the devil.

I could kill him. I could take his life with my own hand, but I see the sweat on his brow, the filth in his hair, the depravation of his soul – and I do not strike. I am a merciful king. It will be for someone else to punish his crimes.

I narrow my eyes and prepare to address him but the men at arms run forward, take hold of him and drag him away.

"Your Majesty, that was rash."

Sheathing my sword, I laugh.

"Rash, my Lord? You've seen nothing yet."

The rain falls unceasing. By the time we reach Thérouanne, the fields around the town are hock-deep in stinking mud. I give the order for a siege and settle down to wait while the beggars are starved from their town.

I have read about sieges since boyhood. Everyone knows that victory by siege lacks the glory of victory in battle. Both the besieged and the besieger can waste away from torment. The long tedious days of inactivity, of plain fare and starvation rations, play havoc with the frail minds of men.

On the third day, I am involved in a game of chess, the wet canvas flapping disconsolately above our heads. It has been a long, dismal afternoon and, since there is an absence of healthy-looking women, I am looking forward to supper to break the monotony. My hand is hovering over my knight when a herald arrives.

I lean back in my chair.

"Show him in."

The tent flap opens to admit a short fellow who snatches off his cap, revealing a balding pate, wispy red hair and a thin miserable beard.

"Sir William Cumming of Inverallochy," my guard informs me. The fellow clutches his hat to his chest and bows low.

"Sir William …"

I am at a loss; I do not know this man. My advisor whispers in my ear, but the visitor cuts in.

"Your Majesty …"

I can tell right away he is a Scot. I sit straighter in my seat and look down my nose.

"I have a message from my King." He holds out a parchment, his hand trembling slightly. I nod to my advisor to take it. He scans it and passes it to me.

It is not so much a message as an ultimatum. The rudest phrases leap out like a slap in the face

Desist from further invasion and utter destruction of our brother and cousin to whom we are bounden and obliged for mutual defence, the one of the other, like as you and your confederates be obliged for mutual invasions and actual war; certifying you we will take part in defence of our brother …

And we will do what thing we trust may cause you to desist from pursuit of him …

"Confounded old fool!" I mutter, forgetting the Scottish herald who stands frowning before me. No doubt he will carry my condemnation of his king back with him but there is no point stopping now. The damage is likely done. I stand up.

"I am the very holder of Scotland – he holds it of me by homage!"

As I warm to the subject, my voice grows louder. I am aware of the horrified faces of my councillors, but I do not stop.

I cannot stop.

"You can tell your king from me, there shall *never* be a Scot to cause me to turn my face. Where he says the French king will be his ally, it would become him better to be married to the King of England's sister, to count the King of England his ally.

"Tell him, if he is so foolhardy as to invade my realm or enter one foot of my ground, I shall make him as sorry of his part as any man ever was that began such business."

I catch my breath, looking around at the surprised faces. Perhaps I should have thought before I spoke, but it is too late now. The words are out and words, once spoken, can never be retracted.

I sit back down, rest an elbow on the table and shrug my shoulders.

"I cannot easily believe that my brother of Scotland would break his solemn oath to Ferdinand not to invade but, if that is his intention, have no doubt he will come to repent it. I shall write to your king, you can carry the letter back to him, but now, be gone and leave me in peace."

He backs out, my guard following to ensure he does not tarry. I lean back, close my eyes and think of Kate. I imagine her in her tranquil garden or sewing with her ladies in the parlour. I see her brushing out her hair, her smiling lips whispering my name and, with a sudden, painful dart of homesickness, wish I were there, in her company. If they do invade, may the Lord God keep her safe.

I am tired of living under canvas. The royal tent is luxurious in comparison to that of other men but even so ... I yearn for a warm bath, a pair of soft velvet slippers instead of boots. I long for roast capon and quail, the soft music of the entertainers, the order and deference to which I am accustomed in my own realm. When I am King of France, when I am ensconced in Paris, I tell myself, things will be different.

The Emperor Maximilian has arranged to meet with me and, in mid-August, when the sun is hot again, we prepare to receive him. This morning, the Emperor's messenger delivered the gift of a fine horned helmet, a thing of exquisite workmanship but intended for display only, not for battle. I send effusive thanks and a gift of equal value before ordering the helmet to be placed on a table where I can admire it throughout the day.

I have further gifts for him and anticipate our meeting with a mixture of nerves and excitement, both of which I conceal from my companions beneath a veneer of indifference.

My tent has been cleaned and adorned with new hangings of cloth of gold. My clothes are brushed, my armour polished and my hair and beard trimmed in readiness. My page is just putting on the last of my plate when news comes of the Emperor's imminent arrival. As soon as my cloak is tied, I quit the tent and step into the bright sunlight.

A clarion of trumpets and a clash of steel salute his arrival. I squint across the camp to see a cavalcade picking its way through the mud. In the midst of his heavy guard, the emperor is easily definable. His bearing is nobler than the rest. He sits easily in the saddle, the feather in his helmet dancing like a will o' the wisp in the breeze.

He remains mounted, so I am obliged to look up while I greet him.

"King Henry ..." he says, his accent thick, his English stilted and his bland expression belying his next words. "I have anticipated this meeting for some time."

I open my mouth to begin my rehearsed speech of welcome but, just at that moment, a shout goes up. A gun fires deafeningly and I turn my head sharply as one of my advisors comes sliding forward through the mud.

"It is probably unrest with the Germans again, Your Majesty. No cause for alarm."

I nod. When so many men are entrenched in one place for so long there are bound to be disturbances, and the German mercenaries have proved troublesome. I turn again to the emperor. "Your ..."

The boom of a gun severs my words. This time followed by the squeal of horse and the unmistakable sounds of skirmish. As one, we turn toward the fray.

"What is happening? Are we under attack?"

My hand is on my sword. I welcome any action that will break the monotony of siege warfare. Ignoring the emperor, I begin to run, my feet slipping, my guard and advisors jogging behind as best they can, calling out words of caution, beseeching me to think, not to put myself in danger.

The site of the disturbance is on the far side of the camp. The closer I get, the louder the noise grows. When I am in sight of it, I pause to catch my breath as I assess the scene.

Although it is difficult to distinguish the two parties, it is not an attack by the French; it is indeed further trouble between the German mercenaries and our own troops.

I snarl a curse.

"The Germans have commandeered one of the heavy siege guns, Your Majesty, and they've blasted a breach in our camp."

A young mud-splattered courier who seems to have lost his hat yells the information from his vantage point at the top of the ditch.

"Our archers are in position now and are shooting in retaliation.... Oh, now the Germans are regrouping into a pike wall. It looks like a stand-off, Your Majesty!"

I lower my sword.

I cannot join in so trivial a fray. As I am sheathing my weapon, I become aware that Maximilian has ridden up to join me.

He wipes his brow and smiles.

"Your Englishmen handled that well," he says. "The mercenaries will soon be overcome. There is always trouble whcn troops become bored."

"I half hoped it was the French so I could wet my sword."

He laughs, one hand on his thigh.

"Your time will come," he says archly. "My spies inform me the French are desperate to replenish the food stocks of the city and plan to breach our defences this very night. I suggest we lay in wait for them together. We may not only vanquish their plans but add to our supply of bacon also."

He addresses me as if we are well acquainted, the rude interruption to the ceremony of our meeting having broken any awkwardness.

"Your spies are trustworthy?"

"I have always found them so."

With a dart of excitement at the impending action, I hold out my hand and Maximilian takes it.

"Midnight then. We will lie in wait together."

While we feast and exchange strategies, I come to like this man, enjoying the company of a wise and seasoned warrior.

"I was great friends with your son, Philip," I say as I gnaw the last scraps of flesh from a capon. "When he was at my father's court."

"You must have been just a boy then."

"Yes, but I was well grown, and Philip gave me the courtesy due to a man. I was greatly grieved at his death.... He was too young."

Maximilian lays down his knife and picks up a cup, drinking deeply.

"Yes," he says at last. "Philip was a good boy, a great man, and would have become greater still, given the chance."

I nod and raise my cup.

"To Philip!"

I do not mention the emperor's wife, Bianca Maria Sforza, who has also recently passed, as I understand the union was not a blissful one. Perhaps he had known too much happiness with his first, Philip's mother, for anyone to replace her. I cannot imagine losing Kate, or ever wedding another. No one else could offer the joy we have shared.

I signal for our cups to be refilled, but the emperor covers his with his hand.

"Not for me," he says. "I will need a clear head if I am to stay awake throughout the night," and, realising the sense of this, I also refuse further wine.

My advisors shake their heads and put forward white-faced arguments against my taking part in the battle. They come at me from all sides, speaking at once.

"You must think of England," they say. "You have no heir. Were anything to happen to you, the realm would be left in jeopardy."

"You must put the good of the country before your desire for glory."

"It is your duty to protect the realm and the people."

"Don't presume to tell your king his duty!" I bellow, leaping up and thumping the table. They cower away, shamefaced and fearful. "Do you think I travelled all this way to sit in my tent? Are you my councillors or my nursemaids?"

They shuffle and bluster, afraid to say more, and I storm from the marquee, my page running behind with my surcoat over his arm.

I do not know what I had expected of war, but it certainly was not tedium. Another long wait follows and, with no end in sight, it is not long before my enthusiasm dwindles to impatience. It is dark and cold, and I crave the comfort of my tent, perhaps a willing wench to warm it, but … it is adventure of sorts.

To show me honour, Maximilian wears a surcoat with the cross of St George over his armour. He grins at me, showing none of the disappointment I feel.

"They will come, we must just be patient," he says, peering into the darkness.

But when the sun finally shows its head, we are still waiting, and the French are nowhere to be seen. I yawn loudly, impatiently stamp my cold feet and wonder if the emperor's spies were mistaken. Maximilian comes close, smiling and rubbing his arms to warm them.

"Now the cover of darkness is lost, I think we should consider extra security. Some light cannon perhaps, placed along that ridge, and archers along the hedge line to give cover to the guns."

It makes sense. I should have thought of it myself. I nod agreement and several of my men creep off to give the orders. A further wait follows.

Maximilian fills the time by telling stories of the days he was held under siege with his parents in Vienna.

"I was a small boy and I'd never known what it meant to be hungry before," he says, wistfully. "I went about the castle begging crusts from the guard, although my father beat me for doing so. I understand what they are going through over there." He nods toward the town walls. "Yet, I inflict it on them just the same. God forgive me."

He flexes his knee, grimacing in pain, and I remember he is well past youth, yet he has waited all through this cold night without complaint. My grandmother suffered from stiff painful joints; she used to rub in a concoction of herbs that stank out her chamber. I remember Mary holding her nose behind Grandmother's back until her face turned puce. She got away with her rudeness, but my laughter brought down Lady Margaret's displeasure on me.

The memory makes me smile.

"My grandmother, Lady Beaufort, suffered greatly with her knees," I say. Maximilian raises his eyebrows and urges me to continue. "She rubbed them with a salve made up of ginger and – and … another herb, I cannot recall. She also drank a disgusting brew made up of rue and vinegar. She always claimed the treatment offered some respite …"

"Perhaps, when this is over, you could send me the recipe. I'd be most grateful."

It is absurd; two great rulers of Christendom huddled in furs against the dawn chill, discussing remedies for whirl bone. I laugh, a little too loudly, and someone down the line, not realising who I am, shushes me.

I could have his head but, instead, I snigger, swallow my humour and peer again toward the horizon.

When daylight finally comes, we are all stiff with cold. I break my fast, pray at a makeshift altar and piss into a hedge like a peasant.

All day, the emperor and I stroll about the camp to keep our limbs supple, our blood flowing, our minds from slumbering. It is not until the sun is past its height and the afternoon is dwindling that word comes that the French have been spotted not far away.

We mount up, the sense of impending glory increasing. My sword is on my hip, my lance at the ready, and it is no tournament this time. This time, it is real. I am riding into battle.

The steady rhythm of pounding hooves is a fillip to my soul. As we near the attack site, I see the French cavalry just ahead. I dig in my spurs, ready to ride, ready to fight. I raise my right arm, filling my lungs to shout the battle cry …

Heavy hands grab my bridle, pulling my mount up short. I dig in my spurs and we tread ground, making no progress.

"What the devil …?"

I turn in fury.

"I beg pardon, Your Majesty. I have orders. I cannot let you go."

"Orders? No order overrides mine!"

My comrades ride swiftly past, looking neither left nor right. Not one of them comes to my aid. Not one of them defends my right to bear arms. Edward IV rode into battle when he was little more than a boy, nobody had any concern for the danger to him. I am governed by pussycats.

Do they not know who is king here?

"This is treason," I hiss, fumbling for my sword, but the other horse is too close; I lack the space to draw it, and I have dropped my lance.

"I am sorry, Your Majesty." His face is like stone, his jaw set with determination.

"God damn you! I am your king!"

The majority of the army is already far ahead; I will never catch them. I should be at their head. I wanted to lead my men into the fray. I feel like a small boy denied his supper, a child sent to his room while a great feast is laid out below.

Thrusting my head forward, I snarl at my guards.

"I will have your eyes for this."

So, I miss it all. I am kept safe behind the lines. I do not witness the French taken by surprise, their army thrown into disarray, their flight from the field so ignoble it has already been dubbed *The Battle of the Spurs.*

Afterwards, I survey our two hundred and fifty prisoners, led by Louis d'Orleans, Duc de Longueville; Renë de Clermont, vice Admiral of France; and Louis, Marquis of Rothelin. I would love to be able to claim their capture, but that glory is for others.

This has not been the second Azincourt I dreamed of. Once more, I have failed my own expectations but, just as I conceal all my disappointments, all I can do is put a good face on it. With great courtesy, I put aside my rage and invite the French leaders to dine.

At least we have the victory, but I had expected it to be more gratifying. Perhaps I expected too much. I thought war would transform me, that God would somehow, through victory, show his approval of me but now it is all over ... everything is just the same.

The battle, which I admit was little more than a skirmish, is hailed as a great triumph and I a great warrior, but everyone must know I have just been playing at war. Of course, I will never admit that, not even to Brandon, who has ridden in with his armies from beyond the palc.

In the weeks that follow, the town is razed to the ground, all but the cathedral, but, despite the praise from Rome and the effusive letters from my queen, I remain heavy-hearted. Nothing is as it should be, and I am sick of this place.

Although I conceal my disappointment from even my closest companions, I think longingly of England, of Richmond Palace and Windsor, the freedom and exhilaration of the wide-open chase.

One of my prisoners is an arrogant Frenchman by the name of Longueville. Captured men such as he bring in a high price and must be kept intact. To prevent him from escaping, I send him home to England where Kate can use him in her household as she fancies. Once we receive his ransom, he will be released.

"Perhaps," I say idly, "we should ride on to take Paris and they can crown me King of France while I am there." But it is idle talk, meant to alarm our foe, but one day … one day.

By return messenger from England, I learn that the Scots have crossed the River Tweed and invaded my realm, laying waste to my lands south of the river while my back is turned. If I were in England, I would ride north and teach James a lesson, but I have obligations here. I must focus on Boulogne or Montreuil and bolster the defence of Calais, but Maximilian now urges me to assist him in a siege at Tournai.

A week ago, I was cursing the tedium of war and now I am overwhelmed with the decision as to which action I should take. Should I look to silencing the Scots in my own realm or aid my newfound friend in securing his?

In the end, I decide to stay. I write, issuing orders to Kate, who means to ride north herself; not to fight, of course, but to be a presence on the field and act as regent in my place.

"Keep yourself safe. Think of the child!" I warn her, and write separately to Wolsey and Surrey ordering them to watch her. Then, instead of strengthening our defences at Calais, I ride with the emperor to Lille.

Lille

I am surprised by the wild welcome we receive. The whole city has turned out to greet us and the route from gate to palace is ablaze with torches. Although I am saddle-sore and weary, the enthusiasm of the crowd rouses me and I almost believe I am the heroic king they think I am. I sit tall in the saddle, raise my hands and whip their cheers to a greater intensity.

The crush is so tight there is scarce room for our cavalcade to pass. I turn to Maximilian, who also smiles and waves but with slightly less enthusiasm, and my heart fills at the realisation that the decision to come here was sound.

For once, I have done the right thing.

We dismount at the palace steps, and Margaret of Savoy comes out to greet us. She curtseys in deep unnecessary reverence and, in return, I take off my hat and bow to the ground. But Maximilian sets etiquette aside and greets his daughter cordially, kissing each plump cheek in turn. I consider doing likewise but, although very fair, Margaret is some ten years my senior and I am suddenly unsure how I should approach her. I am unused to dealing with attractive women of her age. Were she younger or uglier, I would be more confident, but … this woman is the sort I like to bed.

No! I scold inwardly. *She is not a light woman; she is of noble blood.*

If I offend her, I also offend her father.

I do not have the opportunity to ponder this for long. With one last wave at the crowd, she urges us inside, and we pass into the palace. The large hall is crowded, voices fill the vaulted chamber; a sweeping staircase disappears into the upper reaches of the house.

The building and the way it is decorated is remarkable but, not wanting to seem overwhelmed, I do not gawp at the grandeur but act as if I see such things every day.

We have finery in England but many of my palaces are in need of updating; they are dark, and, in some corners, they are also dank. This palace gleams; it is fragrant and well lit. Surreptitiously taking note of the lavish gilding and the large windows that flood the palace with light, I resolve to make similar improvements at home.

"A fine palace!" Brandon murmurs, who makes no such pretence at nonchalance. He turns in circles, pointing out details, exclaiming at the fat golden cherubs looking down from the ceiling.

"Yes, Kate and I have been considering making similar renovations. One day, I intend to build a new palace that will be unrivalled the world over."

His smile is broad. "You are the king to do it, Sire."

Margaret is speaking, congratulating us on our recent victory, laughing at the ignominy of the French army's panic in the face of an enemy.

I warm to her even more.

"But you will want to refresh yourselves," she says. "Your rooms are made ready and I've ordered a fine banquet this evening in Your Majesty's honour."

I kiss her hand and straighten slowly, my gaze lingering on her throat, which is long and elegant, made for kissing. She smiles back at me, a smile that stretches her generous mouth and illuminates her humorous eyes. She is well aware of my admiration, and her returning smile is confident. She is no doubt used to such adoration. There are things this woman could teach me.

Then she turns to Brandon, lately raised to the position of Duke of Suffolk, and I watch jealously as she treats him to the exact same favour she showed me. Mayhap she looks on all men that way. Perhaps that is her weapon; she enslaves us all and uses her charms to bend us to her bidding. I bury my resentment and, by the time we are rested and reassembled in the hall, I have all but forgotten my resolution not to be enslaved.

A fine banquet ensues. A minstrel plays while we dine, and I relish the comforts I have missed during the campaign.

I am seated at Margaret's left side, Maximilian on her right, and I am relieved to see Brandon's seat is farther along the table. As Margaret eats, I appreciate her hearty appetite, watch as she sucks meat from her greasy hands. When her ewerer steps forward, instead of rinsing her fingers she reaches for another capon, her conversation unstilted by hunger.

"Have more wine, Henry … I can call you Henry, can't I? I prefer to dispense with titles; it helps one become properly acquainted."

I nod like a fool, mesmerised by her easy manner. She takes up her cup, swills wine around her mouth and seeks with her tongue to dislodge a piece of meat from between her teeth.

"There will be dancing later. I warrant you are a master of the dance."

She looks me up and down, and I am glad of the cloth of gold and black velvet clothes that enhance my ruddy hair, the cut of my doublet augmenting my fine torso. I nod agreement, reach for a wafer at the same time as she, and somehow, our fingers become entwined. She does not pull away, our eyes lock and her smile spreads.

"I look forward to it," she says, before turning away to speak to her father.

That night, the wine in Lille flows freely. I postpone my appointment with the Milanese ambassador and accept Brandon's silent challenge for Margaret's attention. He may be older and just as strong and handsome, but he lacks my power. He cannot outdo the King of England.

We dance so long and hard that the heat becomes unbearable, and I throw off my doublet and dance in my shirtsleeves – the shirt so lovingly stitched by my queen.

The memory of my sweet Kate has completely faded, her face obliterated by the greater beauty of Margaret. As we dance, I leap higher and higher, like a stag – the king of the forest – and when the musicians take their ease, I lounge decadently at Margaret's feet while I quench my thirst.

Brandon, cup in hand, approaches, swaying a little as he crosses the floor.

"My lady." Unsteadily, he bows low. "I am your mosht humble servant. Pleash take this pledge ..."

With undisguised amusement, the court watches as he drunkenly takes hold of her hand but, instead of pushing a ring onto her finger, he removes one of hers and places it on his own. Spinning on the spot, he roars with laughter and opens his arms to the watching crowd, some of whom shout appreciation, while others frown. Piqued at no longer being the centre of attention, I join the latter party.

Margaret smiles, but not as widely as before. I suspect she is not as relaxed as she pretends. Nothing that happens in a royal court is secret. It is all very well to make merry and flirt, but … to take her ring? He has overstepped the mark and news of this will spread across Europe. The gossips will be out in force. *Is it a clumsy attempt at a proposal of marriage?*

Brandon has married in haste before – and repented at leisure but, at present, he is free. I greatly hope this is not a request for her hand but merely a drunken overture to illicit relations. Either way, his action is inexcusable. Margaret's reputation must not be sullied; not by an Englishman and especially not by a womaniser like Brandon. Fortunately, her father retired some hours earlier. Perhaps we all should have. Should Maximilian hear of this.…

The next morning, complaining of a sore head, Brandon joins me for talks with Maximilian, who seems not to have heard of the events of the previous night. He is keen to move on with our plans to lay siege to Tournai and spreads a large map on the table.

Trying to ignore my aching head and raging thirst, I frown at it and force my mind to the matter in hand.

"We will place the siege guns here …" Maximilian says, and I nod blurry agreement. Brandon merely stares in befuddlement at the plan. He points to a mark on the map and opens his mouth to speak, when the door opens and a messenger enters. From his livery, I see he has been sent by my queen. Anxiously, I scan his face, breathing a sigh of relief when I see it is bright with news.

I take the missive and break the seal. Kate's handwriting has been scrawled in haste …

My Lord Howard has sent me a letter by which you shall see at length the great victory that our Lord has sent your subjects in your absence.

This battle is to Your Grace and all your realm the greatest honour that could be and more than if you should win all the crown of France.

Thanks be to God for it and I am sure Your Grace will not forget to do this, which shall be cause to send you many such great victories, as I trust He shall do.

I send Your Grace a bill found in a Frenchman's purse of such things as the French king sent to the King of Scots to make war against you.

Your Grace shall see how I can keep my promise to protect England, sending you for your banners a king's coat. I thought to send himself to you but our Englishman's hearts would not suffer it ...

"Ha!"

My companions look up from their studies. "Our forces in England have vanquished the invading Scots and killed their king. James is dead and my queen sends forth his bloodied coat that we might be sure of it!"

The messenger holds high the ripped, gory clothes that once graced the back of James V. I grimace and wave it away. I should have been there. I should have led the army against Scotland, for this triumph belongs to Kate and Surrey. While I wallowed in French mud, my army at home slaughtered some ten thousand Scots. I glance down at the message, which estimates: twelve earls, fourteen lords, an archbishop, a bishop and two abbots, as well as the main prize – King James himself. While England has lost just one and a half thousand souls, Scotland is on its knees. If only I had been part of it.

"God is indeed on our side," I say aloud. "With our recent victory in France and another repelling the Scots …" I crush the letter in my palm and throw up my fist in triumph.

"Well, praise be to God!"

<u>Late summer - autumn 1514</u>

When, without warning, Maximilian pulls out of Holy League and the pope seeks peace with France, my hopes of taking Louis' crown are destroyed. Disillusioned and depressed, we travel home.

Back in England, I am hailed as a great victor over both the French and the Scots, but I do not feel like a hero. Kate, on the other hand, sups up the praise as if it is fine wine. I watch her: swollen with my child, the strong Spanish bones of her face proud beneath her flushed cheeks. My ripe, regal pomegranate queen is the real hero and she knows it.

After my return home, the fighting in France continues sporadically. When they trespass across the Channel and the town of Brighton is burned almost to the ground, I send a force to ravage the coast near Cherbourg.

Wolsey and Fox argue against it, claiming peace is vital. I would rather smite the entire French nation but, still smarting from my failure to win the throne for myself, I reluctantly turn my thoughts to seeking amity. After all, I tell myself, in vanquishing the Scots we have at least secured our northern borders and strengthened our position. Peace settlements can always be broken – I will return to France and take Louis' crown another day.

"An alliance, Your Majesty," Wolsey murmurs. "I was thinking … your sister, the Princess Mary, is ripe for matrimony and now that the French king has been widowed …"

I let his words sink in. Mary is almost eighteen, the flower of our court. I would prefer to keep her with us but … when Margaret was wed to the King of Scots, the king we recently killed at Flodden, Mary was adamant that she would never marry a man in his dotage. At the time of their marriage, James was no more than thirty, yet he seemed old to us, who were still in the nursery. Louis is three times Mary's age. Such a marriage will not sit easily with my sister.

I rub my chin.

"Such an arrangement will not please her. She is likely to protest, and she never complains quietly."

"No, Your Majesty. I thought perhaps, rather than call her before the council to break the news, you could have a quiet word."

I give a sharp cough of scorn.

"Indeed, Thomas, and I thought I employed you to do my dirty work, not the other way around."

He closes his eyes in acquiescence.

"Of course, if Your Majesty prefers."

I stand up to look from the window across the parkland, the scudding colours of autumn calling me to hunt before the winter closes in too deep.

"We will do it together, Thomas. There is strength in numbers."

He laughs softly and gathers his papers together, tucking them beneath his arm.

"Concentrate your mind on the dowry, Your Majesty. Two hundred thousand crowns is the figure I have in mind, plus a further fifty thousand a year."

That will not help restore our coffers, I think. A lot to spend on top of my sister's displeasure. I will be the double loser. She will be Queen of France, sleeping with an old man, but I will still be the one to pay the higher price.

Mary screams and rages and I am thankful Wolsey chose to relate the news in my small privy chamber. With tears of anger, she clenches her fists and stamps her foot, but it serves no purpose. It cannot be helped. She is a princess of England and has her duty, just as I have mine.

For a while, I let her rant. I watch her as, like a spoiled child, she snatches off her hood and kicks it across the chamber. Wolsey raises his eyebrows and steps back, his mouth fallen open, and I smile at his alarm. I have witnessed Mary's temper since infancy. She was born angry. If I think hard, I can still recall her in swaddling bands, red-faced and screaming for the wet nurse. There is nothing new or remarkable in Mary's temper.

At length, her anger spent, she collapses exhausted into a chair and glowers at me. Anyone would think I was committing her to a life in the stews instead of the highest honour a woman can have.

"You will be a queen," I observe, "lavished with honour and dignity. Across Christendom, your name will be spoken in hushed tones …for ever more."

"I care nothing for that. You know me, Henry. Titles mean nothing. I want to be happy, not lauded. The betrothal to Charles of Spain was one thing, I knew it would never happen, but this…. And didn't you promise me when you first became king that I could stay in England and take a husband of my own choosing?"

I shake my head, shrugging my shoulders. I have no memory of any such promise.

"As a princess of England, you must do your …"

"Don't!" She holds up a hand, silencing me. I could have her thrown in the Tower for such a thing, but she is my sister … my favourite sister, she always has been.

"If it were in my power …"

She turns and leans over me so threateningly that I almost shrink away. The angry bones of her face harden, obliterating her beauty. My soft sister is suddenly hard and bitter. She looks like Grandmother. I grasp her wrist.

"I have no choice, Mary. It may not be so bad. Louis is old, and they say his health is … precarious. Perhaps, in time, you will be widowed and then you can marry where you will."

She straightens up, her scowl scored deep, but she at least considers the matter. Our eyes are fixed, one to the other; hers are hurt, but her rage is subsiding, overridden by dismay. I wait, my heart sick, for her response.

She folds her arms, striding from one side of the room to the other, and back again. Finally, she halts before me.

"I will do this on one condition only."

"Name it," I say, relief rushing upon me. "You can have anything in my power to give."

"Louis is growing old. As you say, he may not have long to live. I demand, in writing, that on his death, I am no longer yours to barter. Once widowed, my future is to be my own."

She stands back, hands on hips, regarding me. It is a high price. Mary is a beauty, her blood a jewel to be traded. Her freedom will cost me much but … I have to agree. When I glance at Wolsey, he remains noncommittal, staring disinterestedly into a dark corner.

I frown, my mouth drooping.

"Very well."

"In writing."

I incline my head. "Wolsey will attend to it."

"But you are to sign and seal it. I also expect to choose my own accompanying household."

I incline my head again. She can have all she wants as long as the deed is done. If Louis can manage to get a child on her, a nephew on the throne of France will offer some compensation for failing to win it for myself. If he dies, I get my sister back. I win either way.

When she returns to her apartments, she is acquiescent but smarting at what she must do. There is no parting smile, no fond kiss. Instead, she makes an ironic curtsey that is eloquent with disdain. She is stating quite clearly: *if you treat me as your subject then you are no longer my brother, merely my king.*

There is nothing I can do. It is what it is. I might be king, but I cannot change the facts of what it means to be royal.

As I head for the great hall where I am to dine in company, I tell myself that Mary will come round. She cannot stay at odds with me forever. This time next week, she will have forgotten. She will be her old self again. She loves me.

I make a note to send for the finest fabrics, the richest jewels to be had at short notice. She will be a queen, after all. Riches will mollify her. She has always known this would happen one day. I can see her now, a plump and slightly sweaty infant, stamping her foot and shouting at Margaret. "I won't marry a man I have no liking for! You wait and see!"

She has not altered; she is still the brave opinionated girl she always was. It is I who have changed. England has changed me. The crown has turned me from her doting brother into her king ... a king unpleasantly like her father, forcing those I love to act against their inclination.

All I can hope is that her life in France is better than she hopes. With luck, she will be fruitful and content with the joy of motherhood but, if that is to happen, she will have to be quick.

As I near the hall, I come upon Kate and her women processing to supper. She stops when she sees me, the smile she paints on for the sake of the court melting to a frown.

"Henry," she says. "Where have you been? I was expecting you all afternoon. I wanted to speak to you ..."

Resentment rises, lodging in my chest. I am the king, yet she speaks to me as if I am an errant infant? I bite back a reprimand. I must be patient. She is with child and prone to tetchiness. The sooner my son is born, the sooner she will return to normal.

Lately, she has been proud and reproachful in turn. I can do no right. Brandon assures me it is always so with pregnant women.

"Something gets into their blood," he says, "and infects their tongues, making it impossible for loving words to be spoken."

It is mid-September now, only a matter of weeks until her lying-in. For the last month of pregnancy, the mother is always closeted away from court with only women for company. I find I am looking forward to it.

I pray to God that when she emerges not only will I have my son, but that Kate will have returned to her old self. She will nurture me again and think me marvellous.

A blast of trumpets and those gathered in the hall fall silent as we enter. The pipers in the gallery lower their instruments, a further tier of torches is lit, and a company of fools enters, their moon faces shining, their tricolour clothes gay, their jokes ... jaded. I smother a sigh and try to look entertained.

One of them pretends to trip, turns and punches his fellow on the nose. A fray breaks out and the hall erupts with laughter. Merry faces line the benches and many turn toward me to ensure their king is as enraptured as they are. I laugh with the rest, but I find myself weary. I want to get up and leave, retreat from the company to the solitude of my private chambers.

Several dishes are laid before us. I pick up my knife. Kate reaches for a sucket and places it between her lips.

"These players came to court seeking employment while you were in France," she says. "I thought they might amuse you."

Usually, they would, but tonight their antics only irritate. I pick up my cup.

"I am not in the mood," I say quietly, for her ears only. "I am surrounded by fools and supplicants from the moment I open my eyes in the morning to the moment I close them at night. I long for frank conversation, but all I hear are placation and appeasement. Only Brandon speaks plainly ... and Mary, of course."

"Don't be ridiculous," she says, with an arrogant toss of her head. "I speak plainly, do I not?"

Sometimes she speaks too plainly and not just with words. Often her eyes accuse me of crimes I have not even yet committed. She questions me about events in France: with whom did I spent time? Were there women present? It is as if her spies have carried tales about my sport with Margaret of Savoy. The face of the courtesan – what was her name? – floats before me. Kate knows what my truthful answer should be, but when I lie to save her feelings, she curls her lip and silently condemns me anyway. I can never win.

I can bear no more of this. I stand abruptly, the music dwindles, and perplexed faces turn toward me. Everyone rises.

"No, no – sit down. I feel a little unwell. I will retire to my bed. You carry on."

I should have known better than to plead illness. As I make my way across the hall, a crowd of attendants follows, all of them speaking at once. "I will send for your physician, Sire." "A lavender-filled cushion works wonders." "Perhaps a posset can be ..."

I halt and hold up a hand without turning and they are hard put not to collide with my back.

"I do not need all of you. Just three will suffice." A tide of speculation flows at my heels. The doors are thrown open and the guard snaps to attention. I tread the wide corridor and, on turning a corner, come suddenly face to face with a woman. I blink.

She sinks to her knees in a pool of blue velvet and, when I look down at her lowered head to glimpse the cleft of her bosom, recognition stirs

"Bessie, isn't it?"

I reach out and assist her to rise. She flutters beneath my touch like a small bird. "Should you not be in attendance on the queen?"

My servants melt discreetly away. She blushes and bobs another curtsey. I keep hold of her hand, the frail bones swamped in my palm.

"The queen allows us some free time and my rest day is Tuesday – that is … today, Your Majesty."

Her eyes rise to mine and I absorb her face; it is sweet and kind, without recrimination or scorn. I am soothed. She reminds me a little of my mother … not in looks but in temperament.

"Come," I say. "Come with me."

In the privacy of my apartments, I ply her with wine and fancies. She looks about with wide eyes, questioning me about the collection of curiosities and keepsakes I display on my table.

"That was my mother's," I tell her when she runs a finger across a miniature prayer book. "I believe it was given to her by my grandfather, King Edward. They say I am made in his image."

Her eyes wander up and down my frame. "He must have been a finely wrought man, Your Majesty." My chest swells. Her words, so honestly spoken, touch me as no others do.

"Come." I sit down, a flagon of wine before me, and tempt her to rest on my knee. She hesitates before moving timidly forward to perch on my lap as if it is so high she is afraid of falling.

I laugh gently and tug off her hood to see her hair fall in a vibrant cloud to her waist. I test its texture between my fingers and find it fine and soft. I lift it to my face and bury my nose in it, inhaling the sweet fragrance of cardamom and sandalwood.

"Oh, Bessie," I murmur. "You are very fair."

And she is fair, and as fresh and untainted as a summer daisy. She turns and looks unfalteringly into my eyes, allowing me to see the desire she has been concealing. The pulse throbs in the base of her throat and I pull her closer, tasting it with my lips and with my tongue.

"Are you a maid?" I ask and she looks away with an imperceptible nod, as if ashamed.

"That is a good thing," I whisper.

"Is it?"

I kiss her again and she seems to melt in my arms. I want to lift her skirts and take her, but she is young, she is afraid. I must be slow and gentle. Let the thing that is to happen be as easy for her as slipping into a bath. My fingers creep up her skirts; she wriggles and whimpers. I still my hand; our lips part.

"Shall I stop?" I ask, desperate for her not to refuse me. She shakes her head.

"No, I don't think so." And so, I continue. I stroke and tease until she lies naked on my bed. When I finally take her, she clutches my shirt and breathes my name.

"Harry!" she cries, as if I am not the king, not her master, but merely her sweetheart.

At the end of October, the court accompanies the queen and me to Dover to see Mary on her way. It should have been a special day, but the weather is foul. We travel through lashing rain that finds a way beneath the stoutest of coverings. It trickles down the neck, blows up the sleeves, and pays no heed to the grandeur of the company it drenches. Mary, dressed as befits the Queen of France, no longer seems like my young sister. Even somewhat damp, she seems distanced from the Mary of old, icily beautiful and exotic.

There is no sign of my impetuous, bad-tempered sibling; she plays the part to perfection. Accompanied by four earls, four hundred knights and barons and as many ladies, her retinue is breathtaking.

Fourteen great ships wait to take her away from England. A huge crowd has turned out to wave her goodbye. When it is time for her to depart, Kate is tired, so my sister takes leave of my wife at the castle.

"I wish you well, dear Kate," Mary says, kissing her on both cheeks in the French way. "May God smile on your childbed this time. Send me word the moment my nephew is born."

Kate, tearful and trembling, responds in kind.

"It is not forever, dear Mary. We will visit your court and you will always be welcome at ours. England will forever be your home."

I watch them. The two foremost women in my life. They have been friends since Kate first arrived to marry Arthur; they dance together, exchange silk swatches and fabrics. I have never felt jealous of their bond before but now that Mary is displeased with me, I find it difficult. I want to tear their hands apart and demand the attention and affection I deserve.

I accompany her to the waterside where her ship awaits. The water is choppy, smacking against the harbour wall.

"I hope it is calmer out to sea," Mary says. "It would never do for me to arrive in France green-faced and stinking of vomit."

"Stop it," I say. "Don't make jokes. Not at a time like this."

She looks down at her feet and I pretend I do not know she is fighting tears. This is not a king bidding farewell to a fellow queen but simply Henry and Mary not wanting to part.

"You will always be my dearest sister," I say, holding her pale hand.

"And you will always be my overbearing bully of a brother." I know her bravado conceals heartbreak, but I dare not pry open her hard shell for fear her soft inside will be my own undoing.

I swallow the hard knot of grief.

My last link with childhood, my only true friend, the only one who really knows and loves the little Henry who hides beneath my ostentatious mask.

"I will write, of course," she says, "and there will be royal occasions when you can visit. It will be a welcome change to host you in my kingdom. You must bring Kate, and the children."

"You are such a pert madam," I say, teasingly. "I warrant you'll give me the worst room in the palace."

Her laughter warms me, but she sobers quickly, lowers her chin and blinks away a tear. I pretend not to notice.

Taking her hand again, I kiss it. "Try to be more like Mother," I say. "She was truly loved. I never heard a harsh word issue from her lips."

"She was a saint, and I am far from that," Mary says, pulling a wry face. "I can never hope to emulate such a queen, but I shall do my best not to shame you, Henry. You be good too."

She pokes the end of my nose, and I try to grab her finger but, as always, I miss it, clutching at the air.

Earlier, I came across her in conversation with Brandon. They pulled apart at my approach and I noted my sister's wan face, her teary eyes.

"Ah, I was looking for you, Brandon," I said, as if I had noticed nothing amiss. "I wish to discuss an errand I wish you to run."

"Are you out of comfits, Henry?" Mary laughed but, ignoring her and taking Brandon's arm, I led him away. Neither of us spoke until we were alone. He stood uncertainly before the hearth until I bid him sit.

"Am I in trouble, Your Majesty?"

He tried to act as if there was nothing amiss, but … I know him too well.

"I don't know, Brandon, should you be?"

"I know of no cause, Sire." He looked away into the shadows, the trace of a frown between his brows.

"I suspect you harboured some hopes in my sister's direction, but … it would never do, you know."

He sighed and accepted my offer of a chair.

"Not hopes, Harry, but I admit, I will miss her. She is bright; her presence illuminates a room."

"Yes. Well, now she will light up all France and you must forget her. Now, while you are in Paris, I want you to seek an audience with Louis. I want Ferdinand expelled from Navarre, and I need Louis' help in cementing Kate's claim on the kingdom of Castile."

Now, they make ready to sail together to France, where Mary will begin her new life and Brandon will return home to me and his duties in England. I am not fooled by their denial of feelings between them. I can only hope it has not gone too far, for Mary is of Tudor blood and made for greater things.

It is quiet at court with both Kate and Mary absent. I miss my sister, but I admit I am relieved to be spared Kate's sharp tongue, that has grown worse of late.

Although she craves a child, she does not relish pregnancy. Her stomach refuses to tolerate her favourite foods, her ankles and lower legs swell, and she is plagued by backache. I do not know the workings of a woman's lying-in chamber, but at least she will now be allowed the rest she requires.

Men are not permitted to enter the lying-in chamber, but her physicians bring me daily reports of her health.

"Is she content?" I ask. "She has been very low lately."

"She weeps often and copiously," they say, "and complains of discomfort. The bed is too hard, the pillow too soft, the light too dim, the torches too bright. But all that is quite normal, Your Majesty, and we are not alarmed."

Poor Kate. But it will be over soon. The royal nursery is prepared, the cot cleaned and made ready, the wet nurse selected. All we need now is our royal prince.

The palace waits. The country waits. The whole of Christendom waits. And then Kate brings forth a dead boy – my heir.

The fourth dead child in five years.

I cannot bear it.

And if I cannot bear it, neither can Kate. When I finally force myself to visit her chambers, she wails and tears at her own face. I pull away from her, afraid she has lost her mind, but I cannot find it in myself to offer her comfort. My own soul is bereft. My son is dead, my heir, the core of all my hopes and dreams, the future of my realm.

I turn away from the blood stench of the birthing chamber and go in search of Bessie.

"Oh, Your Majesty," she says, stroking my hair and cradling my head as if I am some great baby. "The loss of a child is a cruel thing but one day you will have your son. Do not lose faith."

I close my eyes, rest thankfully upon her soft bosom.

"I sometimes wonder if God is displeased with me. I do all I can to be a good Christian king but … I have wondered …"

She sits up and cocks her head to one side.

"Nothing," I say. "No matter."

I cannot speak of the creeping suspicion that Kate was no maid on our wedding night and, in lying with my brother's wife, I have committed a grievous sin.

Does it not say in Leviticus: *"If a man shall take his brother's wife, it is an impurity; he hath uncovered his brother's nakedness; they shall be childless."*

I do not speak this aloud. I have spoken of it to no one and never shall, but … what if she lied and was no maid on our wedding day? That would mean our marriage was no marriage and our childless state is God's punishment.

January - July 1515

By twelfth night, Kate has left confinement and sits cheerless at my table again. I mourn not only the loss of my heir but also the loss of my bright young wife. Kate is no longer the joyful queen she once was.

Oh, she maintains her gentle manner and a smile is ever on her lips yet, when we are alone, she seems to deflate. She relinquishes all pretence and takes refuge in her misery. She snaps and snarls whenever I speak to her and she spends far too long on her knees.

I am used to women who pray. My mother was pious, and rumour has it that my grandmother's knees were worn to the bone through constant prayer.

Kate's piety is desperate. It is as though she has committed some great offence against God for which she feels she must constantly beg forgiveness. It makes me wonder what she can have done that was so sinful.

The courtiers creep around the palace like churls, afraid of offending us. I am full of rancour at the lack of cheer. I jerk my arm upward, slopping wine on the cloth.

"Light more torches," I cry, "and bring on the entertainments. We are not dead yet!"

Obediently, the courtiers burst into a semblance of celebration. A lively tune fills the room and in the far corner a group of young people begins to dance. *A group of young people?* What am I saying? I *am* a young person. What the devil am I doing sitting here with the cares of the world on my shoulders? I have Wolsey to take the burden of my troubles.

A sennight ago, we had word from the pope that Wolsey is to be made cardinal. That will fill his vain old heart with pride. The house he lives in is grand enough, but I daresay he will now make improvements to befit the grandeur of his status.

I peer across the hall to where he sits in deep conversation with the French ambassador. He catches my eye and raises his cup, gives a bow. Wolsey is a good fellow, a reliable councillor and a good friend too.

I am glad for his success despite the other members of my council grumbling about purses and pigs' ears.

I stand up and the crowd parts to form a passage for me to follow. He and the ambassador turn and make obeisance.

"Thomas," I say, clapping him on the back. "You two are the glummest fellows in the room. You shouldn't be talking business tonight."

"Your Majesty." Thomas' face is pinched and I am unsure whether he is upset or angry; perhaps a mixture of both.

"Your Majesty," he repeats. "I was just on my way to find you. I am afraid the ambassador has grave news. I am sorry to spoil the celebrations but … the king of France, King Louis, is dead."

My cup halts halfway to my mouth. Slowly, I place it on the table.

"Dead?" I repeat. "You are quite sure?"

Of course he is sure. The ambassador would make certain of his facts before relaying it to us. My sister is now Dowager Queen of France – her influence drastically reduced … unless she has managed to get with child.

"And the queen?"

"She is well, Your Majesty, considering her loss …"

I raise one eyebrow. I am sure she is in fine fettle. Probably already packing and arranging her return home. The ambassador clears his throat.

"Of course, the queen must remain in confinement, as is tradition, to establish whether or not … she carries the late king's heir."

"Of course."

Mary will baulk at that. I frown about the room, the colour and gaiety suddenly mocking. The death of a king must never be taken lightly. This will remind the people of my own mortality – and lack of heir.

Louis died without issue and if my sister is not carrying his child, his crown will go to his nephew, Francis of Valois.

"I will write to the queen, expressing my condolences and offering comfort, both as king and brother."

"She will be distraught for the marriage to have ended so swiftly."

I search Wolsey's words for irony but find only sincerity.

"Indeed. Becoming queen of such a nation is an honour every princess dreams of. We must help her find another match after a suitable period of mourning has passed."

He closes his eyes, inclining his head in agreement.

"I must tell the queen," I say and, taking my leave, rejoin Kate whose face is as long as a mule's. It will be even longer when she learns my news.

***

"Oh, poor Mary!" The tidings from France jerk Kate from her self-pity. "Where is she, do you know?"

"Cluny, I believe, or that is where Wolsey claimed she was going. Until we are sure whether or not she carries Louis' child, she must remain there. No hint of scandal must be allowed to touch her."

"Of course not. I don't expect there is much hope of a child though … Louis was ..."

"Decrepit? Yes, he was. I doubt he was vigorous in bed and I very much doubt Mary will be shedding any real tears at his loss."

"I was going to say 'ailing'."

"Oh." I smile sheepishly and resume my seat at her side. "I will write to her tomorrow. Perhaps you would like to add a note to it."

"I will, Harry. Poor Mary, to be widowed at nineteen."

"My grandmother was widowed at fourteen and left pregnant into the bargain. It did her no harm. She took it in her stride and made herself a new dynasty. Mary will survive. She is a Tudor."

"And she will be home soon. It will be so nice to have her at court again; she is always such a lively addition. It may only have been a short time, but I have missed her."

"I might investigate the chance of rekindling a Spanish marriage for her."

Kate perks up at that.

"Oh yes, my husband. Mary would be happy in Spain. Shall I speak of it to the ambassador on your behalf?"

"No, not yet. Let us not be so hasty. She may yet prove to be pregnant."

In the coming weeks, I cannot make up my mind whether it would be better for Mary to be carrying the next dauphin and thus put Tudor blood on the French throne, or to have her back with me so I can put in motion a union between her and the Spanish. In the end, I make lists detailing the advantages and disadvantages of each scenario. It is unfortunate that I do not have two sisters.

***

"She's done WHAT?" The cardinal winces against the force of my roar. "Tell me this is some – some ill-conceived joke!"

"I wish I could, Your Majesty, but it seems … not."

I stand for a while, speechless, as rage reverberates through me, robbing me of coherent thought.

How could she do this?

"King Francis did not object, or so I am led to believe."

"Well, why would he object? This devious marriage has ensured that my sister will not now be used against him in a marriage contract with Spain."

I scowl at a servant who has come forth to replenish the wine. "Brandon: of all the people I thought I could trust. I could have his head for this!"

Wolsey sits forward, his red robes blanketing his knees.

"Your Majesty, I think, perhaps, your sister appealed to his sense of chivalry."

"CHIVALRY?"

He flinches again, linking his fingers over his belly as if fortifying his defences.

"Yes, Your Majesty. You will recall she has been in great distress since the death of Louis these past months. To all intents and purposes a prisoner … a political hostage."

"And marrying my former stable master will prove what, exactly?"

"Try to think, Your Majesty. Mary has known the Duke of Suffolk since infancy. In her travail, widowed in a foreign country, her household sent home, attended by strangers, a hostage to whatever marriage was chosen for her, Brandon would have seemed like a kind hand in the darkness, her only friend."

"Have you spoken with them direct?"

"No, no, Your Majesty. I learned of this only yesterday evening."

I look into his calm eyes and, finding no lies, spin away from him and sink into a seat. My sister, wed to a philanderer, a man with a multitude of failed relationships – a whoremonger! I clutch the wooden arm of my chair, my lip curling.

"You think he persuaded her? You think he had the gall to seduce the Dowager Queen of France into his bed?"

Wolsey flushes and averts his eyes.

"Your Majesty, I am sorry to say so, but … rumour leads one to think it might rather have been the other way around."

Nonsense. Mary is an innocent. Brandon is a notorious womaniser, but I would have laid good coin that my sister, as a royal princess, was safe from him. Surely, he would place our friendship higher than any woman, even a princess.

A lewd picture of my sister's seduction rears before me. Disgusted, I shake my head to clear my mind. I should *never* have agreed that her next spouse could be of her own choosing. *Did she plan this from the beginning?*

"I should never have given her my promise, Thomas."

He shrugs in sympathy and reaches for his pen, the jewels on his fingers twinkling in the candlelight.

"You cannot have known she would be so swiftly widowed, and as for a match between her and Brandon, well, that was beyond anyone's imagining."

Was it?

I think back. Brandon walking with us in the garden, my sister's vibrant response to his conversation. She laughed too loudly at his jests, laid money against him beating me at tennis. In times of debate, she always took his side. I should have seen it. I know her better than any man, yet now it seems I know her not at all.

"Francis will be laughing at us. I would not be surprised if he connived with them."

Wolsey puts down his pen, carefully blotting his words before massaging his wrist. I take a sip of wine.

"I doubt it, Sire. Francis was pushing for a French union. I am informed …" he clears his throat, pulling an apologetic face, "that he went so far as to offer the dowager the position of royal mistress."

I choke, splutter malmsey down my doublet and dab at it fruitlessly with a kerchief. That scenario is even worse than her being in Brandon's stable of women.

"Did he, indeed! The jade! I can imagine how Mary received such an offer."

"As I understand it, if Your Majesty will forgive me, the dowager queen complains that your good self and the French king have been fighting over her 'like two dogs over a juicy bone'. I imagine, being in such a state, she saw Brandon as an easy way out – her only choice."

But I know better. Mary would never have given herself to Brandon unless she wanted to. She has only ever thought of herself. Her rash decision has upset my plans for reviving our relations with Spain and I will see she suffers for it ... Brandon too.

As the weeks wear on, Kate continues to show a brave face to the world, but I know her misery and resent it. I want to forget the past and look to the future. I want to dance and feast and joust. I want to be merry.

My court should be a place of tournament and joy, not mourning. The queen has to rise above it. It is her duty to do so. Am I not as scarred as she?

Usually, I would seek Brandon's advice, but he is in France, arranging to bring Mary – *his wife* – home, so I speak to Bryan instead.

If Francis Bryan knows about anything, it is women. He has the reputation of a rake and Wolsey has no liking for him, but he intrigues me. How must it be, I wonder, to have so little regard for what others might think.

"Perhaps you should try courting the queen again."

Bryan stands at the hearth, one hand caressing the head of his hound, the other twirling a cup of wine. He ignores Beau, who sits at his feet, thumping his stubby tail on the floor.

No one at court will ever come close to understanding the wall that has grown up between me and the queen but, with Brandon away, Bryan is the only one I can talk to. Although I enjoy their company, I could never speak to Compton or Percy in this way.

I sigh and wish again that Brandon were here with me. I might have confided in Knyvet had he not been killed in action in France. I try not to dwell on that. I direct my mind to the matter in hand.

"Court her? Why should I do that? She is my wife, wedded and bedded long ago."

He ceases to knead his dog's ears, causing the beast to paw at his hose.

"Perhaps that is part of the problem, Your Majesty. Women are odd creatures, moody and changeable. It is always difficult to know exactly what they think of us. I have found it beneficial to treat them always as if they mean everything. Give her gifts, send her poetry, posies of flowers, sweetmeats ..."

"Well, I do give her presents. In fact, I gifted her a priceless prayer book for her New Year's ..."

"Yes, and very fine it was too, Your Majesty, but it was a formal gift, part of your kingly duties. Try sending her spontaneous gifts: a rose plucked from the garden hedge with a note claiming its exquisite nature brought her image into your mind."

I raise my eyebrows.

"Really, and where am I to find a hedge of roses at this time of year?"

His tilts his head back, laughing ... but not at me.

"Something else then, Sire. A palmful of snowdrops, their colour an indication of the purity of her soul."

He places both hands on his heart and pulls a lovelorn expression. I frown, look down at my lap and, as if sensing my unease, the spaniel abandons him and comes to me. Beau thrusts his wet nose between my fingers and, obediently, I caress his head. His skull is hard and warm beneath my touch as he turns his soulful eyes upon me.

"The queen will think I've run mad." I address Beau rather than Bryan and, in response, his tail slowly thumps the floor.

The next morning, as soon as it is light, I send a puzzled page in search of snowdrops and, an hour after Mass, I take them myself to give to the queen.

She is not expecting me and looks up from her seat by the fire, her women melting away to afford us privacy. I stride into the room, spy Bessie near the window and send her a secret smile before laying my offering in Kate's lap.

She gasps, not entirely with pleasure, and stares at them for a few moments before scooping them up in her palms. She quirks her brow in silent question. I recite my carefully practised answer.

"I – I saw them growing in the shelter of the hedge and was reminded of the purity of your heart, your goodness …"

The suggestion of a smile blossoms on her lips, encouraging me to stumble on. "It struck me that, these days, since … it struck me that we do not spend so much time together of late. I thought it would be nice to – to walk in the gardens, perhaps hunt ... when you are feeling up to it, of course."

"That would be very fine, my husband."

"And dine. Why do you not dine with me in my chambers? I will send the servants away so it is just the two of us. I will serve you myself."

Her smile spreads. It is infectious and, taking heart, I pull up a chair, toss my cap into a corner and sit close to her.

"Sometimes, I get so tired of all the ceremony. I'd like to dispense with it more often, as we used to do when we were first wed … when you were a maid and I an unschooled youth."

"Those were happy days."

Her eyes shine with nostalgia. I pray God she does not begin blubbing again. In answer to my plea, she shakes herself and smiles. "I'd like that, Henry. Thank you."

"This afternoon then. I've a meeting with Wolsey, then I shall seek you in the privy garden."

When I take my leave, I wince at Bessie's stricken face, the suggestion of moisture on her lashes.

I continue to send the queen daily gifts, and most mornings she opens her eyes to discover some small offering on her pillow. When I run out of ideas, I ask Bryan, who seems to have a list of ways to woo a woman. By the week's end, the queen accepts my subtle suggestion that my visits to her chamber should resume.

We both know it is our duty to beget another child as swiftly as we can, but I see now that it does not have to be a chore. It is not impossible to revive the old relationship I had thought dead. Kate smiles and laughs again and, one morning, I even hear her singing as she takes the early air.

"Did you hear that our cardinal has begun new work on his palace at Hampton?"

Kate takes my arm and beams up at me.

"Yes. He told me of it himself. He is like the dog with the two tails."

"Or maybe three."

We amble between the flowerbeds, full now with spring blooms, early bees, and the scent of heaven thick in the breeze. It has been a long dark winter but, together, my queen and I have thrown aside our sorrow and, by sharing our grief, we have grown closer.

She now anticipates the small surprises I spring on her and delights in the way I leap out from a hedge when she is least expecting it. I make sure I regularly dismiss my gentlemen so we might be alone as husband and wife, not king and queen. The sun is warm on my back. I send my servants away and lead Kate along the lavender -strewn path. Every so often, I pause and pluck a bloom from the garden and she adds it to her posy. We could be mistaken for a knight and his lady instead of the king and queen of England.

She halts, pointing to a particularly pretty rose, and I pluck it for her, hold it to her nose. Her cheeks flush as I fasten it to her bodice, my fingers brushing the softness beneath.

"I have some other good news too, my husband."

I raise my eyes to hers, my senses alert.

"News? What news?"

She bites her lip, avoids looking me in the eye.

"I – I have missed what I should have seen … twice now, and this morning … I couldn't face my breakfast."

Hope floods through me.

"You are sure, Kate? It's not some mistake?"

"Well, I am not certain, but my women keep a record. If they are correct, then the child should be here sometime in January, or perhaps February."

I crush her to me, making her squeal with surprise and, when I release her, I realise she has dropped her posy and I am standing on it, crushing the petals into the gravel. Neither of us remark on it.

"Ah, Kate. This time, God will smile on us. He will appreciate how much we crave a child. This time, he will send our son and our troubles will be over."

"God willing," she whispers as if she cannot quite believe it. "God willing."

I take her hand and we continue our walk to the end of the garden, where the cultivated ground grows rougher before merging with the wood.

"Should we go any farther? Should you not return to the palace? It will not do to tire yourself."

She laughs. I have said such things before. With each pregnancy, I have insisted that she should limit her exercise, rest each afternoon and eat only food recommended by the physicians. It did no good then, but this time ... *this* time it must be different.

1515 — Westminster

I make Brandon and my sister pay for their breach of trust. Not only do I demand a vast financial compensation, but I also ban them from my court.

"Mary will hate to be exiled," I sneer to Kate, during my weekly visit to her apartment. "Brandon too will be aching to return to the limelight. It will teach him not to overreach himself and remind him that his status is dependent only on my good will."

"Yes, my husband," Kate replies, easing her swollen feet onto a stool. In late pregnancy, she holds little allure for me. She is fat, waxy-faced and tetchy, but I visit her nonetheless.

"Between them they have little wealth. In her eagerness to get out of France, Mary signed all her jewellery and plate over to me. She is all but penniless now. Brandon may already be regretting his rash decision to bed her."

I frown from the window, noting the untidiness of the leaf-strewn mead. I must make sure the gardeners are instructed to keep it clear. Sometimes, I fear the palace is going to rack and ruin; yesterday I discovered a dog turd on the throne room floor. In truth, these small niggles are due to me missing my best friend and errant sister more than they are likely to be missing me.

There is no one I like better than Brandon. He understands me and, as for Mary, well, she has always been there, laughing at me, teasing … life is strange and uncomfortable without her. But I will not admit it.

"You can always summon them back to court, Henry. I know how you miss them both."

I turn sharply, my dissatisfaction now directed at my unattractive wife rather than my untended garden. I make a dismissive scoffing sound.

"Me, miss them? There is plenty to keep me busy. Now, I must away. I promised Compton a game of tennis and I've a meeting with Wolsey this evening. Get some rest, Kate; you look like under-cooked pastry."

I kiss her damp forehead and stalk indignantly away, her women bowing low at my approach, their bright skirts pooling like sunshine on a dark lawn.

As I draw near, Bessie dares to look up, her face pink, her eyes gleaming with invitation. I pause, incline my head and give her the benefit of a royal smile.

"I hope you are well, Mistress Blount."

The other women turn startled eyes upon her. She blushes red.

"I am very well, thank you, Your Majesty."

She sinks low again and, when she rises, I notice she is wearing the locket I gave her at our last meeting. It pleases me to see her wear it. The gold chain caresses her throat, drawing my eye to the jewelled bauble nestling in the valley of her breasts.

What day is it today? Wednesday, but no matter, I will summon her to my presence later whether she be in attendance to the queen or not.

It is a cold night, the wind howls about the chimneys and, every so often, the rain patters like a handful of gravel on the windowpane. Inside, it is warm; a fire roars in the grate and candles ward off darkness. I yawn and stretch my limbs.

I have had a full day: an early morning ride, a game of tennis, and a council meeting followed by a vast supper. Now, I am waiting for Bessie to arrive and have sent all but two of my attendants away.

Every time we meet, she is shy for the first half hour, and I put myself out, trying to put her at ease, taking pleasure in teasing forth the girl I have come to hold great affection for. I have ordered light refreshment and send the servers away. I like to play the part of her servant and ply her with wine and wafers as if she is a queen.

"Here, try this."

I hold a sucket to her mouth. She hesitates, her tongue emerging and moistening her lips before her mouth opens, allowing me to place the dainty on her tongue. She nods as she chews, opening her eyes wide and nodding in appreciation of the taste. Sauce dribbles on her chin and, instead of dabbing it away with a napkin, I use my tongue.

When I am with Bessie, I forget I am Henry, King of England. All I know is the warmth of the fire on my naked back and the heat of Bessie beneath me. I am Henry the man, in need of a woman. The trials of state, the want for a son, the myriad problems that blight a monarch's life, all are soothed beneath the touch of this good soul.

Afterwards, naked and rosy in my bed, she lounges on my pillows while I ply her with food and drink. Outside, the rain continues to fall, dripping on the sill in a melodious tune. The rhythm seems to spell out her name. *Bessie is my true love ... Bessie owns my heart ...* I sit up and cock my head.

"What is it, Your Majesty?"

"A song," I say. "Sometimes a tune just enters my mind uninvited and I am forced to make note of it lest I forget."

"A song?"

"Yes ..."

I reach for my lute, pluck a string and reel off the words to the tempo of the rain.

"You see? Do you like it?"

Her hands are on her mouth, her eyes dancing with delight.

"Oh, Your Majesty. Nobody has ever written a song or even a poem to me before."

"Really? I am surprised. You are so very pretty; I'd have thought you'd have been ..."

"Oh, no, Your Majesty. I have never.... When I was young, gentlemen would remark on my prettiness but no man except you ever viewed me as a woman."

My eyes absorb the youthful bloom of her skin, the softness of her chin, the fullness of her breasts above the sheet. I lick my lips.

"Nobody but me?"

She shakes her head. "Only you, Your Majesty."

Only me. My loins tighten. That is how it should be between a woman and a man. If only I could be sure that Kate …

Taking Bessie's cup, I place it on the nightstand and tear back the sheet before pulling her down the bed. I cannot resist her. She makes me feel like a lion. If she were my queen, we would make a dozen sons.

"Your Majesty, I was thinking …" Bessie is lacing the front of her gown. Her face is still flushed from lovemaking, her hair snarled and tangled.

"Yes, my sweet. What were you thinking?"

"The song you composed. While we were … erm … while I was in your arms, I thought of one for you. It isn't finished yet …"

She puts her hands behind her back, lifts her chin and sings like a bird. Her voice spirals up to the chamber ceiling, like a bird seeking freedom. I listen, amazed that such a sound can issue from so small a person.

> *Whilst life or breath is in my breast*
> *My sovereign lord I shall love best.*
> *My sovereign lord, for my poor sake,*
> *Six courses at the ring did make,*
> *Of which four times he did it take:*
> *Wherefore my heart I him bequest,*
> *And, of all other, for to love best*
> *My sovereign lord …*

"Bessie," I exclaim when she has finished. "I had no idea you had such a voice, and you compose music too? Why did I not know of this? Come, come here and talk to me. I want to know all there is know about you. What other secrets do you conceal from your king?"

Over the weeks that follow, Kate goes into confinement, leaving me free to spend more time with Bessie. Sometimes, two hours have passed before I even think to take her to bed. When we are in company, I seek her out, and people begin to remark on how often I lead her on to the dance floor.

During the course of the day, I find reasons to speak to her. I compliment her gown that is nothing out of the ordinary and, on one or two occasions, I invite her to join me on the hunt.

"People are whispering, Your Majesty," Wolsey mutters as a council meeting nears its end. "Mistress Blount's reputation could be …"

"Sullied? By an association with her king? Her family should be honoured, sir!"

Wolsey clears his throat. "I was going to say 'compromised', Sire. I suggest a suitable marriage should be arranged, lest …"

"She is too young."

She is not, of course, too young at all, but I baulk at the thought of sharing her with another. She is mine. She pleases me and I am not yet weary of her.

I wave Wolsey away.

"We will consider her marriage when she is a little older. Rest assured, we will find her a good match when she is ripe to marry."

He bows and backs obediently away. I remain in my seat, my mind lingering on Bessie's laughter, her lightness of heart that always lifts mine to match it. So often, before the court, I have to disguise my lowering spirits behind false laughter, forced gaiety. It is never so with Bessie; she brightens my darkest hours and, when I am in her company, there is no need for pretence.

As if I have summoned her, a door opens and she glides toward me, eyes lowered, hands clasped as if she is an innocent.

"Bessie." I reach for her hand, pull her close, and kiss her cheek so I can inhale her now familiar scent. She wriggles away.

"Sire, I am here on the queen's business."

"Kate? What does she want?"

I grab for her again, peering down her bodice at what I teasingly call her 'twin blessings'. She struggles half-heartedly.

"I am to tell you that the queen's pains have begun. Her waters have broken, and the child's birth is imminent."

My grip on her tightens, making her gasp.

"My son."

She pulls away, straightens her hood and bobs an awkward curtsey.

"Yes, Your Majesty. He will be born very soon, I should think, judging by the queen's cries."

Delight spreads from my belly at the thought of my heir. My son will soon be here. I feel invincible.

I pull Bess onto my lap, push off her hood and try to nibble her earlobe. Her giggles reverberate through me and my fingers creep up her skirts, finding the place that always makes her stop struggling. She becomes compliant and gives herself up to me.

Half an hour later, I am helping her conceal her tangled hair beneath her cap when a babble of voices drifts up from below.

"The king! Where is the king?"

It is Wolsey. He knows well where I am and who I am with. He calls so loud to alert me to his arrival and give us time to make ourselves decent.

Bessie hastily pulls down her skirts, helps me tuck my shirt beneath my doublet and is standing a demure three feet away when Wolsey is admitted.

"Ah, Your Majesty. I wanted to be the first to … congratulate you. Your queen has been delivered …"

"My son!"

His eyes slide away, his chin drooping. "Erm … a daughter, Your Majesty. A big bonny bluff girl with hair as red as an October dawn!"

Disappointment lodges like a stone in my chest. "A girl."

"Yes, Your Majesty. A *healthy* girl, and the queen is doing well. You have both been blessed with a beautiful princess. The whole realm will rejoice."

And Christendom will laugh.

Wolsey is advising on how I should react, what I must say. Once again, I am to act the part of a happy prince. I must receive the gift of a useless female as if it is in answer to my prayers. But I prayed for a son. Kate prayed for a son.

The whole realm prayed for a son.

The celebrations to welcome our royal prince have long been ordered. It was to have been a son, a boy to grace the name of Tudor. Not a girl. A useless girl.

"Your Majesty …"

"Leave us."

I do not watch as Wolsey backs regretfully from the room. I slump in my chair, head in hand, and allow disappointment to wash over me. For just a few moments, before I paint on a joyous face with which to fool the world, I must have time to grieve for my elusive boy.

A tear drips onto my hand. I wipe it away, but another quickly follows so I let it lie until I hear a footstep, a sigh. A gentle hand reaches from the shadows. Small loving fingers sweep away the tear, reach up to touch my hair, gently stroke my brow, as my mother used to do.

I look up into dark wide eyes and let her see into the depths of my sorrowful soul.

"Oh, Bessie ..." I groan.

"Oh, Henry," she whispers. "My Henry."

February 1516

The bells ring out across the country, announcing the birth of a princess, and I somehow find the strength to appear delighted. It is a few days before I visit the queen in the chamber for my first glimpse of the child.

Kate is propped up on pillows, the rich hues of her gown bleaching her face of colour. She looks every one of her thirty-one years, but she seems pleased with herself, despite her failure.

"How are you?"

I stand at the foot of the bed, trapped into polite enquiry when I would really like to shout my frustration. She has not yet been informed of the death of her father, Ferdinand, a few days ago. We thought it better she birth the child before being told of it. It is my place to do it, but I find myself reluctant to break the news. I decide to wait. I will instruct Wolsey to do it, or the Spanish ambassador. I cannot smirch her joy.

Kate beams at me, her hands folded in a self-congratulatory manner on top of the sheet.

"I am very well, my husband, and, as you can see, our daughter is thriving."

She indicates the royal crib. I take a step nearer while Kate continues to prattle.

"They keep advising me to send her to the nursery so I can sleep, but I want to keep her close by. It is too soon yet for us to be separated."

She fears to be parted from the child and no wonder. How often has she got this far into motherhood only for her child to be snatched away? How often have I suffered the same?

I peer into the cot and am confronted with a red-faced infant, tightly swaddled and, by the look of her, quite cross about it. She frowns at me, her pursed lips moving, making a sucking noise. I recognise the piercing blue eyes, the shade of the red curl on her forehead. I also recognise her contained fury.

I recognise myself.

Reaching out, I touch her cheek and she turns her head, searching for the comfort of her mother's teat. Her hot, wet mouth finds my finger and she latches on to it and sucks hard.

Something stirs in my heart, melting the ice-cold disappointment that has plagued me since her birth, and ignites my smile.

"Hello, little one," I whisper, while she frantically attempts to draw nourishment from my knuckle. "Hello, my little pearl."

I am buoyed up by her birth and seem to walk on air. A great weight has been taken from my shoulders. *Who gives a damn if she is a girl?* We will soon provide her with a brother. Even while I am at council, I do not stop thinking about her.

"We are going to name her Mary," I announce to nobody in particular. The gathered privy councillors look up, murmuring appreciatively.

"After your sister, perhaps, Your Majesty?"

I sniff, remembering I am displeased with her. Reaching for my cup, I pause before lifting it to my lips.

"Or perhaps after the good Virgin herself, my Lord."

Amused laughter, shuffling papers, a chorus of coughs.

"In time, we will seek a match with Spain. Young Charles, perhaps. There will be some disparity in age but that is of no matter."

Murmurs of agreement, nodding heads, the occasional shifting eye. There is no hurry. Mary will not be marriageable for twelve years or so yet. Much may change in that time. By then, Kate and I will have filled the royal nursery with boys, and I will be king of both England and France.

If only my coffers would allow, I would resume the war now and snatch the crown from Francis' head before Christmas. Thoughts of France bring my thoughts back to my sister.

I miss her merry laughter, the teasing that I always thought I hated. I have only seen her once or twice since her return to England and have shown her and Brandon no favour. No longer welcome at court, she has installed herself at Bath Place to await the birth of their first child. If she gives Brandon a son, I will never bring myself to bless or look upon it.

"You should forgive her, Henry," Kate says. "I suspect there have been feelings between Mary and Brandon for some years. She was obedient to your wishes and married the French king. You promised she could choose her next husband and you cannot really complain that she took you at your word."

"But the subterfuge! Brandon is ... was my friend. They should have come home and broached it with me. I would have been glad for them and showered honour on the occasion instead of the sleazy, undignified exchange of vows they took. I am disgusted, both with Mary and Charles, and I hope they are enjoying their penniless existence away from my court."

Kate sews in silence for a few moments. I stare from the window, watching the wind chase scudding clouds across the sky. If Brandon were here, we would not be indoors but out on the hunt, or practising in the tiltyard, or I would be trouncing him at tennis. Kate clears her throat, drawing my attention and, when I turn, her needlework now rests in her lap.

"Be careful, my husband. I fear it is you who suffers most from their banishment. There was a time when Brandon was never away from your side. These days, you are like a huntsman who has lost his favourite hound. You should be careful lest he find another master."

I snort humourlessly but, deep down, I fear she is right. Mary and Brandon might be far from court, but they have each other. They are probably laughing at their deception. I can almost hear my sister's mocking voice.

Silly Henry; how gullible he was not to realise we planned to marry all along.

Almost a month after Mary's birth, news comes that my sister has birthed a boy. Sickness bites at my gut. They do not *need* a son. It is *I* who needs a son. *Why is God so cruel?* Couldn't he at least have sent them a girl?

Unable to bring myself to write, I order Wolsey to compose a letter of congratulation. Kate, on the other hand, writes of her joy at the news and tells them how she cannot wait to see them.

"This child," I grind through clenched teeth, "this *boy,* or indeed my sister Margaret's son, may one day sit on my throne if you do not give me my heir."

Her face hardens.

"You have an heir, Henry. You have Mary."

I thump the table, dislodging the pen from its pot. Ink splashes across the board. I watch it slowly soak into the grain of the wood.

"Mary is a girl. There has never been a woman on the English throne."

Her chin is high, her mouth pinched and proud.

"Yet Spain has done very well under a female monarch. My mother …"

I spin on my heel, placing a hand on each arm of her chair, and lean over her, snarling into her face.

"This is *England.*"

But I do not dwell too long on the future. I have an heir, albeit a female. Sons will follow. I determine to stop bewailing the things I lack and enjoy the things I do have.

Despite my disappointment, there follows a time of merriment. Tournaments, feasts, weeks of hunting, hawking and sport. The royal court overflows with gracious company, come hither to enjoy the pageants, but it requires just one more thing to make it perfect. In the end, bullied by Kate, I permit the return to court of my sister and Brandon. And I am content once more.

Spring 1516

At first, Brandon is uncharacteristically deferent. The old camaraderie has vanished. He addresses me as 'Your Majesty' where before, in private, I was usually 'Hal' or 'Harry'. In the months that follow, he does not once best me at tennis or at the tilt. He ensures he is always my close second, never taking precedence in the field. At council, he is careful to take my side, never once putting forward a challenge or offering an alternative.

Mary, on the other hand, is unrepentant.

"I knew you'd forgive me in the end, Hal," she says, sailing into the room and kissing me on the cheek before turning to greet Kate and coo over our daughter.

"I've brought you a gift." She snaps her fingers and her man brings forward a basket. I am wary, expecting trickery, and shift my gaze from the gift to Mary.

"Oh, Henry, you are infuriating. Do you think it is a poison asp? Open it and see what I've brought you," she cries.

I nod to her man, who slowly opens the lid. I peep inside.

Spaniels. Two spaniel pups lie curled asleep on red velvet. She knows me too well. Pleasure stretches my cheeks. I reach into the basket and lift one out. A male, he stretches and yawns, showing his pink tongue. Only Mary would think of giving me such a gift. While offerings of priceless jewels and plate become tiresome, I will never grow weary of the warm fat body of a spaniel. I pluck the other pup from sleep and rub my cheek against the silken coat.

"A dog and a bitch, so you never run out of spaniels." She laughs, pleased with herself.

"I wonder what Beau will make of them?"

"Oh, no doubt he will hate them at first and they will plague him for a while but, in the end, he will come to love them. Do you remember the old spaniel of Father's? I misremember his name. He hated Beau when he first arrived yet, in the end, the old fellow acted like a delighted father."

I watch the proud tilt of her head, the upcurve of her lips, the confidence with which she takes her seat between us. She turns to Kate.

"I've missed you so much, Kate, and have so much to tell you, but I will keep it until we are out of the hearing of Mr Flappy Ears."

I splutter with outrage. Mr Flappy Ears! How has she remembered that old nursery name?

I have missed her as much as I would miss my right thumb yet, now, the instant she is back, I am wondering why. *Are all sisters so irritating?*

She dandles Mary on her knee. "I never thought I'd like babies so much," she confesses, "but I admit I am enchanted with our son. This little thing is so pretty too, Hal. I can see why you've dubbed her your 'Pearl'. She is precious."

Her blithe taunt at my lack of a son does not pass me by but I keep my temper. Gently, I stroke my spaniels, soothing them back to sleep. As they drift off with tiny snores, my lap grows warm and I become concerned lest one of them has pissed on my doublet.

"Her brother will be even more precious," I say, watching as Mary pokes my daughter's cheek to make her smile.

"Oh, is there news?" She turns sharply to Kate, who flushes and lowers her head.

"Not yet, but we hope there will be soon."

"Our little Henry – did you approve of our choice of name, Hal? – is delightful. Strong as an ox and his lungs – I swear, we will hear it from here when he wakes."

Their son, my namesake, has been left at Bath Place, brought from the depths of Suffolk for the occasion of a visit from our sister, Margaret.

In a few weeks, the queen of England, and the dowagers of France and Scotland, will be gathered under one roof. And I will be at the centre while they discuss their wondrous offspring and, no doubt, the deficiencies of their spouses.

Margaret is due to arrive in a few weeks, the first time any of us have seen her in thirteen years, since she departed for Scotland. Kate worries that it will be awkward due to our defeat of their army at Flodden, where we took the life of her husband.

Knowing Margaret, she will keep her tongue civil, but sometimes I think it would be preferable if she were more like Mary. At least you know what she is thinking, even if you wish you did not.

After Flodden, as mother of the young king, she was ousted from her role of regent by the Duke of Albany. In a vain attempt to bolster support, she rashly married Archibald Douglas, Earl of Angus. She quickly realised her mistake for, by remarrying, she forfeited the status due to her as Dowager Queen, and Albany then demanded that her sons be given into his care.

Last month, heavily pregnant, she fled over the border into our realm, and now seeks my help in winning back her Scottish rights. She would have done better to apply to me for help before she remarried in haste. I would have found her a much more beneficial match – one of benefit to both Scotland and England. Now, having recently given birth to Angus's daughter, she is to make a welcome visit to our court.

"Are you looking forward to meeting our sister again?" I ask, breaking the long silence. Mary swivels on her seat toward me, my daughter cradled neatly in the crook of her right arm.

"Yes, I suppose I am. I expect she will be very different. In truth, I remember little of her. She was always too aware of the fact that she was the future queen of Scotland and I just a lowly English princess. It will be different now we are both dowager queens. She will have changed, I expect. From memory, when we were children, while you and I made mischief beneath the nursery table, she spent most of her time hidden away with a book. If we don't get along with her, you and I can hardly resort to hiding under the table now."

Her laughter pulls at my cheeks. Kate leans forward.

"When I first arrived in England, Margaret was already in Scotland. Hal was such a brave little boy and you, Mary, so diminutive and sweet, curtseying as you'd been taught, and Hal so studiously concentrating lest he forget his lines."

The door opens and Beau creeps into the room. Hastily, I replace the pups in their basket and make space for him at my knee. He snuffles at the aroma of strange dogs on my lap.

Kate smiles at me as if she is my mother. I am reminded of that day when I first saw her; so fresh, so young, so full of promise. I remember going out of my way to make her smile, to hear her laugh. Although I was just a child, I wanted her at once, or at least, I did not want Arthur to have her.

The day they rode off to rule over their principality from Ludlow, I was full of envy. I imagined them one day taking the throne, ruling over England, bearing sons and daughters to take the Tudor name into the future, flooding Christendom with our blood. And when the news came of Arthur's death, while the realm sank into misery, and my parents wore themselves out trying to conceive a replacement prince, all I could think of was Kate.

That was the day I realised how dark the future is. For all our dreaming, tomorrow is closed. We cannot turn the page. None of us, not even kings, can predict what is to come. This time next year, Kate might have given birth to twins, or I might be dead.

Or she might be.

I turn my eyes upon her, noting how faded her cheeks have become, how sunken and lined her eyes. She is no longer the fresh young bride that stirred me all those years ago. The many pregnancies, her many sorrows, have taken a heavy toll. If she were to die soon, whom would I marry? Whom would I choose to give me sons?

Suddenly, smothered by the company of women, the talk of babies, and who has married whom and what fine new fabric has just arrived from overseas, I stand so abruptly that my dog falls backward. He scrambles up and rolls over, tongue lolling, not in the least put out by my rough treatment.

"I must go. I need some air." I reach out and stroke little Mary's cheek. "I will see you at supper."

I walk briskly through the antechamber where Bessie waits demurely, our secret blazing from her dancing eyes, and I am tempted to abandon my walk and spend an hour with her. She waits expectantly, but I do not tarry.

I must warn her not to look at me like that when we are in company. She should keep her eyes lowered in my presence or the whole court will know of our trysts – if they do not already.

***

I had expected to see a change in Margaret. I knew she would no longer be the same young woman who rode north when I was just a boy, but I had not expected this.

She clambers stiffly from her litter, looking up at the towering walls of Baynard Castle before offering me her hand.

"Henry," she says. "I'd have known you anywhere."

I would not have known her. She has not just grown into a woman but looks like an old woman, although she can only be … I calculate her age on my fingers. Twenty-seven?

She has grown portly, and her eyes are shadowed and lined, her mouth pursed, reminding me of Grandmother, and I am sure I notice the suggestion of a moustache. They say life is harsh over the border, and she has been ill, of course, her life despaired of at one point.

"And I you," I lie. I hesitate to embrace this stranger with my sister's voice, but she tuts and moves forward into my arms.

"It is good to be home, Henry. My years in Scotland have been hard of late, and my sons …"

Ah yes, her sons. I have long been envious of the ease with which she produced three strong boys for the Scottish king but, a week or so ago, came the news that the youngest, the heir presumptive, had died at Stirling castle. I can relate to that and she has my pity.

"It would not have happened had I been there," she weeps when Kate offers her condolence. The queen raises her eyes to mine, and I look away. We both know her pain, but at least Margaret has the luxury of two other sons. I have only Mary.

PART TWO
MARVELLOUS TO BEHOLD

After dinner, his Majesty and many others armed themselves cap-a-pie, and he chose us to see him joust, running upwards of thirty courses, in one of which he capsized his opponent (who is the finest jouster in the whole kingdom), horse and all. He then took off his helmet, and came under the windows where we were, and talked and laughed with us to our very great honour, and to the surprise of all beholders. (*Sebastian Giustinian- Venetian Ambassador 1515*)

October - November 1518

Two years pass. The cardinal has conceived an idea to unite us in peace with France, Burgundy, Spain, the Holy Roman Empire, the Netherlands and the Papal States. These countries will unite against the Ottoman Empire, promising to aid one another in times of war. To cement the treaty, which Wolsey calls *The Treaty of London*, the heads of these countries are invited to our capital. Preparations are underway to dazzle them with English splendour.

As part of the peace with France, we have agreed that Mary, now almost two years old, will be formally betrothed to the dauphin. We dress her in cloth of gold, a cap of black velvet and smother her in jewels. She stands with Kate, a diminutive gem, trying hard to remember not to suck her thumb while siegneur de Bonnivet takes her hand and, in the name of the infant dauphin, places a huge diamond on her finger.

It is far too big, but she clutches it tightly to her finger and admires the way it catches the light of the candles. A storm of applause erupts followed by smiling faces, shaking hands, and cries of joy.

Jousts and banquets follow in which our finest possessions are displayed. I note the envy in men's eyes when they regard me and when they see the splendour of my palaces, the richness of my garments, the servants that do my bidding, and the power I hold in the palm of my hand. This is my birthright – or it became so when Arthur died.

Would he have made a better king? Had he lived, would he have begotten sons on Catherine? Princes, dukes, future kings, future queens? Would he have succeeded where I have failed?

I have trusted men around me who assist in the running of the realm. Between us, we keep England safe and secure, we fend off would-be invaders and quash all who threaten our stability. If there is a matter of diplomacy or state that puzzles me, I call on Wolsey – we hold a council meeting, and the matter is sorted.

Of late, Wolsey has been keen to purge our court of what he calls 'bad influences'. By this, he means my friends, the younger men of court, those who are likely to lead me into mischief. He sees their behaviour as reckless, damaging to my position.

Under Wolsey's careful governance, the country is as secure as it has ever been in all but one matter. I lack an heir, yet I can hardly call on the cardinal to assist me with that. I protest but, deep down, I know he is right. My friends distract me from duty; perhaps they should be sent from our court.

I seldom admit to sometimes being sickened by their excesses. In my heart, I wage a constant battle between sin and piety, duty and desire. It is as though there are two Henrys – one pious and God-fearing, the other reckless and full of lust.

Every time I stray from the path of righteousness, I sully the ear of my confessor with the details of my sin. Every time, in self-disgust, I swear I will not err again. It has even occurred to me that Kate's prior alliance with Arthur may not be the reason for God denying us a son. Perhaps it is my own misdemeanours that He punishes. What if my lack of heir is retribution for my adultery? I shake myself, dislodging the discomfort of such an idea.

Kate *is* pregnant again, but where I once looked upon her gravid state with hope, euphoria even, I now expect every day to hear that she has once more delivered a useless dead child.

It used to break my heart. I used to weep and berate God for his failure to provide me with the one thing I crave. The one thing I *need*. These days, I am braced against disappointment.

I am ready for it.

When the news arrives that the queen's pains have begun, I do not even pray. I spend the afternoon with Brandon who, sensing my mood, carefully steers the conversation away from women and the childbed. He even goes so far as to make me work very hard to beat him at tennis.

We are recovering from our exertions; Brandon has a towel about his shoulders, his hair sticking damply to his forehead.

"Well played, Hal," he says. "I had to fight hard to best you this time."

He is lying, or flattering, as Kate would call it. Doing his best to boost my flagging ego. I mop my brow, take a long draught of water, rinse my mouth and spit into the waiting vessel.

"Come," I say. "I need a real drink."

Brandon picks up his doublet and follows as I hasten from the tennis court, gentlemen and servants skipping from my path.

"Do you remember when we used to disguise ourselves and take a barge after dark to the stews? We should do it again, while we still have the vigour for it."

His reminiscence conjures pictures of sins I would rather forget. I smile without humour. I already lack the vigour. I certainly lack the joy. Deep in my heart, I am grey, my humour dripping despondently like a wet dog. Of course, I seek to hide it, but it is there. I am like a mummer, concealing my desolation from those around me. I am a lame gelding playing the part of a steed.

The mask I wear must never be removed. Nobody must know the image I see reflected in my looking glass. I do not see the golden boy everyone else sees. I see a child who cannot yet tie his laces without the aid of his nurse. Inside I am still a boy of ten who fears he is not good enough.

"Your Majesty!"

Bessie's voice cuts into my musing. I look up, surprised to find myself in the garden, the assembled courtiers looking on expectantly while I stand like a statue in the middle of the path. Bessie Blount is on her knees before me.

"Yes, what is it?"

My voice is querulous. She looks up, her brow ridged with confusion. I lighten my tone, realising I have been unjust. I have no wish to hurt her. "What do you want, sweeting?" I repeat quietly.

"Your Majesty, I beg pardon. I have some news …" She casts a glance at the assembly, their eager faces greedy for gossip. I take her elbow.

"Leave us."

I wave the courtiers away and, while they depart, I lead her into the winter arbour.

It only seems a matter of weeks since I dallied with her here. The grass was emerald beneath our feet then, the air rich with the scent of blossom, the sounds of bees and birdsong.

I remember kissing the softness behind her ear, peeking down her bodice to admire the rise and fall of her breathing. I feel no such desire now.

The air is dank, my heart is heavy, and I fear her news will be dire.

"Tell me your errand," I say, trying not to mind her disappointment when I fail to remark on the freshness of her cheek.

"I have grave news, Your Majesty. Oh, I am so sorry, but the queen … her pains began suddenly … the child was born dead."

I feel nothing. I cast my eyes over her stone-white face, her sad, dark eyes. I wonder why they sent her to tell me the news.

"A boy?" I ask, unsure whether I want to learn of the loss of a son, or another girl. It scarcely matters.

She shakes her head. A tear falls upon our entwined fingers. I had not realised we were holding hands.

"A girl."

I close my eyes. Pat her hand and feign a smile.

"No matter. God has not blessed us with a son this time. It is not for us to question his will."

Her lips part. She tugs at my hand.

"Henry," she hisses. "Do not pretend to me. I know your heart. I am yours. You can trust me to keep your troubles close. You should talk to me."

I shake her off and stand up.

"Take our condolences to the queen. Tell her, tell her … Oh, do not bother. I imagine she knows my feelings on the matter after all this time."

As Bessie hurries away, I know she is weeping. I know I have been cruel, but darkness is rushing in.

I am drowning in it.

While life in the garden continues around me, I stand alone. A robin comes searching for worms at my feet. He does not bow and scrape. He cocks his head, fixes his beady black eye upon me before hopping off, unimpressed. I shiver, suddenly aware that I am only in shirtsleeves, the November afternoon drawing swiftly in.

As I am about to stir, I glance up to a figure waiting at the gate. Brandon. I take a few steps, then pause for a moment. He stands up straighter, raises his head, fixes me with his consoling eye and waits for me to approach him. I look away when I fall into step with him but, before we enter the hall, I stop and speak over my shoulder.

"Order up that barge, Brandon. Let us revisit our rakehell youth. Just the two of us."

***

Sin does not erase misery. It blots it out for a short time but when the effects of the wine wear off, reality returns in full measure. I feel twice as bad. I wake the next morning, somehow miraculously returned to my apartments, and open one eye. I blink at the blood-red bed hanging and wish I were dead.

Someone has drawn back the curtain and opened the shutters, and judging from the light that streams through the window, I have slept long into the day. I roll over, my head banging, my stomach rebelling, and vomit into a basin.

At once, the chamber is alive with attendants. They help me sit up, someone bathes my head, another offers me a drink, while another produces fresh linen.

"Perhaps you should eat something, Your Majesty, to settle your stomach."

I reek of the stews, offending even myself. Squinting into the light, I snarl at them to back away and they beat a hasty retreat to the farthest reaches of the chamber.

"Bring water that I might bathe, and then send for the cardinal."

Sinking back into my pillows, I close my eyes again and wish for oblivion.

"You have visited with the queen?"

Wolsey's bottom lip protrudes and he turns up his eyes as he nods and shuffles. He has not yet fully recovered from the sweating sickness and his pallor is greenish, his girth narrower than it once was.

"Alas, yes, poor lady," he says. "She was asking for you, Your Majesty. I assured her you would visit as soon as your duties allowed."

I roll a pen between finger and thumb, the white feather igniting a fogged memory of a Southwark whore trigged up in feathers, her full fat lips working their way from my knee to my … I shove the memory away. Shake my head and concentrate on the matter in hand.

"She is out of danger … the queen, I mean?"

"Yes, Your Majesty. The physician reports that the birth was straightforward. Had the child survived, we'd be celebrating the birth of a pr…"

I bring down my fist on the table, making the cups rattle. A parchment rolls to the floor.

"A princess! We have no need of princesses, Wolsey. We need a son. A SON! And it is becoming clear to us that the queen cannot provide one."

"Your Majesty, the queen is …"

"Old. The queen is *old* and will bear me no further children."

"Women older than the queen have given birth to healthy children."

His soothing voice grates on my conscience. Throwing down the pen, I rest my brow on my hands. I know in my heart that Kate and I will have no further children. These days, I can barely bring myself to share her bed. Her tired body, her constant prayers, her desperation to please are robbing me of my manhood.

"I pray you, Thomas, stop seeking to placate me. I will hear no more platitudes. We must be honest with one another. The queen's childbearing years have passed. I need a son. England must have an heir. Find a solution."

"A solution?"

His mouth falls open and his cheeks sag, his skin fading to parchment white.

"Get her to free me from this marriage. A divorce: an annulment. She can retire with all honour into a religious house and leave me free to marry again."

He is aghast. I imagine he is picturing himself relaying this news to Kate … as is his duty.

"I – I will give the matter some thought, Your Majesty, but do not lose faith that God will yet bless this marriage."

Wolsey is Kate's slave. He has taken her part since she arrived on our shores, but he is not the one who has to tup her.

"This other matter, Wolsey," I say, changing the subject. "The excommunication of Luther. I have made some notes on the subject and would like to expand on them. Ask Sir Thomas More to come to court that I may seek his opinion on it."

I deplore the teachings of Luther that are seeping from Europe to our realm. I am told that there are even members of my court who secretly applaud it – they talk of the 'New Learning' as if it is something wondrous, but I know it to be the work of the devil.

In a few days, More obeys my summons, and we are closeted in my privy apartments. He has ever been my mentor and my friend, and it is not the first time I have sought his guidance on matters spiritual.

After the pleasantries have been exchanged, we spend several hours discussing Luther's heresy.

"Why does God impose such men upon us, do you think? As if life isn't difficult enough for princes."

More smiles and shrugs.

"I do not know the answer, Your Majesty. We must see it as a test. Perhaps such men are sent to assess our resilience to the devil in all his forms."

"Luther is the devil?"

I lean forward, elbow on the table, chin in my hand.

"Or, at least, sent by the devil."

"Perhaps it is to force men of God to ponder on the wonders of Heaven. Some men ..." I clear my throat. "Some men fall from grace, from time to time."

More smiles and accepts a cup of wine from my servant.

"We are human and as such all men are flawed. We must constantly battle against temptation. We must set an example for our sons to ... follow ..."

His voice trails off as he realises he has stepped close to the edge.

I look away.

"Yes. Sons. I would seek your advice on that matter also, Thomas. My marriage – I must find a way to beget a legitimate son and Kate is – the queen is no longer able."

"She is barren, Your Majesty?"

Uncomfortably, he puts down his cup, links his fingers, and leans forward with concern quilting his brow.

"Yes. She is no longer of childbearing age. I am told her menses ..."

He sits up, his face colouring. I take a deep breath. "I hope to persuade her to retire to a house of God where she can pray and contemplate. It is not an uncomfortable life for one of her status."

"Yes." A troubled frown hovers above his eyes. "And you think she will welcome this ... suggestion?"

"Why wouldn't she? She is a pious woman. Already much of her day is spent on her knees and she has fasted so much that beneath her shift, she is little but skin and bone."

He flushes at my indelicacy and I turn the talk to other things. When it is time to go, we part as friends. I embrace him and he pats my shoulder as he was wont to do when I sought his counsel as a boy.

November 1518

Alone, apart from the unseen presence of the guard, my page, my fool, and my spaniels, I scratch some notes in the margin of my document. When I am done, I sit back in my chair and discover Beau's head on my knee. I fondle his silken ears and think how old he seems now I have the puppies.

A scratch at the door of my privy chamber has the dogs leaping up and barking, while a messenger, a note held high above his head out of the reach of their naughty jaws, wends his way toward me. I stand up and move closer to the fire, where I tear it open and hold it to the light of the flames.

It is from Bessie. She is outside, seeking audience. I sigh. More trouble from Kate, I suspect. I return to my seat, pick up a pen.

"Show her in," I say, annoyed at the disturbance but, when she enters, I am reminded of her beauty, and my pique fades.

I turn in my chair.

"Bessie," I say, and hold out my arms. She runs forward and sinks to her knees, pushing away Cut and Ball when they leap up and try to lick her face.

"They're even more eager than I," I laugh, pulling her up and onto my knee. I slide an arm about her narrow waist. "What is your message? More bother from the queen?"

She shakes her head, biting her lip.

"No, Your Majesty. I am here on my own account. I am in some trouble."

"Trouble? With the queen? What have you done to upset her?"

"No. It isn't that." Her face flushes, scarlet as the sleeve of my gown. I reach out and erase a tear with my finger.

"Tell me. It can't be as bad as all that."

She sniffs, fidgeting on my knees before breaking into thunderous tears. It is not like Bessie to make a fuss. Her misery throws her beauty into disarray. She sniffs, fumbles for a kerchief, wipes her eye and dabs her nose.

"I fear – I ..." She takes a deep shuddering breath and begins again. "I am with child, Your Majesty, and set to be ruined."

Something explodes in my heart. I think it is joy. I open my mouth, surprised, although I do not know why.

"Is it *my* child?"

She stiffens on my lap.

"Of course it is *your* child, Henry. I was a maid ... you know that."

A maid. Of course she was. She is young. She is fertile. Loving her is no chore; it is pleasure only. Thinking of it makes me want her again. I cup her breast and find it heavier than before, unless I imagine it.

"When, Bessie? When will he be born?"

"I am not skilled at such things, Your Majesty, but I have gathered it takes nine months or so. I have missed ... what I should have seen twice, so I judge May or, perhaps, June."

I let my hand slide to her belly but the stiffness of her gown hinders contact with my son. I *know* it is a son. I can feel it and I know this child will live. He could be my salvation. *Bessie* could be my salvation. Who would have thought it? Little Bessie Blount, the bearer of a future king.

I laugh aloud.

"Will you speak to my father, Henry, to deflect his anger? I am worried he will cast me out. I am afraid I am ruined."

"Nay, Bessie. No woman is ever ruined by the affections of a king. I shall protect you. I will raise you up and find you a good match and, if this child is a boy, as I suspect he is, I will make him a Duke. I will make him my heir."

Her mouth falls open. We stare at one another and, as unlooked-for joy and hope surges in my heart, I do not look away.

The news restores my vitality, and the court returns to its full glory. Wolsey and Norfolk may have expelled my friends from their former positions in the royal household, but this only provides them with more leisure hours. We spend our days jousting, feasting and hunting. But, as Bessie grows stout and Kate retreats almost with relief into old age, I grow lonely for a woman and start to look about for a mistress to soothe me while Bessie is indisposed.

The queen, well aware that Bessie is carrying my child, is nonetheless discreet in her disappointment. My own efforts at concealment fail, for I cannot help but ask after Bessie's health, enquire if she needs a chair, if she wishes to retire.

Kate never berates me, not even in private. She knows a king must have relief. There is nothing unusual in the situation yet still, without saying a word, she somehow manages to make me squirm.

January - May 1519

In January, we receive news of the death of the Emperor Maximilian. I recall our exploits in France; the way he led me, a shallow boy, on a fool's errand. I had liked him. I admired his confidence, his power, and secretly pledged one day to be such a man.

Now, they will be electing a new emperor, and every monarch in Christendom will covet the title. I see no reason why I should not be the one chosen, but Charles of Spain and King Francis will no doubt covet the title also.

King Francis sends word via our ambassador, Thomas Boleyn, requesting my backing, and I prevaricate, promising much but delivering little. At the same time, I send the secretary, Richard Pace, to the Elector in Germany, to create division and sow the seed that I would make the better emperor.

It is a delicate game, a game in which my hopes of winning are dashed when neither I nor Francis are chosen, but instead Charles becomes the next emperor. I send felicitation but there is a new distrust between us all that threatens the stability of the Treaty of London.

I suspect Francis undermined my own chances of election, just as I undermined his. The old enmity is stirring, hackles are rising.

"It is imperative that peace is maintained," Wolsey warns. "We cannot afford another war. Bide your time, Your Majesty. Refill your coffers before we risk another campaign."

I grunt with dissatisfaction. Wolsey clears his throat.

"I've been toying with the idea of a meeting, Your Majesty, between yourself and the French king. A grand affair on such a scale …"

"For what purpose?"

"Amity, Your Majesty, and peace, and it will also provide the opportunity for you to outshine the King of France, who boasts so openly of his prowess in every field. You must show the world this is not so."

He has my attention. Francis is a few years my junior, a spindly man, and I have heard he is so ugly that no amount of finery can disguise it. Gossip says the sharpest thing about him is his nose.

I laughed when I heard that and, a few months ago, I saw a lampoon in which Charles V was using it to slice a side of beef. I would relish the chance to prove myself in every way the superior king.

Kate, as a Spaniard, is delighted that her cousin has been chosen. She has always favoured a treaty with the country of her birth and greatly dislikes the French. When Wolsey announces his proposed meeting between us and Francis at Picardy, she baulks against it.

"Why should we go? It seems a great deal of expense to waste on a show of ostentation. I'd sooner spend it on war."

Ah, I smile at the glimpse of the sweet warlike girl I once wed; the victor of Flodden field. However, even I can see that combat is not the only way to put down one's enemy.

"Wolsey thinks it politic for us to go. We shall take the whole court and put on the most extravagant demonstration of our nation's wealth and power we can. No servants in stained skirts or out at knee hose will be permitted."

She cocks her head, tempted by the idea of a visit to her dressmaker.

"Will Mary come with us?"

I nod. "Yes. It will be good for her future country to have sight of her. You must ensure her clothes match ours."

"And you will leave your whore behind?"

The sudden wave of warmth I had felt for my queen dwindles. I stand up and drain my wine cup.

"Come, Wolsey," I say. "We are finished here."

While Wolsey bows low to the queen, his scarlet robes spreading like blood across the steps of the dais, I walk away without taking leave of her.

***

When Bessie's lacings can no longer conceal her condition, Wolsey suggests she retire to the country until after the birth. Reluctantly, I let her go.

"We must find her a husband," Wolsey says. "To protect her name and that of any future children you may beget on her."

I look up.

"I shall acknowledge this one," I say. "But yes, for the sake of her reputation, she should perhaps be wed."

I stare dispiritedly into the fire, unsure if my conscience will allow me to lie with her once she is handfast to another. It would be adultery: it does not seem right.

As I am dressed for the coming feast, I recall the glister of Bessie's eye as we made music together. How she always seemed surprised when I bid her put down the lute and let me unlace her gown. She was compliant and willing ... and fertile. How I wish I had wed a woman like her. How I wish I had not coveted my brother's wife. With a fertile bride, I could have filled the royal nursery to overflowing.

I stare unseeing into the looking glass while they tie on my sword, ease my coat over my shoulders, and tie the garter about my knee. Someone hands me my gloves and I am ready.

I have never really become accustomed to how the real Henry seems to disappear beneath my garments. The uncertain man is suddenly replaced by a king; a rich, wise monarch, the greatest England has ever seen.

I peer into the mirror. *Greater than my grandfather?* I straighten up, shake my head, and send up a silent prayer that it should be so.

King Edward IV fathered many children, three sons in all, but it did him little good in the end. My mind darts to my unborn son, to little Mary, and I shudder to think of them ever coming to harm.

As if all is well between us, the queen and I process to the hall hand in hand and take our seats on the dais. She inclines her head to the courtiers. I raise my hand, bidding them rise from their knees, and the festivities begin.

"How are you, Kate?" I ask for want of something more interesting to say. I am disinterested in her reply.

"I am well in body, husband, but not so well in spirit."

"Why is that?"

She turns her eyes upon me, scornful eyes, accusing eyes, and there is a slight curl to her lip.

"I miss my husband and mourn the fact that he prefers the company of lowborn women to the comfort of his royal queen."

"Don't be ridiculous."

She looks away, smiling at someone across the hall as if nothing is amiss. We do this often; play the part of a happily married couple when in fact, beneath the veneer of content, the foundation of our marriage is crumbling.

We are tiptoeing through the ruins and, while I am content to take my chances and jump, she clings on, her nails scraping down the ruined cliff face of our former love.

It makes my eyes water.

"I need a son." I grind the words through a forced smile.

"And how am I to conceive you a son when you no longer visit my bed?"

Her physician has confirmed she is no longer fertile, yet she refuses to accept it. Were there the slightest chance of a child I would go to her nightly and force myself to spend my royal seed in her flaccid womb.

Has she always been so stubborn? How has it come to this? What has become of that fresh girl who first stirred my desire? I see no resemblance to her in the lined, barren bitch beside me.

A fresh burst of music and a troop of dancers skips onto the floor. I applaud with the rest. Beside me, Brandon whoops in appreciation as the participants leap and twist in the air. I want to leave the queen to her sulking and join my companions but, just as I am about to rise, my eye is taken by one of the dancers.

I lean forward for a closer look.

I have not seen this one before. She is fair, plump, and so light on her feet. Her mouth is full wide, and her expression merry. I lean on the table, rest my chin in my hand and follow her progression around the room. Her body epitomises the tune to which she dances. It is one of my own songs. It is as if I wrote it for her; as if I knew that one day she would happen along to dance to it. I cannot tear my eyes from her lilting steps.

It is clear she knows she has my attention, for a blush creeps up to mantle her cheek and, every so often, she glances in my direction then, just as quickly, looks away.

When the music ends, she sinks into a curtsey, her honey-coloured hair falling forward in a silken cloud.

Brandon stands up, clapping loudly and ostentatiously.

"Sit down, Brandon!" Mary growls, tugging furiously at his gown.

The dancing girl turns to acknowledge Charles' applause, so I too rise and lend my hand to his. She turns back to me, her face scarlet, her eyes dancing, and puts up a hand to conceal her delighted giggle. I lean closer to Brandon and, speaking from the side of my mouth, ask, "Who is she?"

He nudges me, his chuckling reply tickling my ear.

"Boleyn's daughter. Mary, I believe. You will remember her mother?"

Boleyn. Oh yes, the mother is Elizabeth, a woman I tarried with once in my youth; an innocent enough evening but ... this is her *daughter*?

During the interval, the fools appear. Wolsey's boy, Patch, got up in silk and velvet, apes his betters while all around him the little ones waddle in his wake, playing at courtiers. The younger members of the court fold in the middle at their antics. Their elders smile, having seen it so often before. Ignoring the gaudy attempts to please me, I scan the room.

In the shadows, the girl, Mary, chatters with a group of Kate's younger ladies. I lift my chin, let her see my interest and, hurriedly, she looks away. I stand up to descend from the dais but, before I can leave, Kate takes hold of my sleeve.

With great courtesy and not a little annoyance, I pause, bowing my head to attend her.

"She is a *child*," she hisses maliciously. "Do you intend to despoil *all* my ladies, one by one?"

Would she prefer I take them all at once?

I snatch my arm away.

"Be silent, woman. Know your place."

For all her blushes, Mary Boleyn is no stranger to courtship. She does not faint or pretend to be shocked when I first invite her to my inner chamber. I have sent all but one servant away, and the shutters are open to the summer night. She looks about the chamber.

"How comfortable," she says. "Much cosier than the queen's chambers."

"It is my private sanctum. Nobody comes here without an invitation from me. It is a place where I can dispense with formality and just be myself; the man rather than the king."

"I came here to be with the king."

She turns and discovers I have moved close behind her. We stand very close, her bosom touching my belly, but she does not shy away.

She looks up at me, placing a hand on my jewelled doublet. "And in what way is the man different from the king we all see ... and love?"

"Oh, I am a simple man at heart. I enjoy peace and quiet, a good book, a glass of wine, a few simple comforts."

She giggles and sweeps a hand at the gilded mirrors, the exquisitely wrought books, the plush velvet hangings, the tapestry of cloth of gold.

"So, I see, Your Majesty."

"You may call me Henry when we are alone, if we are to be ... close friends."

"Henry..."

She tries out the name and it flows nicely from her tongue. Her cheeks stretch into a smile that ends in a tinkling laugh. I reach out and touch her lips with my forefinger, silencing her, and she grows still, pliant.

She is bolder than Bessie, her virginity no doubt lost along the way, but I want her badly. Cupping her face, I turn her head upward and lower mine to hers. I keep my eyes open, and see she closes her own. When our mouths meet, she makes a small sound in the back of her throat, a sound that makes my head spin.

Lying with women who are not my wife serves me nothing, of course. I need legitimate heirs and I know that too many bastards will complicate things. The next time I see Wolsey, I instruct him to arrange a marriage for Mary Boleyn so should she conceive a child, it will not be of my doing.

While I continue to dance and joust my way through life, Wolsey's firm governance of the country gives me the freedom I crave, but even leisure palls in the end. Eventually, I have to turn my attention to more serious matters.

I take out the papers I have written in response to the false and wicked doctrine of Martin Luther. Long into the night, I discuss the matter with Thomas More, whose opinion balances the wilder elements of my argument. I make notes and spend time refining my initial work, incorporating some of More's thoughts. I entitle it ***Defence of the Seven Sacraments*** and, when I am done, I make my bold signature at the foot of the page.

"That will make them think again," I tell the two Thomases when we dine privately one evening.

"I do not understand where such heresy comes from, or why it is allowed to thrive." Wolsey shakes his head as he peels an orange.

"God will prevent them from prospering too far. I am certain of that." More's words are innocent enough, but his remark sets me thinking. God does prevent sinners from prospering. Is He so displeased with me that He denies me that which I most desire?

"May all sinners heed God's teaching," I say by way of filling the silence, while my mind hurtles off down another path. Wolsey and More raise their cups and belatedly I lift mine too, and we drink to the health of the true religion.

<u>June 1519</u>

After a week of summer rain comes a spell of warm weather, and I am preparing to join the hunt. The horses chew at their bits, scraping at the gravel with their hooves. I have just pulled on my gauntlets and picked up the reins and have one foot in the stirrup when a messenger arrives. I lift my chin, watching as he weaves a path through the melee. As he draws near, one of the hounds leaps up and leaves muddy footprints on his hose. He pushes the dog away and makes a deep bow.

"Your Majesty, I bring news from Ingatestone."

My heart leaps.

Snatching the letter, I look furtively at the company before hurrying back into the hall. In the privacy of a side chamber, I break the seal and drink in the words.

Bessie has been delivered of a son, a fat, healthy boy. *My Boy*.

I clutch the letter to my chest, close my eyes and thank God for her safe delivery and for the blessing of a son at last – albeit illegitimate.

The messenger hovers outside the door.

"A pen!" I cry. "Fetch me pen and ink."

I want to shout it to the world, let them all know that I, Henry of England, *am* capable after all of fathering a living boy.

I scrawl a brief, loving letter to Bessie.

We must name him Henry and he will be known as Fitzroi, my sweet love, for I mean to honour my promise to acknowledge and raise him as my heir. I shall visit you both as soon as I can get away.

When I emerge again into the sunshine, all eyes turn enquiringly upon me. I feel I will burst with the longing to tell them. *I have a son!* I have a son! Instead,

I mount up, raise my arm and, with a loud halloo, gallop toward the heath.

I set my horse at a ditch. He leaps high in the air, clearing it easily, and we hurtle on into the wood. I duck beneath branches, splash through the mire, my cloak catching at twigs. My hat blows off and is left far behind, caught in the undergrowth. As hard as I ride, I am aware of hoofbeats behind me.

They likely think I have run mad, and if I cannot speak of this, I think I will! The knowledge that I am now the father of a son is like a giant bubble of joy in my heart.

At last, noticing my mount's distress, I slow him down to a walk, and finally a halt. He stands, head down, belly heaving, and I too am breathless. My cheek stings from the lash of a thorn bush and my eyes water. I grope for my hat, forgetting I lost it, and turn in the saddle just as Brandon rides into the clearing with Blount and Percy at his heels.

"Henry, are you hurt, Sire? I couldn't keep up."

He draws closer, taking in the scene. "Your horse is blown; I will summon another."

As I slide from the saddle, a page trots up, having retrieved my hat. He flicks some debris from the brim and hands it to me with a bow. I put it on, turn and beam at my friends.

"Oh, I have had such news, gentlemen!" I laugh, incredulously. "Such splendid news."

"From Mistress Blount?"

My smile is likely to split my cheeks.

"Yes, from Mistress Blount. She has birthed a boy. I have a son at last."

"Oh, congratulations, Your Majesty!"

They forget themselves and form a ring around me, reaching out to pat my shoulder, wring my hand. They are my good friends and can be trusted not to speak of this openly before the queen.

"I can barely contain this news," I say. "I will ride to meet him as soon as I can."

"An official visit from ... the king? Will that not seem ... odd?"

"No, Brandon. I thought perhaps a private visit is overdue to your house at Westhorpe, whereupon I might slip away with a small guard to Bessie, who resides not too far away."

"Good idea, Sire. One might think you'd been planning such a thing for some time."

Good-naturedly, I punch him, and he pretends great injury. I sling an arm about his shoulder and, laughing, we set off to the clearing where tents have been erected and refreshments laid out.

Henry Fitzroi is four days old before I find the opportunity to call upon them both. A blushing maid shows me into the bedchamber, where Bessie reclines upon pillows. I sit on the bed, pick up a lock of her hair and raise it to my lips. It smells different. She smells different. The seductive scent she uses has been replaced by sour milk and infant vomit.

I sit back.

"Are you well, my dear?"

She smiles and nods.

"I feared for a while I would not survive to see you again, Your Majesty, but ... it passed. Our son awaits you in his crib."

The bed ropes creak as I stand up and move hesitantly toward the cot. I peer at the tightly swaddled infant. He sleeps soundly, his crumpled face almost as pale as the bands that wrap him.

I wave a hand at the waiting nurse.

"I want a closer look," I say. "Wake him up, unbind him. I want to see his legs ... his ..."

I want to be certain he is a male child. I want to see the colour of his hair, hear the strength of his cry, test the grip of his fist.

She glances at Bessie as if she can gainsay my command, and Bessie nods her permission. I watch impatiently as the boy is lifted from his cot and his limbs unwrapped. When the chill air of the chamber strikes his skin, he squeals like a pig, then stretches his legs, clenches his fists and opens his mouth.

A stream of piss arcs through the air, anointing my velvet coat and making the nurse jump back in alarm. Bessie's look of horror dissolves when I emit a bark of laughter and reach out to lift my naked son into my arms.

I nestle him in my elbow, let him clutch my forefinger.

"He is straight of limb and seems a good weight," I remark. "The Princess Mary was much lighter, and my son ... m-my first son, Henry ... was smaller still and lacked the hair this one has."

"I think he will be auburn-haired, like you, Your Majesty."

"I think he has the Tudor temper too," I say, raising my voice above his indignant protest. "And a fine pair of testicles, I see. Nothing lacking in that department."

I wink at her and draw the cover over his body, not wanting him to be chilled. He quiets a little, sucks his fist and snuggles into my chest. Gently, I jiggle him up and down, humming a little tune, keeping my eye upon him until he dozes again.

"Little Henry," I murmur. "Little Henry Fitzroi." *May the Lord God let you thrive.*

While our son slumbers in my arms, I spend an hour chatting with Bessie. She is tired, paler than usual, lacking her customary appeal. Maternity changes women. I do not know why, but I wish it was not so.

"You are comfortable here?" I ask. "You want for nothing?"

She smiles. "I am quite content, Your Majesty, now that our son is here at last. The pregnancy was long and lonely toward the end."

"Well, it is over now. He shall lack nothing. I shall ensure his upbringing is fit for an heir to the throne. I would create him Prince of Wales if I could but ... the queen, you understand, still has not given up hope of bearing a son herself."

It is a false hope. Everyone knows that but Kate.

"Of course." She turns her head toward the window, her smile fading, just a little.

"I will honour him. He shall have titles – a dukedom perhaps, and estates and a thorough education. I shall find the greatest tutors in Christendom. And you yourself will be offered a worthy husband, and I shall heap manors and honours on you both."

"Thank you, Your Majesty," she says dully. "And, once I am wed, you will still ... wish to ... I will still be welcomed at court ... as before?"

I clear my throat, offer the child back to the nurse and watch anxiously as she lays him back into the cot.

"Perhaps not quite as before ... the queen, you see? But you will be honoured, and I shall always be grateful, always here if you need anything."

She frowns, struggling to right herself on the pillow.

"Perhaps I could give you more sons, Henry ..." She reaches out, as if to delay my departure. I take a backward step and look away, tugging the front of my doublet, and wet my lips.

"Perhaps, Bessie; we shall have to wait and see. I will call again, as soon as I may."

I bend over her hand and then back away with a last lingering look at my son, wishing I could carry him with me back to court. Then, with a sigh, I quit the chamber, leave the hall and ride back to Brandon's manor at Westhorpe.

Leaving Bessie to recover in the country, I return to court, eager for the merriment of my friends, the warm sensuous arms of Mary Boleyn. There is nothing motherly about Mary; she is intelligent, witty, and her time at the French court has taught her how to please a king. Rumour has it that while she was in France she was a mistress of King Francis, but if it is true, she must have been very young.

She is fair, and unafraid to air her views, even when they are quite incorrect and do not match with mine. I like her. I enjoy the way I can trip her with my intellect and change her point of view until she becomes so entangled that she argues against her original stance.

When I laugh at her, she does not take offence and sulk but kisses me instead. She is a much-needed respite from Kate's reproachful company. I revel in her long, firm legs, her flat, hard belly and high bosom. She is young – a girl, not a matron, a plaything not a penance. Some fourteen years the queen's junior, she makes me feel as though I have left the old bitch slumbering by the hearth while I creep out to sport with the puppy.

June 1520

Christendom has seen nothing like this. When Wolsey and my Lord Chamberlain lay the plans before me, it looks grand enough, but seeing it like this, well, it is beyond my imaginings.

Not just dukes and earls, marquises and bishops, but musicians, fools, poets and choirboys; and each lord has a vast household of his own in tow. Wolsey's three hundred servants rival my own. Worcester's estimated gathering of four and a half thousand was astounding on paper but now, in reality …

"The whole of England seems to be here," I remark, astonished at the crush of people.

"All those that count, Your Majesty … and their servants."

I am gratified to see not just the old guard but the younger set too; my friends, ousted from my service a few years ago, greet me cordially. Carew, Compton and Bryan's zest for the venture is as great as my own.

"A fine sight, Your Majesty!" Brandon calls as he pushes through the crowd toward me. "And all in their best finery. This should show the French king just who he is dealing with."

"Indeed, it will. Where is my sister?"

"I left her with the queen. They talk too much of fripperies for me. Their main concerns seem to be whether the French ladies' gowns will outshine theirs, whether they will be more graceful on the dance floor, blah, blah, blah."

"Ha! As if our women need worry on that score."

I do not mention the recurring dream I have in which Francis eclipses me. In my dream, he is taller, stronger, and more handsome. It makes me shudder to think of it. I turn the conversation back to Mary.

"It must be strange for her to return to the country of which she was once queen."

"She is more worried about leaving the children."

"Ah yes, of course."

Mary and Brandon have three children; two girls and a son: Henry, named in my honour. I misremember the names of the girls.

"And Mary is fully recovered now? I know she's been ailing."

He nods. "Yes, thank the Lord. When she is ill, she never lets me leave her side … not that I want to." He recovers hastily, remembering he is speaking of my sister. "Judging from the conversation between our wives this morning, they are determined to put the French ladies into the shade."

"That will be easily done. I have no worries on that score."

Kate might be plain and staid, but her women will make up for that. I scratch my beard which, since I have remained unshaven since July, is satisfyingly bushy. The French king and I swore not to shave until we met, and I am more concerned than I should be that his beard will be fuller, or more finely laundered than mine.

When I suggested the beard-growing contest, I had expected it to make us kings stand out from other men, but it seems we have set quite a fashion. Almost every gentleman in my court has followed my lead and now, an Englishman has come to be judged by the length of his beard.

Kate dislikes it. She claims it makes me look like a bear, but Mary Boleyn likes the way it tickles when we kiss.

There is no sign of Mary this morning. She has talked of little else in the lead up to the event, seething with anticipation for the voyage. After spending so long at the French court, she has good friends there. I have watched her closely these past weeks for signs she might be carrying my child … although I am now spared the need of acknowledging it so. I know from past kings that multiple royal bastards are often more trouble than benefit to a monarch.

In February, Mary was married to William Carey, a distant cousin of mine; a privy councillor, a dull but well-intentioned fellow. I wonder how she compares his lovemaking with mine. It must be strange to jump from the bed of a king into that of an ordinary man. I have qualms about married women and, somehow, bedding a woman who has pledged herself to another before God seems to increase the sin.

Every morning, after I have lain with her, I spend an hour with my confessor, wiping clean my slate. But I am not finished with Mary yet and will continue to bed her for as long as she pleases me. Carey is well aware that she is my mistress and is content enough. He will concentrate on the manors and favours he has gained by sharing his wife. It is an honour for any man when his wife enjoys royal favour. Besides, now she is safely wed, any child she spawns will not be laid at my door. I must live with my discomfort about sleeping with another man's wife.

Little Henry Fitzroi is costing me a fortune. He must have manors and a household to suit his status: clothes, household goods, and plate for every occasion. Wolsey urges me, for the sake of my purse, to acknowledge no further bastard sons.

We ride slowly from the town toward the village of tents where we shall be housed. These are no ordinary tents; my own lodging, built part of brick, part of canvas, mimics a castle, and nearby is a slightly smaller pavilion for the queen. They are all fashioned from cloth of gold and, together with the clothing of our courtiers, the temporary town glistens in the sunshine.

It is a splendid sight. I look up at the pennants snapping gaily in the brisk wind, listen to the babble of excited voices, inhale the scent of roasting meat and baking dainties that issues from the cookhouse and am well content. Wolsey will be well rewarded for staging such an event that will be talked of for years.

The main pavilion perfectly mimics a house, even down to the brickwork and, when we dismount and enter, we discover that the splendour does not stop at the door. Inside, the lodging is as impressive as any English palace. There are rich hangings, luxurious furniture, carpets and curtains and plate.

"Lavish." Brandon pushes back his cap, the pearl adornments gleaming in the light of the torches. "It is hard to conceive we are in a tent. Is the queen housed in the same way?"

"She is, and Mary too, as Queen Dowager of France. You, though, are to attend me."

"Of course, I am honoured to do so, Sire."

He reaches out to test the quality of the hangings, his approval eloquent on his face. He turns to the cardinal.

"You've done us proud, Your Grace," he says, "and I am informed there are to be jousts, pageants? Is there a schedule?"

"Be patient, Brandon," I say, quirking my brow at the cardinal. "We've only just arrived. There is time for all that. First, I must meet with King Francis and seal our agreement. Do not forget that this is all in honour of the Treaty of Universal Peace. It is not meant to be just a lark."

"No, Your Majesty, I had not forgotten that. I do have some concerns about the wind though. I hope the tents don't blow down or, more importantly, it doesn't interfere with the joust."

No man, not even I, can handle a lance in a high wind. I shrug and test the comfort of the biggest chair, putting my feet on a velvet-covered stool.

"It won't matter if it does, the wind can't last forever and the schedule can be rearranged. We have foot-fighting, wrestling, and archery lined up too and the weather will not impede any of that. And later, there will be the feasting and dancing. It will give you a chance to sample the charms of the French ladies."

I watch his response from the corner of my eye, but he recognises my trap to test his loyalty to my sister. To my gratification, he deftly avoids falling into it.

"I have no interest in other women," he declares. "I have eyes only for my wife."

"So you should."

I lower my brows in silent warning before my mind drifts off to Mary Boleyn, housed with the rest of the queen's household in a nearby pavilion. It will prove difficult to have her conveyed secretly to my chamber; there are more spies here than at home. But a king has his needs. I could openly visit the queen, but … I dismiss the idea. I am here to enjoy myself.

For years I have heard tales of Francis; even before he was king people spoke of his youthful good looks, his noble bearing, but the man I meet is no grander than I. He is clad in the finest silks and fur, and his legs, encased in silken hose, are strong, but his calf is not as well formed as mine. His hair is black and thick and his demeanour haughty and very … French. But the main characteristic, one might say, *the most prominent* thing about him, is his nose. It is long and ugly, and quite spoils his looks. I had heard rumours that his nose was large, but this … this is *larger* than large. I am thankful for my fine wrought Tudor features.

The French queen is small and plain, with ill posture, yet her smile when she greets us is sweet, and it seems the people adore her. I watch the three queens together: Claude, sweet and eager to please; my sister, Mary, bored, her eye darting about the hall in search of Brandon; and Kate, at her arrogant best, is perfectly poised, perfectly polite and perfectly dull.

Bryan is already making eyes at the French ladies, who giggle and whisper behind their hands. They keep to their posts, close to the queens should their services be needed, but later, when the dancing begins, I notice the subtle differences between the French women and English.

Despite the grandeur of their gowns, the dazzling jewels at neck and finger, our ladies are somehow less ... alluring. The French women reveal more hair, their gowns are cut differently, their sleeves are fuller, their throats somehow more on show. And I see my sister was right to worry that they would outshine our English ladies on the dance floor.

"What is it about them, Brandon?" I ask when he takes a seat at my side. "I cannot determine the difference."

He narrows his eyes and watches them dance for a while with an appreciative smile.

"They are younger than our queen's women, Sire. That could be why they seem lighter on their feet, or perhaps it is merely the demands of this particular dance."

I watch more closely. Our women are now joining in, weaving in and out, touching hands, bending knees. Mary Boleyn is laughing; I watch her, my knowledge of what lies beneath the sumptuous green silk gown making me warm. As I watch, she takes the hand of one of Queen Claude's ladies and they hurry onto the floor, where the other girl gives instruction of the steps. After a few seconds, Mary has mastered it and relaxes, laughing often, and loudly.

She is having the time of her life. She is sunny, her joy making the torches seem to shine less brightly in her presence. Beside her, the French woman is darker but, when she smiles, as she seldom does, it is no less dazzling.

Kate remains in her seat, but she sends her women onto the floor in her place. I watch her, tapping her fingers on her knee in time to the music, her head nodding with the steps. It is not so long since Kate and I never sat out a dance. I recall leaping and skipping around her while all eyes were upon us. I remember her grace, her flirtatious smile, the way she would blush scarlet each time I whispered a courtly salutation in her ear.

I sigh for those days.

It seems unfair. I am yet in the full flush of my youth, yet Kate has grown old. It is Kate who has failed.

I dance with my sister first, and when Queen Claude begs to be excused, I lead out one or two of her women. It is plain to me that Mary expects to be invited to step onto the floor with me and, for a moment, I consider disappointing her, just to see what she does.

As I bow over a French lady's hand and thank her for the dance, I feel Mary watching, waiting. Eventually, I give in. I stroll toward her, stand waiting while she sinks to her knees, and then I take her hand and help her rise.

The court watches, the crowd melts away, and Mary and I are alone on the floor. As we move to the music, our hands kissing, our steps in perfect unison, we are both aware of the speculation of the audience. They know she is my mistress. Brandon knows, Mary knows, Bryan knows; but if Kate knows, she gives no sign.

Mary's fingers are light and rather hot in my palm, her desire latent in her downcast eyes. When the music dwindles and the dance is done, I kiss her knuckles. *Later,* I promise silently before I turn away.

Dorset waits at my seat with a cup of refreshment. I take it from him and turn back toward the floor to see that Francis has taken my place and Mary's fingers now rest in his palm. Whatever he is whispering to her makes her blush, and I recall the rumours that when she returned to England she came fresh from the French king's bed.

A wave of jealousy washes over me. *How dare he?* Is it not bad enough that he debauched her in the first place? Does he now seek to steal her back from me? I grind my teeth, my former amity with the French king replaced by simmering resentment.

In the days that follow, the high wind continues to delay the joust. We lounge in the glazed gallery, playing and listening to music, discussing the weather, flirting and feasting. The ladies of the two courts form friendships, while the gentlemen vie with one another as to who is the most handsome, who the strongest, who the greater sportsman. Most often I am granted the victor but sometimes Francis is hailed the better man.

Day by day, my antipathy increases.

I am sickened by his constant flattery, his incessant conversation, his politeness. Etiquette has always been high on my list of priorities, but the French king makes me feel like breaking every rule. I want to kick over my chair, spit on the floor and fart loudly at table. Never before have I been so obliged to button my lip and keep my thoughts to myself. In the end, I confide in Brandon.

No one else would understand.

"I want to punch him, Brandon," I say, "and hard too, right where it will hurt the most."

"I'd not advise that," Brandon laughs, "but I know what you mean. These French fellows are overly polite, and so smooth. It always raises my hackles. It is as if they want to show us up as uncouth blaggards."

"I will have to watch myself at the lists tomorrow. It won't do to go in too hard, even though I long to teach him a lesson or two."

I attend so many dinners that I grow sick of the sight of food, and am filled with ennui. I need exercise. So much leisure is making me testy. I long for the feel of a good horse beneath me, a gallop across a fine heath with the brisk English wind in my hair. I have had enough of these fancy French ways.

When we dine that evening, I listen to Francis eulogising the skill of his cooks. Of course, they have the best food, the best chefs, the best wine, the best women, the best scholars, the best horses, the best artists, the best …

"And the best whores?"

I have spoken aloud. An appalled silence falls upon the company. Someone, Brandon I think, clears his throat and leans forward to refill my cup. Further along the table, I hear Kate loudly congratulating Queen Claude on the beauty of her daughters, the lustiness of her two-year-old son, Francis.

Yes, the King of France has a fine fat son too, an heir to follow after him, while I have … just a girl, and a *bastard* boy.

I know I should beg pardon, pretend to be drunk or something, but pride will not let me. Again, Brandon leans forward to my rescue.

"England has the best wrestlers in Christendom," he announces, and a murmur of agreement breaks out among our courtiers.

Francis sneers.

"I am considered the best wrestler in the whole of France."

"Not today, you're not. Not while I am here."

I glare at him. He puts down his cup and looks down the considerable length of his nose.

"Perhaps we must put that to the test; at your convenience, of course."

He looks pointedly at my wine cup, which I have regularly emptied throughout the evening. He thinks I am drunk, incapable. I will never be so drunk as to be unable to best him in any contest.

I give a shout of laughter.

"A challenge, by God! Then I am ready, sir, whenever you are."

I push back my chair, unfasten my cloak and let it fall.

"Oh, Henry, not here, not now …" Kate's plaintive protest dwindles away. The courtiers leap to their feet, clear a space for the match and begin placing bets on who will win. I regard my opponent, my lip curled, while Francis remains in his seat, his gaze darting uncertainly about the hall. I remain standing, waiting for him to rise.

Reluctantly, he stands, shrugs his shoulders and rolls his eyes as if he is humouring me. He acts as though I am the aggressor when, in truth, he has been goading me from the moment I set foot upon this soil.

I wrench open my doublet, seed pearls scattering to the floor. Fumbling with the buckle, I fling off my sword belt, regretting I cannot just run him through and be done with all this.

Slowly, Francis does the same. Stripped down to our linen, we face one another and begin to circle, eyes fixed, arms at the ready. Somewhere in the hall a woman begins to weep.

He launches at me. I am in his arms; his fragrance fills my head, his muscles taut beneath my hands. Time seems to slow, and an inexorable episode of gripping, gouging, sweating, and grunting follows as he tries to best me. It takes all my strength to hold him fast while he pushes and gasps, grabs for my face, pressing so hard I fear my neck will snap.

I push back harder, managing to force his arm back so far I think it will dislocate. He is stronger than I imagined. Our shirts are sweat drenched, our faces slick. I grab a handful of hair and tangle it around my fingers, forcing back his head, grateful for my own shorn hair. He grabs my beard, making my eyes water until, with a roar, I throw him off and we circle again.

He is not as easily vanquished as I thought. For the first time, I consider what it will mean to lose. I cannot allow him victory. I pounce first, like a cat at a rat, and we fall in a tangle of limbs. Pain shoots through my hip as we hit the ground but I bite back the agony. I wrap my legs about his torso and grab his arms, attempting to tie him in a knot. He breaks free, chops my shin with the blade of his hand, loosening my hold, and rolls away. Gritting my teeth against the pain, I stand again. Face to face, we lean forward, arms akimbo, and circle one another with murder in our hearts.

He shall not best me. I will not allow it. He tosses his head, shaking sweat from his hair, and scowls as he beckons me forward, inviting me to take him if I can. I leap, and we grapple for mastery. There is an interminable moment of straining before I begin to unbalance. I scramble to take a firmer hold, stumble backward and feel myself falling.

As if in slow motion, like a felled oak I drop and, as I go, I see the triumph emblazoned on his face. The crowd stops breathing. Nobody speaks. There is a moment's peace. I close my eyes and drown in humiliation as self-disgust seeps into every fibre of my being. As the French court breaks into roars of appreciation at my defeat, the English stand silent.

Bleeding for me.

"What were you thinking, Henry? Is this any way to cement the peace treaty? And suppose you'd been seriously injured?"

In the privacy of my quarters, Kate's recrimination goes on and on. I want to scream at her to go away. I want to thrust her from the room so I might be alone with my shame. But, after a few moments, I realise the soft dabbing of the cloth in her hand is soothing to my injuries. If only she would not nag so, if only she would not always tell me I am wrong.

"Damn Francis, and his country too." I speak thickly through a swollen lip, spit blood into a bowl. She straightens up, tosses the cloth away and looks at me as if she is my nurse and I an errand boy.

"Where is the wisdom in this, Henry? As if you haven't wasted money enough on this display of – of – this competition about who is the best man, the better king. You are like schoolboys. You are both ridiculous."

I slump back in my seat, wishing she would either be quiet or put her arms around me. I have not felt so bruised since I fell from a high wall as a child. I remember the great fuss my attendants made that day, how my mother came running and bathed my cuts herself. Afterwards, she sat me on her lap and kissed my damp hair. I need my mother's arms now. I need tenderness, yet all I have is Kate and her infernal criticism.

The next occasion I meet Francis, I hide my humiliation beneath a show of etiquette, and he does his best to disguise his scorn. Dislike sits like a vulture on my shoulder, taunting me to offer another challenge, but I ignore it.

At the chapel, before cardinals, bishops, legates, dukes and princes, we mount the platform with our respective queens and kneel at the oratory to hear Mass. Singing fills the chapel, high pure voices that pierce one's soul and bring tears to the eye.

Cardinal de Bourbon carries the gospel forward and presents it to Francis, who waves it away, indicating that I, as his honoured guest, should kiss it first. I shake my head, hold my hands up and graciously refuse, insisting that the honour should go to the French king.

In truth, I would like to snatch up the book and beat Francis about the head with it. The cardinal hesitates, uncertain how to navigate through this royal battle of wills. The onlookers shuffle and whisper at the spectacle we are making of ourselves but, in the end, with a flourish of false gratitude, Francis concedes and kisses the book, and the formalities resume.

I came to France full of hope, full of confidence. I intended to prove to the world that an English king outshines all others. I wanted them to see I was not the snivelling, hole in the wall king my father was. But I have failed, as I have failed in so much else, and the knowledge eats at my soul. The whole affair has been a huge waste of money. I cannot wait to leave.

I do not rouse myself even when a great fire dragon launches into the sky. Taken by surprise, the villagers fall to their knees, thinking the end of the world has come. But the nobles of my party call out in amazement, exclaiming at the wizardry of such a display. My own smile is wooden, my heart full of anger and irritation that even Francis' scientists are proving more advanced than mine.

An interminable meal with the French follows. Francis waves his arms to embellish his droning conversation while I nod and focus my anger on my meal. I eat too quickly and the food lodges in my chest; I try but fail to wash it down with wine. All afternoon, I am troubled with a pain beneath my ribs and I belch often and loudly.

"I'll warrant he poisoned me," I complain afterward when Kate doses me with physic.

"You have poisoned yourself, my husband, with your gluttony and bad temper," she replies, not in the least concerned I may be dying.

There is a further day of combat displays to endure yet; bonfires and feasts to mark the vigil of St John. Then, a meal with Queen Claude, which promises to be a sweeter appointment than dining with her husband. Then, only then, can I quit this place and return home to England, where things are done properly. I cannot wait to leave.

I should not have signed the treaty. I should have known an English and Frenchman can never see eye to eye; we are chalk and cheese, silk and sack cloth, as different as the moon is from the sun.

Of course, when the time comes to leave, I have to pretend great regret. I kiss Queen Claude, then grit my teeth and kiss Francis, the words of camaraderie sticking in my throat. Then we part, he and his royal entourage riding toward Paris whilst I lead mine on the road to Calais.

England is calling me, but first I have a meeting with Charles of Spain. I have no wish to confer with the Spanish, although their derogatory opinion of Francis might salve my hurt. We may well be in agreement, but I am tired of deceit. I long to throw off the taste of false diplomacy and, with just a few friends, ride out on the hunt, gallop off my disappointment and return late to the hunting lodge for a hearthside meal in good company.

A song begins in my mind; a few lyrics I penned some time ago.

> *Pastime with good company*
> *I love and shall unto I die.*

I compose a few more lines in my head. Once I am safely back in England, I must remember to write them down, perhaps set them to music.

Outside Calais, in the town of Gravelines, Charles awaits us. We greet cordially and he listens with interest to my carefully edited retelling of my meeting with Francis. Thankfully, this encounter with Charles will be short, no longer than a few days, and there will be no wrestling.

He is wary of my treaty with Francis and tries to persuade me not to marry little Mary to the dauphin but to enter into negotiations for a Spanish marriage. Kate lifts her chin, alert as she waits for my reply. I know she would prefer an agreement with her home country. When I shake my head and apologise that it will not be possible, she looks away.

Wolsey is determined this treaty with France shall last. It is imperative that I remain neutral and maintain the friendship of both countries. England's wellbeing depends on it. But, when Charles enthuses on the idea of England entering a league with Spain against France, although I am non-committal, I am sorely tempted.

It is so pleasing to be back in England. August stretches ahead with the promise of good hunting and good company. When I wake on the first morning after our return, I am reinvigorated.

"Just one night in England has erased all my megrims," I tell my gentlemen as they help me dress. "I intend to stay in the saddle all day."

Someone groans in mock horror and I laugh aloud. There are few men who can keep up with me on the hunt, when I am apt to wear out five horses and still want more.

When I am laced and buttoned and smell as good as a king's mistress, I snatch up my hat and head for the stable. As I pass through the great hall, I catch sight of Thomas Wolsey. He holds up a hand in greeting.

"Ah, Your Majesty, I was hoping to speak to you …"

"I am late, Thomas! Can it wait?"

He comes closer, lowering his voice.

"It is a matter of some urgency, Your Majesty. You will recall our conversation regarding the Duke of Buck …."

I frown. I do indeed remember it. Edward Stafford has been an irritant since he interfered in our dalliance with his sister all those years ago. Since then, I have kept him at bay as much as possible, putting him in charge of the marcher lands between us and Wales. He failed to keep the peace, and I had words with him about it. A few weeks ago, Wolsey informed me that Buckingham has been 'loose of tongue', and I instructed an investigation into the matter.

I glance at the early morning sun streaming through the open door, hearing the hounds barking in their impatience to be off. My friends are waiting, and I am in dire need of a day on the chase. I put a hand on the cardinal's shoulder.

"Come to me later, Thomas. We will sup together this evening."

He bows his head and, before he straightens to wish me a successful day, I am out the door, my foot in the stirrup.

April 1521

"News from Rome, Your Majesty."
I put down my pen and hold out my hand for the letter, my eyes quickly scanning its content.

"Ah, this is most pleasing."

It is a wet day and, while I peruse my letters with my secretary, Brandon and Compton play chess at the hearth.

"You will recall the piece I wrote in defence of the church a year or two back? The pope has seen fit to honour me with a new title he is calling *Defender of the Faith*."

"An honour indeed." Brandon gets up and comes to peruse the message. "I think it calls for a celebration, Your Majesty."

"If you had your way, Brandon, everything would call for a celebration but yes, on this occasion I agree."

"The queen will be delighted. Shall I inform Her Majesty, or would you prefer to do it yourself, Sire?"

Wolsey never ceases his attempts to bring me and Kate together. I have not seen her for some weeks. She keeps to her apartments and we meet only on official business now. I see little Mary, of course; she is no longer a baby but a fine, red-haired child, strong of feature ... and will.

I sometimes miss the infant I carried with me into council meetings, miss the way she would sit on my lap and play with my jewels, tug my beard, and make the company smile.

If only she were a boy.

Fitzroi is growing up too, toddling about, demanding this and that, and throwing his toys about when he is crossed.

If only he was not base born.

"I've had news back from our informer, Sire. It seems the duke has again been, erm ... indiscreet in his opinions. Your Majesty, I really think we should speak to him."

"To the tower, for questioning?"

I have wanted this for months. Edward Stafford taunts me; it is like knowing there is a wasp in the chamber but not being certain of its exact location. I have been waiting for him to creep close enough for me to swat him.

"What has he said?"

Brandon and Compton are on the alert now; they make no pretence of not listening.

"It seems he was recently heard boasting of – of his lineage and stated that ... should Your Majesty fail ... be unable ... should the queen not produce a male heir, he would be happy to take your place ... should the ..."

He trails off. It is treason to speak of my death or what might happen after, but Wolsey will not be punished for repeating information.

I lean back in my seat and throw down my pen, scattering ink across the board. Wolsey looks down at his ink-spattered hand, takes out his kerchief and wipes it off.

"Ha! I think we have him."

"There is nothing in writing, Your Majesty."

"No matter. He is skulking at Thornbury, isn't he? Have him brought in, without delay."

Stafford arrives in London unsuspecting of our discovery of his crimes against us. When he is taken under guard to the tower, he shouts of innocence, that his arrest is part of a prolonged conspiracy against his Plantagenet blood but, no matter how loud he protests, there are none who can help him now.

He collapses readily under questioning and, early one April morning, he goes to his death. When they bring me news of it, I feel no regret. I breathe a sigh of relief. He had the gall not only to wish for my death but also to imagine himself taking the place of my infant heir. He also sought the prophecy of Nicholas Hopkins, a monk who claims the ability to see the future.

A white-faced Wolsey tells me that the duke was also involved in a plot against him, and everybody knows that to scheme against the cardinal is to scheme against me.

At his trial, a jury of seventeen peers found Stafford guilty; not one man stood against the accusation, not even the Duke of Norfolk who loved him well.

"They say Norfolk wept as he read out the sentence ..."

Brandon sits in the window, a cup of wine on his knee.

"Norfolk did his duty, that is the main thing. He is a good man. He works in my interest whether it pleases him to do so or not. The Staffords have always been traitorous. Buckingham's father and grandfather went the same way. They crave the power we hold. They are destined to reach for it despite knowing very well the penalty for treason."

"Yes." He peers into the darkness of the garden and I sense the regret in his silence.

"His attainder enriches us greatly. I can now add Thornbury to my own list of properties and disperse the rest among my favourites."

I expect him to perk up at this, but he merely nods and sups his wine.

What would he do in my place?

I must consider the vulnerability of my heirs. If I were to die from a blow in the tiltyard, or a fall while out hunting, or a summer plague, what would become of them? They are so very little, so defenceless. There are few I can trust to put the cause of my heirs before their own. I must weed out those who might work against them.

When I look around the court and watch the nobles whose blood places them above other men, I begin to understand the insecurities my father suffered. I wholly trust none of them. Not one.

1525

I yawn, rueing the quantity of wine I drank last evening. Where once I could drink as deeply as a pot man and not mind it the next morning, lately I find it best to limit myself to a few cups only. *Why have I woken so early, after such a night?*

I lie back on my pillows and try to judge the sort of day that lies ahead. Watery sunshine spills between the chinks in the shutters, but whether the day is wet or dry I cannot yet tell. My attendants still slumber, and I am loath to wake them. I am so rarely alone; I welcome time to think.

Today, little Mary is to make her departure for Ludlow, far away on the border with Wales, where she is to head her own household. Kate is grieving before the child has even left. She came to me a week since, weeping and wailing that the girl is still too young. *Ludlow is too damp*.

The castle holds bad memories for Kate, who resided there with my brother, her first husband. Her *only* husband if I had my way.

I have not yet given up hope of finding a way to free myself of Kate so that I might marry again, but Wolsey, who has a deep love for the queen, fumbles and farts around the matter. He is afraid of Spain, afraid of the pope – his *master*. Is he not *my* man? Should *I* not be his *only* master?

"If I were free," I tell him, "I could marry again, I could beget a dozen sons, there is still time." He cannot see that I have not yet reached my prime. *I* am capable of begetting a son; it is Kate who is barren.

Early last year, Mary Carey, that was Boleyn, gave birth to my daughter. Thankfully, since she is now wed, there is no need to claim this one as my own. I have no doubt that she is mine though, and it is likely that everyone else knows too.

The girl looks like a Tudor, with a fine head of red hair and the sort of expression that tells everyone she knows her own mind. She has a look of my daughter Mary about her and I have little doubt the court gossips will take note of that.

While Mary, my pearl, leaves us for her own household, Fitzroi is now approaching six years old and will be established closer to court. The arrangements to honour him with the titles of Richmond and Somerset are underway and, afterwards, he will be educated as befits a prince. I am determined that, should God deny me a legitimate son, Fitzroi will be there, ready to step into the breach.

It will please Bessie and help cheer her in her loveless marriage to Gilbert Tailboys. I had intended to continue 'visiting' Bessie once she was wed but, as I have long since realised, it is a sin to bed another man's wife. Bessie is different now. She is no longer the lithe young girl that first drew me; she is still fair but fleshier and motherly and, in her maturity, no longer tempts me as once she did.

It is the same with Mary Carey. Marriage seemed the perfect solution but once Carey had taken her for his bride, my regard for her dwindled. The birth of the child, leaving her as plump as a Christmas goose, has only terminated a relationship that was already over. I looked elsewhere.

I am not a lewd man. I no longer frequent bawdy houses as I did once or twice in my youth. I admire pure, intelligent women. Ladies who, after I have bedded them, can engage me in conversation, hold their own in a debate, and make me laugh.

I like to pen songs in their honour, praising their beauty, their wit, their poise. It would not be seemly to do that to the wife of another man. So, at present, I am lonely.

I need a female companion, someone who will soothe my soul and help me forget the recent unpleasantness with Charles V, who has rudely broken his betrothal with Mary to marry Isabel of Portugal. The Spanish king is a jade. I will have no further dealings with him.

Kate, of course, who craves above anything a union with Mary and Spain, is heartbroken. I have been toying with the idea of another alliance with Francis but, since he has been imprisoned in Madrid after a battle in Pavia, that will have to wait.

"Perhaps his son, Henri, would be a better match for the princess," Wolsey suggests, and I brighten up a little. I still have a great dislike of Francis. I will never forget the way he bested me and made me look a fool. The son would be far preferable. If Mary is one day Queen of France and her children rule after her, it would be a way of achieving my dream of one day ruling over France, as my forefathers did.

Rolling over, I embrace my bolster pillow and close my eyes, concentrating my mind on other matters closer to home.

There is a woman whose acquaintance I recently made; a woman I would like to know better. I first noticed her a year or so ago when she arrived home from France to be betrothed to the son of the Earl of Ormond. The union is no love match but will serve to settle some dispute over the lands and titles. It seems a shame to waste such a pretty piece on an Irishman.

"Who is she, Brandon? She has a way with her."

He peers across the hall.

"She's fresh back from France."

"Do you think Francis has tasted her?"

I purse my lips, outraged at the possibility, but he shakes his head.

"There is no gossip. It is her sister that Francis dallied with ... among others."

I laugh, uncertainly.

"Forgive me: her sister?"

"Mary Carey," he says pointedly, and I feel myself grow hot.

"Oh, yes, Mary. I had forgotten that rumour."

Indeed, when I chose to take Mary to my bed, I dismissed the suggestion that she was ever a mistress of Francis as tittle-tattle. I hoped to God it was not true; there is no telling where Francis has been.

"They are sisters then: Mary and ..."

"Anne. Yes. Mary is older by a year or two. There is also a brother."

"Yes, I know George. It is only the younger of the girls with whom I am unfamiliar. Anne."

I try out her name and find it rolls neatly off the tongue, no need to find suitable shortenings. There is something familiar about her face, something that warms me. It is as if we have met before, perhaps in life or maybe in some half-forgotten dream.

I resolve to find a way to speak to her and the next time she is among the company, I make sure I bump into her.

When she realises with whom she has so clumsily collided, she begs my pardon and sinks to her knees. I look down at her fine cap, the hint of dark hair that peeks from beneath her veil. Raven black, by the look of it, a change from all the blondes and redheads.

"Get up, get up," I say and offer her my hand. When she takes it, her touch sends a vibration through my body, as if I have touched nettles, but far pleasanter than that.

"Your Majesty." She glances away, dark lashes half-mooned on her cheek.

"Mistress Boleyn, is it not? I don't think we've had the ..."

"You know my sister, Sire. My sister, Mary ..."

She risks much in interrupting her monarch, but I choose not to mind. After all, I have waited a long time for this meeting. A longer wait than I would usually endure.

Since our first meeting, we have become better acquainted, but I do not wish to rush things. Occasionally, I lead her onto the dance floor, where her step is light and elegant. She dances somehow differently to the other ladies. Her step is lilting, soft as a feather, but I know she is not soft, particularly her tongue, and I sometimes surprise myself at the liberties I allow her to take.

1527

It is a particularly trying morning at council; they are discussing the recent treaty with France. Everyone is speaking at once, arguing and hurling insults. I should shout them down, but I cannot be bothered.

I long to escape.

I have arranged for Anne to join me on the hunt. I have no particular thirst for the deer, but my fruitless pursuit of the lady is robbing me of sleep, of concentration, of peace of mind. I wonder what she is doing now. Attending to her toilette, perhaps. I imagine her body being sponged and oiled, her hair brushed to a high sheen. I know her hair better now than before for I have seen her without her coif ...

We are in the garden when she accidentally dislodges her hood. I pick it up, but before offering it back to her, I reach out for a glossy, dark strand that is not as dark as I first thought. She stands stock still beneath my touch and does not move when I untie her coif and bare her head.

"Beautiful," I breathe, running my hands over her hair, barely touching yet making her hair crackle and rise magically to meet my palm. It is not raven black nor merely brunette but a mixture of shades: enlivened with highlights of red and gold.

"George says it looks *rusty*," she says, in her dismissive way.

"No, he is wrong. Shall I have him thrown in the tower, just to please you?"

When she laughs, she throws back her head, and my greedy eyes fasten on her throat, so long and white. I want to kiss her Adam's apple, nibble the softness between neck and shoulder, inhale her fragrance, and tangle my fingers in her hair.

Instead, I chastely kiss her knuckles, clutching her hand close to my heart.

"Mistress Anne, would you ..."

She withdraws her hand and places it on my chest as if it is a defensive rampart keeping me from her.

"Sire, please ... do not ask it of me. I can never be your mistress."

I blink in surprise. "It – it is usually considered an honour."

"I know, I know it is, Your Majesty, a great honour, and I love you above all others, but I – I have a dream of marriage, children, a house in the country. I would marry for love."

"Surely you are not still pining for *Percy*."

The name issues in a sneer, as if he is some peddling player and not the son of the most powerful magnate in the north. She shakes her head with a pained expression.

"No, no. I am quite recovered from that but … I still harbour hopes of a loving marriage."

Silence falls. *I wonder if he had her.* Shortly after she arrived from France, her name was linked with Northumberland's son but Wolsey, who had other plans for Anne, put paid to that as I later put paid to his plans for her marriage with Ormonde.

I watch her pluck a leaf from the hedge and begin to shred it with her nails. I had not expected a refusal, even from her. Nobody ever denies me. I frown, clearing my throat to explain it further.

"As my official mistress, you'd be the highest lady at court, bar the queen."

"I'd be a whore, Your Majesty. A royal whore but a whore nevertheless."

She spins away, repeating the word over and over as if to offend me, but surely … not even Anne would go so far as to purposely goad me.

I am never sure what she will say or do next; perhaps that unpredictability is her charm. I follow her along the path.

"Not a whore: a royal companion, a helpmeet. Think of the good you could do, the people you could help, the scholars you could encourage …"

She halts, turning back.

"What do you mean? Scholars?"

She thinks I know nothing of her Lutheran leanings but there is little that escapes me in this court. My spies are everywhere, and I have discovered there are already many who resent Anne for her radical ideas.

"I know you are curious about the new learning. You could meet some of the best scholars in Europe face to face. Tindale is here in England now, you know."

She frowns, shaking her head.

"But that would be against the law … your law!"

"I know." I snatch up her hand again. "I'd be prepared to turn a blind eye if you were to become my mistress."

I should not have to stoop so low. In truth, I do not mean it. It is a snare to discover her price, to test if she can be bought at all.

I kiss her fingers, one by one, my ardour increasing each time my lips meet her flesh.

"The queen would never let that happen," she says, and she is right. Kate detests the new learning; *Heresy*, she calls it, and for once we are in agreement.

"The queen," I lie softly, "does as she is told."

Anne's laughter is high and mocking.

"She'd never meekly accept an official mistress endorsing the new religion, Your Majesty. Every one of her ladies that has ended up in your bed has ceased to enjoy the queen's favour. I have no doubt that no sooner had you bedded me than I'd find myself sent back to Hever in disgrace."

"But Anne …"

I follow her along the path, back toward the hall. At the door, we encounter Brandon and my sister, arm in arm, about to take the air. They halt and bow their heads.

"Your Majesty. A lovely day," Brandon says, while I kiss my sister.

"You know this lady, Anne Boleyn?" I open my arm to draw her forward and, while Brandon bows stiffly over her hand, Mary sniffs and looks the other way.

"Yes," she says, as if I am introducing her to a snake. "I have had that pleasure. A fine day."

She changes the subject, smiling blithely, but not before I note her sneer of dislike. She cuts Anne rudely from the conversation and I feel a stab of irritation, disappointed by her hostility.

Mary, better than anyone, should know that we do not always love where we should. When she lowered herself to marry one of my servants without my permission, I forgave her for it, and welcomed them both back to my court, showering them with undeserved rewards. She could at least afford me the same consideration.

Brandon covers the awkwardness by describing an encounter with Wolsey earlier.

"One of his servants had dropped a sheaf of papers. They were scattered everywhere, blowing about the draughty corridor when I came upon him. Wolsey's curses were most, erm …unChristian. He cuffed the fellow about the head and chastened him in most unholy terms."

We laugh, my hand on Brandon's shoulder, my other clutching Anne's, which is tucked beneath my arm.

"I must away," I say. "I will see you both at the tilt later, Brandon. Mary …" I take her hand, anoint it and, on rising, note the narrowed speculation in her eyes.

They bid a stiff good day to Anne and I escort her into the hall.

"You see, Your Majesty. Your sister hates me. She'd sooner you bedded a dockside whore than me."

"No – no. You are quite wrong. Mary is always wary of those she does not yet know. You will be friends, by and by."

"I doubt that very much," she laughs, with a hint of bitterness. We continue on our way while Anne continues to number the reasons why she cannot possibly accept my offer. I dismiss her argument just as I dismiss the disapproval of my best friends that is burning a hole in the back of my doublet.

"You were rude! I was thoroughly ashamed." I bite back my anger, letting them see my hurt when I meet them later. Brandon looks down, shaking his head.

"I don't trust her, Your Majesty. She has some agenda. She could be a spy. She is not long back from France, and I've heard she has been most disrespectful of the queen."

"Not in my presence." I pull my coat tight about my chest.

"Of course, not in your presence, Henry," Mary butts in. I knew she would be unable to keep quiet for long. "She is pert and rude, and totally ignores etiquette. Since you've been … showing an interest …

she has overstepped the mark more than once. And it hasn't gone unnoticed."

"What do you mean?"

"I mean, I've seen Kate watching her. How do you think she feels to have another of your indiscretions thrust beneath her nose? Honestly, Henry, it's like she is the madam of your own private brothel."

"There has been no indiscretion," I say, offended, as if I have no intention of any such thing.

"Maybe not yet. It is only a matter of time."

She sits back in her chair, folds her arms and looks the other way. If she was not my sister …

"I like her. She makes me laugh. She appreciates me …"

"She flatters you, inflates your already ridiculous ego."

I scowl at her, glancing at Brandon who is studiously examining some flaw on his sleeve. If he were a true friend, he would support me … in anything, even against his wife.

"There is no need to worry. I offered her the chance of becoming my official mistress but she refused me. I felt like she'd slapped me in the face."

They are both staring at me now; Mary's mouth is open, her face flaccid with surprise.

"She refused you?"

I cannot meet her eye.

"Yes. And it hurt. I don't think I've been rejected before … not by a woman."

In the silence that follows, a wasp buzzes about Mary's head and she tries to swat it away. She has always been afraid of flying things that sting and bite. Brandon, ever the gallant, strikes it away and Mary settles down again, clasping her hands tightly in her lap.

"Well, I trust her even less now. She does all she can to put herself in your way, yet refuses a perfectly honourable position as your mistress. You must ask yourself, Henry, *what is it that she wants?*"

Later, after the candles have been extinguished, Mary's suspicion keeps me from sleep. I toss and turn, thinking of Anne, wanting Anne, wondering what I shall do if she continues to refuse me.

For many months, we play an extravagant game of catch and chase, and she is as difficult to land as an eel. Starved of a woman in my bed, my temper grows short and, in search of release, I exhaust myself by riding hard all day or playing tennis until my opponent drops. I get no ease and wake in the morning to find my sheets damp.

The younger members of court, aware of where my favour lies, gather about Anne like bees at the hive. If not the most beautiful woman at court, she is the wittiest, the most elegant, the most vibrant. Beside her, the queen seems like some fat, dwarfish crone, as she is well aware. Kate berates me at every chance.

I am in my private chamber, going through some private letters, making notes in the margin of my books, and trying not to think of Anne. When Kate is announced, I push aside my irritation and put down my pen.

"Kate," I say, rising from my chair and going to greet her as if I am pleased. "Would you like a glass of wine?"

She nods acquiescence. A good sign. A sign she has not come to berate me.

"I have finished your new shirts, my husband," she says, ushering her woman to place them on a chair.

"Thank you, I am pleased."

She seats herself stiffly and I take a seat opposite. In the firelight, the lines that flank her nose and mouth are graven deep, her eyes shadowed and, beneath her chin, the flesh sags like the loose skin on one of my hounds.

Age is cruel, yet she is just six years my senior. How can she be old when I am yet in my prime? The flesh on my neck is still taut, my torso well muscled, and my calf as hard as rock. I may not be as young as I was, but I am vigorous, virile! The blood still surges through me, and I have stamina enough to put most of the court gentlemen to shame. How has Kate become so grey ... so elderly? Shall I, in six years' time, be the same?

Have I so short a time left?

My stomach turns at the thought. *I have no son.* I must have a son.

"I wanted to speak to you, my husband, on a matter close to both our hearts."

I give her my full attention. "Yes? What matter is this?"

She clasps her hands tightly in her lap, her rings winking in the candlelight.

"I know you love me, Henry. I know you would never want to hurt me, or our little Mary, but ..." She lowers her eyes and wets her lips. I have the sudden memory of a dimple that used to appear and disappear on her cheek. I used to go out of my way to make her smile just so I could see it. I have not seen sight of that dimple for years.

Is it so long since she smiled?

"No, I'd never want to hurt you." I put my head on one side and smile winningly, but still her face is sorrowful. She shakes her head, as if with regret.

"But you have, my husband. You hurt me every day, every moment we are not together. I am your wedded wife yet … we spend no time together. You prefer to be with … with that *woman*."

She spits the last word, leaving me in no doubt as to whom she refers. I look away. She has come here to nag after all. She hopes to persuade me to give up my Anne. She wants me to walk away from the chance of being loved, as a man.

"She is not my mistress. I will swear that on the Bible."

Our eyes clash. Hers are a cold steel grey, as venomous as twin poison-tipped daggers. I turn my face away again.

"If she is not then she soon will be."

"You underestimate her. Unfortunately, she is virtuous and has refused me."

She gasps, as if in pain.

"But you have tried."

I jump up, knocking over a cup of wine. Liquid pools and runs across my papers. I say a foul word that makes Kate flinch.

"I am a man! I have needs. What comfort is there for me in your bed these days, Madam? With your weeping and praying and constant recrimination. Do you think I wanted it to be like this? Do you think I ever imagined you would fail me? Do you think I would have wed you if I had known you were barren?"

A tear escapes her eye and trickles slowly to her chin, but it is her only sign of having heard me. She sits like a statue; grief and betrayal encapsulated in stone. Only her chin trembles, very slightly.

"We have a daughter. A fine daughter, who can rule England after you."

"A girl! And a sickly one at that."

"She is not sickly. The physician says she will soon see the onset of her menses. Then she will be a woman, and able to marry and bear you a grandson."

I turn my back, walk to the window and look out across the darkening garden. *Why are the shutters not drawn?* I see shady figures going about their business. Boys running errands, lovers creeping off on a secret tryst. A dog, escaped from his lady's clutches, yaps at the base of a bush.

"Come back, Troy, come back!"

I turn again. Kate has not moved, her hands are still clasped, her chin is still high, and her face is still wet. I knead my scalp, tousling my hair.

"England has never known stability under a woman's rule."

She shifts in her seat.

"It seems to me that England has known considerable unrest beneath the rule of a man also."

Touché.

"Kate; you know I must have a son. It was the first lesson I was taught as Prince of Wales."

"My mother ruled Castile and Aragon without the aid of a man for many years, and my grandmother Isabella proved she …"

"That was Spain; this is England. We do things differently here, as you should have learned by now. I need a son, a *legitimate* son."

"And how do you propose to get one, my husband, when you shun my bed? Only I can give you a legitimate child."

I turn and look on her in astonishment. She is either ignorant or in denial.

"Kate. You are too old. Your body is … is …"

"Is what, Henry? Disgusting? If that is so it is only because of the many, many legitimate children I have borne you."

I put my face close to hers; we are almost nose to nose. Her features blur. My words blast in her face.

"Dead children; dead sons are no good to me!"

I leave her there, sobbing in my private chamber. I can stand no more of it. I blunder through the palace as if the hounds of hell are in pursuit. Barging servants and courtiers from my path, I holler for Wolsey. As I reach a junction in the corridor, a figure steps from the shadow.

"Your Majesty, the cardinal is at Hampton."

"Then send for him. Now."

It is coming on to dark. I find myself in the stable yard. It has been raining, the cobbles are slick, and the aroma of horses and dogs lies like a thick blanket in the air. There is something soothing about the simplicity here.

I look around at the midden where some chickens scratch, at the trough from which the horses drink. I move slowly forward, pausing at one of the boxes. A pale mare lifts its head, hay poking from its lips, big teeth crunching. I reach out and touch her face, travel up to the place between her ears where every horse likes to be scratched.

"Hello, girl," I say, and she blows through her nose, scattering hay and chaff. "Do you know this doublet you've just ruined cost a king's ransom?"

She nods her head, blinks her eye, and nuzzles my chest, further soiling my clothes.

A stable boy enters carrying a bucket. He halts when he sees me, stands as still as a statue, his face flushed scarlet. With wide eyes, he edges slowly away before dropping his bucket and running, calling for his master. I sigh. He will tell everyone he meets that I am here. I am king of all I survey yet can find no peace, no place where I can just *be*.

Soon, they will come running, start fussing that I might catch a chill, try to persuade me back to my chambers, and I have no doubt my fool will be making jokes about 'the King of the Stable Yard' for weeks to come. I resume my conversation with the horse. She blinks, her great black eyes like agate jewels.

"Do you know how fortunate you are? With your oats and hay, resting here in the warm until the morning. You have all you need, and nobody to tell you what you must do. Oh, the tragedy of a king envying a dumb beast."

She jerks her head, as if she dislikes being called dumb, but then I realise she has heard footsteps. Someone is approaching. I turn wearily to find Brandon leaning against the stable wall.

He smiles noncommittally.

"They said I'd find you here. Is everything all right, Your Majesty?"

Sighing, I run a reluctant hand down the nose of my silent equine friend and accompany Brandon back to the hall. I do not speak until we reach my chambers.

"I've sent for the cardinal, but he probably won't be here for hours."

"Has something happened? Some news from abroad?"

"What has happened, Brandon, my friend, is that I've decided to stop dithering and take action. I have no choice but to rid myself of the queen."

Incredulity furrows his brow.

"Be rid of ... how can you rid yourself of the queen?"

I shrug and take the cup he offers.

"Annulment? She is barren, I need a son, so she must be encouraged to step down, take the veil so I might remarry and get an heir while there is still time. Wolsey must think of a way to persuade her. There must be a way."

While Wolsey attempts to keep the matter of the annulment secret, I turn my full attention to wooing Anne Boleyn. I befriend her friends, I write sonnets praising her looks, songs lauding the turn of her ankle, the subtle beauty of her face. I shower her with gifts: priceless gems, horses, falcons, fancy sleeves and gloves.

While the older, staider members of our court stay close to Kate, I am swallowed up by the young gayer set. Even after spending a long day on the heath, we dance and feast late into the night. We are tireless, grabbing at merriment as if there is a limited time in which to taste it.

Yet it is not all cheer. Anne has enemies. Those who champion Kate whisper against Anne, spreading wicked lies and slander against her family. As the rumours fly, I draw her friends closer. Richmond becomes a palace of two courts.

Although Wolsey has hopes of a French alliance should Kate ever grant me a separation, I have begun to harbour other hopes. A year or so ago I made Anne's father a viscount, and now I plan to raise him further. The improvement of her family's status will make her worthier of becoming my next queen. I misremember when the idea of marriage to Anne began to seem like a possibility, but once I have conceived the idea, I cannot keep it to myself.

As soon as the plans to increase her family's status are under way, I tell her of it.

"Don't speak of it yet though, sweetheart. Until the arrangements have been finalised, we must keep the news to ourselves."

"An earl?" She raises her eyebrows. "He will be pleased, and so will George."

"And you, Anne, does it please you?"

"You know, Sire, anything that pleases my king pleases me also."

I search her face for irony but detect nothing. I had expected her to be more delighted but … I have noticed she takes most of my excessive gestures as her due.

"And will you make me happy, Anne? Will you accept my proposal and become my queen, my wife?"

I must have an answer. Since the pope decreed that my sister Margaret's marriage to Archibald Douglas was invalid because of a pre-contract, my hopes that Rome will agree to an annulment are growing. Once I am free of Kate, I will have Anne – all I require is her consent to my proposal of marriage.

She moves away, lowering her head.

"I have been giving it a lot of thought."

I take another step, closing the gap between us. "And?"

My heart beats sickeningly; my head feels light with the anxiety of anticipating her answer. If she refuses, I don't know … Oh, she is wringing my heart as if it were a lemon.

"I will tell you this evening, Mr Impatient!"

She pokes the end of my nose, as if I am an infant. Then she spins away laughing in her usual fashion, her mouth wide, her head back, revealing that lovely neck. Disappointment hits me like a low belly blow. I wanted her answer now, and my responding laugh is half-hearted, resentful.

I could force her to tell me. I could give her an ultimatum – *tell me now or I will seek a wife elsewhere* but … knowing Anne, she would take me at my word.

May – September 1528

May is the month of love. I should be lazing with my sweetheart near a slow-moving, country stream, enjoying her gentle caresses, her whispered words of love. Instead, we are apart.

She has retired to Hever while I am held captive in a three-day secret meeting with the cardinal and the Archbishop of Canterbury. They ply me with questions regarding my so-called marriage to my brother's wife. Keeping a tight hold of my patience, I quote Leviticus again.

"If a man shall take his brother's wife, it is an unclean thing: he has uncovered his brother's nakedness. They shall be childless."

Wolsey fumbles through his papers as though in search of some illusive text that will thwart my argument. He allows Warham to parry my quote, and his riposte is a passage from the Book of Deuteronomy, which states the opposite:

"When brothers live together, and one of them dies without children, the wife of the deceased shall not marry to another: but his brother shall take her and raise up seed for his brother."

My jaw aches with furious tension. I glare at the archbishop.

"But Leviticus has precedence, as well you know."

I turn to Wolsey, silently entreating his support. He holds up his hands in despair.

"I understand your dilemma, Your Majesty, but there is also the matter of the dispensation, granted by Pope Alexander ..."

"Everyone knows Pope Alexander was Ferdinand's puppet; he granted anything they asked of him."

Both men look shocked.

"Your Majesty, the queen swears her marriage to Arthur was never consummated and she came to you as pure as the day she was born."

I think back to the ripe, pretty girl I courted after my brother's death. I remember the hot kisses, the fumbled caresses, the small liberties she allowed before our wedding day. She was no virgin. I was just too green to realise then.

I shift in my seat, trying not to speak through my teeth.

"She would swear our daughter was really a boy if she thought it would serve her cause. Her one wish is to hold me fast in this marriage, and I am determined to be free of her. She tricked me into wedlock and, if justice is to be served, I will be granted an annulment."

I look from man to man while they avert their eyes and mutter under their breath. We all look toward the door when it opens to admit Wolsey's servant.

"Ah, Thomas," he says with no little relief as he holds out his hands for the message. "Forgive me, Sire." He breaks the seal and draws in breath, a hand to his mouth.

"What is it?" I lean forward, elbows on the table.

He clears his throat.

"It seems ... and I can't quite believe it ... but it says the Imperial army has invaded Rome, sacked the city and forced Pope Alexander and all his cardinals to flee."

"Flee? Where to?"

He squints at the page, scanning the words with his forefinger.

"To Castello St Angelo, Your Majesty. May God protect them."

"By Christ's bones! Is everything against this annulment?"

I stand up, pacing furiously up and down the floor from window to hearth while the two men cringe beneath my passion. In the end, when I have calmed, Wolsey summons the courage to speak first.

"It will give us more time to prepare our case, Your Majesty. There are several matters that should be addressed before we send to Rome, for, we must consider ... the queen is not after all barren. Or she wasn't. She has borne you a healthy daughter, and a son who lived for quite a few ..."

"And what use is a dead son and a useless girl? Do you not see, it is our punishment? I have lived unwittingly in mortal sin with Catherine for years. She was my brother's wife. In sleeping with her I uncovered my brother's nakedness and therefore WE ARE CHILDLESS!"

"But, Your Majesty … the princess Mary …"

Blood sings in my ears and I feel my heart will burst from my chest. I would like to knock Wolsey into next week, yet … I must have his good will. I cannot achieve this without him. I slump into a chair and put my hands to my head. I could weep.

I *do* weep. And when I am done, I take a deep shuddering breath, reload my argument and try a different approach.

"It is a matter of conscience. If ever you loved me, Wolsey," I say at last, "sort it: use any means necessary. Free me from this woman or I will be forced to find a man who can."

Soon, the whole court is talking of the King's Great Matter. Whispers of our impending separation flow swiftly along the palace corridors, out into the street, to the taverns, the cloisters, the whorehouses. It will only be a matter of time before the queen hears of it and comes to reproach me.

I have been advised that for the good of my reputation, I should send Anne back to Hever and continue to live with the queen. Reluctantly, I agree to do so.

I do not think I can bear it. I watch from my window as she rides away. She seems happy enough to go as she waves from her horse, chatting with her escort as if they are there to amuse rather than to guard her life.

Belatedly, she sees me watching and her smile vanishes. She puts both hands to her heart, pulls a sorrowful face and blows a forlorn kiss in my direction. I make no attempt to catch it. I have no heart for games. Then, she kicks her horse and off she goes, leaving me behind … with Kate.

The queen outdoes herself trying to please me. She produces yet another pile of newly stitched shirts, orders my favourite wafers and drizzles on the honey herself, just as she knows I like it. Although I hide it from everyone, I do find some reluctant pleasure in the domesticity of the next few weeks. Despite loving Anne as I do, it is quieter without her.

It is not always easy to be Anne's would-be lover; she is hard to please, sometimes obtuse in her opinion, as changeable as the weather. It is like chasing a will o' the wisp. At least with Kate, I know where I stand. She cannot help being so dull.

She chatters on, about trivial matters concerning her women, or the new horse in the stable that bites and kicks any who come within reach.

"We should send it as a gift to King Francis," I quip before my mind wanders to the fresh green hunting land around Hever.

What does Anne do when she is in the country? I wonder. Does she not die of boredom? All her friends are here. Her brother George is here, her sister Mary is married and has her own concerns. Wyatt is … where is Tom Wyatt? I have not seen him at court for weeks. Perhaps, if the weather stays fine, I will ride to Hever for a few days; the hunting there is almost as good as here at Windsor.

Kate taps three times on my knee, pulling my attention back to her.

"I was saying, my husband, that we must ride to Ludlow soon and visit Mary. We promised her she would see us often."

"Can't she come here? I do have a country to run."

"You can run the country just as well from Ludlow as from here, my husband, and the change of scenery will do us both good."

She drones on, and my mind wanders again. I think of the looks that kindle in Anne's eyes, the way she tilts her head when she is about to say something designed to shock me. The way she wets her lips with her red pointed tongue, her long mobile throat, her high, merry laughter.

As the hours stretch on, I grow drowsy, bored by the conversation and roasted by Kate's infernal fire. After all the years she has been in England, she still detests cold, damp weather and, even on a day like this, she keeps what she calls a 'cheery hearth.' Beau is sleeping blissfully near the fire.

I need some air. I stand up.

"I must walk the dogs, Kate, before they puddle on your rug."

"Oh." Her face falls. "Don't be long then, Henry. I was just going to tell you about Lady …"

I walk out, Cut and Ball bounding after me, leaving Beau to his slumbers. Kate's voice fades as I increase my pace. Outside, I breathe in fresh air. The spaniels bound ahead, tails like banners, barking at the gardener who leaps out of their way. He pulls off his cap and bows as I pass by. As I stride briskly on, he resumes his task.

"Cut," I shout, "Ball!"

The spaniels have dashed ahead, out of sight. If they run off too far ... I increase my pace, calling to them again, and they appear suddenly at the far end of the gardens.

Cut barks as if urging me to run, and I break into a jog. Ball comes bounding to meet me, drops a stick at my feet. I pick it up and throw it with all my strength into the rough grass beyond the garden gates. Both dogs tear after it, barking, their ears and tails flapping, and I run after them, calling to them to return the stick.

They ignore my commands. I should have named them Wolsey and Wareham, I think, or perhaps Cardinal and Archbishop.

Last month, they ran off and, despite my calls, did not return. They were gone all night, I barely slept a wink and, in the morning, issued a vast sum of money against their return. They plague me so much I sometimes wonder why I bothered.

Managing to snatch the end of the stick that protrudes from Ball's mouth, I tug at it. He pulls back while Cut barks, his wagging tail belying the ferocity of his protest.

For a while, it is just me and the dogs, a man and his companions, a boy and his best friends. I forget that I have been living in sin for more than twenty years. I forget that God continues to deny me a son. I forget the dark, forbidden fruit that is Anne Boleyn. I am Henry, who has stolen from the schoolroom to play in the park and soon, my little sister Mary will come and tease me. Indoors, my mother is alive, she is reading a book of King Arthur, and my father is ... my father is ... shouting at me: "Every king needs a male heir!"

The sun shrinks behind a cloud, the stick snaps in two, and I step suddenly backwards into something foul and slippery. I lift my foot and find my good boots are smeared with shit.

"Argh, you horrible beasts!"

Ball leaps around me while I attempt to wipe my boot clean on the grass. I continue the walk, but my former optimism has been tainted. The dogs fan out, sniffing out rabbit trails, but the sun is weaker now and we should return to the palace before they send out a party of searchers.

There are papers to sign, Mass to be heard, and there is always business to attend to. I sigh and call to the dogs, which emerge reluctantly from the nearby copse.

"Come on!" I call. "Dinner time."

The promise of food brings them haring back, barking at my heels, snatching at each other's noses all the way home.

The moment I set foot inside the hall I am besieged by messages. "The queen wishes to ..."

"Yes, yes, I am sure she does."

I take off my hat, pass it to a waiting page and call for a boy to take control of the spaniels.

"Ahh, there you are, Your Majesty."

Wolsey appears at the other end of the hall, holding up a fistful of documents, and bears down upon me. My brief respite is over, and duty swallows me whole.

As we enter my privy chamber, Wolsey is at my shoulder, his face red and hopeful.

"I trust Your Majesty enjoyed his day with the queen …"

I raise a hand, silencing him.

"I believe, Wolsey, that the queen imagines I will join her in her bedchamber later on. I tell you now, that will not happen."

He flushes, as scarlet as his robes. He shakes his head, his jowls trembling, opens and closes his mouth like a fish, but no sound escapes him. I lean closer.

"I will do as you ask and pretend great reluctance at my enforced separation from the queen but only for the sake of appearances, for the sake of the pope. I will never sin with her again."

He nods, places his papers on the table and arranges them in piles. For appearances' sake, I recently wrote to the Vatican expressing great regret of the steps I am forced to take.

Where it not for the great sin between us, there is no woman on this earth I'd rather take as my wedded wife than Catalina but … my conscience simply will not allow it. We cannot continue to sin against Heaven.

When I read them aloud the words sound hollow to me, but both Kate and the pope have apparently swallowed them. She now anticipates my imminent return to her bed, but she will wait for me until the cows come home. I have no need or want for any woman other than Anne, and the moment I can, I will resume courtship of her, not the queen.

But, in June, word comes from Hever that plunges me to the very edge of despair. Anne, my precious, darling Anne has been taken ill with the sweating sickness. There is no time to send for a scribe, so I write to her hastily, in my own hand.

There came to me suddenly in the night the most afflicting news that could have arrived. The first, to hear of the sickness of my mistress, whom I esteem more than all the world, and whose health I desire as I do my own, so that I would gladly bear half your illness to make you well. The second, from the fear that I have of being still longer harassed by my enemy. Absence, much longer, who has hitherto given me all possible uneasiness, and as far as I can judge is determined to spite me more because I pray God to rid me of this troublesome tormentor. The third, because the physician in whom I have most confidence, is absent at the very time when he might do me the greatest pleasure; for I should hope, by him and his means, to obtain one of my chief joys on earth — that is the care of my mistress — yet for want of him I send you my second, and hope that he will soon make you well. I shall then love him more than ever. I beseech you to be guided by his advice in your illness. In so doing I hope soon to see you again, which will be to me a greater comfort than all the precious jewels in the world.
Written by that secretary, who is, and for ever will be, your loyal and most assured Servant,

I sign it *Henry* and ply the messenger with gifts and comforts for her, bidding him return with great speed with news of how my lady fares.

Long into the night, I pace the floor, snapping at my friends, cursing my servants. The spaniels watch me from beneath the table, their eyes sad and anxious. For days, I am out of sorts, off my food. I can think of nothing but losing Anne. If she dies before I have known the pleasure of her bed, I will spend the rest of my days comparing every other woman with her unparalleled charm.

My gentlemen keep their distance, their voices low, creeping about as if I am a dying man. It is not me who is dying; it is my love, my salvation, my hope.

For three days, I hear nothing. My mind fills the silence with grotesque imaginings. *She cannot die, she cannot die, she must not die.*

On the fourth day, the messenger returns, and is ushered into my presence still dusty from the road.

I stand up and go to greet him.

"Well? What news? Speak man!"

He twists his cap.

"The Lady Anne lives, Your Majesty. They despaired of her for a while but she – she fought strongly and is recovering. Her brother-in-law, however, William Carey, was not so fortunate, and word arrived yesterday of his passing."

Relief surges through me.

"Thank God. Oh, thank God."

I bury my face in my palms and give way to tears. Silence falls upon the company. The messenger shuffles his feet and clears his throat. I take a deep breath and smile through my tears at the gathered gentlemen. I have never in my life been so relieved.

Brandon moves closer to whisper into my ear. I look about, alert, remorseful at my neglect.

"Of course, we are very moved by the loss of William Carey. He was a good friend to us, indeed. We shall miss him."

As soon as the threat of contagion has passed, I ride off to Hever, where they tell me Anne is taking the air in the garden. Neglecting the proper civilities to my hosts, I run past them, through the hall and out again through another door.

Anne sits looking out across the meadow. I take one step and then pause, drinking in the wonderful fact of her being there – of breathing when I had feared ...

Despite the heat of the afternoon, she is wrapped in furs. I breathe in her presence and, as if sensing me, she turns, her thin pale face opening like a crushed flower.

"Henry!" She holds out her hand and, obediently, I hurry to her side and cover her fingers in kisses.

"Oh, Anne," I breathe. "I thought I was going to lose you. If you had died I would never …"

"I know, my dear Lord." Her eyes are shining with tears. "I never realised until I was at the door of death just how much you mean to me. It is vital that we be together, Henry …"

I put my arms around her, so hungry for her that, when I cover her mouth with mine, she squeals, deep in her throat. When we pause for breath, I am smiling, happier than I have ever been.

"Do you mean … you consent to be my mistress?"

Her face drops and she looks away, a frown darkening her beauty as she shakes her head.

"I didn't mean that, Sire. I meant that it is vital the divorce happens soon, for I shall die if I cannot be wholly yours."

"It will be soon," I swear recklessly. "I will make it so. Cardinal Campeggio is on his way to England and I will place such a strong case before him that he will be unable to refuse."

In September, after Anne's brief return to our palace at Richmond, I send her home again to Hever while the Legatine Court wrangles over the validity of my union with Kate.

Campeggio has taken months to reach us but finally arrives in October. Once the court is in session, I plead with them to free the queen and I from our sinful bonds.

"I have been advised by diverse great clerks that our marriage is directly against God's law and precept. If it be adjudged by the law of God that she, Catherine, is my lawful wife, there is nothing that could be more pleasant or acceptable in my life. Were I to marry again, if it were not for the sin of our union, there is no other woman I would choose above her."

Kate, seated a short distance away, snorts audibly and rolls her eyes. The greybeards shuffle their feet, cross their legs, and examine every aspect of the hall apart from me, their king. I fear I have failed to convince them, but they do not dare contradict my words.

Wolsey will speak in my support. He owes everything to me. The son of a grocer, risen to the most powerful magnate in the land, my gratitude financing his lavish lifestyle and palaces that rival my own.

I could bring him down, if I so chose.

I glare at him and his jowls droop, his hands fumble with the array of papers before him. He clears his throat but not enough to remove the croak of anxiety from his voice when he speaks.

"Perhaps … forgive me, Your Majesty …" he bows his head in Kate's direction, "the queen could retire … to a nunnery …"

His futile words trickle away to nothing; even he knows his effort is miserable. It has been suggested before, to no avail.

Gripping the arms of her chair, Kate leans forward, knuckles white, her mouth tight and bitter.

"God has never called me to a nunnery. I am the King's true and legitimate wife."

She stands, the legates stumbling to do the same, but I remain in my seat. When she throws herself suddenly onto her knees before me, I draw back into my chair as if fearing she means to bite me, dreading what words she will speak.

"Sir, I beseech you for all the loves that hath been between us, and for the love of God, let me have justice and right, take of me some pity and compassion, for I am a poor woman and a stranger born out of your dominion, I have here no assured friend, and much less indifferent counsel: I flee to you as to the head of justice within this realm. Alas! Sir, wherein have I offended you, or what occasion of displeasure have I designed against your will and pleasure? Intending (as I perceive) to put me from you, I take God and all the world to witness, that I have been to you a true and humble wife, ever conformable to your will and pleasure, that never said or did anything to the contrary thereof, being always well pleased and contented with all things wherein ye had any delight or dalliance, whether it were in little or much, I never grudged in word or countenance, or showed a visage or spark of discontentation. I loved all those whom ye loved only for your sake, whether I had cause or no; and whether they were my friends or my enemies. These twenty years I have been your true wife or more, and by me ye have had divers children, although it hath pleased God to call them out of this world, which hath been no default in me."

Christ, will nobody stop her?

The moment she draws breath, I urge her up with a jerk of my hand, but she shakes her head, forestalling my words. She clings to my clothes and rolls her eyes, the teardrops balanced on her lashes falling like rain. As she speaks through her tears in a voice made ugly by grief, it is as though a statue of Paris has woken and fired an arrow into my heel.

"And when ye had me at the first, I take God to be my judge, I was a true maid without touch of man; and whether it be true or no, I put it to your conscience. If there be any just cause by the law that ye can allege against me, either of dishonesty or any other impediment to banish and put me from you, I am well content to depart, to my great shame and dishonor; and if there be none, then here I most lowly beseech you let me remain in my former estate, and received justice at your princely hand. The king your father was in the time of his reign of such estimation through the world for his excellent wisdom, that he was accounted and called of all men the second Solomon; and my father Ferdinand, King of Spain, who was esteemed to be one of the wittiest princes that reigned in Spain many years before, were both wise and excellent kings in wisdom and princely behaviour. It is not therefore to be doubted, but that they were elected and gathered as wise counsellors about them as to their high discretions was thought meet. Also, as me seemeth there was in those days as wise, as well-learned men, and men of good judgement as be present in both realms, who thought then the marriage between you and me good and lawful. Therefore it is a wonder to me what new inventions are now invented against me, that never

intended but honesty. And cause me to stand to the order and judgment of this new court, wherein ye may do me much wrong, if ye intend any cruelty; for ye may condemn me for lack of sufficient answer, having no indifferent counsel, but such as be assigned me, with whose wisdom and learning I am not acquainted. Ye must consider that they cannot be indifferent counsellors for my part which be your subjects, and taken out of your own council before, wherein they be made privy, and dare not, for your displeasure, disobey your will and intent, being once made privy thereto. Therefore, I most humbly require you, in the way of charity, and for the love of God, who is the just judge, to spare the extremity of this new court, until I may be advertised what way and order my friends in Spain will advise me to take. And if ye will not extend to me so much indifferent favour, your pleasure then be fulfilled, and to God I commit my case!"

On and on she goes.

I am trapped.

There is not a sound in the hall. For a long moment, we stare at one another. I look at her pale, flaccid features, her faded eyes, her slack cheeks and find no vestige of the golden princess I once loved. Involuntarily, my lip curls. I open my mouth to disabuse her, but she forestalls me …

"How can you do this to me, my *husband*?" she says. "How can you put aside your lawfully wedded wife, the mother of your legitimate children, your daughter, Mary? Mark my words, God will punish you."

Her words cut like a curse. Internally, I shy away, but I do not allow my gaze to falter. I match her disgust with hate and deplore the day she came here.

She clambers to her feet and, with her head high, turns and descends the dais. I hold my breath as she takes the arm of Master Griffith and processes from the hall.

Belatedly recovering from the sting of her words, I exhale loudly and leap to my feet.

"You cannot just leave. The matter is not resolved …"

She does not deign to answer. I signal frantically for the court crier to summon her back.

"Catherine, Queen of England, come into the court!"

A moment later, he repeats, "Catherine, Queen of England, come into the court!"

Time and time again, they call her back, her name echoing about the hall, but there is no response. The legates and I stare at each other, each of us stunned by her outburst, and wonder what on God's earth we are to do next.

***

Months pass and we make no progress. My desire to be with Anne is overwhelming. Her fury and frustration is as great as mine.

We walk in the garden at Hever, but it is no tranquil stroll, our hearts and minds entangled by the hopelessness of our plight. Her face crystallises into rage; she clings to my sleeve and speaks with a clenched jaw.

"What are we to do, Henry? Why won't she just accept you no longer want her, and go into a nunnery?"

She scowls at me, as if it is my fault, as if I have not tried to move Heaven and Earth. I shrug my shoulders.

"Wolsey swears he is doing everything in his power …"

"Do you really still believe he is on our side? Can you not see he doesn't serve you; he serves the pope? Rome is his real master. He is afraid of me, and terrified that he will lose his position should I ever become queen."

"No, no, you are wrong. Wolsey loves me and seeks to please me. He has always been more statesman than churchman. He is a politician. If he cannot think of a way out of it, then I don't know who can."

I flop defeated onto a seat and she sits beside me, digging the toe of her slipper despondently into the golden gravel.

"I – I have a book I would like to show you but … it is a forbidden text. You might be angry with me."

She looks up at me through her lashes, pouting like a girl. How could I ever be angry with her?

"A forbidden text? How did you come by that?"

She waves her hand, dismissing my query.

"Oh, never mind about that. It is William Tyndale's *The Obedience of the Christian Man and How Christian Rulers ought to Govern*."

She slides her hand beneath my elbow, snuggling against my arm. I frown, piqued that she should break my laws to read such things.

"You think I require instruction on how to rule? Who is Tyndale to dictate to his betters? He is a low-born knave, wholly unworthy to school his superiors."

As the matter sinks in, my irritation increases. I am tempted to throw off her arm and walk away, leave her there in the garden and ride off back to court without telling her the real reason for my visit.

"No, no, Henry. Of course you don't need instruction but, listen please; there are some passages that might be of use to us. You could add them to your argument ... it might speed up the process."

"What passages?"

I am reluctant to utilise the heretical writings of Tyndale to further our cause but ... we are desperate. It will not hurt to listen to Anne. I do not have to act on her advice.

"I will show you the text later, when my parents have retired for the night. The passage I am interested in says something along the lines of ..." She sits up straighter, links her fingers in her lap and recites a sentence like a schoolgirl remembering a lesson.

"Tyndale believes in the supremacy of scripture over any authority, including what he calls the false authority of the pope, and the supremacy of King. To Tyndale, God is the highest authority and God appointed kings, thus making them the highest authority in the land. He says a king is the judge overall and over him there is no other judge – not even the pope."

I look at her, so pure, so fair, spouting heresy but, as I absorb the meaning behind her words ... I begin to listen.

"This book is in your possession?"

Her dark eyes slide away; a flush of guilt creeps up her neck.

"Yes, Sire. I didn't know what it was at first. I just ... stumbled upon it but, once I began to read, I found I couldn't stop. You should read it too, Henry. It will make you see things anew. There is much to be said for ... some of the new teaching. Tyndale is ... really quite remarkable."

I am discomforted. It is not so long since I wrote in defence of Rome. I am proud of my title *Defender of the Faith* yet ... what has Rome done for me, other than turn its back in my hour of need?

I take Anne's hand and find it is thin and cold. I can feel her pulse, fluttering like the wings of a startled wren. I clear my throat.

"Very well, I will read it. It sounds to me like a book that perhaps all kings should read."

She smiles, her sallow features brightening into sunshine.

"Come," she says. "Let us continue our walk; the breeze is chilly. The last time I was at court I had the strangest encounter."

"Who with? Not a suitor, I hope."

Her laugh startles a small flock of sparrows and sends them flying up in a whirring of wings.

"No, no. It was with Master Cromwell; you know, Wolsey's man?"

"Oh yes, the quiet man. I know him."

"He might be quiet, Henry, but I found him very wise. He has some rather startling ideas himself ..."

"Indeed?"

We wander along the golden paths between the profusion of summer blooms and as I listen to her chatter, I experience a rare moment of exquisite perfection, such as one rarely enjoys.

But such happiness is always fleeting. On my return to court the next day, problems are heaped upon me again.

I brood through the council meetings and escape as soon as I can. Simmering resentment spoils my meals and corrupts my pleasures. I miss Anne. She should be here. The court is insipid without her.

"Where is Brandon?" I demand, forgetting that he and Mary are spending a month at their estates. I ask for Thomas More, my chancellor, my mentor, my erstwhile friend, but he is not here either. He sneaks away from court whenever he can. He loves Kate and dislikes Anne and abhors my attempts to free myself from the queen.

The courtiers who are left are mostly newcomers; they are young men, out to get what they can, they are not my real friends. I am learning that lasting friends are difficult to hold; they slither like eels between my fingers.

I sit alone, my servants at a distance, and ponder the travesty my life has become. I am trapped, bound to Kate by a specious set of rules laid down by a corrupt organisation. I must free myself. But how, how am I to do it?

I need cheering and find myself at such a low ebb that I summon Anne back to court whether the queen likes it or not. Kate has appealed to Rome, and Rome has listened to her. The pope has taken her side in a dispute where right should be on *my* side. She might be content to live in contempt of God's law, but I am not.

I will not.

I refuse.

Anne's arrival is like a bright refreshing breath of air on a stifling day. I allocate her apartments that are close to mine, the finest in the palace, and have them filled with gifts. I no longer care what the court says or what Christendom thinks.

I only wish the gossip were true.

I would give anything to know the luxury of Anne's bed, to taste the delights she will offer once we are man and wife. My body yearns for her but even if she welcomed me, my head would not allow it. I have come to realise that when I get Anne with child, there must be no question as to his legitimacy. If we are to marry, we must remain chaste until we are man and wife. This time, my son will not be a bastard.

Anne's apartments quickly fill with the brightest and the best. The rooms ring with music; there is dancing into the night, afternoons spent in the best company, the exchange of poetry and courtly love. Those closest to us love her and, in every practical sense, she is my queen.

The court treats her with deference; no man flirts with her for she is the property of the king. I provide her with the finest gowns, the most valuable jewels, the most outrageous gifts. I want to show the world that I mean to have her, and I do not care who stands in my way. I will shoot down the queen and the damned pope as if they are skittles.

Anne is practising some dance steps with her ladies, a new style that is sweeping the court. I watch her, smiling at the way she holds the tip of her tongue between her teeth. Her arms are outstretched; each hand clasped by one of her cousins, the Shelton girls.

She moves three steps forward, turns and processes toward me. Her head is tilted to one side, her smile wide and wonderful. Then Madge Shelton loses time and turns the wrong way, so they crash together inelegantly and fall to the floor in a heap of velvet petticoats.

Anne's laughter rings out and I sink back into my chair, relieved that she is unharmed. She rocks back and forth, a hand to her breast. Then she looks at me, her face relaxes, and she blows me a kiss, mouthing the words 'I love you'.

There is a brief silence. Everyone in the chamber has read her lips. Then the company breaks into chatter, like a cage of finches, while our eyes remain locked.

I could die for the love of her.

Reluctantly, I tear my eyes from hers. I sigh, looking down at my fingers as they drum an impatient tune on the arm of my chair. It cannot be much longer. I am not sure how I can restrain myself.

She is so ripe, so much in love with me. I know that if I were to abandon my wish to wed her honestly, I could scoop her up now and take her off to my bed. There is no one who could stop me.

She could not stop me.

I stare at her, imagine pulling off her hood, freeing her dark hair, unleashing those small firm duckies ... I shift uncomfortably in my chair, blow out my cheeks gustily and force my mind to other matters.

For now, I must tolerate the queen who is still in residence in her old apartments. A few weeks since, she came to me complaining of the favour I showed Anne, the shame I bestowed on her, the rightful queen.

"God will punish you, Henry. Are you not afraid to burn in hell? Although I am on earth, I already suffer the pains of purgatory. Never was a queen so badly treated."

The old recrimination I have heard so many times washes over my head. I look at her and feel no compassion. Her tragic face, with greying hair peeking from beneath her cap where once it was gold. *Was ever a man so cheated?*

I fix her with my stare, letting her see my disgust.

"If you do not like it, Madam, return to your own country. Your nephew will welcome you, I am sure. You know I am not your legitimate husband. I have scholars, doctors, and canonists who will swear to it. Why don't you retire to a nunnery as your betters have done, or go back to Spain? England is done with you."

Her nostrils flare and her chin juts forward.

"England *is* my country. I have been here for most of my life. I hardly remember Spain. And you know very well that we were married truly. That foul *woman* has cast a spell over you, turned you from the sweet boy I married into a despot, a – a bully! You think the pope is against you, but he merely seeks to save you from yourself."

I thrust my face close to hers.

"If the pope refuses to agree with me, if he does not declare our union null and void, then I will denounce the pope as a heretic. I will free myself of him and marry where I will."

Her face falls and she pales, a hand to her chest. She shakes her head, her tears running like molten wax.

"Oh, my Henry," she says, as if fearful for my soul. "My dear husband, may God save you."

After that, whenever we happen to meet, we greet each other coldly. I keep my distance, paying her only the merest of courtesies if we should be forced into shared company.

Christmas is fast approaching; the new year is on the horizon and I will be obliged to spend the season with her. While I must attend the feast with Kate, my heart will be with Anne, who will hold the celebration elsewhere.

I swear before God that this will be the last year that Kate reigns as queen over my court. I will see an end to it. The end of the marriage, the end of her queenship, the end of Kate.

To rub the queen's nose in the precariousness of her position, I honour my promise to Anne and create her father the Earl of Ormonde and Wiltshire. I also make him my Lord Privy Seal.

As my intention to be rid of Kate and marry Anne becomes clearer, the division in my court widens, and old friendships disintegrate.

Tom More, who has loved me since childhood, wears such a long face when he has to attend me that his chin almost grazes the floor. Brandon is no longer my merry companion. He is reluctant to spend time in the same company as Anne and finds excuses to remain on his estates.

And so, to my great misery, does Mary.

<u>January 1530</u>

The year opens, a slow creaking door giving way to the new and the fresh. As the festivities draw to a close, I resolve that this year I shall be merrier; my court will be joyous again. There shall be a new beginning.

I will throw off the trivial traditions that bind me to the wife I abhor. I shall play and sing and joust, for life is for living. From now on, I shall cease to envy the sons of other men and concentrate on begetting my own.

Ignoring a papal edict that I acknowledge her as my queen, I no longer admit Kate into my company. While she keeps her own dull court, in my part of the palace I surround myself with young, energetic companions.

Although I lack their youth, there is still no one who can best me on the tennis court or in the saddle. We hunt all day, dance all night and create an atmosphere that is brittle with joy. If life with Anne lacks the warmth I knew with Kate, it makes up for it with delight.

To all intent and purpose, Anne is my queen already. It is she who sits beside me at the feast, she who orders the entertainments, and she is the lady I lead onto the floor to open up the dancing.

My advisors whisper that I should be content with that. I have the woman I love at my side, why not let matters lie? There is no need for an annulment. Let Kate rot in her apartments like some forgotten cat. There are few who will care.

Yet I want more than that. I want to show Anne off as my wife, my queen and, besides ... she continues to refuse me the pleasures of her bed. Sometimes it is not easy for her to refuse but she is strong; her will is so much more determined than mine.

I am so eager for her that I often overstep the boundaries. It is clear from the way her heart patters beneath my hand that she wants me too. When she allows me close and my lips graze her skin, she groans and writhes with wanting. But we go only so far. We both recognise the moment we must draw back, for there is more at stake than the slaking of our lust. We need a son, but he must be born in wedlock; there can be no question as to his legitimacy.

Wolsey continues to fumble his way through the meeting of the privy councillors. Norfolk, who has ever looked down on him, smirks beneath his hand, shuffles his feet noisily beneath the table, and coughs loudly to further interrupt the cardinal's flow.

"What can you expect of a butcher's boy?" I hear him remark as Thomas quits the room when the meeting is over. "It isn't the king he works for. His paymaster sits in Rome …"

I rest my chin in my hand and tell them to go. I watch as, one by one, they take leave of me. When the room is empty, Norfolk's words repeat in my head. His opinions of Wolsey's low beginnings and compromised loyalty echo those of Anne. It is the only thing she and her uncle agree on.

At first, I wonder if he sowed the seed in her mind or contrariwise, but then news comes from Francis Bryan, whom I sent to Rome on my behalf. He too believes Wolsey and his cardinals have done me a great disservice. He reports that it is widely believed abroad that had the matter been properly dealt with, I would have been free of the queen long ago.

These findings make sense. When all is said and done, Wolsey is a cardinal, and as such, he must carry out the wishes of the pope. He also has little love for Anne and, if I were successful in ridding myself of the queen, would sooner see me wed to France.

I am at a loss, lacking dependable advisors whom I can trust. Brandon can no longer be relied on; his hatred for Anne is surpassed only by his love for

Kate. I mourn the days when our friendship was carefree, and I could confide anything to him.

What can I do about Wolsey?

I have trusted him since my youth, yet he has failed me; his loyalty is conflicted. He cannot serve both the pope and his king, that is …that is *premunire* – a crime against the crown.

If I were to take him down, strip him of his titles, his positions and remove his properties, not only could I elect a more trustworthy advisor, but my coffers would also be the fatter for it.

I have long envied his palace at Hampton. It is wasted on Wolsey; it needs a woman like Anne to grace its elegant halls. It should be mine. What right has a subject to own possessions that outshine the king's?

I call a secret meeting with the few I trust … or perhaps, those I know who crave Wolsey's fall.

Norfolk scratches his long nose and addresses me without making eye contact.

"Of course, the cardinal is in the pay of the pope, and so is Campeggio, who is no doubt sneaking from the country as we speak with his baggage full of incriminating papers."

I look up sharply.

"He has embarked?"

"Not as far as I know, Your Majesty."

I snap my fingers at a scribe who stands ready with a sharpened pen.

"Order Campeggio stopped; order his baggage searched, order that he is not to leave until every cranny of his luggage has been investigated."

"But what of the cardinal?" Norfolk is eager, his face wolverine. "He is a traitor, Your Majesty. He has deceived you and England by putting Rome before the good of our realm."

For a long moment, I stare into a corner, haunted by the wraith of my younger days, when I was newly king. I recall walking with Wolsey in the gardens; he laughed at my jokes, praised my skills, and made little of my failures. He was my friend, my mentor, the first one I would turn to when matters of state seemed overwhelming. *What happened to sway his allegiance?* Was it me? Was it Anne? Or was his eye always on the higher prize?

I remember joking once that he would be pope one day. I recall the way his laughter had faded, how he peered into the distance as if imagining it was so. Perhaps he never loved me for myself, but only for what I could provide.

And has he not risen high at my expense? Without me, he would still be gutting rabbits at his father's butcher shop. I thump the table so hard that pain shoots up my arm, then I stand up, my chair tipping to the floor.

"Strip him of his diplomatic position," I say, before storming from the room in search of Anne.

Even as I hover on the edge of despair, she soothes me, her honeyed voice salving my pain, erasing the inner fear that I am running headlong down the wrong path. I cannot stop it now. I try not to think of him: *Thomas, my friend ...*

Against my will, I imagine the guard approaching him. I envision how he will turn, surprise turning to horror as he realises why they have come. He will drop his bundle of papers, throw up his hands, cry out a protest and beg an audience with his king, but ... they will not listen.

His day is done. His fate is sealed. I wonder what Kate will say when she hears of it.

"You must take Hampton for yourself," Anne says, running her hands down my chest, tweaking the buttons on my doublet as though she intends to loosen it. "I have always thought it too grand for Wolsey. The gardens are wonderful. When you travel along the river and come upon the palace suddenly from the water, it takes one's breath away."

"There is no need. He has made me a gift of it," I answer distantly.

Events are running away with me. I try to turn my mind from the enormity of what I am allowing to happen. I must concentrate on the here and now, the future with Anne. I can never go back to how things were before ... even if I wanted to.

"I will need a new chancellor. I will ask Thomas More – I trust him. He is a good fellow."

She sits up, pouting, her prettiness marred by a frown.

"He has little liking for me. He is Catherine's man."

She never gives Kate the title 'Queen' and although I should not, I resent it a little.

"He loves *me*. He is my man. He will always be my good servant."

"Hmm."

She turns to me, her dark eyes glinting in the shadowy light. "You should speak with Thomas Cranmer. I find him very eloquent, very wise. He believes there is no need for you to beg permission for an annulment from the pope at all. He says there is no reason you cannot just put Catherine aside and marry me at once …"

She sits up, yawning and stretching, so the fabric of her gown pulls tight to her body. I yearn to undress her. One day, one day very soon, I will do so. I will lie naked with her in my bed and I will get a son on her. Every inch of her body screams of fertility. I can smell it in her hair, in the musky sweetness of her neck. I know, the first night that we finally lie together, I will get her with child.

Wolsey accepts his dismissal from court and takes himself off to York to attend his duties as archbishop. Rumour says he is sick, weeping often, complaining of cramps, but I know it is an attempt to change my mind. He imagines that when I am told my old friend is at death's door, I will forget his crimes and pardon him.

But I will not. I cannot.

Instead, I have a warrant made out for his arrest and order the Duke of Northumberland to travel to York and bring him to London under guard for questioning.

Yet the prospect is unsettling. I am not sure what I will do without Thomas. But surely losing the cardinal is a small price to pay for having Anne.

Anne and our closest companions have gathered with me for an evening of song. The chamber is warm and merry. The windows are shuttered to keep out the frigid November air and a musician plays his lute unheeded in the corner.

I sop up the laughter, the gentle chatter of my friends. It is as if they have no cares in the world. How wonderful it must be to have no worries.

I am their centre yet feel separated from them, not by my kingship, but by my inability to relax. My conscience has ever been my enemy, stealing my joys, my laughter. My own smile is forced, a layer of gaiety thinly masking my inner sorrow. It is a long while since I was truly happy, but once I have Anne, once we have our son, our heir, then the world will be bright again.

I look around. William Brereton and Henry Norris are singing a duet. Brereton is out of tune and Anne and her brother George boo and hoot at the discord he makes. Her entire family is here: her cousins and friends. I never realised how large the Boleyn family was. They are good company, yet, where are mine? Where are my own friends?

It is a month since I last saw Mary and Brandon. They use Mary's ill health as an excuse to stay away from court, but their lie is feeble. Mary has rarely been sick a day in her life. I sigh, missing her honest constancy. Her horrible teasing. She is probably the only person in England who knows and understands the real me.

A page creeps close to refill my cup, and I sip warm ruby wine. Perhaps I should sink a barrelful, drown myself in it like my mother's uncle, George of Clarence.

What a way to die ...

A scuffle sounds at the door, and a messenger is ushered in. Turning blearily from my musings, I see Northumberland's badge on his sleeve. I break the seal, my eyes scan the page ... I drop my cup.

With my hand to my mouth, I cry out, like a dog whose paw has been trodden on. The paper crumples in my fist. The rumpus in the chamber falls suddenly silent; the only sound is that of Cut slobbering as he licks his own balls.

"What is it, Henry?"

Anne leans over me, her perfume filling my head. I close my eyes as she prises the letter from my hand. I blink to see her friends turned as one toward us; greedy faces, their curiosity blurred by my own tears.

Anne's voice is too loud, it sounds rude and brittle in the silence of the chamber.

"The cardinal is dead. He died on the road from York … of a broken heart, so they are saying."

The murmur of scandalous surprise increases to a babble – a deafening cacophony of ill-concealed gleeful astonishment. Their feigned regret sickens me. I rise and quit the room without taking my leave of Anne.

My heart is heavy, my throat aching with grief. I should have stayed true to my friend. *My good friend, Thomas!*

As I make the stumbling journey back to my apartments, I glimpse the flash of scarlet robes as Wolsey's ghost falls into step beside me. I smell the incense and sacramental wine that always clung to him.

"Oh, what have I done?"

A sob escapes me and he puts his arm about my shoulder as if I am his friend and not his king, not the harbinger of his disgrace.

"What am I to do, Thomas?" I sob. "Tell me what to do."

But, as in the matter of my conscience, Wolsey fails to provide a solution, just as he failed to free me from Kate. Perhaps there is no answer.

I call together clergymen and lawyers of England to ascertain whether, in virtue of the privileges of this kingdom, Parliament can act on the findings of the Archbishop of Canterbury on the matter of the annulment.

I sit in desperation, waiting for the answer they *must* give. There can be no other. Their king is in torment. Their country needs an heir. Why should some overfed pope, the spawn of de' Medici, hold the welfare of my country in his sinful hands? Does he think the rumours of sodomy have not reached us? *Who is he to accuse me of sinfulness?*

The meeting rumbles to a close, a show of hands answering in my favour, as I knew it would. I stand up, still with a heaviness in my heart, but also a wider smile than I have managed for many months.

I hurry off to tell Anne.

"Oh, Henry!" she cries. "I can scarce believe it. After all this time. Catherine is not and never has been your wife. We could marry tomorrow!"

I pull back and her face drops.

"Not just yet, sweetheart. We must think of the people. They must first become accustomed to the idea of you being queen. The people are slow to accept change, but I will give you a more prominent position at court. You will be at my side always, for state occasions too, and Kate will have no further role. If she argues, I will separate her from Mary, refuse to let them meet."

As the words tumble unbidden from my mouth, a pain stabs me high up in the ribs. I have never properly considered what affect this might have on Mary.

My little pearl is half-grown now and has become an awkward angular girl, prone to pimples and melancholy. The last time I saw her she was taking part in a dance, and grace and beauty were not the attributes that marked her from the rest.

She will grow out of it, I know, but she lacks the appeal she owned during her infancy and, if matters do not improve, finding her a husband will not be an easy matter.

I scarcely listen as Anne chatters on about accompanying me on a state visit to Calais; something that is as yet only in the planning stage.

"Of course, sweetheart."

Idly, I kiss the top of her head and beam at her brother, George, who has just entered our presence. He gives a deep obsequious bow.

"George!"

She pulls away and dances toward him, throwing her arms about his neck. "The king and I are to be married! Can you believe it?"

"What? That is splendid news!"

He bows his congratulation. "And when is the happy day to be, Sire?"

"Oh, not – not for some time. I was just explaining to your impetuous sister that these things take a while to arrange. It isn't just ourselves we have to please …"

"No, you will need to persuade the queen to leave court first."

He looks innocently at Anne, who frowns at his use of Kate's former title. Then she sniffs, folds her arms and puts her nose in the air.

"If she continues to refuse to go, then we will be the ones to leave. We can take the whole court with us and let her wake up to an empty palace. She will be welcome to this place once we move into Hampton Court."

Of course, I would never consent to that. Kate might not be my true wife, but she is still the Dowager Princess of Wales. As my brother's widow, she is due some respect. I will, of course, allocate her appropriate lodgings.

Had she only agreed to step aside, I would always have treated her as a beloved sister, a valued family member.

She has brought all this on herself.

"I shall order new garments to be made," Anne says. "I must have clothes to suit my status."

I do not point out that she is already attired like a queen. Some of Kate's jewels are now in Anne's box, but I have asked her not to wear them yet in public. We must be discreet. It will not do to alienate the people.

There are already far too many who love and support Kate. I do not need to encourage them to scorn me for supposed crimes against her. They do not understand that I do what I must for the sake of my country.

Anne is happy; that is the main thing. Soon, we will be husband and wife and she will waste no time in providing me with an heir. I close my eyes and envision the day. She is smiling; I am smiling; and my parents and grandmother are smiling down on us from Heaven.

But the next day, our smiles fade when another edict from the pope arrives, ordering me not on any account to remarry.

"The pope is threatening me with excommunication." I read the words aloud in disbelief.

Anne snatches the letter and runs a scornful eye across it before letting it flutter to the floor.

"No matter," she says. "The pope is not your master. This is England. He no longer has jurisdiction here."

She struts about the room, her chin high, her eye narrowed but, as much as she dismisses it, I can see she is annoyed. I, on the other hand, am filled with fear lest the pope does in truth speak in God's stead. If I were to be excommunicated … it doesn't bear thinking. Just suppose that in severing my realm from Rome, he also cuts us free of Heaven.

I quit Anne's presence and seek the comfort of the chapel but, although I pray for nigh on two hours, He provides no guidance. There is no sudden blinding clarity, only darkness, cold, and a sharp pain in my knees.

Never in the history of the realm has such trouble been heaped upon a king. I am allowed no sleep; all night the matters spiral in my head, growing worse at every turn. I cannot appease Rome, I cannot appease Kate, I cannot appease Anne, I cannot appease my country … when I awake, heavy eyed and heavyhearted, I realise there is only one person I can please.

Myself.

"Send for the queen," I order. "I would speak with her."

My messenger hesitates. "Queen C-Catherine, Sire?"

I had forgotten my orders that she is no longer to addressed as queen but her old title of Princess Dowager. I flip my hand.

"Yes, yes, the Dowager of Wales."

Once he has gone, I pace the floor while I ponder on how to begin the conversation we must have. How I can appeal to her better nature one last time ... if she has one?

She keeps me waiting so long that I have plenty of time to think. It is almost three hours later when she finally puts in an appearance, yet she makes no apology and does not curtsey as she was always wont to do. Her respect for me has been eroded by years of unhappiness.

"Henry."

She greets me with no tenderness in her voice. She stands upright before me, revealing no trace of pleasure, bestowing no smile of welcome.

I can see she has come well prepared for battle.

"Kate. Won't you sit?"

Sharply and firmly, she shakes her head, just once.

"Very well."

Politeness forces me to also remain standing. For a long moment, silence pulses between us; time in which I struggle not to remember other, happier days of our courtship. Once, we were too shy to speak, too shy to begin our romance, and now ... now, we are too afraid to end it.

"Kate," I say at last. "I really don't want it to be like this between us. There is no need ..."

She turns tragic eyes upon me.

"Then come back to me. Look upon me as your wife again and all will be well. I have overlooked other women before this. I can do so again."

"Anne is not like other women ..."

"No, she isn't. Your other women knew their place. Your other women didn't rise above themselves and they didn't insult their anointed queen. Your other women had the grace to know themselves for what they were – whores!"

Her composure explodes into anger.

"Kate, don't fight with me. Why must you always fight?"

Startling in their hostility, her eyes stab me.

"Because I am fighting. I am fighting for my rights, and for my daughter's rights. If I were to agree to this – this travesty of an idea of yours, what would become of Mary – our legitimate daughter, your heir? Will you be the one to tell her she is now a bastard, or would you like me to do the deed for you?"

I open my mouth to speak but she forestalls me. Holding up her hand to halt my speech.

"You are not just annulling our marriage, Henry; you are marking me as a whore. We have lived blissfully together for many years; we were married before God. He blessed us with many children, perfect children that He saw fit to take from us.

"But he gave us Mary too – your *precious pearl*. You maintain she was conceived in sin, Henry. You want to name your only legitimate child a bastard? The happiest years of our lives – annulled? Our blessed union besmirched, our daughter dishonoured, and all for the sake of a jumped up trull!"

She is shaking; there is spittle on her chin and tears on her cheek. Her words blossom into memories. Kate and I, newly crowned, young and fertile, the joyous world at our feet and the whole of Christendom in love with us.

Why couldn't that blessing last? Why did all our little boys die? If only just one of them had lived, just one …

"There is still time," Kate says, seeing my regret. "You can put this right. Dismiss your concubine, take me back as your queen. I will forgive you. The pope will forgive you. We can make England merry again …"

She steps forward, but I retreat from her, drop into a chair, and she falls to her knees before me, burying her head in my lap. She plucks at my gown; her breath is hot on my thighs; her tears soak through my hose.

Her grief matches mine. She is so desperate that I am tempted to rip off her hood and offer her comfort for, surely, we are the most miserable pair in this realm. When she looks up again, the tears that have gathered in my own eyes impede my vision. They dilute the harsh bitter lines that now etch her face and, for an instant, she turns into the Kate of old, the woman I comforted after each failed pregnancy. Without thinking, I reach out, trap a tear on the tip of my finger and look at it.

"Oh, my husband …" she mouths silently, her face mangled with grief, "… do not forsake us …"

There are always moments in life. Moments when we can pause; when we can turn a corner or retrace our steps to take a different path but, too often, we let such opportunities pass. I recognise that this is such a moment. I could relent. I could give up on Anne and reconcile myself to giving up the fight. I could embrace Kate as my truly married wife, and Mary as my heir. Yet something stops me.

"I must, I am sorry," I whisper and, as I say it, I know the opportunity will not come again. My path is set and all I can do is follow Anne.

My life with Kate is over.

Author's note

Henry's marriage with Catherine of Aragon ended as abruptly as the narrative in this story. For months, the king and his two 'wives' had lived in a sort of *ménage à trois*, with Catherine trailing in the wake of Henry and Anne. But in June 1531, Henry and Anne rode away from Court, leaving the queen behind.

For a few weeks, the couple visited several hunting lodges with Anne playing the part of consort. It had long been Catherine's habit to write to Henry every few days when they were apart, enquiring after his health, but this time her letters also expressed her regret that he had not bid her farewell on his departure. Henry's response was that he 'cared not for her adieux.'

Catherine's reply illustrated admirable restraint, but Henry did not answer; instead, she received a letter from the Council which, for the first time, failed to address her as 'Queen.'

It also ordered that she was to remove herself to The More in Hertfordshire, and ordered the Princess Mary to go to Richmond. Henry was not only abandoning Catherine but also their daughter Mary, who was never allowed to see her mother again.

Of all the 'difficult' Tudor characters I have written of, Henry is the most complex. On one hand, he was loving, generous, romantic and sentimental; on the other, he was callous, brutal and murderous. The deeds he carried out later in his reign read like some sort of monstrous fairy tale, but I have not believed in monsters since I was a little girl. It is easy to label someone a brute, but I am in search of the inner Henry.

I have tried to imagine his thoughts, his pain, his reasoning. This trilogy takes a fresh approach to the king we all love to hate because it looks at events from the inside. The opinions expressed in this novel are not my own, they are what I imagine Henry may have thought.

Henry was a vulnerable man. He was needy, demanding admiration in every aspect of his life, and he was also easily persuaded. Throughout his reign, his ministers waged a private battle for supremacy over the king; each with their own agenda. Henry was merely the fulcrum on which politics rose and fell. We often talk of the 'victims' of Henry's reign but, in some respects, the king was a casualty too.

Henry's reign was long, it was complex, and even covering the early part of his tenure as this novel does, I had to omit many details. I have focused on his relationships because I believe it is our personal lives that define us.

Henry was a magnificent figure, his image instantly recognisable the world over, but I am more concerned with the man that lay beneath his carefully created facade. Since I write in the first person, the primary question I had to ask was: How did Henry see himself?

In writing this first volume of what I hope will become *The Henrician Chronicle*, I have walked at the king's side. I have played the part of an unqualified psychotherapist, reading and thinking deeply about his childhood experiences, his aspirations, and his absolute belief that he would be a perfect king.

In this narrative, he starts out as an unblemished boy, endures a troubled adolescence, and ascends the throne to take on a role for which he is poorly prepared; a role at which everyone expects him to excel.

Juxtaposed with the merriment and splendour of his early days was failure with a capital F; his campaign in France ended in ignominy, he failed to beget a son, and failed to embody the shining royal figure that Henry had promised to be. Looking for someone to blame, he turned on his wife. The real Henry hid behind a blindingly magnificent facade. It was failure that eroded Henry's golden dream.

In walking with Henry, I have found, not a monster, but a man drowning in self-reproach. A perfect prince tarnished and on the edge of despair; an amiable man made dangerous by his own impossible expectation.

Henry's story will continue in the second volume of The Henrician Chronicle – A Matter of Faith

The year 2020 was like no other I've experienced. We were all at home all the time, the outside world became a frightening place. I spent much of it in my study with only Henry for company and he isn't always a comfortable companion. I'd like to thank my readers and author friends on social media who kept me going and spurred me on when I began to falter. If it wasn't for my readers, I'd not be able to write full time and I am immensely grateful for each book they buy.

If you have enjoyed A Matter of Conscience, please leave a short review on Amazon or Goodreads.

About the Author

A lifelong history enthusiast and avid reader, Judith holds a BA in English/Creative writing and an MA in Medieval Studies.

She lives on the coast of West Wales where she writes both fiction and non-fiction based in the Medieval and Tudor period. Her main focus is on the perspective of historical women but more recently she is enjoying writing from the perspective of Henry VIII himself.

Judith is also a founder member of a re-enactment group called *The Fyne Companye of Cambria* and makes historical garments both for the group and others. She is not professionally trained but through trial, error and determination has learned how to make authentic looking, if not strictly HA, clothing. You can find her group *Tudor Handmaid* on Facebook. You can also find her on Twitter and Instagram.

Judith Arnopp's other work includes:

The Heretic Wind: the story of Mary Tudor, Queen of England
The Beaufort Bride: Book one of The Beaufort Chronicle
The Beaufort Woman: Book two of The Beaufort Chronicle
The King's Mother: Book three of The Beaufort Chronicle
A Song of Sixpence: the story of Elizabeth of York
The Kiss of the Concubine: the story of Anne Boleyn
Intractable Heart: the story of Katherine Parr
Sisters of Arden: on the pilgrimage of Grace
The Winchester Goose: at the court of Henry VIII
The Song of Heledd
The Forest Dwellers
Peaceweaver: the story of Eadgyth